Break Neck

Ex-National Hunt Champion Jockey John Francome is now a frequent broadcaster on racing for Channel 4 and is fast establishing himself as one of the front runners in the racing thriller stakes.

His previous bestsellers, *Outsider*, *Rough Ride*, *Stud Poker*, *Stone Cold*, and with James MacGregor, *Blood Stock*, *Declared Dead*, *Eavesdropper* and *Riding High*, have been enthusiastically praised:

'The racing feel is authentic and it's a pacy, entertaining read' *The Times*

'Francome knows how to write a good racing thriller' *Daily Express*

'Pacy racing and racy pacing . . . Francome has found his stride as a solo novelist' *Horse and Hound*

Break Neck

John Francome

HEADLINE

First published in 1994
by HEADLINE BOOK PUBLISHING

First published in paperback in 1995
by HEADLINE BOOK PUBLISHING

10 9 8 7 6 5 4 3 2 1

ISBN 0 7472 4704 8

Printed and bound in Great Great Britain by
Cox & Wyman Ltd, Reading, Berks

HEADLINE BOOK PUBLISHING
A division of Hodder Headline PLC
338 Euston Road
London NW1 3BH

Prologue

'Don't bother searching the cupboard for skeletons, because there aren't any.' Eland's visitor sounded completely sure of himself. 'So you'll have to provide one – a totally convincing one.' The word 'totally' was emphasised.

On the day after St Valentine's Day, two weeks before the Thames Land Trophy, England's most valuable amateur chase, was due to be run at Kempton, two men talked in a house near Slough.

Beneath a dismal February sky sat the unexceptional house, built in the early sixties, like hundreds of others on drab estates all over England. Externally, it had little to say about its occupier. Inside, however, among the discordant smells of rich Havana tobacco and stale frying fat, among the cheap modern furniture and the banana-leaf-patterned carpet of the front room, the occupant's interests were more apparent.

Pornographic video tapes stacked from floor to ceiling, lurid covers of magazines strewn across a teak coffee table and purple sofa, framed, signed photographs on the walls of unforgiving women wearing few clothes and hard smiles while they brandished whips and leather straps were evidence of the owner's preoccupation.

There wasn't anything particular about the man himself to suggest it. He was a little shorter than average. His colourless hair, moist with sweat, was thin across his scalp. A few red spots glowed livid on his pasty face. His pale blue shirt was dull with infrequent washing and strained across a waist six inches wider than it should be.

Arthur Eland sat nervously picking at a scab on the back of his hand as he listened to his visitor and watched him suck the last few moments of pleasure from a Bolivar corona.

He had dealt with hard men before, but the man sitting opposite him was more than hard. From the calm, icy smile that spread across his thick lips, Eland recognised that here was a man who could be completely unpredictable and very dangerous.

The foundation of this man's fortune had been the international trading of human lives; acquiring them, despatching them, smuggling them: African maids, Filipino prostitutes, Indian houseboys; even well-bred English girls for demanding Middle East clients.

And he had found through long experience that the best way to manipulate such stock in trade was to hold something of theirs that was dear to them – their passport, their identity, their family, their reputation.

It was to talk about a reputation – at least the destruction of one – that had led him to Slough.

Eland made a living by his skill with a camera and an

ability to pose his subjects in unlikely but convincing attitudes and circumstances. Taking photographs of people engaged in unusual sexual congress was his job, as well as his hobby. And it paid him enough to indulge his own particular and expensive sexual tastes.

'So, your job is to provide a skeleton.' Eland's visitor's deep voice was just perceptibly foreign, though too well disguised to place. 'I want pictures that would disgust a King's Cross pimp.'

'But,' Eland whined, 'how the hell am I supposed to get someone like that into the studio? I'm a photographer, not a kidnapper.'

His visitor's eyes narrowed as he took a last long drag on his cigar until the end glowed like a furnace between the tips of his thumb and forefinger. He glanced down at a large ashtray on the coffee table between them, leaned forward to stub out the cigar then paused for a moment. Staring deep into Eland's moist blue eyes, he moved his hand to one side and crushed the glowing butt straight on to the table top.

Eland blinked and his face twitched with unease.

His visitor smiled again, satisfied. Sometimes he had had to hurt people's children to gain their cooperation; with Eland it had taken no more than a cheap, nasty coffee table.

'Say it's a vicar's tea party,' he said. 'I don't care; that's your problem, if you want to earn enough to keep you wallowing in little boys for a month.'

'It . . . it'll be expensive,' Eland stammered, '. . . and risky.'

'If it was easy, I'd ask my secretary to do it, wouldn't

I?' The big man reached inside his jacket and pulled out an envelope which he put on the table. 'Here's a name and address, and a photograph taken last week. Get on with it. I need the job done by the end of the month and I need this person so tight in my fist they won't want to take a shit without asking me first.'

'It all depends how sensitive . . .' Eland said.

'Don't you worry about that. You just take the dirtiest pictures your nasty little mind can think of.'

Eland shrugged. 'Okay. But . . . the money?'

'Two grand for the shots, when I get all the prints and the negatives. I don't want you looking for bonuses elsewhere.'

He gazed with distaste at Eland's sweaty face. He wrinkled his nose at the smell that seemed to hang around the photographer, but he knew that men with unwholesome passions and no family or friends could be pushed much further than most. 'Then there'll be more money,' he said. 'I want no one else involved – understand?'

Eland understood; more money was more interesting. He nodded.

The other man stood up and started towards the door. 'Get those shots by the end of the month. Then I'll tell you what to do with them.' He walked out into the narrow hall, taking a closer look at the stained carpet. 'Why do you live in this hovel?'

Eland followed him towards the front door. 'No one bothers me here.'

His visitor shook his head in disgust, let himself out and banged the front door shut behind him.

Eland muttered a few obscenities as he heard the Mercedes start up and drive away. Why the hell did everyone think they could push him around? They always had – his parents, his brothers, the kids at school. He still hated it, and loathed himself even more for not having the courage to stand up for himself.

Then he thought of all the young boys he would be able to buy and bully with the money he would earn for a few hours work, and he sighed.

He went back into the living room. Ignoring the cigar butt on the table, he picked up the envelope and carried it across his narrow hall, through a door which led to what had been built as an integral garage. Now it was a well-equipped studio.

His neighbours didn't know about the studio; they thought he always left his car outside because he was too lazy to open the garage doors. But this was where he most liked to be alone, immersed in the sickly-sweet smell of developing fluids and his own stale sweat.

He sat down on a cantilever chair in front of his light box and switched on the bulb beneath the opaque surface which he used to view transparencies. He noticed that, through lack of recent use, a large spider's web had been spun between the box and the wall.

A fat, evidently replete spider crouched in the middle of the filigree pattern. Gleefully, Eland felt in his pocket for a box of matches. He struck one and held the flame to the bottom of the web. He watched in delight as the silk threads flared and disintegrated. The dozing spider sensed the conflagration too late. Eland let out a strange cackle of childish laughter. The creature was frazzled to a small black ball and fell to the ground.

Satisfied, Eland opened the envelope which had been left for him.

The kind, compassionate face which stared up at him from the first photograph also displayed a strong sense of purpose.

This wasn't going to be an easy job.

But a smile crossed Eland's pale grey face as he pondered his prey, a trap and an approach which he had found from experience worked well for both male and female victims.

Chapter One

That same February morning, Laura Mundy drove half a mile down an avenue of lofty, waving limes from the noble Tudor manor house in which she lived to the stable yard where she worked.

When Laura had first suggested to her husband, Luke, that she knew enough about training racehorses to take out a public licence, he had responded by ordering the construction of a set of racing stables that would surpass every other jump-racing establishment in the country in both elegance and technical facilities. He didn't care how much he spent, as long as Laura got the best. Then, if she failed – he told his friends – she could blame no one but herself. Those who knew him well knew that he wasn't joking; so did Laura. At first that had been her greatest incentive.

Now she wasn't thinking about Luke; she had trained herself to ignore the discomfort that he had once caused. The pain had become no more than a dull ache, easily displaced by concentrating her mind on her horses.

As the Land Rover rumbled along the smooth black Tarmac on their private road, she threw a quick glance at the small, weathered face of the man beside her – a glance which showed affection and respect.

'If you're happy about Jimmy, that's good enough for me,' she said.

'He's sound as a church.' Patrick Hoolihan spoke with the cadence of an Irish jig. 'That sore heel has cleared up quicker than I thought it would; he pulled Tony's arms out when he went for a canter yesterday.'

Laura never suffered from overconfidence in her horses. 'He's got to give Fancyman nearly two stone this afternoon. Those couple of days without exercise might just swing the balance against him.'

'Fancyman'll not trouble him; so long as Dai gets our horse settled,' her head lad reassured her.

'Who's riding Fancyman?'

Patrick consulted the *Sporting Life* on his lap. 'Rory Gillespie.' He gave a respectful sideways nod of his small head. 'But he'll have trouble doing ten stone.'

Laura didn't answer at once.

Rory Gillespie.

It seemed strange now, and absurd, how the very syllables had once made her tingle. And yet, despite more than ten years of avoiding him – tricky in the small world of jump racing – she still couldn't suppress a slight tremor.

It had been easier at first, after she and Rory had split up and Luke Mundy had swept into her life. Luke's was a presence which allowed no room for competition. But, she remembered, she had felt physically sick the day Rory had married Pam Fanshaw – sick and bewildered.

Rory had been the star apprentice then in old Mick Fanshaw's yard; his boss's daughter had been the stable tart. When Laura heard eight months later that Pam had given birth to a baby boy, it was no surprise, but no more comprehensible.

She had asked Dai Price's opinion when he'd joined her yard as stable jockey. He and Rory had been apprentices together at Mick Fanshaw's, but Dai didn't offer an explanation. 'Can't think what he saw in the old slapper,' he had declared in his grating Valleys accent. 'Wham-bam-thank-you-Pam we used to call her. Wouldn't touch her myself.'

Laura had recently recalled Dai's opinion of Pam. She had seen the little Welshman talking and laughing with her in the bar at Ascot sales, and not behaving as if he found her at all repulsive. There was no denying, Pam was a desirable woman. She'd had no more children, had kept her figure by race-riding herself – quite successfully – and had become a bit of a personality.

Laura wondered how much Rory suffered from his wife's overt flirtations and the rumours they provoked. She knew how it felt, after ten years of marriage to Luke. All her instincts were to sympathise with Rory, despite the misery he had once caused her.

'It'll be a good race,' she said to Patrick, 'if they jump the last upsides. Dai always rides better when he's against Rory.'

'What is it between them two?' Patrick shook his head, not really needing an answer.

Laura swung the Land Rover beneath the clock tower arch into the yard, and didn't offer one.

The lorry was parked with its ramp down, ready to take their three runners to Newbury. The first wasn't due to run until two forty-five, and it was only half an hour's journey. Patrick got out and gave the order to load. He always liked the horses to arrive at least three hours before a race, so that they had time to settle.

Laura watched the horses being led from their handsome brick stables, gleaming with condition, carrying a little more flesh than was fashionable, all three of them alert but unruffled. She looked closely at Flamenco Dancer, her star six-year-old chaser, known in the yard as Jimmy. He walked out with long strides from his well-muscled back end, with no hint of soreness.

'Just trot him up for me, please, Tony,' she called to his lad.

The lad proudly geed the horse into a leisurely bouncing gait. Patrick stopped to watch, too.

'What did I tell you?' He turned to his guv'nor with a grin.

Laura nodded. 'You've done a good job, Pat. Look, as we've got no late runners, why don't you come to the races with me – get away from the yard for a change?'

Patrick took a moment to consider what horses had to be looked at, what jobs had to be done, then nodded. 'Good idea.'

Laura drove to Newbury in her new Mercedes Sports, with Patrick nestling in the bucket seat beside her. As head lad, Patrick rarely had a chance to go racing; his job was to look after the horses at home. But when he did have an afternoon away, he always went with Laura. It gave them a chance to have a really good talk about what was happening in the yard. Over the years Patrick, though he didn't know it, had come the closest to being her confidant.

Laura knew she could rely on Patrick's discretion without reservation; it had been implicit in their relationship since the day she had taken him on when she had started her yard. At that time, no other racing stables in the country would touch him – none of them would believe he had finally given up the booze, which had been responsible for him losing every post he'd ever held. He'd come to Laura, frankly pleading for the chance, vowing in the name of the many things that were sacred to him that he had beaten the bottle. His skills and knowledge weren't in question: he'd been the main man behind two Champion trainers. Laura wasn't normally interested in gambling, but she'd taken a punt, despite everyone else's advice, and she had won. In the eight years he had been at Langlands, Patrick had once again become the most respected head lad in the business.

When he had asked Laura if she would also take on his son, Declan, as an apprentice jockey, and she had agreed, Patrick's gratitude was such that he would willingly have killed for her.

As they drove to Newbury, Laura talked to him about their runners that day and some of the other seventy horses back in the yard.

'How are the six that came from Mick Fanshaw's yard settling in?' she asked.

Patrick laughed. 'They're a lot happier than Mick Fanshaw. He drove them over himself yesterday and was

11

trying to have a good snoop around. He's sore as a fox in a trap now we've had ten away from him. I thought he'd never leave. But the horses are fine – just carrying a little too much fat. We'll have them right in a week or two. I don't know if any of them are any good but they certainly look the part.'

Laura nodded, but she felt a pinch of guilt at being the principal beneficiary of Fanshaw's bad luck. She'd always liked the old scoundrel.

Like every other National Hunt yard in the country at that time of year, their ambitions were focused on the festival meeting at Cheltenham. With over three weeks to go, Laura still had six runners entered. One of her first intake of ex-Fanshaw horses was heavily fancied for the Ritz, and her husband's horse, Midnight Express, was widely considered the form horse for the Two Mile Champion Chase. Patrick was concerned about a possible hiccup in his preparation.

'Will Mr Mundy still want to ride him in these two hunter chases before Cheltenham?' he asked in a way that made it clear that was the last thing that should happen.

Laura made a face. 'I hope I've convinced him there'd be more glory in being a winning owner at Cheltenham than the winning jockey of an amateur chase. But I'm afraid he may insist on riding in the race he's sponsored – the Thames Land Trophy, I ask you! He thinks it'll be the biggest hunter chase in the calendar and he's set on winning it himself. But I should be able to talk him out of running the horse in the Grand Military.'

'He shouldn't run him in either.' Patrick replied with more authority than he had intended. 'The horse takes a long time to recover; if he gives him a hard race over three miles, even as much as two weeks before, it'll spoil him for the Champion.'

But, as they talked, Laura found her thoughts returning to Rory Gillespie, Mick Fanshaw's son-in-law, riding the danger in Flamenco Dancer's race that day.

With a feeling of confusion, she realised she preferred the idea of Rory winning rather than her own jockey, Dai. But she quickly pushed the sentimental thought from her head.

It was Patrick who brought it back as they drove into the trainers' and jockeys' car park.

'There's yer man,' he said and nodded in the direction of Rory Gillespie climbing out of a fast-back Rover with his name and that of the sponsoring garage plastered along the side of it. 'He's wearin' well for a jump jockey.'

Rory Gillespie was feeling well. He had worked hard to do the weight for that day's race without losing any strength. He hadn't sweated it off, just cut the booze for a week and taken a lot of light exercise – nothing that would put heavy muscle on as any surplus fat came off.

It wasn't a big race, but it was an important one in Fancyman's campaign, and he was glad of the work. Although the horse's trainer, Jack Suter, had wanted to use his own stable jockey, the owner had insisted that Rory take the ride.

Since Rory had taken the risky decision to go freelance two seasons before, it was usually owners who were responsible for booking him. Experienced, knowledgeable owners liked Rory's honest opinion of their animals' abilities; this sometimes resulted in a horse being taken out of training. Trainers were less enthusiastic about frank assessments which contradicted their own stated views – 'he needs a little more time'; 'he'll win a race for you'; 'he needed the run' – anything to keep the owner in promise land and the horse in the yard.

Rory had already spotted Laura's Mercedes glide into the car park. He gave her a quick glance as he walked briskly past, heading for the jockeys' changing room with a leather grip over his shoulder. It was a month since he had ridden Fancyman, but Jack Suter had told him on the phone the night before that the horse was as fit as he had ever been. Flamenco Dancer was a better horse – Rory knew that – but he was sure he wasn't two stone better over three miles; and that Dai Price was riding the favourite was in itself a strong incentive to win.

The other jockeys welcomed the sandy-haired Scot. At five feet nine, he was taller than most of them but managed to avoid that half-starved look even when he was doing his bottom weight. His good looks were enhanced by the self-confidence he had developed through the knowledge that, given the right horse, he was more than a match for anyone.

Rory Gillespie had upset few of his colleagues in his fifteen-year career. He never crowed when he won and seldom blamed anyone else when he lost. If a younger jockey asked his advice, he gave it willingly. If he didn't think he got on with a particular horse, he was never too big to say so. 'Best to get someone else to ride it,' he would honestly advise.

He was almost universally liked and had the kind of smiling face and blue eyes that made it hard not to smile back.

Only Dai Price, sitting under his peg at the far end of the room, let his mean features curl with hostility.

Rory deliberately didn't look at him, and sat down to pull out his tobacco tin and create a tidy roll-up.

'How's the weight?' a young jockey next to him said with a grin. 'I see you've got ten stone to do.'

'Is that all?' Rory widened his eyes with surprise.

'You'll never do that, will you?'

'I'll tell you when I'm sat on the scales,' Rory said.

'Won't make any bloody difference whether you do or not,' Dai Price called across the room.

Rory looked at him briefly and nodded. 'You could be right.'

Laura Mundy stood in the parade ring with Flamenco Dancer's owner, George Rutherford. They inspected their horse, then Fancyman.

'He looks well,' Laura admitted.

'Ours is in a different class,' Rutherford drawled, giving an impression of experience he didn't possess. 'Why do they use this chap Gillespie? He's a bit long in the tooth now, isn't he?'

'Not at all. He's still one of the best.'

'He doesn't win that many races.'

'He doesn't get the rides. He's too independent. Too honest.'

Rory passed the scales at ten stone one pound and walked into the ring relaxed and animated as he joked with one of the other jockeys.

As she half listened to her owner rumbling on about Flamenco Dancer's chances, Laura thought that Rory wasn't showing much sign of suffering from his wife's infidelities. She wondered just how much was concealed by his famously incorrigible sense of humour.

'Is your husband here today?' she heard Rutherford ask.

'No. He usually only comes when he's riding himself,' she answered without emphasis.

'I wonder how much longer he'll be doing that,' her owner mused.

'As long as he thinks he stands a chance of winning.'

'Hmm,' Rutherford grunted, as the bright-coloured pack of jockeys split and mingled with small groups of drab brown- and khaki-clad connections around the ring.

Dai Price strutted across to get his instructions from Laura.

'Afternoon, ma'am, sir.' He held out a hand to Rutherford who shook it perfunctorily. The jockey turned back to Laura. 'There's a couple that want to be up there, so they're sure to go a good gallop. He ought to settle all right.'

Laura looked hard at her jockey. Recently she had found that she was trusting him less. She'd been getting the impression that he was losing his nerve. There was nothing she could seriously reprimand him over, but enough to worry her.

'Good,' she said. 'Get him switched off at the back and try not to hit the front too soon.'

The bell rang to mount up.

'You shouldn't have any trouble,' Rutherford boomed at the jockey.

'That's what the man who built the *Titanic* said to the captain,' Dai muttered just loud enough for Laura to hear.

Laura smiled, but thought Dai would need to come up with more than a few old jokes if he was going to keep his job.

Connections bustled around the paddock to their horses. Jockeys got mounted and their lads led the horses out along the path to the course. The ten steeplechasers, all experienced, knew what was coming and got on their toes as they stepped on to the grass. They jig-jogged their way across the track to the centre of the course, before cantering down in front of the huge number board towards the start.

Jumping is always the name of the game, but the adage is never more apt than at a Grade One course like Newbury where the fences are that much stiffer. It was on just this type of course that a big rangy horse like Fancyman excelled. He was one of those rare equine athletes blessed with the ability to stand off a long way from a fence then somehow stretch again in mid-air.

As the starting tapes flew up, Rory eased the horse ahead of the pack to take full advantage of his jumping and the light weight he was carrying.

Two horses took him on at the first fence but Fancyman pricked his ears and took it like a greyhound over a hurdle, while the other two fluffed their takeoffs and jumped awkwardly.

That first fence set the pattern. From then on, Rory was able to dictate the race at Fancyman's cruising speed. This was plenty fast enough and, with his jumping, much too good for the others.

At the big open ditch on the far side and at the downhill

cross-fences, Fancyman put in jumps that had everyone gasping, including the jockeys sitting in the changing room watching the race on closed circuit television.

As they raced round the bend into the straight for the second time, it was obvious that only Flamenco Dancer was travelling well enough to make a race of it with the leader. Dai was closing the gap slowly but surely. Flamenco Dancer's jumping wasn't as quick or flamboyant as Fancyman's but he had class. At each of the four fences in the straight, Fancyman gained at least a length, only for Flamenco Dancer to claw it back with interest on the flat until the run from the last became a desperate battle.

Rory could feel how tired his horse was. He could sense a challenger, too, but dared not look back. He clenched his jaw; if only there were another fence to jump. Up ahead, he could hear the crowd roaring. He urged Fancyman on with everything he had, trying to keep his tired legs from rolling. The winning post appeared like a mirage as the brown head of his challenger came up by his right boot. But that was as close as it got.

Fancyman dug to a depth in his reserves that only the bravest horses reach for. There was no way he was going to let anything pass him now. Rory grinned at the animal's sheer bloody-mindedness while Fancyman held on to win by half a length.

Rory leaned forward and gave the gelding a grateful pat down his sweaty neck. As he gently reined back to a trot, Dai Price cantered past.

'You're a lucky bastard!' he shouted.

Rory didn't answer and turned the weary Fancyman back towards the stands.

18

Jack Suter, with no owner to bother him, came up and took Fancyman's head at the side of the track and led them back towards the winner's enclosure. Laura and a rock-faced Rutherford were already waiting there for Flamenco Dancer.

To Rory's surprise, there was genuine sincerity in Laura's voice as she called, 'Well done, Rory' – the first words he could remember her addressing to him in nearly ten years. He did a double take before he could stop himself. Though he would never admit it, there was still something about Laura that tugged at him.

Rory didn't have a ride the next day, so there was nothing to stop him having a couple of drinks. As he walked through to the bar, he met George Rutherford.

'That was a very good ride you gave Fancyman,' he boomed with pompous affability, while blocking Rory's path.

'Thanks,' Rory acknowledged with a modest nod. He didn't even know this man's name. He wondered if he would introduce himself. Rutherford didn't; he knew who Rory was and he expected the same in return.

'Come up to my box and have a drink. It's quieter up there.' When he saw that Rory was going to turn him down, he went on quickly, 'I own Flamenco Dancer. I wanted to talk to you about riding him in future.'

'Thanks for the offer, but the horse would have to change yards before I'd ride him. And I'm okay for a drink.'

Beyond Rutherford, Rory could see his father-in-law Mick Fanshaw, trying to catch his eye and toting an imaginary glass in invitation. Mick could be dangerous if he'd had more than a couple of drinks, but anything was better than the self-important, oversized Jack-the-lad he now faced.

Rutherford didn't take rejection well. His eyes blackened as if someone had flicked a switch.

'When I make an offer, I only make it once. You'll be sorry you turned it down.'

Rory felt the full force of the man's personality, and it shook him more than he would have liked; but he wasn't going to let it show. He raised his eyebrows a fraction, muttered an excuse and brushed past Rutherford towards Fanshaw.

'Rory!'

He had nearly reached his car. He stopped walking. She had always had an unmistakable way of saying his name. He didn't turn.

'What do you want?'

She caught up with him and had to walk round in front to face him.

'I wanted to talk to you.' She was slightly out of breath and there was a warm flush on her face despite the damp chill of the winter evening.

Rory was both shamed and elated by the sense of triumph this gave him. He showed nothing; just raised an eyebrow.

'Your owner's already asked me if I'll ride Flamenco Dancer for him,' he said. 'I said No, and I haven't changed my mind.'

A flash of regret crossed her face. 'Okay, but there are a few other rides you might like. I mean – you're not getting as many as you should.'

'What makes you think I'd ride for you?'

'Why shouldn't you? You're not under an obligation to anyone else, are you?'

'No one, except myself.'

'What does *that* mean?'

Rory shook his head and stepped sideways to carry on towards his car.

'Rory! Hang on.' She turned and caught up with him. 'What's the point in being like this? You're a professional jockey; I'm a trainer with some good horses – some very good horses – to ride, and from what I've heard you could do with a few.'

'I get all the rides I want on horses I like from yards I like. Thanks for thinking of me, though,' Rory added with a forced smile.

He felt her hand suddenly grip his upper arm with surprising strength. He stopped walking and looked at her.

There was nothing in her eyes or her attitude to tell him what she was really thinking. She had always had a lot of self-control.

'Why are you being like this?' she asked quite calmly.

Rory stared back at her. 'Why the hell do you think?'

'For goodness sake, Rory, what happened between us was years ago. Don't you think it's time we forgot all that? And anyway, it was you who cheated on me, remember?'

'I don't want to talk about it.'

'Rory, please, I *need* to talk to you.' Her big brown eyes were soft as velvet now. 'Come on,' she grinned. 'It's not a lot to ask.'

Rory shrugged. 'Okay. I'm listening.'

'Not here. Could you come to Langlands? This evening?'

Rory hesitated for a moment. 'I suppose so. What about your husband, though? He won't be too pleased to see me.'

'Luke won't be there. He hardly ever is. He's rather busy at the moment. Come at about eight. I'll give you some dinner.'

Rory thought about his wife; she'd be quite happy if he rang to say he'd be late getting home. But he'd promised his son Tommy they would put the finishing touches to the station on his Hornby track that evening.

'I won't be able to get to you until nine,' he said, and was surprised by the look of relief in her eyes.

'Great!' she said, leaned forward, put warm lips on his cold cheek and was gone.

He climbed into his car and watched her for a few seconds, picking her way through the puddles towards her Mercedes.

Luke Mundy signed the bill for lunch at Le Gavroche. For the first time in years, he looked at the amount and privately winced. He shouldn't have ordered the Dom Perignon and Petrus '66. But then the bill would probably never be paid, so he might as well enjoy these things while he could.

Of course, he didn't let his thoughts show. To the man sitting opposite him – a still impressionable investment banker – Luke was as confident and optimistic as ever. This was not the first time Luke Mundy had wallowed in a business trough before hauling himself back to the crest of the wave with uncanny foresight, and a lot of luck – luck which he gave the impression of having created for himself.

Johnathan Martin's bank had made considerable profits in joint ventures with Thames Land, Luke Mundy's development company, and Luke had been Johnathan's find. The banker had a proprietorial pride in his client which muddied the waters of his normally clear thinking.

What he saw facing him now were the familiar male-model, chunky good looks and dark eyes which creased and sparkled with amused cynicism. In the ten years Johnathan had known Luke, it seemed to him that his client hadn't changed at all. At forty-five, Luke's hair was as thick and black as ever, and his waist as trim. Ten years of indulgent living seemed to have preserved rather than ravaged him. And he still approached each new deal and each new crisis with the same detached air of knowing all the moves long before it was his turn to make them.

'I'm glad it was your turn to pay,' Johnathan thanked Luke. 'We've all been encouraged to cut our peripheral expenses by half, or pay them ourselves.'

'That bad, is it?' Luke said with a smile that dissociated him from the prevailing gloom in the City.

'If you knew how many people have had to restructure,' Johnathan said confidentially. 'You're one of my few clients who hasn't come crawling back to ask for a little kindness and understanding. If it weren't for the profits our foreign exchange boys are making, we wouldn't be too comfortable ourselves; though it's rather degrading having to rely on barrow boys and Greek spivs – and they don't let us forget it.'

'As long as you're not going to want your money back from me in a hurry,' Luke grinned.

'Lord, no. You'll be all right, provided the repayments keep coming.'

'No problem,' Luke said with confidence.

Johnathan was satisfied that he'd made his point and turned the conversation to a less sensitive topic.

'I read in the *Mail* yesterday that you're riding Midnight Express in this race you've sponsored.'

Luke nodded. 'As we've put up twenty grand in prize money, I thought I ought to try and win some of it back,' he grinned. 'And I'll be surprised if I don't. Either way, it's turned out to be a great stunt. It's worth twice as much as any other hunter chase and it's getting tremendous coverage which won't do our public image any harm. In fact, I'd go so far as to say that if I win, it'll probably give our price a bit of a boost. And we can do with all the help we can get in this bloody awful climate.'

Johnathan thought privately that it would need more than the chairman winning a horse race to boost the stock of any property company at the moment, but he agreed that any positive media coverage would help.

'Should I have a bet on you, then?' he asked.

'Put a few of your best shirts on it.'

Luke kept a smile on his face until he had clambered into the back of his Bentley and settled where his chauffeur couldn't see him.

He wondered how Johnathan would have said goodbye if he had known that he'd already had his last repayment. It would be three weeks before the bank would find out, but then, unless Luke was the beneficiary of a miracle he didn't deserve, he had no moves left.

He had sold every last acre of undeveloped land – dog land, some of it, without even the inkling of planning permission – at prices it hurt him to think about, just to keep the money coming in. And his Thames Valley Business Park was as resolutely unlet and unsold as it had been a year before. For the bank's benefit, he had managed to put flesh on to the vaguely expressed interest of the multinational companies he had approached with suicidally discounted terms. It surprised him a little that Johnathan still hadn't smelt a rat, but then, he had spent many years, and many thousands of pounds developing Johnathan's trust.

Why the hell, he thought, was the man so gullible? If Johnathan hadn't been so convinced that he, Luke, was infallible, he wouldn't have lent the money in the first place – at a time when every indicator said he shouldn't.

Luke cursed the performance he'd put up then. 'There's no question,' he had predicted with a flourish, 'that when this Gulf War's over, public consumption and business confidence will surge, and land prices with it.'

If only Johnathan and his colleagues hadn't believed him; had told him to wait, like every other experienced developer. If only they had said No, he wouldn't be wallowing, not just in a trough, but beneath the surface of a turbulent sea with no shore in sight.

It was their bloody fault, their own tough shit if they lost their money. He had never claimed to be a prophet . . . or had he?

He wanted to bury his head in his hands and weep, but

it was unthinkable, so contrary to the public image that had become his private self, that he was incapable of it.

And he thought of the women who would laugh and sneer at him, however bold a face he put on the catastrophe of being broke. How they would titter at the stark announcements in the broadsheets, and the snide crowing of the tabloids, who so liked to kick a man fallen from a great height.

Just thinking about the women made him sick, more even than his grand racing friends, or the MPs and television faces he liked to entertain at Langlands and who were only too happy to drink his champagne, laugh at his jokes and make him feel like a prince.

Sod them!

He didn't care. He'd started with twenty quid, thirty years before. He'd do it again, much quicker this time, with all the knowledge and wisdom he had gained first time round.

What knowledge?

What wisdom?

After thirty years, he had still managed to go out and dig himself such a deep hole in such a mountain of shit that his crowning achievement would be to break a few records for personal bankruptcy.

And he thought about Laura.

Guilt was a sensation unfamiliar to Luke Mundy. Yet now, when he thought of the one person who would care about him and offer gentle, tentative sympathy when he fell, he knew that she, of all people, owed him nothing.

True, he had given her a beautiful home in which to feel miserable and lonely; true, he had funded the racing yard which had enabled Laura to build considerable self-respect and recognition in her own right.

But while he had regarded the state of marriage as no more than a mildly restricting social category and had been as free with his attention to women as he had ever been, she had never stopped loving him and longing for him to be the kind-hearted, eager twenty-six-year-old he had been when she, just sixteen, had first met him. She hadn't told him that for several years now; he had discouraged her, cruelly and with none of his famous charm. But he still knew she felt it, and he really didn't want to let her down.

At first, Laura Mundy had treated her horses and the business of training them as an anaesthetic – something to deaden the bitter realisation that she ranked in her husband's scale of priorities somewhere below his newest Bugatti and his latest property deal.

She had not even the compensation of children to rear. At considerable cost to her own self-esteem and Luke's personal bank balance, she had submitted to many and various fertility clinics in London, Zürich and Houston. No clear reason had been found to explain her lack of conception. Although she had pleaded with Luke to have his own functions scrutinised, he had absolutely rejected any possibility that the trouble might lie with him. At first she had been heartbroken; now, she was relieved.

Without children or the demands of a sensitive husband to distract her, she had chosen to throw herself into the job of training horses to the exclusion of everything else, and that very single-mindedness had been the key to her success.

But it was Luke who arranged the weekend parties,

and told their cook what to serve. It was Luke who was the host and decided who would sit beside whom. Laura, the leading lady jump trainer, was paraded with the same easy pride as were the horses in the yard.

Because he didn't like awkwardness, Luke always made sure that Laura had an owner or two at the dinner table beside her, while he concentrated on the wives or daughters of the influential men he asked to stay in his vast, labyrinthine Tudor manor house.

During the week, of course, he was never there. He lived in Cheyne Walk by the Thames in London, in a house lavishly decorated by a woman who had been a lover until there was no more decorating to do. Laura hated it and rarely stayed there. Nowadays the only time she saw her husband during the week was at the races, where, with great flamboyance, he liked to ride his best horses in the big amateur races, as he fully intended to do on Midnight Express in those critical weeks before the Cheltenham Festival.

Chapter Two

'But, Dad,' Tommy said, with tears in his voice, 'you promised we'd finish it tonight.'

Rory knew it didn't matter to Tommy whether his model railway station was finished tonight or next month. That wasn't the point – the boy just didn't want him to go. His mother was out. The babysitter, a bulky girl with a face like lard, was glued to a can of Coke and *The Bill* downstairs – about as stimulating as a dead cod to a boy of ten. Kids thrived on stimulation, Rory thought, and this one got none from his mother.

Rory looked down at his son and smiled. The boy wasn't yet ten years old but was already just like his father; same golden hair and blue eyes, and just as devious at getting his own way. 'All right. I'm supposed to be down at a trainer's house in half an hour to fix up a few rides but she can wait. Only I don't want to do all the work on this station myself. You start doing the roof while I do the walls, okay?'

Rory disguised his impatience and was rewarded with

a spell of strong, silent communion between father and son as each concentrated on his share of the job.

When the small wooden building was constructed, Tommy knew that he'd had a generous helping of his father's time, and he didn't object when Rory got to his feet.

'Right, Tommy, I've got to go and see this trainer now. And it's time you were thinking about bath and bed. Tell you what, if I sort out some good rides, I'll take you for a couple of days' fishing up the Wye, like I said I might, okay?'

Tommy's eyes lit up. 'Brill! You won't forget, will you?'

'Of course not. I'm looking forward to a bit of fishing myself. You'd better check that all the lines and rods are working. I'll see you in the morning.'

In the car, Rory told himself he wouldn't let Tommy down. God knew, he spent enough time with the boy, but somehow he had to make up for Pam's constant lack of interest. He felt, unjustly to himself, that he should have stayed this evening until Tommy was tucked up in bed.

Pam hadn't told him where she was going. He hadn't asked and he found that he no longer cared. She was a selfish woman; she always had been, though for the first few years of their marriage Rory pretended she wasn't. It was when Tommy had been diagnosed as a diabetic at the age of two that she had made it plain that she had no time for a boy who was dependent on a daily shot of insulin. Now she was a lousy mother and a worse wife. Rory had thought about divorce, but he knew the statistics: over ninety-five percent of cases ended with the mother gaining custody of the children. Rory couldn't expose Tommy to that.

But what the hell was he doing, he asked himself, almost allowing himself to jeopardise his own relationship with Tommy so that he could see Laura?

Laura – who had been the *raison d'être* of his early adult life and had filled it with overwhelming sensations of pleasure and tenderness, pain and guilt.

Rory had told her at the races that he didn't want to talk about it. Now he didn't even want to think about it. Abruptly, he leaned forward and switched on the radio to listen to whatever Radio 4 offered to block further thoughts from his mind.

Laura, with a docile and devoted yellow labrador in her wake, opened the front door of the huge house. She looked small and young against a background of a massive carved oak staircase and gallery, panelled walls and hanging tapestries.

There was a short moment of awkwardness. It seemed too unreal that after years of animosity and slander they should be meeting without hostility.

'Hello.' Rory felt a shy boyish smile on his face.

'Come in,' she invited, with a hint of apology for the grandness of the place.

They didn't speak as she led him across the hall into a small panelled sitting room where logs blazed in a broad inglenook, and the flames sparkled off a battery of Waterford glasses and decanters on a Jacobean table. The only lights in the room shone on a pair of classic eighteenth-century equestrian paintings. Midas, the dog, flopped down in front of the fire and gazed at his mistress.

'Glenmorangie?' she offered, going to the drinks table.

'Yes, please.' Rory nodded. 'I haven't changed that much.'

'I hope your taste in food hasn't changed either. There's a truck-load of Chinese on its way up from the takeaway in Andover. The cook nearly walked out when I told her. Sit down if you want to.'

Rory thought about asking if she'd ordered a 69er but decided now was not the time for smutty jokes. Instead he smiled. Pam hated Chinese food. He was glad that Laura hadn't forgotten the takeaways they'd shared in the cosy fug of his little room at Mick Fanshaw's. He sat in a deep, tapestry-clad armchair and reached into his jacket pocket for his tobacco tin.

'Still smoking those nasty little roll-ups, then?' Laura asked.

'Sure. I'm quite good at it now. D'you want one?'

'Why not.' She put a full tumbler of pale whisky on a table beside him. 'I'll swap it for a Monte Cristo after dinner.'

Rory meticulously rolled two thin cigarettes, passed one to Laura and lit it for her.

She sat opposite him in a high winged chair.

'So,' he asked, 'what makes you suddenly want to talk to me?'

She gave him a smile, not the self-conscious, seductive look of her early twenties, but a wide, generous grin. 'There wasn't anything sudden about it.'

Rory looked at her, the firelight on her long, rich black hair and the shadows cast by her large, well-formed breasts in a cream silk blouse. He tried to remember her naked body, and wondered if it had changed.

'No,' she went on with a short laugh, 'I've been thinking about talking to you for a long time. Rutherford going mad and blaming me because you won't ride his horse just gave me an excuse – that and the fact that Dai isn't riding too well.'

'It's not business, then?'

'No. I mean – I *do* want you to ride for me – but that's not the main reason I wanted to see you.' She paused, she seemed to be having difficulty getting to the point.

Rory picked up his glass and sucked in some of the single malt whisky. He waited; he couldn't help her.

She leaned forward in her chair and waved a hand round the room. 'What do you think of the house?'

Rory shrugged. 'It's magnificent, like something in a movie. Way beyond what I'm used to.'

'You're right. It's very beautiful. I suppose it's one of the best Tudor houses in England.' She gave a tight little smile. 'My gilded cage.'

Rory frowned. 'You, in a cage? It doesn't sound too likely. You're a successful woman, you could leave any time you pleased.'

'Maybe, now. You've never met Luke, have you?'

'You didn't ask me to the wedding.'

'But you've seen him at the races, when he's been riding?'

'Sure.'

'One of the boys; all macho charm and healthy ambition. When the mask's down, he's a different beast. He's got an almost manic need for power and control over the people around him, and he uses any weapon he can lay his hands on to achieve it.'

'He beats you?'

'Only mentally.'

'But you can handle that.'

'For God's sake, I was twenty-three, and feeling incredibly unsure of myself after you'd gone off with Pam, when he reappeared in my life. Luke's got a very forceful personality and if he can't dominate someone head-on, he undermines them, knows all their weak points and how to exploit them. When he married me, I was a pushover.'

'Our splitting up wasn't entirely one-sided,' Rory said quietly.

'Okay,' Laura came back more gently. 'There's not much point going over that now. As you say, I'm a successful woman, in my own right. And I think I probably am strong enough to walk out. I just need someone to convince me. Unfortunately, though I've got all this,' she waved her hand around the room, to take in the whole house, the pictures and tapestries, the park outside, the stable yard, the seventy-five thousand pound Mercedes in the garage, 'I haven't got a single close friend.'

'You must have been scraping the barrel if you had to resort to me,' Rory chuckled.

'Yeah,' she said with a grin, 'but I'm glad I have, aren't you?'

Rory picked up his glass and tilted it towards her before taking a drink. 'Sure,' he smiled.

They looked at each other, bridging a gap of ten years in their lives. In the gentle silence there was a tap on the door and a tiny Filipino woman came in.

'Mrs Mundy, your dinner ready.'

Laura glanced up at her. 'Thanks, Maria. We'll come straight in.' She turned back to Rory. 'I've ordered masses, so we're eating in the dining room. I hope you're not riding tomorrow.'

'I'm not, and I haven't had a proper meal for three days.'

An hour and two bottles of Burgundy later, Rory laughed at the remains of their Chinese feast.

'I already feel like a Sumo wrestler, and there's enough left to feed a football team.'

While they had eaten, by the light of two silver candelabra and another log fire, they had taken themselves back to the time when they had first met at Mick Fanshaw's mucky yard on the Sussex downs.

Rory, just nineteen, had arrived a month before from his home village beneath the mountains in the upper Esk valley. It was his first visit to England, undertaken despite the anxiety and disapproval of his strict Presbyterian parents. He had never sat on the back of a horse before leaving Scotland, but Mick Fanshaw had taken him on without any hesitation; one glance into the good-looking boy's bright blue eyes had told him all he needed to know. Before the end of that first month, Rory was riding work, and Mick had already decided that he was his best discovery in a decade. But he didn't tell Rory that.

Rory knew even less about girls than he did about horses. There had been little scope for experimentation in his village and his parents' small house beside their post office. Girls were something admired and desired from afar, mostly on a television screen.

When one of Mick Fanshaw's owners, Edward Brickhill, had come to visit the yard, he'd brought his daughter Laura with him. One glimpse had sent the blood rushing around Rory's body and struck him dumb when Laura and her father reached the horses he looked after for them.

After that, Laura always came with her father whenever he visited the yard. It wasn't until her fourth visit that Rory spoke to her.

In some ways, Laura Brickhill could not have been a more unlikely candidate for his first love. While he was from a poor Scottish Presbyterian family, her parents were rich English Catholics. He had been to the village school in Eskdale and a comprehensive in Dumfries; she had been to Lady Eden's in London and St Mary's Convent, Ascot.

But, in common, they had both possessed streaks of rebelliousness against their respective backgrounds. Laura loathed her mother's small-minded snobbishness, which gave more weight to a person's accent than their intelligence and Rory was reacting to the unforgiving narrow-mindedness of his parents' faith.

Nevertheless, these influences had left on both of them indelible and conflicting attitudes which they had never been able to reconcile and which became the last resort in any arguments between them. It was her scathing personal criticisms, issued with the complacent confidence of her class, which stung hardest; Rory was too naive then to deflect and discredit them, in a way he could easily have done now.

But their rapport was sustained by a fierce physical attraction which always overcame the differences between them. They revelled in newly discovered mutual pleasures and tacitly acknowledged the equal strength of each other's personality.

They had known one another for nearly three years, while Rory's career as a jockey was beginning to take off, when a trivial argument about his attitude to her father so stung him that he cancelled a date with her and went instead to a party at Fanshaw's stable.

He arrived a little drunk and was foolish enough to tell his junior colleague, Dai Price, the reason. Dai, malicious and more worldly than Rory, had plied him with double strength vodka before challenging him to 'score' with Pam Fanshaw, the guv'nor's daughter.

It wasn't much of a challenge.

Rory, though he hadn't learned to appreciate it, was by then a very good-looking man, already fancied by most of the girls in the yard and village. If Pam had any thoughts about resisting, she kept them well under control. And, either by instinct or experience, she knew what men liked and how to provide it.

Still smarting from Laura's criticism, Rory didn't find it hard to go along with what Pam was offering. Next morning – a Sunday – the thought of how Laura would react if she found out quickly replaced his sense of euphoria with a vicious, guilty hangover.

He left Pam sleeping in his narrow bed in the loft above the stables and went to find Dai Price to beg him not to tell Laura what had happened.

Before he had even finished asking the sharp little Welshman, he knew he had been betrayed already.

Rory tried to ring Laura throughout the day. Her mother answered each time with the implausible statement that she didn't have the slightest idea where Laura was.

That evening, Laura appeared at the yard in her twenty-third birthday present, a Golf GTi. She drove right into the yard and skidded to a halt. Some of the lads were giving their horses the last feed of the day. They told her Rory wasn't about. With a sour smile, she spotted Pam emerging from a stable with an empty feed rubber in her hand.

'I was looking for your little Scottish lover boy,' Laura said loudly. 'But you'll do.'

Pam confronted her rival with a hand on her hip and a big grin on her face.

'That's what he said,' she jeered.

Laura shook her long black hair and angrily tugged off the small gold earrings that had been Rory's one, modest present to her in all the time they had been going out together.

'You can give these back to him. If you're lucky, he'll give them to you – they're worth at least a fiver.' She hurled the earrings on to the ground at Pam's feet. She couldn't avoid a convulsive heave of her shoulders as her voice broke. 'And tell him I never want to see him again.'

'I don't suppose he'll want to see you again after last night,' Pam said triumphantly, to the laughing cheers of the two or three lads who had stopped working to watch.

Their ridicule gave Laura strength. She stiffened herself, glared at them haughtily and walked as calmly as she could back to her car. She climbed in, started it and drove quietly away from the yard.

When Rory got back to the stables late that evening, still hung over and slightly drunk, he listened with a tightening of the guts to the story of Laura's visit and public rejection of him. He lay in bed that night, half sleeping, torn between anger and remorse. When he woke next morning, he knew that if she came, he would beg her to come back. He sat down at the rickety table in his room and spent a pen-chewing hour composing a letter to her. He posted it early next morning but never received a reply.

A month of silence from Laura passed before Rory finally accepted that it was all over between them.

Pam Fanshaw watched and bided her time. She didn't hurry him or tease him over his loss like Dai and the other lads in the yard. She just told him quietly that if he wanted someone to talk to, she was around. She knew that sooner or later, Rory's sexual urges would bring him to her.

Losing Laura was more than just a blow to Rory's pride. He knew that he had really loved her. And he had made it clear to her that as soon as he was on his feet as a jockey, he would marry her. Despite the difference between them, she had been just as keen, and Rory had scarcely been able to believe his luck.

Now he was baffled and hurt by her rejection, because he was sure there was still something between them. Until he heard that Luke Mundy, a rising star of the gossip columns and the burgeoning property market, was taking an interest in her.

It was Dai Price who first showed him the picture in the *Daily Mail* of Laura at a party in Berkeley Square, hanging on to Luke's arm, grinning happily.

It never occurred to Rory that he was the one person in the world who Laura hoped would see the picture.

Pam Fanshaw skilfully took her cue.

Rory was the jockey on the up in her father's in-form yard, and a good catch. Mick Fanshaw made it clear that he thoroughly approved of the idea of Rory as a son-in-law. To have a jockey of Rory's calibre in the family could only have advantages, which he made sure to spell out.

From Rory's point of view, to marry Pam would be to marry guaranteed employment, with the pick of the rides. Besides, he had no complaints about their physical affinity, and Pam had made it her business to nurse and revitalise his battered ego. Any pangs of guilt that troubled him he quelled with the thought that it was, after all, Laura who had taken the initiative in terminating their affair.

Rory had tried to make the most of his new marriage, and to be fair to Pam, she hadn't been a bad wife to begin with.

She was certainly decorative, in an obvious way. She had big eyes, full lips and large breasts, and knew how to make the most of them. She cooked surprisingly well and was never too tired for sex. She worked hard, keeping spotless the tiny cottage Fanshaw had given them. When, after eight months, Tommy appeared, she dutifully performed her maternal tasks. She even gave up her own race riding career and helped Rory with his, hustling for rides when her father didn't have one for him.

She was ambitious for Rory, always a few steps in front of him. She spotted corners he could cut, deals he could do which would increase his income and advance his career, and which caused him agonies of self-disgust, until, after two or three years, he refused to go along with them any more. That was when he and Pam had ceased to communicate beyond the practical.

She was already bored by her toddler son and the extra care his diabetes required. But she stayed with Rory for his status as a leading jockey and for the income he brought in, which was steadily increasing in spite of his refusal to respond to her urging to ring up trainers for other jockeys' rides.

Rory stayed with Pam for Tommy's sake.

Over the years that followed, his father-in-law's yard suffered from an intermittent virus and the winners began to dry up. Rory took the unilateral decision to move on and ride as a freelance jockey. He worked hard and with the money he had carefully saved he bought Camp Farm, a sixty-acre property near Lambourn, with a brick and flint house.

Philosophically, he had resigned himself to his deteriorating relationship with his wife by devoting his energy to his son, his brood mares and more recently the building of his new barns and stables – until today, when Laura had asked him to Langlands.

Now, looking across the broad oak table and the debris of the Chinese dinner, she smiled at him.

'I think I've talked to you more tonight than in all the time I knew you before.'

'I hope it's been some use to you.'

'You know it has, and more than just useful. Apart

from the men in the yard I never have a good discussion with anyone, and I can't really ask them whether or not I should leave this place, even if I can find somewhere else to take them all.'

'It's none of my business, but if you left Luke, would you be sure of having the money to start elsewhere?'

Rory sensed an evasiveness in her reply. 'Well, if the worst came to the worst, my father would always back me.'

'You mean, you think Luke might not cough up?'

'There could be problems.'

'Nothing that a good lawyer couldn't deal with, surely?'

'The way I'm feeling now, that's a secondary factor. I've just come to the absolute end of my tether, being the chattel of an arrogant, pig-headed megalomaniac who still thinks he's a god. I just can't stand any more fighting. I should have gone years ago.'

'Despite all the fringe benefits?'

'Give me some credit, Rory. I've never been that mercenary. After all, I was prepared to marry you when you had nothing.'

'But you're older and wiser now.'

'Older, certainly.' Laura made a face.

'And twice as beautiful,' Rory added.

Rory nodded to himself as he drove through the blustery night and the narrow lane that led away from Langlands. She was more beautiful, all right. And somehow, there was more depth to her, too.

Thirteen years ago, he felt the beauty had only been on the surface, which was all that had mattered to a healthy young man finding his first real taste of sexual adventure.

He gazed through his busy, swishing windscreen wipers and was glad nothing serious had happened between them tonight. Just the warm moistness of her lips on his had been enough. Besides, with Luke still on the scene, however sporadically, it would be a mistake to get involved. He wasn't convinced that she really would leave Luke. If and when she did – that would be the time to think about it.

He smiled to himself again.

He would take Tommy on the fishing trip, even though, as far as his racing career was concerned, the evening had yielded nothing. Apart from the few words when he had first arrived, they hadn't talked about his riding for her. He thought now that he didn't mind; he didn't really want to ride for Laura, until Luke was out of her life.

If he was going to stray from Pam, he wasn't going to do it lightly.

Rory's farm lay in a valley in the southern slopes of the White Horse Hills below the ragged double rings of an Iron Age hill fort. The wind was less fierce here, but the rain still fell in large drops as he ran from his car towards the back door. He saw that Pam's car was already back and slowed to a walk. He wasn't in the mood for a fight.

He let himself in and looked at the messages on the pad by the phone. There wasn't anything important – no one had rung up in a panic needing his services the next day. He poured himself a small whisky and sat down to look through the plans which had been drawn for the new barns and stable-block he was building.

It had long been his aim, his long-term career strategy, to make himself a toehold in the bloodstock breeding business so that he had something to go on to when his body had taken enough of a hammering from jump riding. He had seen too many other National Hunt riders carry on longer than they should have done simply because they hadn't organised any other way of making a living.

Since he had moved to Lambourn, Rory had used his spare time in the summer to track down good quality mares at bargain prices. He had developed an excellent eye for a horse and had intensively studied the history and many arcane theories of bloodstock breeding. Now he had five brood mares and had sold a dozen home-bred foals. This season he had had the intense pleasure of seeing the first of these, a four-year-old gelding called Camp Follower, winning his first two races over hurdles.

This success had encouraged him to look for a good-quality jumping stallion to stand at his yard. It was to accommodate Long Run, the stallion, and mares who would be coming to visit him that he had planned new brick buildings to replace the old existing timber-clad stables.

Long Run was a big, rangy, rather unfashionable sort of horse. His only wins had been in two-and-a-half mile Cup races. No one breeding flat horses would have looked at him. But Rory judged him ideal to put a bit of bone and muscle into the offspring of slighter, quicker fillies.

Long Run had had two crops when Rory bought him and those of his yearlings which had come to market had fetched depressingly less than his stud fee. The stallion's owner hadn't needed much persuasion to part with him.

But Rory had made a particular study of Long Run's progeny, and he was convinced that the potential would be realised as they grew.

Another reason for Long Run's cheapness was that he took a lot of handling. He was well behaved in the field but in the stable he could be a savage. Rory attributed this to an incident in the horse's youth which had made him associate people in his box with imminent pain. With patience and gentleness, though, Rory was slowly convincing the animal that the connection wasn't inevitable and he was pleased that the first few coverings that season had gone as well as they had. When the new covering shed was ready for the next season, it would be even easier.

But looking at his plans now failed to absorb him as it usually did. His mind kept straying back to the soft brown eyes of the woman alone in her bed in the grand Tudor manor house.

'Rory, what the hell are you doing?'

Pam was wearing a short nightie, too flimsy for warmth or modesty.

'Just studying my plans.'

'If you spent as much time hustling for rides as you do looking at the plans for those bloody barns, you might make enough money to build them.'

'I've already bought most of the materials, and I'm going to do the bulk of the work myself,' he said, not for the first time.

'And I see you're drinking again; you know what that does to you and I might want a bit of action tonight.'

'You mean you haven't had any?' Rory raised an eyebrow.

'I don't know how you've got the nerve to say that! I

know bloody well where you've been.'

'Do you? How?'

'Just putting two and two together. You're spotted in the car park being kissed by Laura Bloody Mundy when you say you haven't spoken to her for over ten years, and Sharon says you've gone off to see someone about some rides.'

'You just said I should be hustling for more rides.'

Pam looked at him speculatively for a moment. 'Did you get any?'

'No, as a matter of fact, I didn't.'

'Well what the hell did you get?'

'A couple of drinks, and some Chinese takeaway.'

'Christ, is that all she can run to? I expect she's as useless at cooking as she is at training. She didn't want you to ride her, by any chance?'

'She didn't say so.'

'Everyone says what a frigid bitch she is. Come on, are you coming up?'

'I don't think so; not until you're asleep.'

'Bastard! I bet you screwed her.'

She turned her head angrily and spun out of the room, banging the door behind her.

Rory put his head in his hands, prayed for patience and wondered for the hundredth time how he had ever come to marry Pam.

The rain had blown off in the night, so Rory took advantage of the fine, crisp morning to get out early and begin lining up the footings for his new stable-block. It was a job that really needed two people, but he had plenty of time and just wanted to be out of Pam's way. The site was a hundred yards up the valley from the house, in front of the old stable block. In the paddock beyond, his five precious brood mares, bulging with imminent birth, grazed quietly in the sunshine. In the stand of beeches beside him, a pair of jays clattered through the budding branches. It was a peaceful scene in which Rory found refuge from his marriage and the duplicitous world of racing.

'Rory!' Pam's voice fanfared up the valley.

Philosophically, he stopped what he was doing and turned to walk back down to the house. If he didn't, he knew, she would only pursue him up here.

She was waiting at the back door as he neared the house.

'Telephone!'

'Couldn't you take a message?'

'I thought you'd want to take this one now. It's your new favourite trainer.'

Rory walked past his wife into the kitchen to pick up the phone.

'Hello?'

'Rory, it's Laura. I meant to talk to you about this last night, but there was so much else to say, I never got round to it. We never discussed your riding for me.'

'You know me, never known to hustle.'

'You should, you know.'

'So my wife says.'

'I expect she does. But what I wanted to say was that I'm not happy with Dai at the moment.'

'Isn't he obeying orders, or should I say, isn't he obeying *your* orders?'

'No, it's nothing like that – no more than usual. I think he's got a bottle problem.'

'He's always boozed a bit.'

'No, I don't mean that. I mean I think he's losing his nerve. He won't have a real cut at a fence any more, and he's getting windy about riding the novice chasers.'

'It's funny you should say that; a couple of jockeys have mentioned the same thing to me.'

'He'd have beaten you yesterday if he'd really committed himself at the last two fences.'

'What can I do for you then?'

'I want you to ride Midnight Express in the Two Mile Champion Chase at Cheltenham.'

Rory didn't answer for a moment. He was booked for eight rides at the festival, so far, with a strong chance in the Ritz, a modest chance in the Champion Hurdle but nothing in the Champion Chase. Laura was offering the possibility of a very lucrative double – just what he needed with the building work beginning.

'What would your husband have to say about me riding? It's his horse, isn't it?'

'That's my problem; I'll face Luke.'

'You mean, he'll object?'

'I mean I'll deal with it. Will you take the ride?'

Rory took a deep breath. 'Yes. Of course.'

'Great! And there could be some others.'

'Let me know.'

'I will. I'd like you to come and work on Express, just to get the feel of him. He's a really smashing horse – the best I've ever trained – but he takes a bit of getting used to.' Rory could hear the pride in Laura's voice as she spoke about a horse that promised to be a true champion. 'He takes a hell of hold when he wants to,' she went on, 'and he can get himself worked up if he's worried about anything. Once you've ridden him at home, you'll know what I mean.'

'Okay. When do you want me to come?'

'Next week, Monday or Tuesday. Can I let you know?'

'It'd have to be Tuesday. I'm working at Richardson's Monday.'

'I'll ring you to confirm. Thanks very much, Rory, and thanks for last night.'

'No problem.'

She laughed. 'No problem? Oh well, 'bye.'

'Cheers.'

Rory put the phone down to find, as he had expected, his wife looking at him.

'Well?' she asked.

'I've got a nice ride in the Champion Chase.'

'What? Midnight Express?'

Rory nodded and walked out of the door to get back to his new barn.

Chapter Three

'Would you stop the car please, Taylor.'

Luke Mundy's chauffeur half turned in surprise. They were still a mile from Langlands, but surely, if Mr Mundy wanted a pee, he could wait. He decelerated in the narrow lane, and pulled into the side of the road.

'I'll walk down to the yard from here,' Luke said. 'You go on to the house and get the bags up. Then I'd like you to help out with drinks and things when the guests arrive.'

'Right you are, sir.' The chauffeur showed no surprise at his employer's desire to walk across the fields on a drizzling February afternoon. It would be dark and a lot damper before he reached the stables. But Mr Mundy didn't pay him to give advice on health matters.

Luke climbed out of the back of the Bentley and set off along the lane towards a stile which marked a path down to the valley bottom where he had sensibly placed his wife's stable yard, screened as it was by a horseshoe of old oaks.

In the fading light, he gazed down at the avenue which

51

led his eye up to a riot of roofs and the irregular chimneys of the great house which showed above the tops of the limes.

He half smiled. There was a tidy irony in knowing that he had bought Langlands and its thousand acres in a forced sale – a result of Black Monday in 1987. All his friends had congratulated him on his bargain, at the time. It didn't look such a bargain now, especially if, once again, it was to be the object of a forced sale.

Indifferent to the wet grass that heightened the gleam on his spotless Lobb shoes, he struck off down the hill, and thought about how he would break it to Laura.

The lads in the yard had to look twice before they recognised the bedraggled, wet-haired figure as their guv'nor's husband. Luke walked into the floodlit quadrangle where the final jobs of the day were being finished off before their two runners got back from Worcester.

'Is Patrick here?' he asked.

'Yes, sir, he's in the tack room.'

Luke walked across the yard and found Laura's head lad staring at the exercise board on the wall watched silently by four or five lads. Down the left-hand side of the board was a column of white magnetic name tags for everyone who ever rode work at Langlands – lads, jockeys and owners. Besides these, mostly arranged in columns for each lot, were yellow tags with the names of all the horses in the yard.

Patrick was clutching one of the yellow tags, trying to decide which lad would get on best with a nervous grey filly which had just arrived. He looked round, ready to issue some instruction or reprimand to his visitor. When he saw who it was, he fumbled for something to say, unable to hide his astonishment.

'You're looking a little damp, sir, if I may say so. Can I get you a towel?'

'No. I'll dry off when I get to the house. I walked down from the road but it was raining rather harder than I thought. Anyway, it doesn't matter,' he dismissed the problem. 'I wanted to ask your opinion before I talk to my wife about running Midnight Express in the Thames Land and the Grand Military.'

'You want my honest opinion?'

'If possible.'

'He has a tremendous chance in the Champion Chase, but he'll have none at all if he's had a hard race over three miles a week or even two weeks before, let alone both.'

'Irrespective of that, what I want to know is how good you think his chances are of winning the Thames Land?'

'I'd say he'd walk it, even, if you'll not take offence, with you on board.'

Luke laughed. 'Fortunately, there won't be any great jockeys on board any of the opposition either.'

'I had taken that into consideration.' Patrick nodded.

'Thank you for your honesty, Patrick. I'll definitely declare him, then. I'll give Sandown some more thought.'

Patrick didn't hide his disapproval. 'It would be much better for the horse's career if he were to win the Champion Chase. It seems a terrible shame to deprive him of that for the sake of an amateur race. He's the best horse I've ever had anything to do with.'

'You're too pessimistic, Patrick. You'll have him back

on top form in time for Cheltenham, I've no doubt, and then we'll all be happy.'

The head lad shrugged his narrow shoulders. 'He's your horse, sir. Was there anything else?'

'No. Just get the horse right for Kempton.' He paused. 'I've a feeling this might be my last ride for some time, and I'd rather like to go out on a winner.'

He turned and walked out into the wet evening.

Patrick looked at the lads, who had all been listening to the conversation. 'That's the first time I've ever heard him talk like that. Something must be up.'

'If 'e's that keen, it's got to be worth a tenner,' one of them said.

'Nah,' another disagreed. 'I wouldn't back anything he was riding. Any case, I don't think the horse will stay three miles.'

This comment provoked a loud argument among the lads. Each had his own view to put. The one point they all agreed on was that they only wanted the best for Midnight Express; he was everyone's favourite.

This prompted Patrick to go outside and check that their star performer had eaten his supper.

Midnight Express was stabled in the biggest box in the yard, next door to the feed house. Here he received a lot of attention from anyone while the feeds were being mixed. If he didn't get his own meal first, he stood and kicked the door with his front foot until something appeared.

Patrick pulled back the top door and looked in at the magnificent bay chaser, who had his ears back as he licked the remains of his evening feed from his manger. Putting on an angry face was just a show. A couple of quiet words from Patrick brought him over eagerly to take a sugar lump that the head lad always had ready for him.

Patrick let himself into the stable and felt inside the gelding's thick, striped under-rug to make sure he was warm enough, while Midnight Express nuzzled his pocket for more sugar. Patrick stroked the big bay head with real affection; there was something about this horse that he had never felt with any other. And he certainly didn't want to see his chances spoiled by the vanity of a rich amateur jockey.

Pride, vanity, inflated ego. Luke Mundy thought of these failings as he walked in the dark beneath the scanty cover of the towering, leafless limes, and for the first time in many years he was inclined to feel humble.

When his débâcle became public knowledge, which couldn't be avoided beyond another fortnight, he would blame other people and cite a dozen causes beyond his control – from Lawson's budget to the collapse of the Berlin Wall.

He had always taken the credit for his achievements, but he didn't have the stomach to admit the blame for this failure. Though privately he knew he was the only culprit, he would tell no one. Except Laura.

The lights of the ancient house glowed warmly, and now that he was on the point of losing it, he saw qualities in it he had never appreciated before.

He didn't walk up to the front door, as he had planned. He went round to the rear of the house and let himself in by a back door that opened into a warren of gun

rooms and fishing tackle stores. In the luxury of a deeply
carpeted cloakroom, he dried his hair and discarded his
sopping jacket. He opened the door and checked that no
one was about, then slipped up a service staircase to the
main landing and hurried along a broad corridor to his
dressing room. In the quiet and rich colours of the large,
low-ceilinged room, he shook off the rest of his wet
clothes, wrapped a towel around his waist and walked
through to the adjoining bathroom to run a hot bath.

When he came back into his room, Laura was waiting
for him with a look of nervous triumph in her eyes.

'You must have crept in.'

'I did. I walked down to the yard and got caught in
the rain.'

'That seems very unlike you.'

'Nonsense. I often walk.'

'I meant getting caught in the rain.'

Luke shrugged his bare shoulders. 'A bit of rain never
hurt anyone. Anyway, I'm glad I've seen you before
anyone else. I wanted to talk to you.'

'Goodness, I am honoured! I suppose it's about your
riding Midnight Express?'

'There was that too . . .'

Laura's eyes flared. 'It's out of the question. He's my
best Cheltenham horse and if he has to do either of these
bloody hunter chases, he won't stand a chance.'

Luke's new humility retreated fast. 'May I remind you
that he's my horse; I paid a hundred thousand guineas
for him, despite your advice to the contrary, so that I
could win races on him myself.'

'He'll be worth a lot more than a hundred thousand if

he wins the Champion Chase; and I gather that, right now, you might find that useful.'

Luke looked at her with the arrogance and disdain she knew so well. 'He's already worth double that; and who the hell told you I might need the money?'

'I'm not telling you. If it's not true, that's fine.'

'Was it George Rutherford?'

Laura didn't answer.

'You can take no notice of anything he says. He's still sore about the deal I did with him on the Chelsea Gaming Club. He knows he sold it too cheap. That's his problem, not mine.'

'I don't know anything about that,' Laura said. 'Anyway, you can ask him yourself. He's invited himself for dinner tonight.'

Luke's eyes blazed and his fists knotted. For a moment, Laura thought he was going to hit her. 'What the hell do you mean?' He forced himself to be calm. 'It'll mess up all the numbers and he'll have nothing in common with the other guests. Why didn't you tell him he couldn't come?'

'Because, in case you've forgotten, he's my biggest owner.'

And because – she added to herself – he'll come up with the money for a new yard if I decide to move out of here.

Luke, becoming at once furtive and remorseful, took a deep breath and a couple of paces towards her. He put a bare arm around her shoulder. 'Look, I'm sorry. I didn't want to be angry with you this weekend, but I'm really determined to ride in the race I've sponsored, and the

Grand Military – I don't spend fourteen days a year messing around in the TA for nothing. And frankly, yes, I do have a cash-flow problem. I'm telling you, because you should know, but it would make matters a lot worse if anyone else did.'

Laura quivered at his touch. Luke, misinterpreting, smiled. 'We've got a bit of time and there's something going on beneath this towel that needs attention,' he murmured.

'Well I'm sorry. I can't do anything about that now. I've got to get down to the yard. One of the horses has got a temperature.'

She didn't look back at him as she left the room.

His surly voice followed her. 'Just try and be back before my guests arrive.'

An hour later, Laura had transformed herself into the perfect hostess. She wanted Rutherford to see how well she could cope. There was nothing about him that she liked, but she recognised several useful characteristics in him. He was rich – so rich that nobody quite knew the extent of his wealth; he was the only man she'd ever met who frightened Luke; and he made it very obvious that he fancied her.

She loathed his unsubtle leering and innuendo; but she was, by now, a thoroughly pragmatic woman.

Rutherford was the last guest to arrive. As he walked into the room, Laura saw Luke stiffen but carry on talking as if he hadn't noticed.

'Luke,' Laura said loudly, 'here's George.'

Luke turned unwillingly, flashing his irritation at Laura.

'Oh hello, George. I'm so glad you could come.'

'I'm glad to have been invited. I wanted a word with you – in private.'

Luke shrugged easily at his other guests, suggesting that a small but essential bit of business had to be dealt with. 'Sure.' He led Rutherford from the hammer-beamed hall into the small sitting room where Rory and Laura had sat and talked before dinner two evenings before.

Luke carefully closed the door behind them.

Twenty minutes later, Laura sensed that the other guests were beginning to get restless and huffy that their host had abandoned them. She walked over to the sitting room door and let herself in.

To her surprise, Rutherford and her husband looked as though they were about to shake each other by the hand. But they didn't complete the gesture. Rutherford tucked a folded piece of paper into his breast pocket, which he patted. 'Right,' he nodded.

'Come on, you two,' Laura chided them. 'You're rather conspicuous by your absence. If you stay out much longer, people might start spreading rumours about you.'

Both men gave her an indulgent smile.

As they walked back into the hall, Laura wondered what they'd been discussing. A loan, perhaps, or – more likely – some kind of settlement over the Chelsea Gaming Club. Certainly, if Luke had somehow acquired the club from Rutherford at less than its real value, Rutherford would have had his reasons. At least, he would want redress.

For the rest of dinner, Luke was quieter than usual, answering his neighbours mechanically and without any of his normal dazzling, skilfully wielded charm. Laura almost felt sorry for him but she didn't let him into her bed later without protest.

That night, though, he didn't persist as he would normally have done and after ten minutes climbed out and went to sleep in his dressing room.

He had never done that before; Laura guessed his problems must be bigger than she thought.

Pam Gillespie shook her implausibly blonde and curly head across the table at Rory.

'You know you said you were riding Midnight Express in the Champion Chase?'

Rory glanced up from the paper he was reading, chewing on a piece of lean, tender sirloin steak his wife had cooked for his supper. He nodded. 'Yes.'

'It's still declared to run in this ridiculous Thames Land race.'

'So?'

'I saw Dai at Ascot on Saturday and he told me if it runs at Kempton, you can forget it winning at Cheltenham.'

'Why's that?'

'He didn't say. I suppose he takes time to get over his races.'

'Did Dai know I was booked to ride him at Cheltenham?'

'No, but I told him.' She giggled. 'He wasn't too happy.'

'You really have an incredible taste for stirring things up, don't you?'

'Well, he would have found out sooner or later,

60

wouldn't he? Anyway, he says the horse hasn't got a chance if he's run the week before.'

'I'm going down to ride work on him tomorrow morning. I'll ask Laura about it then.'

'Lucky bitch had two winners at Fontwell today.'

'That makes her a lucky bitch, does it?'

'She is a lucky bitch.' Pam didn't conceal her loathing. 'She'd be nothing if her husband wasn't a millionaire.'

'She works hard at it; she's always had a good eye for a horse,' Rory said quietly, knowing it would annoy Pam.

'And a jockey.'

'Has Dai been obliging her, then?'

'God, no! He says he wouldn't touch her with a barge pole.'

Rory laughed. 'He'd be lucky to get that near.'

'You fancy her again, don't you? There was a time when you used to call her a snotty bitch.'

'I never said she was a snotty bitch, but anyway, people change; or, at least, some people do.'

'What's that supposed to mean?'

Rory shook his head. 'It means whatever you want it to mean.' He turned his attention to the Welsh collie lying on his feet. 'Come on, Taffy, let's go and take a look at the horses.'

Arthur Eland knew from the dossier he had been given where his victim would be at about twelve on that Monday morning. He decided to set his trap for half past ten.

He had arranged over the phone to take a stable in a scruffy livery yard. He had sent the rent, two weeks in advance, using a post office money order.

To bait the trap, he needed a horse.

'Good home wanted for much-loved old family friend,' the advertisement said.

Eland grinned. They'd rather give it away than let the knacker have it.

'15.2hh dun cob; 18 y-o, but sound, ideal quiet lady's hack or suit teenage beginner.'

He took a boy with him. 'Try and look like my son,' he said.

'That's a bloody joke,' the boy said with a hoarse, coarse laugh. He was just twelve, but hardened by exposure to Arthur Eland and clients like him.

'What d'you think of him, then?' Eland had inspected the horse; he'd run his hands nervously down one of its hairy legs and asked the sad-faced woman who was selling the cob to trot it up for him.

''E's lovely, Dad,' the boy said. Eland had rehearsed him in the car coming over. 'Can we get 'im?'

'I dunno. He *is* nice, but I don't think I can afford him.'

'Oh, Dad!' the boy whined.

Eland turned to the woman who was holding the horse's head and looking with compassion at the slight, pretty child who didn't look as though there was much joy in his life. 'Would you take four hundred?' he asked. The broad-backed horse was worth more than that in meat.

'Well, my husband did really think we should get six hundred for him.'

'That's a real shame,' Eland said, shaking his head. 'The

boy really likes him, and he'd have done him very well.'

'Yes, he'd be a lovely first horse; even though he's a little big, he's very kind.'

'I can see that.' Eland allowed his voice to quiver with disappointment. 'But I just couldn't go higher than four hundred.'

The woman smiled, pleased at the decision she was making. 'To be quite honest, the money's not all that important. I think he would have a very happy home with your boy, so you can have him for four hundred pounds.'

Eland and the boy bubbled with gratitude.

'That's great, Dad! Can we take him now?'

Eland smiled indulgently at him. 'If the lady will let us. I've got the cash and I've got the trailer,' he addressed the woman, who nodded with a soft smile.

'What do you want the bloody thing for anyway?' the boy asked as they drove between the silver birches that lined the drive from the cob's old home.

'That's none of your business. I'm taking you back now.'

'What about my money?'

'Here's twenty.' Eland produced a note and passed it to the boy, who disdainfully tucked it in his shirt pocket.

Eland dropped the boy outside an arcade in Slough. A few minutes later he was unhitching the trailer from his Jaguar and hitching it back on to a nondescript, untraceable Japanese pick-up.

Twenty minutes after that, he arrived at the livery yard. He didn't drive straight in. He wanted to be sure there was no one around to see him; it had been enough of a risk to use the boy, and Eland wanted no more – no chance of a finger being pointed at him once the photos were taken and put to work.

After the last time, he'd vowed never to spend another day in prison. It had only been an eighteen-month stretch, but eighteen nasty months of persistent and painful sexual harassment by the harder inmates. Just thinking about it made him gag.

When he was sure there was no one around, he backed the trailer into the yard. Quickly, he grabbed a leading rope and a whippy plastic crop he had brought with him and went round to lower the trailer ramp. He clipped the rope on to the head collar which he had bought with the horse and unloaded it to lead it into the box he had identified over the phone.

But the horse had another plan. There was a paddock full of fairly fresh grass on the far side of the railings beside the trailer. He quickly slipped his head through and stretched down to chomp. Eland tugged hard but fruitlessly to bring the horse's head up. The horse moved its back end around, squeezing Eland against the fence.

"'Ere, what're you doing?' Eland squealed in panic. He had experience of dominating only very small creatures. Letting out the rope, he began nervously to sidle past the horse's hefty quarters. Transferring the rope to his left hand, he raised the thin crop with his right and brought it down as hard as he could across the animal's back.

The cob was taken by surprise. He lashed out his rear offside leg. The freshly shod hoof caught Eland a glancing blow on the thigh.

'You fuckin' bastard,' Eland yelled and cut viciously

with the crop at the cob's flanks.

The horse had never known this kind of treatment. He tried to tug his head back through the railings, caught it for a moment before getting free, then jerked it up to loosen the rope from the man's grasp.

Eland, despite his terror, hung on. If he let the animal escape now, all his efforts at anonymity would be wasted. But the cob was several times stronger than he. It headed for the open space in front of the stables, dragging Eland behind. Eland stumbled, fell to the ground but hung on as the cob reached a concrete forecourt in the 'L' of the stable block. Here it checked and gave Eland time to get painfully to his feet, still clutching the rope and the whip in both hands. He rushed at the animal, snarling, with the crop raised.

When he was near enough, he laid about the animal's face and head with a manic, unrestrained force until the beast was backed into a corner, terrified. Then he stopped. The sudden outburst had left them both blowing heavily, Eland's eyes bulged and he began to sweat as he stood regaining control of himself.

The cob was frightened but submissively it consented to being led in through the open stable door of Eland's box. Eland secured the end of the rope to a ring on the wall, and stood back, well out of range of the horse's rear end.

'Right, you bastard. Don't you do that to me again,' he said, still panting slightly.

He stayed for a moment in the stable, listening for sounds of anyone outside. The house to which the stable block belonged was a hundred yards away. With luck, the fracas hadn't been noticed. When he was satisfied that no one had been alerted, he let himself out and walked swiftly back to the trailer. He heaved a bale of straw from the front of the box and dumped it outside the stable door, under cover of the overhanging roof. He filled a hay net and took it in. The cob snorted his appreciation and Eland surveyed his new purchase with wary satisfaction. It would serve its purpose next day, then he'd collect it and drive it straight to the knacker. He judged he should even make a profit out of it.

Next morning, clad in the khaki uniform of a countryman, he left the pick-up and trailer in a public parking place, and walked a mile to the yard. This time, he made very certain there was no one to see him before he slipped into the yard and let himself into the cob's box with the crop in his hand.

The horse, still tethered, sidled away from him and set back his ears. Eland swished his crop through the air. 'That's right, my son, you know who's boss now, don't you?'

He walked across, plucked the hay net from its hook on the wall, went out to refill it and brought it back in.

Once the horse was busy munching in the corner, Eland settled down beside the door, like a spider waiting for a fly.

From the pocket of his khaki jacket he pulled a single black nylon stocking.

From his other pocket, he took a large wad of cotton wool and a small bottle of chloroform.

Prepared, he clambered up between the wooden roof trusses of the stable.

Eland heard the car pull off the road into the top of the

track. His face twitched and he lifted the stocking to his head and pulled it over, stretching it down to his neck. He unscrewed the top of the bottle and tipped most of the contents on to the wad of cotton wool.

Instinctively, all his muscles tensed to spring.

The car's engine was turned off. A door slammed with an expensive-sounding clunk. Firm footsteps crossed the concrete apron of the yard, hesitated a moment as the box was identified.

A moment later, the light from the open upper door was obscured. The bolt was drawn back.

Eland held his breath as the door opened and he saw his victim in the flesh for the first time.

Laura had phoned Rory at the weekend and asked him to come to Langlands at ten on Tuesday morning, in time to go out with the second lot.

A morning mist was beginning to lift to reveal a pale, low sun as Rory drove south to the Hampshire hills. He had heard about the spectacular private gallops at Langlands, and he looked forward to seeing them. And each mile closer he came, the more he realised how much he was looking forward to seeing Laura.

Rory arrived early. He took the back drive to the yard and parked his own car among the lads' old Capris and rusting pick-ups behind the main block. He spent a moment admiring the architecture of the place and the details – the corbelling and old roof tiles – which might have been specified for a high-grade private house.

The first lot was coming back to the yard as he walked in. He was impressed with the quality and condition of the horses as they walked past him into the yard. He also noticed how unusually clean and tidy the lads looked – each in matching dark blue cap and jacket.

Following the horses in a long Land Rover was Patrick, the head lad. He jumped down from the vehicle and walked across to Rory with his hand stretched out and a broad smile on his face.

"Morning, Rory. And it's a pleasure to see you here.'

Rory took the Irishman's hand and shook it. He knew who Patrick was, of course, but he didn't know him. His instinct was to like him, but he had been disappointed too often by Irishmen with more charm than scruples.

'Lovely yard you keep here,' Rory said.

'Thanks. I helped Mrs Mundy with the planning of it, so she always blames me if something doesn't work,' he laughed. 'But it's worth it. Now, I was to tell you that you're riding Midnight Express up to the gallops. You're to go with Declan on Jimmy – that's Flamenco Dancer. Hack up the shavings gallop and then let him stride along for five furlongs on the grass. Declan will look after you, and you look after the horse; he's the best we've got.'

Rory smiled at the Irishman's enthusiasm.

'Isn't Mrs Mundy coming down herself?'

'She will be on the gallops and she said you're to have breakfast with her after, up at the house.'

'I see. Is Dai Price here this morning?'

Patrick gave half a smile. 'He is not.'

Feeling a discontent at not seeing Laura which he didn't want to admit, Rory was legged up by Midnight Express's lad and followed the first two horses out of the yard and on to the green lane that zigzagged through the oak woods up the steep hanger.

Declan was Patrick Hoolihan's twenty-three-year-old son. He had started at Langlands five years before, with a little persuasion from his father. At first, as an apprentice, he had become a competent horseman, but seemed to lack the competitive edge that would turn him into an effective jockey. He still held a licence and Laura gave him the occasional ride in a race, though it was two seasons since he'd had a win. Philosophically, and without rancour, he had accepted that he was never likely to make the grade, and now put all his energy into getting to know and schooling the horses of which he had particular charge.

Now racing was Declan's life. He had happily settled for a job in a good yard with a lovely cottage which he could never have bought himself. It was also a yard where he felt appreciated. Although his race riding ambitions had come to nothing, he took a lot of pride in the ability he had developed to judge at an early stage which horses had any real talent. Using this knowledge, he liked to bet, and he was one of the few who made it pay.

As they approached the bottom of the all-weather gallop, he turned to Rory.

'That's the best horse you'll ever sit on,' he said with complete conviction. 'He'll try to run off for the first twenty yards, but if you just ride him on a long rein and sit quietly, he'll settle; then you can do what you want with him.'

Rory nodded, confident of Declan's advice.

'Just sit ten lengths behind me,' Declan went on. 'We'll pull up after the bend.'

Laura's gallop man stood at the bottom of the all-weather track, leaning on a long-handled divot fork. Midnight Express used his presence as an excuse to whip round to his right, and almost drop Rory in the mud. Declan, seeing it, grinned at Rory, now back in the saddle.

'I forgot to tell you,' he said. 'He can drop his shoulder when he's feeling well.'

There was nothing lads liked more than to see jockeys fall off.

Rory smiled back. 'Funny with kids, I expect.'

Midnight Express behaved just as Declan had said he would. Once he had settled into his stride, Rory began to appreciate that he was sitting on something special. The horse was cantering as effortlessly as if he were out for a walk.

Rory pulled up quietly behind Flamenco Dancer. His horse squealed with well-being as he patted him on the neck.

'What a tool this is!' he shouted to Declan.

'Wait until you let his head go on the grass; then you'll know what he's all about.'

In the ten minutes it took to walk back to the bottom of the gallop, Declan filled Rory in with everything he knew about Midnight Express's likes and dislikes. It seemed, as the stable favourite, there wasn't much the horse wasn't allowed. He liked, for instance, to be let loose during evening stables to graze on the lawn in front of the yard – a privilege granted to none of the other inmates at Langlands.

When they reached the bottom of the slope, Declan's conversation reverted to the job in hand.

'I won't be able to lay up with you for long when we turn in, so just let him run along on the bridle in his own time. Then pull up just after you've passed the boss.'

It occurred to Rory that Laura must have immense confidence in her staff; although he had seen her in the distance at the top of the gallop, she still hadn't spoken to him.

He wheeled his horse around on to the grass gallop.

For the next fifty seconds, he experienced a feeling he hadn't had for so long that he'd almost forgotten it.

Power, balance, comfort, control – Midnight Express had everything, even brakes.

They flew past Laura and the small group with her at the top, before Rory slowly eased back to a walk. He headed for home as he'd been instructed and let his thoughts dwell exuberantly on the prospect of his ride at Cheltenham.

Half a mile from home, Rory loosened his girth, ran his irons up the leathers and hopped lightly to the ground. He led Midnight Express the last part of the journey, allowing some air under the horse's saddle to cool him off.

Back in the yard, he let him pick grass for a minute or so until a lad came to take over.

'How'd he go?' the lad asked.

'Incredible, once he settled. Do you do him?'

'No, Declan does. I just help when he's busy.'

'He looks great,' Rory encouraged him.

Patrick had walked over to join them.

'Everything okay, Rory?' The two enthused over the horse for a while until Patrick told the lad to put him back in the box. 'D'you know your way up to the house? It's straight out of the yard and up the avenue. You can't miss it,' he laughed. 'And use the front door.'

Rory thanked him and walked out of the yard to collect his car. He felt a vague uneasiness that he hadn't spoken to Laura yet. He had expected her to have come down from the gallops by the time he'd ridden back. Still, she'd asked him to breakfast. He hoped – though it was a lot to expect – that there wouldn't be anyone else there.

At the house, the Filipino maid who had served the Chinese dinner the week before showed him into an empty room with a big round table laid for breakfast for an indeterminate number. It was a large, softly decorated room, lit by a pair of French windows which gave on to a broad flagged terrace and semi-formal gardens beyond. Even with only clusters of snowdrops and a few early roses to brighten it, it was still an exceptionally lovely view.

Rory walked across to a sideboard where a coffee per-colator gave off a seductive aroma. He filled a big French cup and walked across to look out of the window.

He didn't hear Laura come in.

He was lifting the cup to his lips when she spoke.

'Hi, Rory.'

An involuntary jerk of his hand spilt a little coffee down his chin. He turned and smiled ruefully, reaching for a napkin from the middle of the table.

'Sorry, you gave me a start.'

Laura was looking as fresh as she had the last time he'd seen her, wearing a large Arran sweater and a loose-fitting pair of Levis. Her long black hair was gathered up in a grip at the back of her head and the pile of folders and papers she carried made her look incongruously businesslike.

'I hope Express didn't,' she said.

'No. Declan told me how to ride him and he was fine.'

'He settles better for you than Dai.'

'Who doesn't?' Rory grinned.

'Who indeed?' Laura said meaningfully.

Rory didn't answer.

There was, he had already noticed, something slightly reserved about Laura's manner compared with the way she had said goodbye to him five days before.

'Sorry,' she said. 'That was meant to be funny. Have I put you off your food?'

'I only want coffee and a wee slice of toast anyway.'

'Help yourself. Patrick and Henry Straker will be here soon.'

She poured herself some coffee and sat in the nearest chair. Rory followed her lead and placed himself opposite her.

'So, what do you think about the Champion?' she asked.

'Provided the ground doesn't come up like a bog, he must have a great chance. But what about these hunter chases – are you going to run in them too?'

'No way,' Laura laughed. 'If we have to, we'll induce a temporary condition that will convince the vet he can't go. He's had corns on his feet before.'

'That's a bit risky, isn't it? Wouldn't the vet just veto him if you asked?'

'Not Henry Straker. He's as straight as a die, and Luke

knows that, so he won't quibble.'

'The only problem I've got,' Rory said, 'is that I've just been asked to ride one of the Irish horses – a bit long in the tooth, but he might have a squeak. It's not a great race this year, you know.' Laura was going to interject, but Rory went on, 'But provided your horse doesn't go to Kempton or Sandown, of course I want to ride him – who wouldn't? How did Dai take it when you told him?'

'Someone else had already told him. He's not too happy, but I said Luke had insisted, and even Dai wouldn't argue with Luke.' She laughed. 'Luke actually talked about riding him himself at Cheltenham. If he wasn't so bloody vain, he would, but even he realises he'd just make a fool of himself if he did.'

The big panelled oak door to the room swung open. Midas the yellow labrador trotted in, followed by a tall man in his mid-forties with an air of great dependability and strong blue eyes of amiable directness. He wore a pair of slightly furry cavalry twill trousers, a houndstooth tweed jacket and a BFSS tie. Rory recognised the Jockey Club's Chief Veterinary Officer, Henry Straker, well respected and universally liked by the racing community – a rare distinction. He had a boyish sense of humour but he had won the Jockey Club's utter confidence in the High Court recently. He had appeared for them in a case against an owner who had contested the validity of their blood analysis. If Henry Straker had failed, racing's rulers would have lost not only a vast sum of money, but also, more importantly, their credibility, then under serious scrutiny.

''Morning, Laura, Rory,' he greeted them warmly

'Gosh, that bacon smells good.'

''Morning, Henry. Help yourself,' Laura invited.

'I wish I could, but I haven't got time. If you could just let me have a list of the horses you want tested, I'll go and get on with it.'

Laura handed him a sheet of paper from the pile beside her. 'Here you are. Sorry you can't stay.'

'I've got the results of the last tests in my car. They're all normal. Shall I leave them in your office?'

'Yes, if you would. Not that they'd mean anything to anyone besides a vet.'

'You're right. Anyway, nice to see you, Rory. I hope Laura's going to give you plenty of rides. 'Bye.'

He left the room with his long, busy stride.

When the door had closed behind him, Laura said, 'He doesn't think much of my stable jockey.'

'I wonder why,' Rory laughed.

Laura didn't. 'Henry thinks he's bent, but I don't agree. He hasn't stopped any horses I've wanted or expected to win.'

'Maybe he's more of a craftsman than you realise. There are all sorts of strokes you can pull.'

Laura glanced at him. For a moment in her eyes there was a hint of the old haughtiness. 'I have learned by now to recognise when a jockey isn't trying.'

'Maybe, but it's a lot easier than you think.'

'How do you know? Have you done it?'

'What do you think?' Rory was indignant.

Laura looked at him for a second or two, then smiled. 'Probably not.'

'And I won't, ever.'

'All right, I admit, I am worried about Dai. But I can't give him the elbow without a plausible reason, and he's still giving some of the horses a good ride.'

'Why does Henry think he's crooked?'

'I don't know. He's never mentioned any particular horse or race. You know what he's like – he's a good man and unbelievably honest. He adores horses and racing and just hates the idea of anyone cheating.'

'You've got to admire him for it,' Rory said.

'And the way he's handled his own personal disasters.'

'What disasters?'

'You know. His two little boys were killed in that car crash – three and five, I think they were – a couple of years ago.' Rory suddenly remembered, their mother was driving, and was so badly injured she was unable to have any more children. Henry had been absolutely devastated. Laura continued, 'I spoke to him about it a while ago; he said he still thinks about them every single day. His wife hasn't really got over it – Henry says she's still racked with guilt – but he's determined to pull them through it. He's really thrown himself into running the boys' club in Reading and has done brilliantly with it. Their soccer team's been winning everything. They're his pride and joy now.'

Rory nodded, and thought of Tommy. 'Yes, of course; I had heard about it.'

The door swung open again, and Patrick walked in.

'Hello, Patrick,' Laura greeted him. 'Grab a chair.'

'I will,' he said but walked over to the sideboard first.

'Now,' Laura said, 'Rory's worried about Luke riding Midnight Express in this hunter chase, so we'll have to make sure he's off games for the day, and somehow we'll have to get Henry to confirm it.'

Patrick grinned. 'I was hoping you'd say that. Leave it to me. There's a lot of stable money on him already for the Champion Chase, and I'd hate to see the lads miss their spring bonus.'

The Irishman poured himself a large cup of coffee and sat down next to Rory.

'I suppose you want your usual fry-up, Pat?' Laura asked.

Patrick nodded. 'I do. Thank you. This is the best part of my job.' The Irishman winked at Rory then turned to tell Laura that her assistant trainer had gone to oversee the blood tests.

Laura stood up and pressed a buzzer above the sideboard. When the maid had taken her instructions, Laura sat once more, looking across the table at the jockey.

'Patrick and I,' she said to Rory, 'would really like you to ride every horse in the yard. That's not possible yet, but there are quite a few where I can say the owner wants you. If we run through their entries for the next few weeks, you can tell me which you can do.'

Rory drove away from Langlands with the fullest diary he'd had for a long time, and a feeling of emptiness.

That morning there had been none of the intimacy of the previous week's Chinese dinner. But after all, they had been talking business. Rory had to console himself with the knowledge that he had deprived Dai Price of a few good rides. He also felt that he had gone some way to justifying his decision at the beginning of that season to do without the services of an agent to fix his rides. At least when he fixed his own, he always knew exactly what he was taking on.

He picked up the A303 at Andover and headed for Wincanton thinking of the time when he and Laura had been together.

As he drove his Rover into the westerly wind towards the Somerset racecourse, he knew with certainty and misgiving that everything he had ever felt for Laura, and more, had been revived; it was already too late to reverse the process if it turned out that all she wanted was a replacement for a stable jockey who had lost her trust and his nerve.

In a haze of anger at this lack of control over his emotions, Rory produced two winners from three moderate horses. On both he was brave to the point of foolishness at the tricky downhill fence before the straight. But the risk paid off; it was always hard to peg horses back once you had them running from there.

Later that evening at home, he grudgingly told Pam about the improvement in his prospects for the rest of the season, knowing that the irony that Laura should be the provider of this bounty had eluded neither of them.

Chapter Four

At twelve thirty on the day that Luke Mundy was due to ride Midnight Express in the Thames Land Trophy, Laura turned her Mercedes into the owners' and trainers' car park at Kempton. She was feeling guilty and irritable. She hadn't told Rory that the horse was still running and she hadn't worked out exactly what she was going to do.

Patrick hadn't been happy either when she'd announced that the horse was going to run. She knew as well as he did that they were throwing away their chances in the Champion Chase by asking Midnight Express to do two races so soon before it at a distance he didn't like.

Irresolute and uncertain, she parked her car. She was jerked out of her thoughts by a loud blast on the horn of the car that had pulled up beside her. She looked across to see George Rutherford grinning at her with his thick lips. By the time she had got out, he was beside her, offering her a camel-hair-clad arm.

'I hear you didn't want your husband to ride today,'

Rutherford said blandly. 'Don't you think he'll win?'

'Frankly, he should piss it,' Laura said with deliberate coarseness. 'But that's not the point. He joined the TA and kept up his fourteen-days-a-year service just so he could ride in the Grand Military next week, but he has to enter this one as well – and why the hell ride this horse? He's got four others he could have gone round on. He just wants to be absolutely certain of winning. I think he loathes the idea of having to give all that prize money to somebody else.'

'So you think I ought to have a bit on him?'

'That's up to you. You won't get much of a price, though. I think he's had a big one on himself.'

'Has he indeed?' Rutherford seemed interested. 'Then I think I'll back his judgement, though I must say, there are a few malicious rumours going around about his lack of judgement in other areas,' he added softly, without any particular rancour.

Laura glanced at him. 'So you said the other day, but I don't think he's suffering any more than anyone else in this recession.'

'I sincerely hope not, for your sake.' Rutherford paused to look at her meaningfully. 'But I must tell you, if you ever did find that Luke was forced to sell up, I'd be more than willing to help you out. I'm delighted with the results you've given me so far.'

He had made this suggestion before. Laura had been hoping he might have been able to flesh out the rumours he had hinted at, but she suspected they only related to whatever bad experience Rutherford had had in his dealings with her husband over the Chelsea casino. His desire to take Luke's place as her backer was probably motivated by bruised macho pride as much as anything else. But she was sure the offer would stand, and that was comforting to know.

Laura was still, reluctantly, on Rutherford's arm as they walked towards the weighing room. She extracted herself as subtly as she could when she saw Henry Straker striding briskly towards her.

''Morning, Laura; 'morning, Mr Rutherford,' he said with a professional politeness which showed no distinction between those he liked and those he did not. 'I need to have a word with you, Laura.'

Rutherford gave no sign of leaving their company.

'Would you mind awfully if I had a chat with Mrs Mundy alone?' Henry asked.

'No, of course not,' Rutherford said smoothly with a smile. 'I'll leave you to it.' He walked off, parting the crowd before him, towards the stand.

The vet was looking worried.

'What's the matter, Henry?' Laura asked.

'I'm not sure. Something rather odd has come up. I received a call in the office a few moments ago telling me that your horse had been got at.'

'What!' Laura couldn't contain the shock in her voice. She wanted to ask a question, but the vet continued.

'It's probably just a hoax. I've spoken to the stewards and we've agreed it's most likely that somebody's trying to get him withdrawn. They don't want a big fuss. I mean, it could set a terrible precedent. So they've asked me to take a blood sample, then let the horse run provided we're both happy that he looks all right. Of course we won't have the results of the test for a week or two, though I dare say they'll rush it through faster if anything sinister happens. Either way, you're perfectly in the clear.'

'I'm glad to hear it. But I don't see how anyone could have got at him. There should have been a lad with him all the time since early morning and surely he'd be showing signs if he'd been doped before then.'

'Well, I'm sure you're right, it's almost certainly nothing but I've still got to take this test. The Jockey Club security man has to be present, of course; I'm meeting him over at the stables in a few minutes.'

'Okay.' Laura spoke in a way that implied she was more than a little concerned about the news she'd just received. 'I'm just going to check he's been declared, then I'll come down to make sure he's all right.'

'I'll need to examine him thoroughly,' Henry said. 'I must give the Stewards my honest opinion. After all, you do see what could happen if we don't let him run? The next time these people want to stop a favourite, they know they only have to make a phone call.'

'Yes,' Laura sighed, 'I do see that.'

Ron Rowland, the Jockey Club security officer, had left the Met. ten years before, but he had retained the speech habits and mannerisms of a policeman. Outwardly, it was only his checked tweed suit that now set him apart from his former colleagues.

Henry Straker found him standing outside Midnight Express's box chatting to Declan Hoolihan.

Straker and Rowland nodded at one another in recognition of their official positions.

'So how does he seem?' Henry asked as Declan pulled back the stable door.

'Pretty normal; a bit on edge maybe, but then he knows where he is.'

'Stick a head collar on him and trot him up for me, would you?'

The lad had to take off the muzzle which Midnight Express was wearing to stop him eating his bed. He took him outside and jogged the horse twenty-five yards up the tarmac and back again.

Henry Straker stroked his chin. 'He looks bright enough to me. Let's have him back inside.'

Ron Rowland followed Straker into the stable and stood with his back to the door.

The short burst of exercise had made Midnight Express come to life. He fidgeted while the vet looked into the corners of his eyes.

'They look normal,' Straker declared as he went to get his bag from the doorway. 'I'll just take his temperature and some blood, and that'll do.'

Midnight Express resented having a thermometer pushed into his rear end. He rushed his hind quarters over to the other side of the stable.

Once he and Declan had managed to settle the horse enough to get the job done, the vet had difficulty in reading the result. 'Bloody thermometers! Why don't they colour the mercury so you can see it properly?' After a few moments' scrutinising it at different angles, he announced, 'A hundred and one – normal.'

Extracting a blood sample from the horse seemed to be more difficult than taking his temperature.

'It's no good; we'll have to put a twitch on him,' Straker said testily.

While Declan kept a cord twisted tightly around the horse's top lip, Straker disappeared the other side of his head, where there was more room to work, to jab a needle into a vein in his neck.

He soon reappeared with two plastic tubes full of thick crimson fluid. 'Right, that'll do, lad.' He patted Midnight Express on the neck. To Declan, he said, 'Okay, you can let him down now. If you're at all worried about him, come and find me.'

Laura arrived as the vet was closing his bag.

'What's the verdict?' she asked.

'He looks perfectly all right to me,' Straker answered. 'Here's your phial of the blood sample; I'm sending this other one off straight away for analysis; I'm sure it'll be clean.'

Luke Mundy sat in the jockeys' changing room, quivering nervously. He'd had no trouble doing the weight this time; the mounting pressure on his business had made sure of that. The flesh had been falling off him and his face was drawn and dull. For the first time in his career, matters were beyond his control and the influence of his bullying charm.

The other jockeys, all amateurs, were for the most part too nervous themselves to notice the absence of Luke's normal boastful ebullience. When they were called into the parade ring, Luke went with the rest of them as if he were in a trance. He saw Laura's stony face in the centre of the circle and tried to put a spring in his stride as he crossed to her.

The closer they were to the race, the more Laura resented having her hand forced.

'I don't know why the hell you're doing this,' she hissed when he reached her. 'The horse is too good and you're not good enough.'

'I'm doing it for you, actually,' he replied.

'The day you do anything for anyone besides yourself will be the day the world stops turning.' Laura made no attempt to disguise her bitterness.

Luke ignored it. 'I heard the stewards asked for a dope test?'

'Yes. Henry had a phone call with a tip-off that he had been got at.'

'And it was negative?'

'I presume it will be. At least, Henry said he couldn't see anything wrong with him, otherwise the horse wouldn't be here, would he?'

Luke didn't need a lot of convincing. 'Thank God. I thought maybe . . .' He gazed around at the other owners and trainers.

'You thought maybe what?'

'Nothing. It's okay. Henry would never have let him run if he had any doubt.'

'No, you're right. He wouldn't. Frankly, I wish to God the horse *couldn't* run, so make sure you pull him up immediately if he's not feeling all right,' Laura pleaded.

'Look, Laura, winning this race means more than you'll ever know, so I just hope to hell you've done your job properly.' There was naked desperation in Luke's voice. Laura softened; she almost wanted to encourage him.

'I've done everything I can, despite the fact that I never wanted him to run. Whether he lasts three miles or not . . .

Well, you'll know sooner than me.'

Luke Mundy clenched his jaw and whispered, 'He'd fucking better.'

Rory Gillespie was looking down from the back of the members' stand.

He saw the horse and, numb with anger, glanced at his race card again. Of course it was on the card; Laura and Patrick had said they were only going to get it pulled out that morning. But they hadn't. What the hell was going on?

He glanced at the paddock again, looking for the jockey. He spotted the colours of red with orange disc and watched Luke walk into the parade ring with the other amateurs, and his blood seethed.

Rory shook his head, perplexed. Laura had been so adamant, when he'd talked to her about it, that Midnight Express wouldn't run; but there she was, legging up her arrogant pig of a husband to flog round in a race of little value to anyone except himself. The horse would never recover in time for the Champion Chase. Why the hell was she doing it?

It wasn't just the fact that Midnight Express was running that was hurting; it was the duplicity of the woman who had promised to keep the horse fresh for Cheltenham.

The jockeys were called to mount up and Rory watched in final disillusionment as Luke and Midnight Express were led on to the course. He saw Laura heading back towards the stands. Almost at a run, he hurried to catch her on the way to Luke's box.

He reached her at the top of the stairs. Still hoping for a logical explanation, he kept his voice calm.

'Hi. I thought you were going to miss this race?'

Laura looked embarrassed. 'I was. Come with me to the box and I'll tell you about it.'

'I haven't got time,' Rory lied. 'Tell me now.'

Laura glanced round to see if they were being listened to. Satisfied that they weren't, she said quietly, 'Look, don't worry. I'm still going to run him in the Champion, and he'll be all right. Luke won't give him a hard race.'

'What the hell's he running him for, then?'

'I'll explain it all to you afterwards, I promise, but I can't now, Rory.'

Rory shook his head and pretended to make light of what she was saying. 'Okay, but I don't like being told one thing, then seeing exactly the opposite going on.'

Laura touched his arm, seeking his trust and patience. 'You'll understand. But look, I've got to go and watch the race.' She gave his arm a quick squeeze, released it and turned to take the last flight of stairs to the top of the stand.

Rory looked after her for a moment, and tried to work out what he was feeling. Sighing, he decided to trust her, but angry doubts still crowded his mind. He walked back through the stand to the box of the owner for whom he had won the previous race and, against all his professional instincts, accepted another large tumbler of Scotch.

A gambler knows – or ought to know – that he has become an addict when, with only ten pounds in the world to his name, he is prepared to stake fifteen on the turn of a card, the spin of a ball or the result of a race.

Luke Mundy was in just that position, only playing for vastly greater stakes.

The confidence he had felt when he had struck the bet was deserting him, being replaced by an insistent doubt that perhaps he'd got it wrong. The effect of this doubt is one of the reasons why so many people like to bet – the sweaty palms, the tightening of the colon, the constant licking of the lips; gambling to lose all is a very efficient stimulator of adrenaline. But never does the gambler quite allow himself to consider what might happen if he loses; that would be sanity, and sane people wouldn't put themselves through this self-inflicted torture.

Luke wouldn't admit even to himself that, for him, this race was a matter of shit or bust.

'Fuck it! I *can't* get beaten! Think positive!' he urged himself as Declan led Midnight Express out on to the course. The lad grudgingly winked at him and wished him luck. Luke didn't reply.

Luke had ridden Midnight Express often enough. He knew how the horse liked to be treated. He knew about his idiosyncrasy when it came to being settled. He gave him a long rein and let him hack past the stands before pulling up and turning back to the three mile start, round the bend behind the water jump.

He tried but failed to push to the back of his mind the nagging thought that the horse might have been got at.

Maybe he was on a horse which couldn't win, no matter what he did.

But then, he reasoned, Henry Straker wouldn't have let the animal run if he hadn't been a hundred percent certain about it.

And Laura, he knew, would have withdrawn the horse at the slightest excuse.

He thought of the party with whom he'd struck the bet. Would they cheat? There was more than enough money at stake for most people to have considered it; but few people had any idea how to go about doping a racehorse in the conditions of security that now prevailed on British race courses. It was a lot more difficult than the general public realised.

Down at the start, a handler tightened Midnight Express's girth and surcingle before he slowly walked round with the five other runners, waiting for the starter to call them into line.

Up until that moment, Midnight Express had behaved quite normally, getting a little warm on his neck. But as Luke pulled down his goggles and jogged across towards the inside of the track, he knew something was wrong.

The horse would usually have been tugging his arms out in eagerness to get on with the race, and Luke should have been struggling in his amateurish way to get it settled. But Midnight Express felt alarmingly as if he didn't want to go anywhere.

They were under orders.

Would he lose the bet if he shouted 'No' to the starter and didn't race?

He didn't have time to decide. The sight and sound of the tapes jerking up suddenly brought the horse back to life. Luke's confidence returned with a surge as he felt his horse spring forward with the rest of the field.

Within five strides, he found himself in the lead and being run away with – just what he did not need.

Though he would never have accepted it, Luke's riding

ability was, at best, basic. He should have given the horse
his head and let him settle in front; instead he tried to
fight with him. He was still struggling to pull him back
to the others when the first fence loomed.

Midnight Express got in close to it, going too fast to
give himself time to tuck his front legs up beneath him.
Luke braced himself as the horse hammered the fence.
But, such was the animal's momentum, he parted the
birch two feet from the top and carried on through. The
unusually steep drop behind the fence caught him out
and he pecked slightly as he landed.

Luke, still desperately trying to hold him up, had such
a tight grip on the reins that when Midnight Express
stretched his neck to recover his balance, the jockey was
yanked forward and almost out of the saddle.

There was a split second when Luke thought he'd gone
beyond the point of no return before his horse bobbed
his head back and caught him full in the face.

Luke's terror momentarily subsided when he felt his
feet in contact with the stirrup irons. In the next instant,
his body balance was violently overcorrected by the speed
of the horse galloping on. Midnight Express took a vicious
tug in the mouth and Luke would have turned a backward
somersault if he hadn't still had a limpet grip on the reins.

By the time he was balanced again, he'd lost all control
of the horse. Midnight Express wasn't just running freely
towards the next fence, he was bolting. Luke had never
experienced this before; it was like careering downhill in
a loaded lorry with no brakes or steering. Worse, the
horse seemed unaware that it had anyone on its back.
For the first time in his life, Luke knew raw fear.

He knew that something terrible was going to happen at any moment. But even in his terror, he knew what he should do and forced himself to do it. He sat as quietly as a nun and prayed to an unfamiliar God.

But Midnight Express galloped on as if he'd gone mad and would have run blindly into a brick wall if he'd met one.

Luke was too petrified even to think about bailing out, or the outcome of his bet.

Three strides before the next fence, he prepared himself for the inevitable shattering fall.

Miraculously, as if someone had tripped a switch, the horse suddenly regained his senses. He popped over the fence accurately as if that had always been the plan.

Luke heaved out the lungful of air he'd been holding in.

There were approximately three hundred yards before the next fence: an open ditch. It was just enough to get the horse settled.

Now the danger was past, Luke's thoughts quickly reverted to his bet. He was alive, his horse was running; there was still a good chance he could win.

He was almost back in control as they jumped easily over the ditch and began the long turn into the back straight. The ground here was well worn and rough on the inside from months of racing. Midnight Express faltered slightly as his feet adjusted to the new conditions. Luke grasped the chance to get him properly anchored. If the horse's erratic behaviour hadn't taken too much out of him, he could still win. The elation at having him settled lasted as long as it took to gallop the hundred yards to the apex of the bend.

When he reached it, Luke knew without any doubt that Midnight Express wouldn't be winning anything.

The absurd sickening sensation that only gamblers know surged through his body – a sensation of complete and utter hopelessness, failure and despair. And bubbling up beneath was a violent anger.

It was obvious even to Luke's limited experience that the horse had been drugged.

His tongue was hanging from the right-hand side of his mouth; his legs seemed to be made of rubber. Common sense and an instinct for self-preservation were screaming at Luke to pull up, but they were outvoted by a desperation to claw back the disastrous bet.

Reckless, vain hopes filled his head.

Just let him jump one more fence; maybe he's swallowed some mud, Luke pleaded.

Midnight Express stumbled in a patch of soft ground. With instinctive bravery, he tried to save himself, but he'd already lost control of his limbs. As his nose crashed into the soft turf, his big frame carried on rolling. His neck snapped.

Luke, still clutching at implausible hopes, felt the horse's legs buckle beneath him. The big, honest head dropped from his sight and the ground rushed up to meet him as he was catapulted from the saddle. His instincts bade him put out an arm to save himself, an instant too late. His helmet hit the ground like a cannon ball as the dead horse took its last, almost gentle turn on to him. The scissor action – the dread of all jockeys – snapped Luke's neck an inch below the base of his skull.

The release of death was longer coming to Luke than

it had been to his horse – several pain-racked seconds in which every nerve end in his body was rubbed raw. As he lay in paralysed agony, his only thoughts were of bitter hatred for the person he knew had been responsible for his fall.

He opened his eyes. An ambulanceman was leaning over him, telling him not to move. Luke struggled to open his mouth to speak.

The ambulanceman saw the jockey straining and tried to calm him. A soft, voiceless gasp escaped the white lips of the suffering man before he gave up and his head lolled to one side. No more breath came; eyes stared blankly across the damp turf.

Rory Gillespie, seeing it all from the nearby stands, couldn't stifle an outraged gasp at the sight of one of the nastiest falls he'd ever seen. Accidents on the flat, when one was least expecting them, were always the worst. If the jockey survived at all, he wouldn't be on the back of a horse for a very long time, unless he was owed a miracle.

Beside Luke, the horse, once a beautiful, highly tuned athlete of an animal, a personality in his own right, was now a motionless mount of so much skin and flesh. The rest of the field thundered past the stricken horse and jockey and on round the bend towards the next fence; they had a race to win.

Laura, not many yards from Rory in her husband's private box, uttered a horrified scream as Midnight Express crunched down on to Luke. She gripped the rail of the balcony to hold herself up as the blood drained from her face.

When it was obvious to all his guests that Luke Mundy was not going to get up, they looked at Laura with appalled embarrassment, guiltily putting down their drinks, uncertain now about accepting Luke's hospitality. A few moved towards her tentatively, offering comfort.

George Rutherford was the first to take control. 'Come on, Laura, I'll take you down to see what's happened. Let's hope they're both just winded.' He sounded genuinely concerned.

She stared at him for a moment, numb with horror, shaking her head. Wordlessly, she fled from the box and along the corridor to the stairs. Reaching the ground floor, she ran blindly through the bar at the west end of the stand, down the track where the horses walked to the course, and out on to the soft turf.

Her view of the prone horse and the smaller red and orange bundle beside it shook and juddered as she ran. She accepted a lift from the course doctor, who was already in radio contact with the St John's ambulancemen at the scene.

Laura felt tears streaming down her cheeks as the doctor solemnly said, 'All right,' into the handset, his eyes confirming what Laura had been dreading. 'I'm sorry but your husband's dead.' The doctor slowed the car and firmly clasped Laura's hand.

Henry Straker was climbing out of the duty Range Rover as they pulled up. They stood quietly as the field came round on the second circuit and were flagged around the bodies on the ground. Then Straker walked straight across to the horse and knelt beside it. He looked up at Laura and shook his head, tears of regret in his eyes. He stood and turned to the knacker who had arrived to remove the carcass.

'They'll want him up at Hawkshead,' he said quietly, 'for an autopsy. He's obviously died from a broken neck. Just tell them to check his heart. I'll get on to them later.'

Fred Willis, the knacker, nodded and started to sort out the winch in his trailer to get the horse out of sight and off the course as fast as possible. 'And treat him with some respect,' Straker added solemnly.

Laura stared, still not wanting to believe it, as the big bay body was dragged across the grass. Reluctantly she turned away and walked the few yards to her husband. Two St John's ambulancemen were lifting him on to a stretcher. They began to lay a blanket over him. When they dropped it gently over his face, she felt as if her stomach had been wrenched from her. And she was struck by the bizarre fact that she cared more about the man dead than she had when he was alive.

Before they picked up the stretcher, she knelt beside it and lifted back the blanket. She gazed at the familiar face, softened in death, and prayed that now he would be at peace in a way he never had been in life. She let the blanket fall back and stood up to find Patrick Hoolihan beside her.

'Is there anything I can do, ma'am?'

She looked at his weathered, dependable face.

'Yes. I'm going to go with Luke. Can you get my car and bring it to the hospital?'

'Of course.'

'The keys are in my Puffa, up in the box.'

Patrick nodded, then reached out and squeezed her

hand before taking a last look at Midnight Express in the trailer for his final journey and turning to go back to the stands.

'Would you like me to come with you?' Henry Straker asked.

She shook her head. 'Thanks, Henry, but I'll be all right. I know there's nothing I can do; I just want to be there and hear it confirmed.'

Midnight Express had started even-money favourite. The punters who had backed him, deprived of any further involvement in the race, carried on gazing at the flurry of activity around the dead horse.

Some – the regular racegoers and professionals – had a feeling that something just wasn't quite right about the way Midnight Express had performed. But then maybe the amateur jockey had simply got the horse upset. Most accepted it as one of those horrible, tragic accidents that happen from time to time in racing.

For Rory, there were too many questions that couldn't be ignored.

He was shocked by Luke Mundy's death, even though he hadn't known the man. It brought home to him bluntly the risks which he and every other jump jockey took each time they rode. But he had two more rides that afternoon.

By the time he had weighed in and changed after winning the last race of the day, he wasn't surprised to hear that Laura had gone.

He considered, then rejected the idea of driving straight to Langlands. Instead, he went home, confused and apprehensive. Luke Mundy was dead; so was Rory's best prospect for the Cheltenham Festival.

As a matter of course, Luke Mundy's crushed body was taken to the hospital in Esher which had seen a hundred broken jockeys pass through its doors. Laura listened in silence as a registrar told her that her husband had died of a broken neck. He would – the doctor said – have died very quickly. The hospital staff were justly proud that few left the way Luke Mundy did, in an undertaker's van.

With rather less ceremony, the body of Luke's horse was driven off the course. Unlike most of the equine victims of the race-track, Midnight Express's last journey was not to the abattoir. Fred Willis had to fulfil a contract with the Royal Veterinary College's pathology lab at Hawkshead in Potters Bar, and this horse would require an autopsy.

His order was for a fresh carcass of a horse killed while racing. The consultant pathologist and his students were studying the effects of trauma on an animal's organs.

At the service doors of the college labs, two porters and the knacker expertly winched the half-ton carcass into a cavernous cold store, and Professor Douglas, the head of the pathology department, was phoned with the good news.

The morning after Midnight Express fell and killed Luke Mundy, the back pages of the papers gave the event full coverage.

The Jockey Club had confirmed the rumour that before the race the stewards had received a tip-off that Midnight Express might have been doped. They had ordered a pre-race sample to be taken and tested. In the light of the fatal accident, that test had been processed without the normal delay of ten to fourteen days and the results were expected to be announced shortly. It was also reported that the duty vet who had inspected the horse before the race had given his view that there was nothing wrong with the horse before it raced.

For many people, the reason for Midnight Express's unusual behaviour became obvious; towards the front of the papers, other aspects of the event were being considered.

The flamboyant 'Lucky' Luke Mundy, it was reported, had timed his demise well. It had just been revealed that Thames Land, the development company he controlled, had substantially defaulted on major loans. A mole at a crisis meeting of the remainder of the board the previous evening had supplied the information that their assets, conservatively valued, fell short of their liabilities by several hundred million pounds. After Canary Wharf and other spectacular failures of large property companies, it wasn't an uncommon sort of story, but Luke's picture, with his famous, macho grin as he held high yet another racing trophy, added an extra dimension to it.

Rory drove down to Lambourn to buy the papers as soon as the shop in the High Street opened at six-thirty. He tried to eat his breakfast, but his system wasn't taking in food. He wanted to believe what he was reading, that what had happened the day before was a simple, though tragic matter of a tired horse stumbling. But every line of thought led him back to the probability that there was more to it than that.

He went out to ride work in the last lot for one of the local trainers. As he rode out, and that afternoon, driving to Worcester, he couldn't rid himself of his doubts about Laura. He scarcely noticed he'd ridden a winner and two thirds.

Driving home, twice he picked up his mobile phone and dialled the number at Langlands. Both times, he failed to push the 'send' button.

Three days later, after a weekend that seemed to have stretched itself into a fortnight, Laura received a telephone call from the Jockey Club.

She was alone in her study at Langlands, staring out at the wet afternoon.

'Could I speak to Mrs Mundy, please?'

'Speaking.'

'This is Major Caswall from Portman Square.'

Laura tried to disguise her anxiety. 'Oh good,' she said. 'Have you got the results?'

'Yes, I'm glad to say we have. We've had the sample taken from Midnight Express analysed and there are no irregularities.'

Laura let out a gasp of relief. 'You mean it was clean?'

'Yes. No problem there at all. I thought I'd let you know right away, what with all the ghastly speculation there's been in the gutter press.'

Laura composed herself. 'Thank you very much indeed. That's great news.'

'I thought it might be. I'm posting you a copy of the lab report; you'll have it in the morning.'

With a brisk, though not unfriendly, 'goodbye' Major Caswall rang off.

Laura held the phone to her ear for a few moments, listening to the hum on the open line. After a moment, she pressed the plunger to get a dialling tone. Slowly, she punched out Rory's number. She reached the last digit, allowed her finger to hover over it, and, with a shrug of regret, cleared the line and dialled Patrick Hoolihan at the yard.

Professor Ewan Douglas tried not to gloat over his unexpectedly fine carcass. He was not interested in the sport of horse racing, but he was passionately interested in the physiology of the animals which took part. Very often, when he came into contact with them, they had died carrying little fat, at the peak of their fitness; they were fine specimens to handle.

The blood in the vessels of this animal – killed on course, not in an abattoir – was coagulated and of no autoptical value. But there were plenty of other fluids and secretions to examine.

Carefully he oversaw the dissection, removal and isolation of the animal's internal organs. He instructed a group of three of his students to carry out a detailed analysis of the contents of the animal's bladder.

'As you know, we can tell a lot about the condition of a mammal from the state of its urine. That's why the first thing you're asked to do in a medical is to pee in a jar,' Professor Douglas announced as he inspected the bottle of thick yellow fluid before handing it over to his students.

The professor walked back into the lab after lunch. The

two students – a man and a girl – detailed to analyse the horse's urine looked up excitedly.

'How are you getting on, then?' he asked.

'Well,' the girl said, 'the specific gravity seems low.'

Their professor nodded. 'Within reason, that's what you'd expect – a direct result of a high level of exercise. Nothing odd there. What else have we found?'

'Well, sir,' the young man ventured eagerly, 'it seems rather odd in a horse that's just come off the racecourse, so maybe I've got it wrong, but I thought I found traces of a pre-med.'

'That sounds more than odd; it sounds bloody impossible. But what exactly do you think you've found?'

'Well, er, I *think* it's xylazine.'

'Do you now? I don't think it can be. You'd better run your tests again in the morning.'

After they had gone, Professor Douglas carried out a series of his own tests.

Jim Knight, the official whose job it was to arrange the acquisition of appropriate animals, dead and alive for the lab, had gone home. Professor Douglas badgered the college switchboard into giving him the man's home telephone number, wrote it carefully in his diary and drove home to Barnet. On the way, as was his habit, he bought an *Evening Standard* from a paperboy at the lights on the Great North Road.

By the time he had settled down in his small tobacco-smelling study, he reckoned Jim Knight would have arrived at his home in Richmond and telephoned him.

'Hello, Mr Knight. It's Professor Douglas here. I'm sorry to trouble you at home, but I've rather a particular enquiry about the horse that was delivered at the weekend.'

'Yes?'

'Yes. I wondered if you could tell me the horse's name, and where it died?'

'Good heavens, I'm afraid that's not the sort of thing I normally carry in my head. I've got all the details in the office. As you know, we're required to do a partial autopsy on the animal. All I can tell you off the top of my head is that it fell while racing and broke its neck. I can tell you the rest tomorrow.'

'I need to know tonight, please.'

He could almost hear the resigned shrug at the other end of the line. 'I suppose I could ring Willis from here. I've got his number.'

'Who's Willis?'

'The knacker who usually supplies us with equine carcasses.'

'I'd be most grateful if you would, and let me know right away, as much as you can.'

The professor gave the man his telephone number and wished him a polite goodbye. He walked to the gramophone in the corner of his study, put on a record of Bruckner's Third Symphony, and sat in a large armchair to light his pipe and open the *Evening Standard*.

After he had read the front page, he started to leaf on to the arts section when his eye was caught by a small half-column.

The piece was following up the speculation that had been provoked about the plight of Thames Land Plc in the wake of Luke Mundy's death. And Luke Mundy, he read, had been killed after a fall on his horse at Sandown

Park in an amateur race the previous week.

It was the final edition of the paper, published late enough to include the news that the blood sample taken from the horse before the race had now been analysed and found free of any introduced substances.

Professor Douglas read the piece again, then got up to fetch his battered briefcase from the hall where he'd left it.

In his chair once more, he pulled out the notes he had made of his readings and conclusions on the analysis of the horse's urine and shook his head with pleasurable excitement.

The telephone beside him rang. He picked it up unhurriedly.

'Professor Douglas?'

'Speaking.'

'Knight here. I got hold of Willis. He knew right away what the animal was called. Apparently it died in a fairly dramatic fall.'

The professor broke in. 'And it was called Midnight Express.'

'You knew anyway?' Knight sounded tetchy.

'Not when I last spoke to you, but I've been reading the evening paper since. Thank you for confirming it. I'm most grateful.'

He replaced the receiver, then stood and turned down the strident brass chords of the third movement before consulting the directory and picking up the phone again to dial.

'Hello. Is that racecourse security? ... My name is Professor Douglas, from the Royal Veterinary College,

Hawkshead. I'd like to speak to whoever's in charge, please ... Good evening. I've just read a report in the paper about the horse, Midnight Express, which fell and died last week ... I see that a blood sample that was taken before the race has been declared by the Jockey Club to be free from any introduced substances. Is that right? ... I see. Well, the carcass of this animal was delivered to our labs, and we started work on it today. Our preliminary analysis of the urine shows clearly that the horse died with significant traces of the drug xylazine in its system. This is not what actually caused death, but there is no question that it would have affected the horse's performance very radically ... Yes, I'd say that whoever introduced it could be held responsible for its fall, and therefore its rider's death.'

Two men called at Langlands that evening. Ron Rowland, the head of security at Kempton, and Detective Inspector Stuart Wood announced themselves soberly to the small Filipino woman who opened the door to them.

'Is Mrs Laura Mundy at home?' the policeman asked.

'Sure. I get her for you.'

The maid ushered them into the sixteenth-century hall and scuttled up the stairs to find her mistress.

Laura came down looking tired but resigned. She had been to the stables that day, but hadn't been able to face going racing – not to anyone's great surprise.

She recognised Ron Rowland from Kempton.

'Hello. What can I do for you?' she asked.

'Good evening, Mrs Mundy.' Ron Rowland knew her

face well. 'We're sorry to have to trouble you at a time like this, but I'm afraid it's come to light that there are circumstances surrounding your husband's death that lead us to suspect foul play.'

Laura looked blank for a moment. 'I'm sorry? You mean you think it was planned in some way?'

'We've got new information that makes it look that way.'

'I don't see how. It was just Luke and the horse out there. And we know the horse went off all right. Portman Square have already phoned me to say the blood test had shown up negative.'

'I'm afraid subsequent tests on the carcass of the horse have shown otherwise,' the policeman said.

'What do you mean?' Laura asked indignantly. 'You were there when the sample was taken.' She looked at Rowland.

'Please, don't get upset, Mrs Mundy,' the security officer said. 'But the lab which carried out the autopsy found traces of a drug in the animal's urine.'

'What drug?'

'Xylazine.'

'That shows in the urine?' Laura asked with surprise. 'But it's used as a pre-med; it would knock a horse out completely.'

'That would depend on the size of the dose, of course,' the policeman said. 'So you can see that we do need to ask you a few questions. Is there somewhere convenient?'

Laura glanced at him with annoyance. She had always disliked pompous officials. 'What's wrong with here?' She waved the two men to a large Knole sofa in front of the great empty fireplace.

105

Ron Rowland smiled gratefully. 'After you,' he said, gesturing at a chair opposite.

Laura walked across and flopped into it under sufferance. Rowland and the detective inspector perched themselves on the front edge of the deep sofa.

The detective was a tall, lean man with lank brown hair falling over his forehead. He wore a thick patterned pullover beneath a drab grey anorak. He looked more like a schoolmaster than a policeman. But there was a restlessness in his eyes that gave him a furtive, faintly hostile look to anyone whom he was questioning, however innocent he thought them.

Having got this far in the proceedings, he evidently considered that Rowland had served his purpose and took no further notice of him.

'Can you tell me who was with the horse from the time Mr Rowland and the official vet . . .' he glanced at the notebook he had pulled from his pocket '. . . Mr Straker left?' The policeman subjected Laura to an intense scrutiny as he asked the question.

Laura glared back at him. 'Am I right in thinking that you think *I* might have had something to do with this?'

'You're right in thinking that I think somebody must have got at the horse between the time the blood test was taken and when it reached the course. Unless, of course, it was trained to inject itself.'

Rowland winced.

Laura stood up. 'I'm sorry, I have absolutely no intention of answering questions on the basis that I am a suspect. I will tell you this, though. The whole time, from the moment Henry Straker left the stable, there were at least two people with the horse. Either myself, Declan Hoolihan, his lad, Terry, the travelling head lad, or Pat Hoolihan, my head lad who had come to the races for the day . . . to watch Midnight Express run. He was a bit of a favourite in the yard, and the best horse I've ever bloody trained.' Rowland turned his eyes away from the sight of tears in her eyes. The policeman continued to gaze at her superciliously. 'And you come here suggesting that I might have given him the drug which killed him!'

Detective Inspector Wood didn't blink. 'It wasn't the drug that killed it, Mrs Mundy. That just slowed it down, anaesthetised it a little. It died by breaking its neck when it fell.'

Laura glared at him with irritation. 'I know that! I was there when he was winched on to the trailer. You know perfectly well what I mean! Now, if you want to talk to me again, you can make an appointment and my solicitor will be present. I've heard about what you people can do when you've made up your mind you've got a culprit.'

The detective shrugged his shoulders to imply that Laura was being very foolish, and stood up. 'If that's the way you want it, Mrs Mundy. I take it you've no objection if I question some of your staff?'

'I don't suppose I could stop you if I wanted to, but just don't give them a hard time. They've taken it extremely badly. When you've lavished a lot of care and time on a horse like Midnight Express, you feel it when they go. It's like losing a close friend.' She turned and walked back towards the stairs. 'You can see yourselves out.'

'We'll just have a brief word with your maid before we

go,' the policeman said and nodded his colleague towards the nether regions of the house where he guessed the little Filipino was to be found.

Maria was reading a Spanish magazine when they walked into the kitchen. She put it down and leaped up on her short legs.

'It's all right. No need to stand up. Mind if we join you?'

The maid sat down. 'What you want?'

'Just to ask you a few questions about Mr Mundy, and Mrs Mundy?'

'I don't know nothing.'

The two men smiled and sat down at the table opposite her.

'Don't worry. All we want to know is how they got on.'

Maria looked blank.

'What I mean,' the policeman pressed, 'is whether you ever heard them arguing.'

The maid looked back at them both for a moment before she spoke. 'They argue,' she nodded. 'Some time, he shout, *very* loud. And she too. He make her very unhappy, I think.'

'Did he ever hit her or anything like that?'

Maria shook her head. 'I don't know. I never see.'

'But they used to argue a lot?'

She nodded. 'Very much.'

'What about?'

The little woman shook her head again. 'I no listen.'

The policeman smiled at her. 'Never mind. You've been very helpful. If we have to come and see you again, try to remember if you can recall anything you ever heard them say, okay?'

The maid nodded glumly, aware that she had somehow betrayed her employer's trust, but more scared of this gimlet-eyed policeman.

The two men left silently. Laura heard the great oak front door clunk home behind them, and sighed. She'd handled them very badly, she knew, but she never had been able to control her temper.

The security officer and the policeman drove down to the stable yard. They were told by a small, tight-lipped Irishman that the horse's lad had been with him from the moment he left the yard that morning to go to the races until he had let him off on to the course to canter down to the start. The lad in question was Declan Hoolihan, the Irishman's son, and he could be found at the Axe and Cleaver.

There were half a dozen lads in the pub, sitting around a pool table. They had been there a few hours. One of the novice hurdlers in the yard had won earlier in the afternoon. It had come as no surprise to the lads, and the small bookmaker in Andover was cursing his lack of prudence in not laying off some of their bets.

But the celebration that would normally have followed a win like this was dampened by the death of the most popular horse in the yard. There wasn't one among them who didn't feel upset by what had happened; Declan, in particular, trying to drink away his depression, had become loud and maudlin.

He had just lost a game of pool when the two men walked in, looked around and came straight across to the bench where he sat banging the end of his cue on the wooden floor.

'You're not going to feel too good getting up for first lot tomorrow,' the racecourse security man remarked.

'What's it got to do with you?' Declan challenged, recognising him.

'Is this him?' the policeman asked.

'Yes. Declan, this is Detective Inspector Wood from Surrey CID. He'd like to talk to you about what happened at Kempton.'

Declan looked up sulkily. 'What for?'

'Because your father told us you were with the horse the whole time until he raced and we need to clear up a few details. The horse had been doped,' the policeman said. 'Do you want to talk here in front of your mates, or shall we go back to the station where it's a bit more private?'

Although Declan was drunk he could detect the hard edge behind the man's friendly manner. He shuffled to his feet and hitched up his faded denims. 'How long will it take?'

'I doubt you'll be back here by closing time. You come in our car; we'll drop you back at the stables.'

The detective sat opposite Declan at the tubular-framed table in a small room in Andover police station. He checked that there were two cassettes in the tape recorder that he'd placed in front of him, and switched it on. He cleared his throat.

'DI Stuart Wood interviewing Declan Hoolihan, twenty-one forty-five, Monday, March fifth. Now, Declan, I want you to tell me everything you did from the time you woke up that morning until the moment you led Midnight Express out on to the course for his race.'

'What's the cassette for?'

'So that we've got an accurate record of what you tell me. You'll have one of the copies to take away with you. Now, tell me exactly what happened yesterday.'

Declan looked at him. Although he spoke with the rural accent of the Berkshire Downs where he had been reared, his Irishness gave him a natural enthusiasm for talking. All right, he thought, you want to know what happened; I'll tell you.

'I got up the usual time, just after six. I was down in the yard by six thirty. I looked on the board to see if any of the horses I look after were going out with the first or second lot. I knew Midnight Express was running, so I mucked him out first, gave him half a bucket of water then let him down to relax. I left a clean bale of straw outside his box so that once we'd left for the races someone else could shake it up – otherwise he'd have been stuffing his face with it.

'The other two horses I do were both going out first lot, so when I'd mucked them out, I left them tied up. Then I went off to tack up the horse I was going to ride, but when I went to pick his feet out, I found he'd got a loose shoe, so I had to see Dad – he's head lad – and put my tack on something else. I got a bollocking for not picking his feet before I'd tacked him up. I just had time to get his hay and a bucket of warm water to wash him down before we pulled out at seven thirty.

'I was going racing at nine thirty, so I had to get my skates on, we didn't get back in from first lot until ten to.

I had to wash and change then get Midnight Express ready – you know – the usual things; grease his feet, put his travelling sheet on. Terry – he's travelling head lad – he'd already plaited his mane and picked up his passport and my stable badge, and he'd got my tenner – day's expenses. Then we loaded and went off to Sandown.'

The policeman raised his hand to stem Declan's flow. 'Hang on. Let's just go back a bit. When you got back from riding out, were you with the horse until you loaded it?'

'Not in his box, like, but around the yard.'

'Did you see anyone else go into his box – another of the lads?'

Declan shook his head vehemently. 'No one at the yard would have touched him.'

'But did you see anyone besides yourself go into the horse's box?'

The lad thought for a moment then shook his head again. 'No. Just Mrs Mundy.'

'Why did she go in?'

'She's the bloody trainer, that's why. She nearly always has a look at the horses that are racing that day, before we load 'em.'

'Okay, so you put the horse in the box, then what?'

'Checked we had everything – there was three of them went to Sandown Tuesday.'

'And who went with them in the lorry?'

'Me, Terry and Lofty.'

'Another lad?'

Declan nodded.

'What did you do when you got to Sandown?'

'Us lads unloaded the horses while Terry went off and found which stables we were in.'

'What then?'

'Terry said for me to stay with the horse.' Declan shrugged. 'He usually does – so me and Lofty hung around outside the boxes sorting the tack.'

'Did you have to do anything to the horse?'

'Yeah. I put a muzzle on him and gave him a quarter of a bucket of water, then I put his stable rug on and let him loose. I locked his top door and went to the lads' canteen with the others. I hadn't been there five minutes when Dad came in – he'd driven up – and told me to get back to the horse.'

'Was there anyone around your box when you got back?'

'No. Dai Price was chatting to the lad who looked after the horse in the box next door – he was riding him later.'

'Dai Price is Mrs Mundy's stable jockey,' Rowland interjected.

'Yes, but he was outside the wire security fence; he didn't have a stable pass.'

'Right. Did Mrs Mundy come to see the horse?'

'Not then.'

'Not at all?'

'Oh yeah, but not till the vet came with the security bloke.'

'Right. What time did the vet come?'

'I dunno – about one, I should think. He and that bloke,' Declan nodded at Rowland, 'came up and said they had to take a sample. I didn't know what was going on – I mean, the horse hadn't even run. Anyway, they checked that the horse had been locked up all the time and been behaving normally.'

'What did they do?'

'The vet asked me to put a head collar on the horse and trot him up. Then I put him back and Mr Straker came in and tried to take his temperature. The horse played up a bit, but I settled him. Mr Straker said he'd take the blood sample, but Express wasn't too keen, so he told me to put a twitch on him.' Declan shrugged. 'Normally he's all right, but he was getting a bit excited. Anyway, I put the twitch on and held him, while Mr Straker took the sample.'

'That's correct,' Rowland nodded. 'I was present throughout. It's all in my report.'

'Thanks, Ron,' the policeman said. 'I'd like to hear the lad's version, though.' He turned back to Declan. 'Have you seen the vet take a sample before?'

'Yeah, 'course I have. They're always testing their blood these days; everybody does it.'

'And do they often need this twitch?'

'Not often, but sometimes, and the horse was a bit on his toes, knowing he was going racing.'

'Okay. Then what happened?' The detective had become more tense.

'Mr Straker told me to take Express out and trot him again, so he could check him. I led him out and trotted him up and down a few times. He seemed all right and Mr Straker said to put him back in the box and not to take my eyes off him. Mrs Mundy came up and said, "What's the story?" Straker said he couldn't find nothing wrong with him. So I put the horse back in the box.' Declan shrugged.

'What did Mrs Mundy do?'

'She had a chat with Mr Straker and the other bloke, then they went off and she came up to me and said, "How does he look?" I said, "Fine." She gave a funny sort of laugh and said, "That's a pity, I'd rather he didn't run today." '

The detective's eyes narrowed fractionally. 'Do you know why she said that?'

Declan laughed. 'Yeah. None of us wanted him to run; he had a bloody good chance in the Champion Chase – two miles, better distance for him – and quite a lot of us had money on him for it. But this bloody hunter chase would knacker him ...' Declan faltered at the thought that it had indeed knackered the horse. 'He was a horse that didn't want too much work; he lost a load of condition after a hard race and took two or three weeks to put it back on. But Mr Mundy didn't want to know. Even Dad told him straight he shouldn't waste the horse in a race like that.'

'And Mrs Mundy didn't want him to run either?'

'No, 'course not. It's much better to win at Cheltenham than some poxy amateur chase.'

'I see. Then what did she do?'

'She went in the box to have a look at the horse.'

'Did you go in with her?'

'No. While she was with him, I went off to get my grooming kit.'

'Were you gone long?'

'I dunno. A couple of minutes.'

'Was Mrs Mundy carrying anything when she went in?'

Declan thought a moment. 'I can't remember. 'Ere, you don't think she gave it something then, do you?'

'I don't think anything yet. I'm just getting all the facts together.'

'But we heard the blood test showed up clean anyway.'

'Yes, but Mr Straker had already taken the sample by then, hadn't he?'

Declan's jaw dropped. 'No. She wouldn't have. Not to Express. She's not like that; besides, Express was one of our best horses.'

'You may be right, but I just want to ask you a few questions about Mrs Mundy. Now, you've said she didn't really want the horse to run that day, but her husband who was riding it, insisted?'

'That's right.'

'Do you know if there was much disagreement between them about it?'

'I dunno. I should think so. I mean, it was common knowledge they weren't getting on too well.'

'Common knowledge?'

'Well, some of the lads had heard them arguing; he could be a helluva sod when he wanted. Dad reckoned there was something up between them and he's often up at the house with Mrs M. We didn't like him down the yard. He was always throwing his weight around. Whenever he got beaten on a horse, it was always someone else's fault. He wasn't much of a jockey – hands like a fork-lift truck.'

'Interview terminated at twenty-two-o-three.' The detective switched off the tape recorder and leaned back in his chair. 'Right, Declan. That'll do for now. But I'll need to speak to you again. Here's your copy of your interview. And I don't want you talking about it or playing

116

it to anyone else – understand? Right. I'll get one of the local bobbies to take you home.'

Next morning, with no arrangements to ride out, Rory slipped out of the house before his wife came down. He got into his car and headed for Langlands. He hadn't rung Laura to tell her he was coming. He knew she wouldn't be surprised but he wondered if she was ready to see him yet.

He spotted Laura's second lot walking in single file from the trees below the ridge, up on to the wide bend of pale and dark green stripes that curved and rose gently towards the horizon. He squinted into the bright sun in an attempt to see if Laura was among the three figures standing beside the Land Rover at the top of the gallop, but he couldn't identify her without binoculars.

He decided, anyway, that he didn't want to talk to her in front of anyone else. He carried on towards the back entrance to the yard.

Rory sensed a subdued air about the place as he walked in. There was none of the normal banter and laughter as the few lads who weren't riding out went about their chores. Patrick came out of his office with no hint of his famous grin.

''Morning, Rory. I didn't know we were expecting you this morning.'

'You weren't.'

'Well, you're not the first unexpected visitor, by any means. I've already sent a few up to the house.'

'Journalists?'

Patrick nodded. 'And police. They were here last night

too. They went and got Declan out of the pub and took him to Andover. He was gone an hour or more. Of course, they had to let him go. They'd already been up to the house but I heard Mrs Mundy sent them packing with a flea in their ear.'

'That doesn't sound too clever,' Rory said.

Patrick shrugged. 'She's nothing to hide. I suppose it's their job to be suspicious, but, God knows, the poor woman has just lost her husband.'

'Is she at the house or on the gallops?'

'She's at home. Michael's in charge today,' he said with a measure of sarcasm.

Rory nodded. Michael Thynne was Laura's young assistant, the son of one of her owners, and a lot more keen than knowledgeable.

'Right, well, I'd better go and join the queue.'

'I'm sure she'll give you priority,' Patrick said. 'She'll want to see you. It's a terrible shame about the horse,' he added gloomily.

Rory drove up the long avenue, queasy with foreboding. The police wouldn't have come without a reason. And yet, no one could have deliberately planned an accident like Luke's.

As he turned on to the large gravel forecourt of the house, a Daimler swept up to the front entrance and stopped alongside four other cars. A tall man in a pinstriped suit leaped out of the car and almost ran round to the front door. His noisy bell-ringing was answered at once and he was let in, with the door closing behind him before Rory had left his car.

Rory hadn't seen the man before, but he guessed he was Laura's solicitor. If a highly paid professional man was running around, Rory thought, there was already trouble. The churning in his guts quickened as he walked across and rang the bell himself.

The maid recognised him with a half-smile and showed him into the small sitting room where he and Laura had talked so intimately two weeks before.

There were already three other men waiting – the journalists Patrick had spoken of, Rory guessed.

They looked up, and knew at once who Rory was.

One of them, the youngest and fittest, was on his feet in an instant. 'Rory Gillespie, right?' He had a quick, London delivery – streetwise and free of glottal stops.

Rory nodded.

'What are you doing here?'

'I came to ride work.'

'But you're not dressed for it.'

'My gear's in the car. I usually have a chat with Mrs Mundy first, but she's not up on the gallops this morning.'

'You thought it would be business as usual, did you, despite her old man getting killed and all the fracas that's going on?'

Rory shrugged. 'Horses have to be exercised. Owners pay a lot of money for it.'

'What d'you know about her relationship with Luke? People say they weren't getting along too well.'

'If you know people who are saying that, ask them. I don't know anything about it. I've only just started riding for her. I don't think I ever spoke to him.'

An older man, more conventionally dressed, whom Rory recognised from one of the racing papers, reckoned he had better questions to ask.

'You must be disappointed about Midnight Express. He

had a good chance in the Champion Chase.'

'Sure, I'm disappointed, but a man's been killed. That's a bit more important than winning a bloody race.'

The younger man didn't like being outmanoeuvred. 'Never mind the philosophy, what we want is the story. I mean, did it look like a regular racing accident to you?'

'I don't know what you're trying to say. A horse came down in a race; it happens twenty times a day during the jumping season. Once in a while, the jockey gets hurt bad. This accident was a lot worse than usual, that's all.'

'But it came down on the flat, and that hardly ever happens. And why are the police here?' the young hack challenged.

'Ah, there you have me. I was as surprised as you when I heard.'

'And some heavyweight-looking brief just ran in. He wouldn't have got himself in a sweat without a good reason.'

'Look, I don't know anything about it. I don't want to talk to you people. I'll wait somewhere else.'

Rory turned and walked out of the room, shutting the door firmly behind him. Out in the great panelled hall, he didn't know where he was going to go. He thought he'd find out from the maid where Laura was and simply butt in. He was looking around for the way to the kitchens when a procession appeared from across the hall.

Laura, white and damp-eyed, was being escorted without being touched by two casually dressed men. The pin-striped lawyer was walking quickly, close behind them, like a tall, thin, worried hen.

Laura glanced at Rory, with a twitch of her tight lips.

The policemen ignored him until he spoke.

'Laura, for God's sake; what's going on?'

'Mrs Mundy's coming in to help us with our enquiries,' one of her escorts answered. 'That's all I can tell you at this point in time.' He evidently thought Rory was a journalist.

Laura, halfway across the hall, turned back to him. 'Don't worry, Rory, I won't be there long. Do you think you could just hang on to Midas until I'm out of the house – I think he's rather worried.' She gave a faint smile. 'I'll ring you as soon as I get back.'

The faces of her escorts didn't show what they thought of her view. Rory watched in glum silence as the party went out through the front door and two of the cars were driven away.

The journalists, seeing this from the window of the sitting-room, burst out and ran through the hall to their own cars.

Rory waited until the sounds of their departure had faded completely before leaving the house and walking down the lime avenue to the stables.

He found Declan just back from the gallops, but the lad couldn't tell him much more than he already knew, beyond the fact that Luke had been unusually nervous before his last, fatal ride. He hadn't expected much but he had to try and find out what was going on. He wanted desperately to believe that Laura's arrest was a case of overzealous police bungling. But he couldn't entirely rid himself of a niggling doubt about Laura's attitude and motives.

He drove away from Langlands bewildered and resenting these uncertainties, knowing that his judgement was being subverted by the revival of his old feelings for Laura.

He hadn't brought his racing gear with him; he hadn't even thought about it when he'd left the house that morning. Now he had to make a detour home on his way to ride at Stratford. He was in a hurry when he arrived at Camp Farm, but he took the time to go up and chat to Tommy, who was home from school with a touch of flu. He wished he could have stayed longer. But Pam came up too, wanting to know what was going on at Langlands. Reluctantly, Rory went downstairs with her. He didn't want to talk about it in front of his son.

'I told you there was something dodgy about that woman,' Pam declared triumphantly when Rory told her about Laura's compulsory visit to Andover police station. 'She probably knew her old man was in trouble and she's going for the insurance.'

'Don't be ridiculous!' Rory snapped. 'Nobody could have planned an accident like that.'

'Not to the jockey, maybe, but she'll get the money for the horse, won't she?'

'She never planned it; it's out of the question,' Rory said, suppressing his own uncertainty.

'You're still taken in, aren't you? Just because she's got a posh accent and lives in a bloody great mansion, you think she's above all that. But she pulls strokes, same as anybody else; Dai's told me.'

'Dai seems to be telling you a lot these days. Are you having some kind of scene with him?'

'He's just a friend,' Pam replied indignantly, but then couldn't control her spite. 'At least he's got bollocks.'

Rory forced himself to stay calm.

'Dai Price is a second-rate little shite and if it took any bollocks to pull horses to order, he wouldn't be doing it,' he said, barely keeping the anger from his voice.

'He's still managed to get more winners than you this season.'

'The season's not over yet.'

'That's why you're so keen on Laura Bloody Mundy, isn't it, because she's giving you some of Dai's rides. She won't be able to if she gets locked up.'

'Of course she's not going to get locked up. Now, I'm late; I'm not going to stand here arguing with you. I'll be back about seven.'

'Well, I'm going out to play squash at seven, so you'll have to look after Tommy.'

'Fine.' Rory picked up his kit and walked out of the house.

The gossip in the changing room at Stratford was dominated by Luke Mundy's death. Dozens of different versions of the event were circulating, most of them based on hearsay or the shoddy reporting of the tabloid papers. Rory was more worried by another rumour beginning to take shape – that the dead horse had been the subject of a formal autopsy, despite the negative results of the pre-race blood sample.

After riding a no-hoper in the novice hurdle for his father-in-law, Mick Fanshaw, Rory slipped into the press box to find the one journalist he trusted. Arthur Brian, wedged comfortably in his seat, was battling with his mobile phone and his lap-top PC. He greeted Rory warmly and beckoned him to sit down in the next chair.

'Hello, Arthur,' Rory said, pulling out his tobacco and papers. 'I didn't think you'd be here today.'

'I wanted to see Moon Chariot run once more before the Triumph.'

'Is she your big nap for Cheltenham?'

'That depends on how she runs today.'

'She'll beat my horse,' Rory said.

'Yes, she will. I'm sorry you've lost your ride in the Champion Chase. Though I see Laura's definitely running Flamenco Dancer now. Maybe you could jock Dai off that one too?'

'Maybe.' Rory lowered his voice. 'I think I'll still be able to ride the Irish horse in the Champion, but I wanted to talk to you about Midnight Express. There's a story going round that someone's already done an autopsy on the horse.'

Arthur nodded. 'There's been a little leak from Portman Square.' It wasn't the first time Arthur had been the recipient of information from the Jockey Club – they trusted him to stick to the facts they gave him and not to speculate. 'In a manner of speaking. There wasn't a complete autopsy. After all, the horse had only been tested an hour before he appeared in the parade ring. And that test was clean. But the poor animal was delivered to the veterinary college in Hawkshead and a professor and his students carried out some standard tests on it, researching the effects of trauma, and found traces of xylazine, which, as you may know, is a fairly common pre-med. Even a very small, discreet dose would have made it pretty dozy and certainly slowed it. I've already done my piece on it for the *Standard*, you can read all about it this evening.'

'So the horse was got at, after the sample had been taken?'

'So it would appear.'

Rory looked at the journalist; he couldn't quell the churning in his guts.

In those circumstances, it was hardly surprising that the police had felt Laura might be able to tell them something.

Rory rode two more races that afternoon, but he rode without conviction, while Dai Price barged his way through to win the handicap hurdle for his absent trainer.

Rory arrived home as Pam left to play squash, with a 'girlfriend'. 'We'll probably have a drink after, so don't expect me back too early.'

Rory shrugged, and thought of Dai Price. The Welshman hadn't been able to look him in the eye that afternoon but Rory couldn't have felt jealous if he'd tried. He cajoled Tommy back to bed and read him a Roald Dahl story without taking in a single word of it; his mind was full of Laura's predicament. But he didn't let his preoccupation show. When he reached the end of the story he left the boy to read a couple more himself while he went downstairs to feed his dog and do what he had been wanting to do all day.

Laura answered the phone herself. Rory felt absurdly relieved at the sound of her voice.

'The police let you go, then?' he said.

'Yes, thank God, I think they eventually believed that I had nothing to do with what's been going on. But what I can't understand is how anyone managed to get at him. At least, they've accepted that nobody would plan to kill someone that way.'

'How are you feeling about it?'

'Pretty miserable.'

'I'll come over.'

'No . . . no, Rory, don't, not now. I don't think that's a good idea. But come and ride work tomorrow. I'm really sorry about Midnight Express, but I still want you to ride the others.'

'All right,' Rory said flatly. 'But if you want me to come before then, just ring, okay?'

'Thanks, I might do that.'

Rory put the phone down, shaking his head with frustration. He wished he could understand what was going on and why the hell Laura had let the horse run. Of course, she was very shaken by what had happened – anyone would have been – being questioned about Luke's death. But a gap seemed to have opened up between them since the intimacy of their evening two weeks before.

He went back up to Tommy's room and settled down to talk about the kind of flies they should take with them to tackle the Wye salmon. Tommy wanted to tie some himself, so they wrote a list of what he would need, which Rory promised to get for him.

As he talked with his son, Rory resigned himself to the fact that Laura wouldn't ring him that night and stayed with Tommy until he went to bed two hours before his wife came home.

There was a palpable tension at the yard when he

arrived at Langlands next morning. Everyone knew, of course, that Laura had been to 'help the police with their enquiries'; the journalists had obligingly come straight down to tell them and to try, unsuccessfully, to get their reactions. The mood in the yard now was one of confused outrage.

Laura hadn't been down to the yard yet and Michael Thynne gave Rory his instructions. On the way up to the gallops, the lads and work riders relaxed a little, joking clumsily about Declan being taken in by the police. None of them believed he had anything to do with what had happened. Although they didn't say so, Rory sensed that they were less sure about their guv'nor's involvement.

Rory rode work on Rear Gunner, an ex-flat horse entered for the Triumph Hurdle at Cheltenham. At the top of the gallop he was almost surprised to see Laura standing by the Land Rover with Michael. She beckoned him over. Rory wheeled his horse round and walked back to her.

'Rory, that was great. If you get down, Mike can ride Gunner back.'

Rory swung out of the saddle and legged Michael into it.

As Michael and the horse walked away to join the rest of the string circling beneath a cloud of steam in the crisp morning sun, Laura turned to Rory.

'I'm sorry I've been so cagey,' she said with a sincerity that made Rory's head sing with relief. 'I think there's a tap on my phone, and I don't want to give anyone any grounds for suspicion.'

'Do you really think so?' Rory said, alarmed. 'What kind of suspicion?'

'That I might be involved with you, again.' She gave him a crooked smile.

Rory nodded. 'Okay, but I still want to know what's happening.'

'Let me deal with this lot, then I'll drive you back to the yard.'

When she had had another look at the horses and a quick word with some of their riders, she and Rory climbed into the Land Rover with Midas and bounced across the soft turf to the green lane that led down to the valley.

Laura, concentrating on the rutted route, didn't look at Rory as she spoke.

'I know you think I had something to do with what happened at Kempton,' she said bluntly.

'Not at all,' Rory said, a little too quickly. 'But after the conversations we'd had about your withdrawing the horse, I couldn't understand why you were still running him.'

'Listen, Luke promised me that if he won, he'd transfer the horse into my name. Now I realise what he was doing. He knew he was in trouble and he wanted to be sure I'd go on training the horse. In fact, I discovered afterwards that he'd already transferred him. Midnight Express was officially mine that morning. Luke shouldn't really have ridden him in his own colours.' She shrugged. 'His only condition had been that he rode in that race. Besides, he was threatening that if he didn't, he'd ride him in the Grand Military *and* the Champion Chase, and I wouldn't get the horse. In the circumstances, I didn't have much choice.'

'But you'll get the insurance money, I presume?'

'I may not. I knew Luke had problems, but I had no idea that they were as bad as they are. When the whole mess is cleared up, if there's not enough money in the kitty, his creditors could come after me for the money.'

'It seems like an unusually generous gesture for him,' Rory said.

'Not very characteristic, I admit.'

'But somebody killed the horse, Laura!'

'And Luke.'

'Do the police think Luke was murdered?'

'No, not now. They realise that it would be far too chancy a way of trying to kill someone. I mean, how many falls end in fatality? They've ruled out suicide for the same reason.'

'Do *you* think he might have tried to kill himself?'

'No. To give him his due, he wasn't a coward.' There was the hint of a break in Laura's voice. 'It's funny, I still can't quite accept he's dead, even though I'd been dreaming of leaving him, getting free of him for the last few years. Now, suddenly, the problem's gone and I haven't really got used it it.'

'I can understand that,' Rory said quietly. 'There must have been *some* good in him; I mean, he must have meant something to you once, or you wouldn't have married him, and when people die, at first we block out the negative things about them.'

'I suppose so. I suppose he must have meant something, as you say, but I couldn't tell you what. I just feel as if a chunk of me has been removed, because he was part of my life for such a long time.'

'Yeah, I can see that, but you'll get used to it.'

Laura gave a short, bitter laugh. 'I hope it doesn't take too long.'

They had arrived at the yard. Laura stopped the Land Rover and looked at Rory. 'Do you mind if we don't look *too* friendly? I just don't think it's sensible for the moment.'

Rory nodded. 'Sure.'

'So, I'll see you at the races tomorrow afternoon – your first ride for Langlands!'

Chapter Five

George Rutherford drove into Langlands by the South Lodge as Rory was leaving. Rory gave him a surly nod. Laura hadn't told him that Rutherford was coming to see her.

He felt a quick jab of jealousy. He was sure Laura didn't have any physical feelings towards the other man, but he resented the influence Rutherford seemed to wield over her yard. And Laura had already told him of the businessman's offer to finance a move to another stables if the crisis Luke had left behind made that necessary.

The sight of Rory leaving Langlands was a source of irritation to George Rutherford, but he wasn't going to let Laura see that. He burst into the house as if he were family, ready to commiserate and offer advice.

'Things aren't looking good for you, Laura,' he said when he had poured them both a glass of the champagne he had brought with him. 'As far as I can tell, Luke didn't have a single asset that wasn't hocked up to the eyeballs, including this place and most of his horses. And whatever wasn't formerly charged will have to be sold to clear the personal guarantees he's left all over the City. His creditors will see to that. As it happens, I'm one of them. He owed me a final tranche for the Chelsea Gaming Club. Mind you, under the terms of the contract of sale, if there's a default on any of the payments, I get the club back and he loses the payments he's already made.' He couldn't resist boasting a little in front of Luke's widow. 'I must admit, I had rather foreseen that might happen, but Luke was so insistent. I'm afraid he thought he'd got a bit of a bargain out of me. He thought the gaming board would automatically renew the licence. I knew for a fact that there would be a doubt. He's sailed too close to the wind in the past, and you need to be whiter than snow to hold a gaming-club licence. But his estate is going to be so in the red, it wouldn't have made any difference to the final outcome,' he added quickly.

'I'm glad you're going to do so well out of it, George,' Laura said with sarcasm.

'Don't worry, we'll both do well, I'll make sure of that, even if he didn't have the good sense to provide for you.'

'Surprisingly enough,' Laura said, 'he did do me one good turn the day he died. He transferred Midnight Express into my name. At least I should get the insurance for that.'

Rutherford didn't speak for a moment. His lips tightened and he turned sharply to look out of the window. 'Did he indeed?' he said quietly. 'That was very generous of him.' He turned back to face Laura, wearing the avuncular smile with which he had entered the house. 'But very unlike him, and rather extravagant, given his circumstances. I'm afraid, my dear, that his creditors may judge it to have been an evasive tactic and claim any proceeds from you. But don't worry, I'm here to help.' He placed a fleshy hand on her shoulder with a light squeeze.

Laura tried not to flinch.

Eland stared, white-faced, at the front page of the *Sporting Life*. It contained a speculative rehash of Arthur Brian's piece about the autopsy on Midnight Express which had appeared in the *Evening Standard* the day before.

There was no mention of it, but it was clear to him that if the police weren't already looking for a murderer, they soon would be. And if they found a culprit, they'd find a motive.

He picked up the telephone on the coffee table, then hesitated. He had been told – ordered – not to make contact under any circumstances. But that was before anyone had been killed.

He dialled.

'Well?' His client didn't sound pleased to hear from him.

'I've got to see you.'

'Why?'

'You know fucking well why!' Eland shouted, bold with fear.

There was a silence at the other end of the line. Eland trembled. He could almost feel the other man's fury.

'Listen,' the deep voice growled at him, 'Get yourself up here, right now, and I'll tell you just what you can and can't do.'

Then the line went dead.

Eland was let into the top-floor apartment by a secretary who looked as though she normally worked in the Raymond Revue Bar. He stood nervously in a large reception room, furnished without taste or regard to expense. Monstrous white leather sofas sat either side of glass and brass coffee tables. Full-length orange slubbed silk curtains were drawn across a window which stretched the whole height and breadth of the far wall.

'Some drum,' Eland tittered fatuously.

The woman looked at him disdainfully. 'Haven't you ever been in a place like this before, then?'

'Yeh, 'course I have.'

'He only has the best,' the woman said proudly, smoothing her skirt over her hips.

While he waited, Eland began walking around, in an attempt to take his mind off the quaking in his guts.

He glanced through a door into the next room, a crude replica of a Victorian library, and beyond that a bedroom containing a round bed, more brass and glass tables and heavy, Victorian mahogany chests and wardrobes.

'Is there a toilet?' Eland called back to the secretary. She barely looked up as she pointed towards the other side of the bedroom. 'Yeh, over there.'

Eland started to walk towards one of two doors on the opposite wall.

'Not that one,' she said impatiently. 'That's the sauna; the other one.'

'What, a sauna with no window,' Eland quibbled to justify his mistake.

134

'That's because the boss doesn't like people peeking, 'specially if he's got a crowd in there,' she added with a titter.

Eland went through the second door in the far wall of the bedroom and entered a warm, humming, deep-carpeted palace of a bathroom. He used the black lavatory bowl and flushed it with a gold-plated handle.

'Feeling better?' the woman asked with a grin, when he returned. 'Don't worry, he won't eat you.'

She was waving him to one of the vast sofas when the door opened and his client walked in.

'Okay, Samantha, you can go now.' The big man nodded towards the door behind him.

She didn't question him and walked out with a provocative swinging of her hips.

Eland looked at him nervously, wishing he'd followed his instincts and turned this man's business away. His client wore a pair of navy blue mohair trousers, held up by a pair of broad bright red braces over a cream silk shirt open at the collar.

'This, my friend,' the man growled, 'is the last time you come here – understand?'

Eland nodded. 'Yeah, yeah. But I had to talk to you, didn't I? I mean, now the filth's involved. Of course, I knew the bloke would fall off, but I didn't think he'd bloody die. And they've found the dope in the horse. They're going to get on to us. We've got to point them in another direction before they turn up on my doorstep.'

'Stop panicking. They're concentrating on the trainer. They've already had her in for a day. What you've got to do is give them a reason for getting her back to the nick.

Use your head, give them a bit of help. That shouldn't be beyond your nasty imagination. And there's nothing she can tell them that'll put them on to you.'

'There might be. She might work it out for herself, 'specially if they charge her with something.'

'Not if you've done your job properly. And don't forget, even if they do come sniffing round you – God help them—' he wrinkled his nose, 'it's got fuck all to do with me, remember? That's why you got paid so much.'

'Look,' Eland said with a burst of courage, 'the thing's got out of hand now; it wasn't my fault. The horse must have had too much of that stuff to make it pack up like that.'

'I paid you to make sure it went right. If you want any more money and you want to keep the skin on your back, you deal with it. I'm sure you'll think of something. Just don't get caught, and remember, if you point the finger at me you'll be in terminal trouble.' Eland quivered before the unequivocal message in the black eyes. 'I don't want to hear from you again. Understand?'

Eland twitched and nodded.

But his client's faith was justified; he had already thought of something.

He made the first of two calls from a public phone in the street outside.

Rory's first two rides for Laura Mundy were at Hereford. On a Saturday with half a dozen meetings around the country, the big races were at Kempton, where Laura had three more runners, to be ridden by Dai Price.

Rory had managed to fix a couple of other rides for

himself at the West Midlands course, and he would be the most experienced jockey there. That would shorten the bookies' prices and heighten the punters' expectations for his mounts, Rory thought ruefully as he drove between the dripping apple orchards and red-brick hop kilns of Herefordshire towards the small cathedral city.

Before he crossed town to the race course, he stopped in a small medieval side street outside a fishing tackle shop which he knew from past trips. He had remembered to bring a list of what was needed to make the flies he and Tommy had decided to use when they came back this way for their fishing.

A few minutes later, he drove off the old Roman road on to a grass car park. Despite Laura's parting words this morning, he didn't expect her to choose to come to this unfashionable little course rather than Kempton.

But he was wrong. One of the horses he was due to ride that afternoon was owned by a local farming baronet, an old friend of Laura's father and her longest-standing owner. She gave this as her reason for being there. That was just about plausible, but Rory suspected she had chosen to keep away from the crush of journalists who would be looking for her at Kempton. She greeted Rory with a formality that he hoped was put on for the sake of anyone who might be watching.

In the parade ring before the three-mile chase, she gave him his riding instructions as she would have done any other jockey. 'All he does is gallop, so keep him as close as you can. I don't mind if you make the running. He only cost ten grand, so Sir Ralph isn't expecting miracles, but you should be able to get him in the frame.'

Rory looked with approval at the big, old-fashioned Irish-bred horse striding easily around the ring. The animal was fit and he had a good jumping record. 'If he's halfway willing, he should give me a good ride,' he said to the owner who came up to join them. 'And the opposition doesn't look much.'

The baronet looked pleased. 'He needs someone like you on him, just to give him some confidence. I was delighted when Laura said she was booking you instead of Price.'

'She needed Dai for her Kempton runners, but I'm sure he would have given it just as much of a chance,' Rory said with a generosity he didn't feel.

A few minutes later, he was mounted and jogging down towards the track. When the lad released them to canter round to the start, Rory found the horse keen but well mannered – just the sort of horse he liked, with big wide shoulders and plenty of neck in front of him.

It was always a problem, trying to find suitable races for slow horses. The big galloping tracks, like Newbury and Ascot, were perfect for them but the horses they would have to compete against would be far too good. Therefore one had to run them in their class at the gaff tracks and just hope that they didn't get out-paced.

From the feel that he got on the canter to the start, Rory knew that Commoner – as his mount was intuitively named – wasn't going to do anything in a hurry. The chances were that if he wasn't careful he'd lose not only valuable lengths at the start, but also his position against the inside rails. Once all of the runners were ready, Rory used his experience over the younger jockeys, gave Commoner a crack with his whip and hit the tapes running.

The sudden flourish took the horse by surprise, sparking him into life to such an extent that Rory found himself almost going too quickly. The fences at Hereford came quite fast, and Rory felt as though he was almost constantly on the turn, with Commoner gaining ground at every one. His long, powerful stride lengthened to measure each fence precisely, before neatly flicking through the top couple of inches of birch.

The horse was as close to being a perfect jumper as one could get and for a circuit and a half Rory sat on board and enjoyed himself; Commoner needed barely any assistance at all. Then, as the race began to hot up halfway down the back straight on the last circuit, the other runners started to close in. Rory felt certain that nothing would be able to pass him quickly but Commoner's jumping was now more important than ever as he struggled to keep in front. One horse briefly came upsides as they raced flat-out to the downhill fence, the second from home, and Rory, by this stage, trusting Commoner with his life, rode towards the fence as if it wasn't there. He knew that if he couldn't trust the horse he was on now, he would never be able to trust any other. Rory saw Commoner's big, noble head lower slightly as the horse prepared itself and then it put in a mighty leap that landed him far from the back of the fence while the other horse bottled out and threw away any chance of winning. Another spectacular jump at the last had the race completely sewn up, allowing Rory to coast home as he liked.

'What a perfect piece of riding!' The horse's owner

beamed in delight. 'I thought you were cooked at the top of the hill.'

'The horse deserves most of the credit,' Rory said as he jumped down after steering the animal to the winner's spot in front of the changing rooms. He removed the saddle, pulled the breastplate over the horse's head and patted it on the neck.

Inside, the other jockeys were generous too, though their congratulations were tinged with doubts about Langlands' future.

By now, it was common knowledge that Luke Mundy had died in a state of spectacular insolvency. His every personal asset was reported to have been pledged – several times over – against the various loans he had raised to keep his companies alive through the recession. There wasn't much doubt that Langlands would have to be sold.

Rory pondered the irony of renewing his friendship with Laura and getting some good rides just as it was all about to come to an end. Or was it coincidence?

Sitting on the changing-room bench, taking in the gossip, he realised just how much it mattered to him that Laura should carry on training, whatever happened to Langlands.

Laura, in contrast to the hot debate going on behind her back, was calm and cool, ignoring any references to the sensational events earlier in the week. Rory was impressed, and determined to add his support.

He made another contribution to her record by winning the seventh race – a well-subscribed handicap hurdle – on an unfancied outsider carrying bottom weight. Laura smiled her thanks once again in the winner's enclosure, but by the time Rory had weighed in, showered the mud off and changed, she had left.

Sir Ralph Devereux, the owner of his earlier winner, invited him back for a drink at his house. Rory thought for a moment; one of the Lambourn trainers was holding a big party to celebrate his fiftieth birthday. Laura's problems would certainly be the central topic of conversation and he didn't want to miss any useful snippets of information, but it was possible that Sir Ralph might know a little, too, so Rory accepted his invitation and twenty minutes later followed the baronet up his long drive to an ungainly red-brick mansion surrounded by untidy parkland.

Sir Ralph Devereux wasn't as out of touch as his red face and thirty-year-old tweed suit suggested. After he had introduced Rory to the dozen friends he had also invited to celebrate his win, he led him away from the main group and took him to a quiet corner where they could talk privately.

'I can't tell you how glad I am that you're going to ride some more for Laura,' he said. 'Of course, I know that you and she haven't seen eye to eye for quite some time but I'm delighted that you have buried the hatchet now.' He was looking out of the window at the dying sun. Suddenly he turned round and fixed Rory with a stern eye. 'But don't do the dirty on her again.'

It was the first time anyone had articulated the guilt which had nagged Rory for over ten years. He shook his head with embarrassment

Sir Ralph looked back at the setting sun. 'Frankly, if

you ask me, Laura's going to need all the friends she can get over the next few months.'

Rory nodded. 'It looks as though she's got problems.'

'That bastard Luke Mundy!' Sir Ralph exclaimed with unexpected venom. 'The man had a strange sort of hold over her, you know. I don't think so much recently, but earlier on, she was terrified of him.'

'Terrified? Sounds a bit strong.'

'I've known Laura since she was wearing nappies and I know just how independent she was, believe me. I had to sit and listen often enough to her father worrying about his lack of control over her. Her affair with you wasn't the first he hadn't approved of – though I don't suppose he'd disapprove at all now. But Luke Mundy was a very domineering sort of a man. Oh, he was fine at a party – charming and quite amusing, provided he was the centre of attention and everyone deferred to him – but he was an absolutely ruthless shit if he didn't get his own way. I never had any dealings with him, except once when I had a horse he wanted. I sold it to someone else for less money than Luke had offered, and I told him so.' Sir Ralph laughed. 'Taught him a lesson.'

'Why do you think he transferred Midnight Express into Laura's name on the morning of that race?'

'I've no idea, but, whatever the reason, I can tell you that it wouldn't have been out of the goodness of his heart. It's my guess that she was supposed to do something for him.'

'But who the hell had the horse doped, and why?'

'That's what everyone wants to know, isn't it? Especially the police and the Jockey Club. And frankly, I think Laura's still on a pretty sticky wicket until they can pin it on someone else. I had her father on the phone for an hour last night and he's worried as hell about it. I must say, I was very impressed by how calm she was today, as if nothing had happened; it seemed almost unnatural. Anyway, what I wanted to say was that Eddie Brickhill would be very grateful for anything you can tell him now that you're seeing something of her, even if it is only in a professional capacity – which I suspect it isn't.'

'I don't think anything I could do would please her father.'

'Nonsense. He forgave you a long time ago for what happened. I don't think he blames you at all, particularly when you consider the bastard she did marry. Give him a ring; he wants to hear from you.'

Rory thought about Laura's father as he drove away from Sir Ralph's mansion, twenty minutes later. When he'd first started seeing Laura, Edward Brickhill hadn't been keen. On the half-dozen subsequent occasions they had met, Rory got the impression that Brickhill hadn't changed his mind. But he felt inclined to trust Ralph Devereux's view.

Pam was waiting impatiently for him when he reached home. She was dressed to make the most of her more obvious physical attributes, and Rory wondered if this effort was aimed at anyone in particular, or the Lambourn racing crowd in general. He went upstairs to change and to show Tommy all the kit and feathers he had bought to tie their flies. As he talked, he thought again that if it weren't for his son, he'd end his farcical marriage tomorrow.

Rory and Pam walked into the large barn which was

normally their host's indoor school. The interior had been decked out in pink cloth, like a vast marquee, and the sand floor had been covered with carpet and a dance floor. The tables scattered around the barn were already packed and the sound of noisy, drunken laughter echoed up to the roof. It looked as though anyone who was anyone in Lambourn was there, but the first person Rory spotted was one of the last he had expected to see.

His father-in-law, Mick Fanshaw, had been one of jump racing's heroes when Rory had first arrived at his yard, but a long run of bad luck and worse management, combined with ever heavier drinking, had changed all that. Pam's mother, no martyr, decided she'd had enough and ran off with an amateur jockey, putting in her alimony bid while there was still something left to claim. Mick had been forced to sell the freehold of his land in Sussex and now rented a small, run-down yard outside Lambourn where he trained the dozen or so second-rate animals which a few loyal friends had left with him. He still knew as much about training as anyone else in the business, but his will to win seemed to have faded, and he spent most of his time pottering around the racetracks, living on his past glories and trying to earn a living from his betting.

As far as Rory could tell, Fanshaw had never completely forgiven him for leaving his yard but still rated him the best jockey in jumping. He also, Rory thought, gave him credit for having stayed married to his daughter.

'Hello, Rory, you Judas,' Fanshaw greeted him with his customary sourness.

Rory, rolling a cigarette, watched Pam dive off into the

crowd towards a gang of similarly clad women before he answered.

'What have I done now, Mick?'

'First you ride two bloody horses for Laura Mundy, and then you go and win on the bastards without telling me. What kind of son-in-law do you call yourself?'

'If I'd had any idea they were going to win, I'd have told you, you know that; and if I get offered rides, who am I to turn them down?'

Fanshaw scowled. 'Bollocks! You've never ridden for her before. Why start now? The only reason the bitch has got the horses she has is because her old man bought lots of them for silly money, and her other owners are only there because they think they can get her into bed. I've lost ten horses to her this season, and a couple of those were just coming right when they left me; of course she's gone on and got all the glory. I mean, look at Flamenco Dancer!'

'It's a pity they weren't winning when they were in your yard, Mick, but what can I say? I've got an expensive wife to keep, I can't turn business away.'

'I wish you'd keep her on a rein as short as her skirt,' her father growled. 'Look at her, looks like a French floozy, waggling her tits all over the place. I don't know how you stand for it. She's turned into a right tart; she's been egging on her mother to try and get more money out of me – as if I had anything left, for God's sake! And I know she's been giving you the runaround. But look, it's not helping you, or me, you riding for Mrs Mundy. Anyway, things are going to happen there, I can tell you. She'll get her comeuppance. 'Specially after the mess that bastard Luke left behind.'

'I don't suppose she'll have any trouble finding the money if she has to set up a new yard,' Rory said lightly.

'No chance. This business at Kempton is going to leave her with mud over her face. I mean, the police are going to have to charge somebody with Luke's murder, aren't they?'

Rory stiffened, then tried to remind himself of Fanshaw's vindictiveness and colourful imagination.

'Don't be crazy, Mick. They're not going to blame anyone for a jockey getting killed in a steeplechase.'

'Oh, no? The horse didn't fall at a fence, did it, like they usually do. It came down on the flat, because someone had a go at it. And that someone had to be Laura Mundy. I heard back from one of her lads that she's even getting the insurance for it – that'll be a few hundred grand.' The old man's eyes were shining. 'They'll have her,' he nodded. 'And if they don't get her for that, they'll find something else.'

Rory was startled by Fanshaw's certainty and spite, which did nothing to quell his own doubts.

'I think you're going a bit over the top, Mick.'

'Just don't reckon on getting too many more rides out of her,' Fanshaw growled before turning abruptly and heading back to the bar.

Rory stared after him for a moment, half wanting to press him for a few facts, though he knew it would be a pointless exercise.

After an hour, he decided he was wasting his time at the party if he expected to hear any more plausible theories about Laura and the future of Langlands. He'd picked up nothing but a lot of wild speculation – too much of it along the same lines as Mick's. Philosophically, he assumed a brightness he didn't feel, and threw himself into the event with enough of his usual good nature to disguise his anxiety over Laura. He saw Pam across the room a few times, laughing loudly at other men's jokes and making it clear to anyone who was interested that she was her own woman. Rory found that this time he didn't care and quietly left the party without telling her.

Rory woke next morning to find his wife in bed next to him. He didn't feel like a confrontation about his leaving the party, so he slipped out and was tiptoeing silently out of the room when he heard Pam's voice.

'What are you getting up so early for?' she said softly.

Rory turned. She had propped herself on one elbow and there was a seductive smile on her sleepy, sensuous features.

'I heard Tommy wandering about downstairs. I thought I'd take him with me to get the papers.'

'Well,' she said, with uncharacteristic winsomeness, 'if I'm not going to get a cuddle, the least you could do is make me a cup of tea.'

'Okay.' Rory nodded willingly, wondering if her attitude was a perverse reaction to his having left her at the party – something he had never done before.

By the time he arrived back with the Sunday papers, Pam was asleep again. He settled down to read the new revelations that had been dug up about Luke Mundy. A liquidator had already been named to wind up Thames Land, and not a stone would be left unturned in his efforts to recover the vast debts to the banks who had appointed him. Every corner of the late Luke Mundy's empire would be subject to scrutiny, 'including his considerable dealings in international bloodstock'. Rory winced. That had to be bad news for Laura.

He thought about ringing Laura, but his instinct now was not to press her. He was sure she had only told him part of the story. He would probably learn more if he waited until she contacted him in her own time.

When Pam appeared at midday, he told her that he and Tommy were going to the pub to play pool. There was a warm, welcoming crowd at The Harrow. Rory and his son stayed for some roast beef, then settled down in front of the television with everyone else to watch the British Lions trounce the French.

Driving back through a blustery, sunlit late afternoon, he thought that, although he'd achieved nothing tangible that day, he'd felt closer to his son than he ever had before. As he walked in through the back door, the phone was ringing.

Pam picked it up before he reached it.

She listened for a moment with a supercilious expression, then said, 'He's here.'

She looked at Rory. 'Your friend's in a bit of trouble,' she mocked with hint of triumph.

Rory grabbed the phone.

'Laura? What's happened?'

There was a moment's silence during which Rory sensed that Laura was trying to get a grip on herself. 'I'm sorry to ring, Rory, but I can't get hold of my father and I can't tell my mother what's happened. I've been . . .

arrested. They've charged me with manslaughter.'

Rory heard a quick intake of breath, almost a sob.

'I'll come now. Where are you?'

'Andover. Rory, I'll be so glad if you come. I've got to appear in front of the magistrates tomorrow. They should give me bail, but I don't know how much for. Could you try and get hold of my father, and get him to come?'

'Leave it to me. Have you spoken to your solicitor?'

'Yes. He's on his way.'

'So am I. Don't worry; we'll get it sorted out.'

'God, I hope so. Thanks, Rory.'

'That's okay,' he answered awkwardly. 'I'll get there as fast as I can. 'Bye for now.'

Rory put the phone down and turned to Pam. 'You heard?'

'She's got what she was asking for.'

'Oh, for Christ's sake! She's been charged with killing her husband. There's no way she did it! I don't know what went on with that bloody horse, but I just don't believe she was responsible.'

'I told you, it's obvious; she was after the insurance money.'

'I'm not going to discuss it with you. I'm getting down there to sort things out.'

'Why the hell should you? And what do you think you can do?'

'Laura and I may have fallen out over you a long time ago, but she needs help, and she's asked me for it. I made the mistake of letting her down once before; I'm not going to do it again. Anyway, I'm not arguing about it. I'm off. I'll ring you later.'

'Rory,' Pam was pleading now, 'don't get involved.'

He looked at her and spoke without emphasis. 'I'm already involved.'

The rain that had been promising all day had arrived with a fury. The wind howled up the valley as Rory set off. Driving fast, he tried to concentrate on the road as he stabbed numbers on his car phone.

First he got the number of Edward Brickhill's home in East Sussex. When Laura's mother answered, it was the first time he had heard her voice in over ten years. It still had exactly the same uncompromising superiority to it. But it didn't daunt Rory in the way it had years before.

'Good evening. Could I speak to Mr Brickhill, please?'

'Who is that?'

'This is Rory Gillespie.'

There was a pause. 'Oh. I'm afraid he's not here.'

'Can you tell me where I can contact him? It's very urgent.'

'What's it about?'

'I'm afraid I can't say. Can you tell me where he is?'

'No, I can't. But I'll be talking to him later and I'll tell him you rang.'

'I'll give you the number of my mobile; I'll keep the line open.'

'Oh, all right.' Mrs Brickhill made some play of her exasperation at being bothered by anyone as unimportant as Rory. 'What is it?'

Rory gave her the number and rang off with a scowl. With a mother like that, it was surprising that Laura wasn't more difficult.

He dialled the police station at Andover and asked if

he would be allowed to see Mrs Mundy. He was told
that he would. He put the phone back and made no more
calls so that Edward Brickhill could get through to him
if he tried.

The black, wet night slid by with Rory's eyes fixed on
the end of his headlight beam. He was surprised that he
felt as calm as he did. He thought that his brain should
be in turmoil, but the gravity of Laura's position seemed
to have focused his mind. The first thing to be done was to
make certain that she got bail. No doubt her lawyer was
already working on that. It would be harder to do the
next job – finding proof that she hadn't doped Midnight
Express. That would mean finding out who had.

A few miles before he reached Andover, his phone
bleeped at him in the dark. He picked it up.

'Hello?'

'Is that Rory Gillespie?'

'Yes.'

'This is Edward Brickhill. I gather you wanted to speak
to me urgently?' There was none of his wife's reticence
in his voice.

'I do. Thanks for calling back. I can't give you details
over the phone. It's about Laura. She's been arrested.
Can you get to Andover this evening?'

'Andover? In Hampshire?'

'Yes.'

'Where shall I meet you?'

Rory named a pub two miles out of the town on the
main road. 'How long will it take you?'

'Make it an hour and a half. I'm on my boat.'

'Right. I'll see you later.'

Rory was on the outskirts of Andover now. He headed towards the centre where he guessed the police station would be. Ten minutes later a policeman was showing him into an interview room. Shortly afterwards, Laura came in.

She stood for a moment just inside the door. Her face was pale and there were worry lines on it which Rory hadn't seen before. Her expression was embarrassed and nervous.

'Hello, Rory. Thanks for coming.'

'No problem,' he said as he walked over to her.

The policeman who had ushered her in left the room and closed the door.

Rory had never seen her so helpless. He wanted to wrap his arms around her and stroke her hair, but he didn't.

'At least they're letting us talk in private. Are you being treated all right?' he asked.

She gave a faint smile. 'Yes, they couldn't be more polite. The man who arrested me was almost apologetic. And my little cell is reasonably civilised. Not much of a view, though. Simon Agnew's been.'

'Your solicitor?'

She nodded. 'He says he'll get me out in the morning. There'll be bail, of course, and they may take my passport away, but I wasn't going anywhere anyway.'

Rory sensed she was showing more bravery than she felt. 'Here, let's sit down. I'll make you a roll-up.'

She gave a weak laugh as they sat on two tubular steel chairs at a plain square table. The top was covered with scratches and a few barely eradicated obscenities. There was a half-full ashtray on it. 'I suppose I'll have to get used to roll-ups again.'

'Don't be stupid,' Rory said, more sharply than he'd intended. 'They can't make this charge stick.'

'Rory, they found an empty xylazine phial in my car. I don't know how the hell it got there, but the police say it was the stuff that was found in the postmortem. Unless somebody comes in and confesses, everything's in their favour. I had the opportunity to dope the horse, and I had several possible motives. Declan told them he'd left me alone with the horse for a few minutes after Henry had gone.'

'Did he?'

'Yes, but only for a moment, and for God's sake, Rory, whose side are you on?'

'I need to know as much as possible if I'm going to help you.'

'I don't see there's much you can do. I think they're going to charge me with conspiring to defraud the insurers as well. I'm afraid they're convinced I did it, and they're not looking too hard anywhere else.'

'Where else should they be looking?'

Laura looked away for a moment without speaking. She sighed. 'Look, when I get out tomorrow, I'll tell you what I think. I've already told the police, but they just think I'm lying.'

'If there's anything that needs doing, I'll do it.'

'Oh, Rory, why should you? You don't owe me a thing. I felt bad enough asking you to come here this evening.'

'I want you back training. You promised me a few good rides, remember?'

'Sure.' She looked at him. The slight smile on her lips showed confidence in him, guilt in herself. 'God, I'm sorry to drag you into this. Did you get hold of my father?'

'Yes. He should be on his way up from the Hamble now. He was on his boat.'

'Is he coming here?'

'No. It'll be too late. He's meeting me at a pub. I'll break the details to him gently there. If we want to, he and I can stay the night there and come in tomorrow to sort out your bail.'

'Thanks.' She shook her head. 'The other thing is to try and keep the press off the scent. Of course, they might pick up something at the hearing tomorrow, but with luck we'll get away before they're on to it.'

'They'll only come and pester you up at the house.'

'I'll worry about that then. Would you mind talking to them for me?'

'I think it would be better if your solicitor was your spokesman.'

'He's not a great communicator, but I suppose you're right.'

'What does he think?'

'I think he thinks I did it. In so far as Luke had any friends, he was one of them.'

'Try not to worry. If the police aren't going to follow any other lines, then I'll have to and maybe you'd better think about getting another lawyer.'

'That wouldn't look too good, would it?'

'No, I suppose not,' Rory shrugged. 'We'll see what he's like tomorrow.'

They were interrupted by the shirtsleeved constable who had shown Laura in.

'I'm sorry, Mr Gillespie, sir. That's your lot, I'm afraid. She's already had one more visitor than she should have.'

Rory didn't quibble. 'That's okay. She should be out of here tomorrow.'

'I couldn't say, sir.'

Rory turned to Laura. 'I'll see you in the morning. And don't worry, you'll be all right.'

Laura suddenly looked defeated again, but she wanted to believe him. 'Thanks,' she said in a small, tight voice. 'Thanks for coming.'

Rory nodded, and turned away quickly to leave the room. He couldn't let her see what he was really feeling.

Chapter Six

Rory arrived at the Dog and Badger half an hour before Edward Brickhill. It was a large pub, still crowded with drinkers and diners at eight o'clock on a Sunday evening. Rory hadn't eaten since lunch with Tommy, but the smells of hot food didn't tempt him.

He ordered a Scotch, then borrowed a *News of the World* from the barman and tried to read it while he waited for Laura's father. But the only item that held his attention was half a page of sensational revelations about the life and loves of the late Luke Mundy. The paper's indefatigable hacks had dug deep to unearth the identities of half a dozen women who claimed to have had affairs with Mundy. There was in the delivery of the piece a thinly disguised admiration for the scale of the dead tycoon's philandering. Rory wondered what Laura's reaction would be to see his activities so exposed. He hadn't forgotten Ralph Devereux's words – 'He had a strange sort of hold over her.'

Edward Brickhill made his commanding presence felt

the moment he walked into the pub. He stood for a moment in the doorway, looking around for Rory, and strode straight over when he spotted him.

'Hello, Rory. How are you?' He held out a hand, as if they were old friends who hadn't seen each other for a few weeks.

Rory bought drinks for them both – a Glenmorangie for himself, a large Hine for Brickhill. They settled down either side of a small round table, and satisfied themselves that they wouldn't be overheard.

'Okay, what's happened to Laura?' Brickhill asked.

'They've arrested her and charged her with man-slaughter,' Rory told him bluntly. 'Maximum sentence, ten years.'

The older man didn't react or speak at once. Rory waited.

After a moment, Brickhill asked, almost as if gossiping about a stranger, 'Did she do it?'

Rory wasn't taken in. With surprise, he realised that Brickhill was prepared to accept his answer whatever it may be, and that that would affect his whole attitude to Laura's position.

Rory shook his head firmly. 'No. No way. Luke's death was a pure accident; no one could have planned it, and Laura certainly didn't want that horse to die.'

Brickhill took a pipe from his pocket, and filled it slowly. 'But the police think she did. And they must have some pretty strong evidence to charge her. And I dare say, as far as they're concerned, she had a strong motive. Laura is the beneficiary of a very substantial insurance policy on Luke's life.'

Rory paled. Why hadn't she told *him* that? But he stuck to his conviction. 'That may be so, but like I said, no one could have planned to kill Luke in that way.'

'No,' Edward Brickhill agreed, 'but they could have taken a chance on it. And Laura told me that she could benefit from a disability policy as well. A hundred thousand a year. It's a lot of money.'

'Do you really think she could do a thing like that?' Rory asked incredulously.

'No, of course I don't. Unfortunately, what you'd have to do to convince anyone else she didn't is to find hard proof – in other words another culprit.' He lit his pipe and raised an eyebrow. 'And you're going to do that, aren't you?'

Rory met Brickhill's steady eyes and knew that Laura's father wasn't ordering him, nor was he pleading with him; he was simply stating a fact. Rory nodded slowly.

'Are you still in love with her?' Brickhill's question took Rory by surprise. He gulped a mouthful of whisky before answering.

'I don't know. I honestly don't. I'd be lying if I said I had a happy marriage myself, but I've tried to stick it out, for my boy's sake. I really don't want to put my son through a divorce.'

'Frankly, though I was delighted at the time, I can't think why you married Fanshaw's daughter.'

'Well, I did.'

'And did Fanshaw keep all the promises he made you?'

Rory smiled at Brickhill's shrewdness. 'After a few years he wasn't in a position to, was he? But I did well enough while I was at his yard. What you've got to remember is that I was an uneducated, working-class boy; I wanted to get on. I'd have done anything for the chance of a good ride. If Laura had only let me talk to her, it might have been different, but she wouldn't even get in touch. I tried hard enough, and after a while Pam seemed like the answer to a lonely man's prayers. I guess I've grown up a lot since then. Anyway, you and your wife didn't do much to encourage me.'

'I've had cause to regret that since. I might say, I was no keener on Luke Mundy than I was on you, but Luke offered my daughter a glamorous alternative, and he had a very overpowering charm, if you could call it that. Still, he's had his just deserts, and I don't suppose anyone is mourning much.' Brickhill took a sip of brandy. 'That's not our concern, though. What we've got to do is get Laura off the hook.'

Rory nodded. 'Sure, but what do you mean by "we"?'

Brickhill ignored the question. 'If the police have arrested Laura, they aren't going to spend too much time looking for another culprit. You're going to have to find the leads to tempt them. Circumstantially, the evidence is stacked against her, I can see that. I spoke to her two days ago, and she told me then that she thought she was in trouble. What made the police charge her today?'

'They found a phial of the drug that was used on Midnight Express in her car. She told me it was planted there; she told the police too but they didn't believe her. It's ridiculous; I mean, for God's sake, if she had done it, the last thing she would do is leave the stuff lying around in her car.'

'I wouldn't say that. I wouldn't have thought anyone

was trying to kill the horse, just stop it. The way it was planned was quite ingenious, but either by bad luck or the wrong dose, the animal died, which prompted an autopsy. So it was pure chance that anyone discovered that it had actually been doped. The subsequent revelation – that the Jockey Club had had a tip-off, had the horse tested and found it clean – I'm afraid only compounds Laura's apparent guilt.'

Rory nodded. 'I realise that, of course. I'll do everything I can. I let her down once before, I won't do it again.

'Luckily, I'm not getting that many rides at the moment, which is why I was prepared to go and see Laura when I did. I've got a few this week, and then half a dozen at Cheltenham, but I'll do everything I can.'

'It might be a good idea to start with the professor from the vet college.'

'I will; then there's Declan, the lad, to talk to, and, of course, Henry Straker. He might be able to tell me more about the tip-off.'

'Any help you need from me,' Brickhill said, 'let me know. I'll give you a number where you can always contact me. Now, let's see if we can stay the night here. Then we'll go to court in the morning and get my daughter out of prison.'

Laura Mundy was formally charged with the manslaughter of her husband, and remanded to appear before a sitting of a high court judge at Winchester at the next sessions. The police did not object to her being bailed on her father's surety of £50,000, though they stipulated that she should yield up her passport.

To Laura's relief, only the regular duty journalist from the local paper was in court. They didn't doubt that he would be quick to earn a healthy bonus by selling the story to the agencies, but at least there were no photographers waiting outside. Laura, her father, her lawyer and Rory drove out of town to talk the situation over in the Monday morning quietness of the Dog and Badger.

Edward Brickhill behaved as if nothing worse had happened to Laura than her being expelled from school, which had happened twenty years before. His attitude was that it was an embarrassing misunderstanding which should be cleared up as quickly as possible. Simon Agnew, the solicitor, was less happy, but did his inadequate best to disguise it. Edward Brickhill proposed that Rory should take on the job of looking for evidence for the defence, until he had something concrete to offer the police. They would not at this stage instruct another investigator.

The solicitor noisily sucked air between his teeth. 'With respect to Mr Gillespie,' he said, turning to Brickhill, 'I think I'd be inclined to hire an investigator right away.'

'Under normal circumstances, I would leave everything to the police, but I've lost faith in them during the course of the past few years. We're talking about the possibility of my daughter going to prison for a very long time.' Brickhill stared hard at the solicitor and paused for a moment. 'I don't want her to spend one more minute behind bars. I want someone who is as keen on her acquittal as I am.' The tone of his voice indicated that this was the last word on the matter.

After half an hour of discreet conversation, it was

agreed that Rory would start his enquiries as soon as he'd driven Laura back to Langlands.

The cloud cover that had started the day was breaking up, letting in shafts of sun to light patches of the Hampshire Downs. For the first few miles of their drive, Rory and Laura didn't speak. Laura sat in the passenger seat gazing straight ahead, wincing every so often as they drove into a patch of sun. At last, she broke the silence.

'It's a terrible thing to admit, but I'm more upset about losing Midnight Express than losing Luke. I hope you're not too upset about losing your ride in the Champion Chase,' she said.

Rory turned his head quickly and glanced at her, to see if she was being serious, but he couldn't be sure.

'It's a pity you ran the horse at all. Even if he'd survived, he'd never have got back in shape for Cheltenham. You were going to have him withdrawn; it wouldn't have been hard to fake something.'

'That was the plan, until Luke threatened to ride him in the Grand Military as well, and even the Champion Chase. I told you, I had no choice.'

'Couldn't you have talked him out of it?'

'I tried. I told him I didn't think Express would get the trip, but he's won over three miles in modest company several times before, and frankly, in a field like that, it wasn't asking much. Anyway, it didn't make any difference what I said. Luke didn't actually tell me, but I think he'd had a monster bet; thank God they can't pursue a dead man for his gambling debts.'

'What sort of a monster bet?'

'I don't know; I'm only guessing he had, but I've never seen him so nervous, and considering the mess he's left behind, it seems likely, doesn't it?'

It did, Rory nodded. It also gave someone a reason for stopping the horse.

'Who did he bet with?'

'I haven't the slightest idea. I don't think he bet much. He certainly never referred to it. But he had his back to the wall in a way he never had before, so I suppose he was desperate.'

'Do you know what's going to happen to Langlands yet?'

'Not precisely, but I can't imagine I'll be able to stay there long. I mean, there are people howling for money, especially now they realise there isn't much left.'

'But you'll get the pay-out on his life insurance.'

Laura didn't answer for a moment. 'Only if I'm cleared of manslaughter.'

'How much is it?'

'Quite a lot.'

'Why didn't you tell me about it last night?'

Laura glanced at him, guiltily. 'I don't know. I suppose because it might be considered a motive.'

'People have been accused of killing their husbands without any financial incentive. And the rubbish papers were making quite a thing about Luke's affairs. Some people might think that was enough of a motive.'

'I haven't been charged with murdering Luke, for the simple reason that if I had wanted to murder him, there would have been less chancy ways of doing it. The police don't think I murdered him, they think I doped the horse and that he died as a result.'

'You could,' Rory echoed her father's proposition, 'have been taking a gamble on it, though.'

'Yes, I could have been – a million to one chance – but I wasn't,' she snapped.

Rory raised a hand from the steering wheel in a calming gesture. 'Look, I'm only trying to see it from the police's point of view. If I'm going to help you, I've got to know how they're thinking. I know you didn't do it.'

'Do you, really?' she asked, subdued.

'Yes. I do. And you've got to believe me and tell me *everything.*'

'Why are you doing this, Rory?' Laura held his gaze, already sure of his answer.

'Hmm,' Rory grunted. 'I'll tell you another time.'

'So, you're a *jockey*, then?' Professor Douglas asked as he poured Rory a whisky.

'Aye. Do you mind if I smoke?'

'No. I'll join you.' The professor carried the drinks over to a table placed between two chairs. He waved Rory into one of the chairs and sat in the other himself. 'As a matter of curiosity, do you have any authority to come here asking me questions?'

Rory had pulled his tobacco and papers from his jacket pocket. He began nimbly to roll a twig of a cigarette. 'Only the authority of natural justice. I'm here for Laura Mundy. Her father has asked me to help.'

'I see. What do you want to know that you haven't already read in the newspapers?'

'I wanted to be sure of what you found, and your opinion of how it would have affected the horse.'

'That's simple enough. What we found in the animal's

urine was a trace of a drug called xylazine which is commonly used as a pre-med before operations. Obviously, a smallish dose was used here, enough to make the horse drowsy, and from the report of the race, it didn't take long to work its way through. It shouldn't have had any damaging effect whatsoever. Unfortunately the horse died as a result of a fracture to the neck sustained in the fall.'

'So, I'd be right in saying that whoever gave it the stuff was intending to tire it, not kill it?'

'In principle, yes, though from the films I have watched of steeplechasing, it would be a pretty fair assumption that it would be in the act of jumping that the horse was most likely to come to grief, which has been known to result in death.'

'Usually, when a horse shows signs of becoming that tired, a good jockey would pull it up,' Rory said.

'But I gather this man, Luke Mundy, was an amateur?'

'There are amateurs who know what they're doing, but he wasn't one of them. Besides, it was a bit of time before the drug seemed to take effect. Before it tired the horse was going like a runaway train, and apparently Luke was desperate to win the race.'

'It's extraordinary the lengths to which vanity will drive some men.'

'In this case, it wasn't only vanity. Could you say how long it would have taken to administer the xylazine?'

'A dose of a few millilitres? No time at all – a few seconds perhaps, from a small syringe.'

'And where would it be injected?'

'Any convenient artery.'

'Right, that's very helpful.' Rory got to his feet. 'Thank

you very much, Professor, for the drink and the information.'

'Before you go, Mr Gillespie. There's something about this case that puzzles me, and I've already mentioned it to the police. The horse had been given far more xylazine than was necessary just to stop it from winning.'

'What are you saying, exactly?'

'I doubt very much that the drug was administered by a professional.'

Rory's heart sank.

No wonder the police were reluctant to spend time looking for another suspect.

The scientist showed the jockey to the door and they shook hands warmly. An open invitation to further scientific questions was swapped with an invitation to the races. Rory climbed into his car knowing that though it had been time well spent, he'd learned nothing that would help Laura.

He had called in at Douglas's house on his way back from Towcester races. It was now half past eight on Monday evening. Rory reckoned he just had time to get to Henry Straker's house in the Kennett Valley in Berkshire.

As the ten o'clock news started on his radio, he turned into the neat gravel drive that led up to the Strakers' handsome Georgian rectory.

A light still showed in a ground-floor window, so he climbed out of his car and crunched up to a large front door with a fine fanlight above. He pressed the discreet brass button and waited.

It was a while before the door was opened.

Susan Straker, a strong, good-looking but disappointed

woman, greeted Rory warmly enough. They didn't know each other well but had met and chatted at a few drinks parties.

'Sorry to call so late, Susan. I was hoping I might catch Henry in.'

'I thought it would be Henry you wanted to see,' she said with mock disappointment. 'But I'm afraid he's in bed. He came back from a session of five-a-side soccer with the boys' club feeling pretty knackered and he's got a very early start tomorrow.'

Rory judged it unproductive to press, and quelled his impatience. 'That's a shame; I did want to talk to him quite urgently. Look, do you think I could arrange to see him tomorrow night, after the races, say seven o'clock?'

'I don't see why not. I'll tell him. Just check first to make sure he hasn't got held up anywhere.'

'Right. Thanks. I'll see you tomorrow then.'

At seven the next morning, Rory was walking back from his stables with his dog, Taffy. He was surprised to see Pam leaning out of their bedroom window. It was early for her to be awake.

'Phone!' she yelled hoarsely.

Rory quickened his pace. He guessed it was Laura.

'Who is it?' he shouted back.

'It's my bloody father. He wants to know if you can do ten-two this afternoon. Micky Fortune can't ride because he's hurt his back.'

Rory slowed down. 'Tell him I'll ring him back in quarter of an hour.'

Pam's head disappeared. Rory thought about his father-in-law. Fanshaw had mentioned he might want Rory to ride a moderate mare in the handicap hurdle at Warwick that afternoon. Without giving it too much thought, Rory had looked up the form. Carrying almost bottom weight over three miles, it was in with a very slim chance – no more. If Mick was planning to have a punt on it, he must be feeling bloody desperate. Rory had forgotten all about it.

Inside, Rory checked his weight on the scales in his bathroom. To get down to ten stone two pounds he'd have to be in a sauna for an hour or so – time for which he had much better uses.

Downstairs he said to Pam, 'I don't think I can ride your father's horse. I won't be able to do the weight.'

'I don't care one way or the other. Anyway, he must be mad if he thinks he can win with her.'

Rory picked up the *Sporting Life* that the postman always brought up for him. 'The betting forecast's got her at thirty-threes; maybe he's going for a place. There are nineteen runners – she only needs to come in the first four. At eight to one, that's not such a bad bet.'

'I'm all for him winning something, then he might be able to pay Mum some of the money he owes her.'

Rory shook his head in despair and picked up the phone.

'Hello, Mick?'

'Rory! Can you do it?' Fanshaw didn't believe in preamble.

'No, I won't make the weight.'

'That won't matter. All you have to do is get her in the frame.'

'That's what I thought.'

'Look, you'll have no problem. She's not a bad horse and there's fuck all to beat.'

'Having a big one, are you?'

'I've got to, Rory. There isn't a feed merchant left that'll deliver here. Your mother-in-law's lawyers are getting heavy and I haven't paid the rent for four months.'

Rory sighed. 'I might put up a pound or two overweight.'

'So long as it's only a pound or two.' There was real relief in Fanshaw's gravelly voice.

'See you there then,' Rory said and put the phone down, not sure whether he'd agreed in order to please his father-in-law or annoy his wife.

He poured himself half a cup of black coffee, which in the circumstances would count as breakfast, and glanced at the other paper.

There was a photograph of Laura on the front page of the *Daily Mail*, standing at her husband's graveside at his funeral the day before. She looked good in black and though she wasn't smiling, she didn't look particularly heartbroken. Rory wondered why she hadn't made more of an effort.

He thought of her, and Professor Douglas and Henry Straker, as he drove up to Warwick at midday.

He hadn't expected to see any of them at the races, but Henry Straker was there, talking to Laura and George Rutherford by the paddock before the first race.

Rory clenched his jaw. Rutherford seemed to be moving in fast. He hoped Laura knew what she was doing.

Although the news of Laura's arrest and subsequent

charging with the manslaughter of her husband had been on the front pages of every national newspaper for the last two days, with pictures of the funeral getting star billing in most of them, it was clear she planned to carry on as though nothing had happened. The Jockey Club helped by holding back from making any comment or ruling on Laura's position, on the advice of their lawyers, as her case was now *sub judice*.

Rory couldn't help admiring her courage as she went about the job of saddling five runners, dealing with their owners, and ignoring the rubbernecking of the crowd and the occasional harassment by journalists. She showed no sign of the doubts he had seen when he had driven her home the day before.

Rory had one ride for her, on her second string in the second race, a handicap chase, where Dai was on the favourite for her, with the weights against him.

She didn't disguise her pleasure when, in the face of the Welshman's open hostility, Rory returned to the winner's enclosure.

Rory was riding his father-in-law's horse in the last race, the handicap hurdle. Fanshaw was waiting for him on the way to the jockeys' changing room. Rory reflected that he seemed to have aged ten years in the last six months. He looked drained and his thick hair, once a rich brown, was almost white now.

'Everything okay, Mick,' he said in an effort to get a spark out of the old man.

Fanshaw tried to put a smile on his worried face. 'Not so bad. Nice win you had there. Hope you make it a double on mine. She's come on terrific since her last run, the top weight's giving her two stone and the rest are all beatable. I got a monkey on her each way at thirty-threes. She'll be lucky to win, but she can't be out of the first four,' he said with a hint of desperation in his voice.

'I'll do my best.' Rory tried to sound confident and took the colours Fanshaw was holding for him. 'I'll see you in the ring.'

Fanshaw's owner, one of the few still loyal to him, was standing with the trainer when Rory marched out into the parade ring.

Fanshaw turned to Rory. 'I was just telling Mr Vickers here that if anyone can get his mare to win, it's my son-in-law, eh, Rory?'

Mr Vickers didn't look convinced. 'As long as she gets in the frame in this company, she can stay with you and I'll be happy, Mick. But I must have some kind of result or the missus'll just carry on moaning until I get rid of her – the 'orse, that is, not the missus.' He laughed. 'Though, Gawd knows, the mare's cheaper to run.'

'Look, Mr Vickers, if you can still get her at twenties, you have a good each way. There's nineteen runners – they'll pay to the fourth. That'd be good value.'

'She certainly looks well,' Rory said, watching the horse being led around the ring. 'And the ground will suit her, if I remember from last time.'

'It will,' Fanshaw said eagerly.

Jogging down to the start, Rory was thinking more about Laura Mundy and his date that evening with Henry Straker than Fanshaw's bottom-weight hurdler. But as they approached the start, his mind automatically applied itself to the job in hand. Despite everything Mick Fanshaw had ever done, from talking him into marrying his daughter to systematically welshing on almost every verbal agreement they had ever made, Rory still liked him. Mick had always been a real racing character, and there were few enough of them around now. He also had a natural affinity with horses. A few seasons with a virus in the yard and not many winners didn't suddenly make him a bad trainer. And, perversely, they had become closer as a result of Pam's behaviour.

Rory had almost subconsciously been assessing the opposition in the ring and on the way down. He guessed he had a reasonable chance of getting home among the first four. To help Fanshaw keep one of the few horses left in his yard and take £4,000 from the bookies, he'd make sure of it.

That the mare was going to struggle began to show as she landed just behind the leader at the second-last flight. Rory felt her begin to tie up. He had brought her over to the better ground on the stand side and had the rail to help her, but she was tired and her legs felt heavy. The winning post was still two furlongs away. Rory sensed another horse waiting to pounce. It came past him quickly, followed by another. Whatever happened, he couldn't let one more by.

At the last flight, the mare, with a heart bigger than her small frame, tried to stand off, landed in a heap and lost all momentum.

Rory did everything legal he could think of to keep her going, to make her stretch out and quicken, but with a sense of failure out of proportion to the event, he watched helplessly as another horse moved up into fourth place twenty yards from the line.

Pulling the mare up past the post, Rory turned and walked her back towards the stands. He caught up with the horse which had passed him into fourth place. With relief, he recognised its jockey as a hungry young hustler who had just lost his allowance and already fancied himself hard and worldly-wise. He hadn't been racing long enough to appreciate Rory's reputation for honest riding.

'Hey, Bruce,' Rory whispered hurriedly, wanting to talk before the lads took hold of their horses, 'do you want to earn five hundred quid?'

The young jockey swivelled quickly in his saddle with a greedy grin on his face.

'S'long as it's easy.'

'It is. Just forget to weigh in.'

A big, knowing smile crossed the other jockey's face. 'No problem.'

'Good lad,' Rory said, feeling sick. 'Are you at Folkestone tomorrow?'

The young jockey nodded.

'Fine, I'll pay you there, okay?'

Bruce nodded briefly and turned to talk to the lad who had come out to greet him.

Rory reined back his horse and let the other get ahead. Once in the unsaddling enclosure, he headed back to the weighing room, not wanting to show any presumption about the imminent announcement that the fourth horse had been disqualified on account of his jockey failing to weigh in, with the fifth horse being promoted.

Mick Fanshaw was too old a hand to show any open

appreciation for what Rory had done for him. He wouldn't have placed the bet in his own name, had probably anyway placed it in half a dozen shops. No one would notice a connection. The only reference Mick made to the outcome later on was in a quick whisper out of the side of his mouth. 'Tell me how much it cost you, and I'll see you about it.'

'I'll tell you another time, Mick,' Rory said quickly.

At the same time, he saw Laura walking towards him, and he didn't relish a confrontation between her and his father-in-law. Mick gave him a nod and walked off to deal with his horse.

There was quite a crowd outside the weighing room. Laura conveyed with a look that she knew exactly what Rory had done, and that he'd made nothing from it.

Aloud, she said, 'Can you come and work Flamenco Dancer tomorrow?'

'Yes, of course. What time?'

'First lot. Be in the yard by seven thirty.'

'I'll be there.'

Chapter Seven

When he had showered, Rory went to the big steamy bar under the main stand to look for his wife.

Pam had wanted to come to the races that day, and they usually met in this bar afterwards. Rory's search was held up by friends and complete strangers wanting to congratulate him on his win earlier in the afternoon. He answered them all with his usual good nature. He gave no sign of impatience as he evaded an interview with a journalist anxious to know what he thought about Dayglow, the horse which it had just been announced he would ride in the Champion Hurdle the following week.

But he didn't find Pam and he had no intention of scouring the other bars. He left briskly, clutching his bag and wearing a purposeful expression to deter more conversation.

Pam had arranged for Tommy to have tea with a school friend in Lambourn, but their son would be waiting to be picked up at six and Rory knew that Tommy fretted if he thought he had been forgotten – a result, Rory guessed,

177

of having a father who was away a lot of the time and a mother who didn't give a damn.

Tommy was pleased Rory had come to pick him up. Though he was used to his father being a jockey, he had become acutely conscious that, in a town dominated by racing, to be the son of a leading jockey meant a lot to his peers. As they drove the few miles up the valley to Camp Farm, Tommy took advantage of his father's undivided attention.

'Dad, can we do that fishing trip this weekend? You did promise we'd do it soon.'

Rory felt guilt tugging at his guts. He wanted to devote every available moment to uncovering the truth about Midnight Express and Luke Mundy's death.

He sighed to himself as he spoke. 'Sure, Tommy. I'll fix it. We'll drive up Saturday night and spend all of Sunday fishing. Okay?'

The boy's eyes gleamed. 'That'd be brill, Dad. Thanks.'

Taffy wandered out of the house to greet them, wagging his tail, but there was no sign of Pam. Rory phoned Henry Straker's house to confirm that Henry would be back by seven. He dialled the farm in the next valley and spoke to the bovine babysitter, who agreed to come down and take charge of Tommy while he was out.

He arrived at Henry Straker's house a little before seven. Susan showed him into their old-fashioned drawing room, spotless through lack of children.

'Can I offer you a drink?' she asked.

'A wee Scotch, please.'

She poured a large one and a matching gin and tonic

for herself. They sat down in large chintz armchairs either side of an empty fireplace.

'Do you mind my asking why you're so anxious to talk to Henry?' Susan asked.

Rory made a sucking sound through his lips. He looked at a framed photograph on the small round table beside him – Henry with twenty or so of the boys from the youth club to which he devoted most of his spare time. He turned back to look at Susan. 'I'm sure you can guess.'

'Midnight Express?'

Rory nodded and took a sip of whisky.

Susan looked a little distraught. 'Poor Henry. It seems to have upset him no end. He had the police here for hours last Friday. The whole thing has really shaken him. He's always hated that side of racing.'

'I know,' Rory said. 'He's a very decent man, and I'm sorry to have to go on about it, but now the police have charged Laura . . .' He shrugged.

'You're doing this for her, then?'

'Aye.'

'But I thought you and she didn't really get on.'

'We didn't.'

Susan looked surprised. 'Oh, I see,' she said knowingly.

'Anyway, I wouldn't want to see her locked up for something she didn't do, would you?'

'But how can you be so sure she didn't? After all, I gather from Henry she stands to get nearly two and half million from the insurance company.'

Rory was startled to hear the sum. 'As much as that? Well, she certainly wouldn't get it if they found she had a hand in what happened. Anyway,' Rory continued, trying to build his confidence, 'I'm bloody sure she didn't do it and I intend to find out who did.'

'But Henry's told everything he knows to the police. If he'd given them any other leads, they'd have followed them up, surely?'

'I guess so, but I just wanted to see if there was anything else; I might be able to jog his memory a bit. I mean – I was riding that day.'

They both looked up at the sound of the front door being unlocked.

'Here he is,' Susan whispered. 'Try not to go on too long.'

Rory nodded.

As he walked in, Henry assumed his normal, cheerful manner, but couldn't entirely hide from Rory the strain he was feeling.

'Hello, Rory. Nice to see you. Ah, good, you've got a drink. Susan, ready for another?'

'No, thanks,' she answered, rising to her feet. 'I've got a few things to get on with, if you'll excuse me.'

She left and shut the door behind her.

Henry poured himself a small glass of amontillado, and remained standing in front of the fireplace.

'Well, Rory, I gather you dropped in last night after I'd gone to bed; sorry about that. Anyway, what can I do for you?'

Rory started hesitantly. 'I'm afraid I want to ask you about Midnight Express.'

A fleeting look of consternation flashed across Henry's face.

'Oh,' he said, and sat down where Susan had been.

'What a ghastly business. It's been hell being caught up in it. And to think I wasn't even supposed to be on duty that day; Charters cried off – flu or something.'

'Laura and her father asked me to find out more about what happened. I mean, though the circumstantial case against her looks pretty bad, I know she didn't do it.' Rory made the statement vehemently, as much to convince himself as Straker. The vet winced slightly.

'I admit, I was rather surprised. I wish I knew who else it could have been, or why.'

'Okay, but you know her well enough. She's a tough woman, I'll grant you, and Luke Mundy was a bastard, but there's no way any sane person would try to murder someone like that – on the off-chance they might be killed in a fall.'

'Well, no, that's not what the police think, but they found a phial of xylazine in her car. Why on earth would she have it otherwise?' Henry looked puzzled.

'It could easily have been planted. Even if she left her car locked, any experienced car thief could have opened it, put the stuff in and locked it again – no problem. Even easier at the yard.'

'I suppose so, but as the police said, why should anyone want to pin it on her?'

'Can you think of anyone who might?' Rory asked sharply.

Straker looked taken aback by Rory's tone, but didn't protest.

'Er, well. No, I'm afraid I can't.'

'Someone who might be jealous of her, maybe?'

Straker wrinkled his brow. 'Well, it's rather embarrassing to say it, but there's always your father-in-law or, for that matter, your wife.'

Rory laughed. 'It certainly wasn't Pam. Nothing's happened between Laura and me since I married Pam, and even if it had, I don't think Pam would care much.'

'All right, I'm sorry to suggest it, but what about Mick Fanshaw? He's lost a lot of horses to Laura's yard over the last season.'

'And to a few other yards,' Rory added.

'But most to Langlands. I think he's probably quite a bitter man now.'

Rory thought of Fanshaw's face after he had squeezed his mare into the frame in the last race. He had to admit that Fanshaw was quite capable of harbouring a grudge. 'He's bound to be feeling sore about it, but he wouldn't bother to do anything like that, not if he wasn't going to make any money out of it.'

'I'm not so sure. Anyway, he's the only person I can think of. Maybe he thought if Laura's horse was found doped, she'd lose her licence and he might get some of his horses back.'

Rory considered this for a moment. 'I don't know. Of course, Mick's an old rogue, but I really don't think he's that vindictive. Now, are you absolutely certain that you sent the right blood sample to the lab for testing?'

Henry, looking gloomily into the fire, jerked his head up to give Rory a sharp look. 'What are you implying?'

'I'm not implying anything. I'm just wondering if it was possible you got the sample mixed up with another.'

'Of course I didn't,' Straker said, indignant now. 'I label each phial as soon as I've filled it, and anyway, I didn't do any other tests that day. There's absolutely no question that the horse was completely clean when I tested it – no question at all. The xylazine shots must have been administered during the hour or so between my taking the test and the horse being led to the pre-parade ring.'

'Did you happen to see anyone who looked out of place hanging round his box?'

'Well, there are always people milling around – lads, trainers, transport. Obviously, I don't *know* them all, but I don't recall seeing anyone who looked particularly alien. Anyway, the horse's lad – Declan, I think – told the police that he had been with the horse or near its box all the time, and no one besides Mrs Mundy went near it.'

'Yes, I know he said that, but he could have been lying, couldn't he? I mean someone might have paid him to lie, and he's quite a sharp little guy.'

'Well, I suppose if Fanshaw had done it – and he was around; he had a runner that day – he might have got at the lad, yes.'

Rory put his empty whisky glass down and stood up. 'Well, thanks very much for your time, Henry. You've given me a few ideas. Would you mind if I got back to you if I think of anything else?'

'No, not at all, but I don't really think you're going to find much. As you say, the circumstantial case against Laura is very strong.'

'But only circumstantial. I can tell you, I don't intend to give up until I've found out and proved who's done this.'

Henry Straker nodded slowly. 'Well, I quite understand. I just hope you can prove she *is* innocent. But I don't think you'll get any further than the police.'

'We'll see. Thanks for the drink. I'll see myself out.'

Rory was intending to drive into Langlands by the front entrance next morning, but the gates at the lodge were shut, and two cars were parked outside. Their drivers were leaning on one of them, smoking. It didn't need the camera with a 600mm lens hanging round the neck of one of them to tell Rory that they were reporters. He drove on and in by the more discreet entrance to the stable yard.

Up on the downs, with Flamenco Dancer stretching out under him, he was able to forget for a while what had now become almost an obsession with tracking down the truth about Luke's death. Laura was waiting at the end of the gallop; the few brief words they exchanged were limited to the gelding's performance and Rory's opinion of him.

But later, driving from the yard up to the house on the internal road, all the conflicting information he had gathered so far crowded back into his head.

Laura, still displaying the same calm she had shown at Warwick the day before, was concluding a deep discussion with Patrick Hoolihan over the breakfast table.

She looked up from the *Sporting Life* and smiled as Rory walked in.

'I see you've already got yourself another ride in the Champion Chase,' she said.

Rory nodded. He'd fixed it with the Irish trainer en route to Warwick the day before. If the ground came up soft, it would definitely have an each-way chance.

'Do you want to get off it and on to Flamenco Dancer?' Laura went on.

'Yes,' Rory said. 'But I won't.'

'Why not? There's no need to worry about Dai. I'm going to announce that we're parting company as soon as Cheltenham's over.'

Rory walked to the sideboard to pour himself some coffee. 'It's not that. It's loyalty: I've arranged to ride another horse, and I don't want to let people down.'

Laura raised her eyebrows with a rueful smile. 'For God's sake, Rory, no one would blame you.'

'Except me.' He sat down at the table and helped himself to some lukewarm toast.

Laura shrugged. 'Well, if anything goes wrong with your mount, the offer stands. I feel I owe you, and George Rutherford's very keen for you to ride. It's not as though you've got much else with a chance.'

Rory grinned. 'The bookmakers don't agree with you. Have you seen how Dayglow's been backed?'

Patrick Hoolihan laughed. 'That's a red herring.'

'We'll see.'

'I see you're riding against us this afternoon,' Patrick went on. 'You should beat us as easily as a nun gets to heaven.'

'Do all nuns get to heaven?'

'My mother used to tell my sisters they did,' Patrick shrugged. 'Anyway, our chap's not ready yet; he needs a couple more runs, for experience, does he not, Mrs Mundy?'

Laura nodded. 'But we'll win the first, as long as Dai does as he'd told. He's riding Pan Piper, another of George's that came up from Mick Fanshaw's yard.'

'And we don't want to give Mick the chance to bad-mouth Langlands in the bar afterwards,' Patrick added. 'I see, by the way, that you're riding Camp Follower. You bred him, didn't you?'

Rory nodded. 'Yes. And he'll be the very first winner I've ridden that I've bred myself,' he added confidently.

Rory's first ride at Folkestone that day wasn't until four o'clock. Edward Brickhill had rung the evening before to ask if they could meet on the way.

'I don't suppose you'll want any lunch, but we can talk while I eat mine.'

They met at a small restaurant on the river at Windsor. Once there, Rory couldn't resist the smell of cooking, and ordered a small, lightly grilled sole. He was, he excused himself, riding top weights in both of his only booked races and he had a good stone in hand.

'How was Laura this morning?' Edward asked when they had disposed of the formalities.

Rory answered him against the background murmur of people enjoying expensive food. 'I can't believe how calm she is. Yesterday at Warwick, she behaved as if nothing had happened. Of course, everyone's talking about it, but she just paid no attention.'

'She's a girl with a lot of guts, my daughter. I also think it's the right way for her to play it. These days, when a case like this gets so much publicity, it's as important to convince the media you're innocent as it is the judge and jury.'

'I know, but . . .' Rory paused, 'she's almost *too* calm.'

'That worries you?'

'It's just that I don't know what she's thinking. I haven't had a chance to talk to her alone for a few days; it's as if she doesn't want me to. And there are things she never told me, like the amount she stands to gain on Luke's life insurance.'

'That's a side issue, Rory. After all, the police haven't charged her with murder, which they would have done if they thought she'd planned it.'

'Aye, but they still could.'

'Look, don't get negative about it. You've known Laura for long enough to know that she's always been rather secretive. Some people are; they feel they're giving too much of themselves away if they let others know what's inside. I understand that; I'm the same.'

'Yes, I know what you mean, but I'm doing this for her, for Christ's sake. She's got to trust me.'

'Fair enough. I'll talk to her about it, but in the meantime, how have you got on?'

'I saw Henry Straker last night and Professor Douglas on Monday. The professor confirmed that the horse hadn't been given anything like enough xylazine to kill him, but more than enough just to slow him down. His opinion was that it wasn't done by a professional. It looks as if it was a simple case of stopping it winning. Nothing particularly unusual about that. Laura told me she thought that Luke had had a bet on it, but she didn't know how much, or who with.'

'That's odd,' Edward Brickhill said. 'I was never aware of Luke gambling on the horses, not seriously, anyway. The odd tenner for interest's sake. I've a strong suspicion that he gambled on the stock market, or at least on the movement of share prices with one of these outfits that makes books on that kind of thing.'

'Are there many who do?'

'I think that anyone with a bookmaker's licence can do it, but I don't know which do. I could find out easily enough. So, since we're agreed that Laura didn't do it, it seems obvious that the horse *must* have been doped to stop it winning, and the police ought to be talking to the bookmakers.'

'I agree.'

'And what did Straker have to say?'

'Poor old Henry, he's well shaken up by the whole thing. He's absolutely certain there was nothing wrong with the animal when he took his sample, which leaves about an hour for someone to have got at him. He said he didn't see anyone around the stables who shouldn't have been there. He suggested it might have been Mick Fanshaw; he had a horse a few boxes away.'

'Why the hell did he think Mick would do it?'

Rory shrugged. 'To get at Laura maybe. If she loses her licence the horses will have to go somewhere. Mick probably thinks he would get them back in his yard. He's lost almost a dozen to her already.'

'I suppose that's just possible, but I had horses with Mick for a long time, and I knew him well. He certainly never used to be someone to harbour that kind of a grudge. But then, that was a few years ago when he was having a good run.'

'There's no question he's turned pretty sour over the last year. I mean, everything's gone wrong for him. I don't see him that much, though. He and Pam haven't got on for years, and I think he embarrasses her now.'

'And how are you getting on with Pam, if that's not too personal a question?'

'Like I told you the other day, it hasn't been much of a marriage for a long time now, but I won't leave her, not till Tommy's older and able to look after himself. He's insecure enough as it is.'

'Should one believe the rumours that occasionally do the rounds?'

'About her flirtations? I've tried not to notice, especially recently. To be quite honest with you, I don't really mind any more. She didn't leave with me after a party the other night, and didn't get back till about four in the morning. I pretended not to wake up, so I never asked her what she'd been doing.'

'Have you any idea who she might have been with?'

Rory made a face. 'I've got a nasty suspicion it was Dai Price, but then, they're two of a kind.'

'You don't think Mick's annoyed with you for letting that happen, and the fact that you're riding for Laura again?'

'No.' Rory shook his head. 'I really don't think so.'

'Okay, but we have to consider every possibility. Human nature can lead people to do the most unexpected things.'

As they ate their lunch, they went over the same ground. Rory agreed to follow up the Mick Fanshaw line by talking to Declan Hoolihan and one of Mick's lads with whom he was still on good terms.

He arrived at Folkstone to be greeted by the news that Dai had won the previous race on George Rutherford's ex-Fanshaw horse. The favourite had unexpectedly weakened and fallen three from home.

Rory saw Dai in the changing room. He made sure nobody saw him passing an envelope to Bruce for forgetting to weigh in the day before. From the embarrassed way in which Dai was behaving, he knew that what had once been a flirtation between Dai and Pam had developed into something more. Despite the indifference he had declared to Edward Brickhill at lunch, he couldn't avoid a spasm of jealousy. He gritted his teeth and tried to remind himself that this was a simple case of slighted male pride, but he felt a violent surging in his guts, and had to quell an urge to walk over and confront the flashy Welshman.

But he fought back the feeling, pushed it out of his consciousness, tried to enforce complete emotional dissociation from a wife for whom he had long ago lost what little respect he'd ever had.

Rory's mount, Camp Follower, a young gelding that Rory himself had bred and named, was the first foal he'd had from his first mare. Like most breeders, he retained a proprietorial affection for horses he had bred long after they had left his farm, especially the first one, and the closer it got to the race, the more Rory realised how much he wanted to win.

In the parade ring, the affable Lambourn trainer who legged him up into the saddle had no inkling of what had been going through the jockey's mind. He saw only the usual chirpy smile and uncomplicated attitude to the job for which Rory was famous.

'How do you want him ridden?' Rory asked.

'You know the horse, you bred him; he likes a late run. In this small field, hold him up until the last fence, then let him go. He'll have no trouble with the weight over this trip.'

Rory nodded. He hadn't identified any serious dangers and this was reflected in the price that was being offered about his mount. He was never complacent these days, but he cantered down to the start reluctantly confident that he was about to ride his forty-eighth, and most memorable, winner of the season.

Rory joined the other six in the field to inspect the first fence. Dai Price still hadn't looked at him, and Rory behaved as if he hadn't seen him either – it was easier for them both that way. This became more difficult as the horses circled behind the start, waiting for the starter to call them up.

When Rory did meet Dai's eyes, there was a look of such shifty guilt in them that he almost felt sorry for him.

He thought about it again as he cruised along at the back of the field, a couple of horses behind Dai's. Camp Follower was a well-balanced, experienced jumper who could see his own stride and needed little help from his pilot. Rory had schooled him regularly from the age of two.

Rory found his mind wandering, going back over the conversation he had had at lunch with Edward Brickhill.

Was there any possibility that Mick Fanshaw would feel so vindictive about Laura's success that he would want to remove her from the game? That certainly wouldn't help Mick or, as Rory had pointed out to Straker, make him any money. Still, he thought, he may as well talk to a couple of the lads, sound them out on Mick's movements that day at Kempton.

Rory's thoughts were interrupted by the need to concentrate on the big open ditch they were approaching, where horses always found it harder to judge their stride. In front of him, Dai's horse hit the guard rail with a massive crack and parted the birch on the way over. The mistake shot Dai up the horse's neck. Camp Follower momentarily lost concentration, took off a pace early and launched himself into a massive leap, just clearing the fence.

They landed to the right of Dai Price, who was scrambling to regain his balance. Dai was on the point of getting back into the saddle, when the horse picked itself up and galloped on towards the next fence. As Dai teetered on the horse's back, Rory noticed immediately that Dai's right boot had been forced through the narrow aluminium stirrup. In the next instant, he'd dropped over the side and his inverted body was being bounced viciously on his head and shoulders, caught every few strides by a galloping hoof.

Even if he survived to the next fence, he'd be seriously injured when the horse tried to jump it.

Rory took a quick look round and cursed; Camp Follower was going easily but he was the only one in a position to help. He had no option. His conscience wouldn't let him race on, even though this was the last man in the world he wanted to help.

He drew alongside and a little ahead of Dai's mount. To the confusion of Camp Follower, he started to pull him to the left, off the steeplechase course, away from the leaders.

Dai's horse had to come with them. They carried on turning in a wide arc within the confines of the running rails of the flat course, still deep and lush before mowing for the coming season. Rory was careful not to take too tight a curve, to avoid Dai's horse kicking the jockey any more than it had already done. As they turned, the horses lost momentum and the urge to follow. Rory was able to reach over and grab the bridle and pull up both horses to a trot, then a standstill.

He glanced back down the course and saw an ambulance already on its way. He leaped off his horse, hanging on to the reins, and walked round to unhook Dai's foot from the stirrup. Dai was conscious, and groaning as Rory lowered his legs to the ground. His eyes were closed, but he opened one for a moment, saw Rory, and groaned again. 'Thanks.'

Rory ignored him and led Camp Follower away. He'd chucked the race, and all for the man who was trying to take his wife from him.

Chapter Eight

The racing press next day reported that Dai Price hadn't been badly injured – bruised and cut by his horse's flying hoofs, half concussed, but with no bones broken. He hoped to be back in action in a couple of days.

One thing was certain, Rory thought as he drove once more across the Berkshire Downs in the grey morning light, Dai Price wouldn't be at Langlands today.

Patrick Hoolihan was the first to see him walk into the yard.

'Good morning, Rory. Bit of a hero yesterday, I hear?'

Rory laughed. 'A moment of madness, Pat.'

'So we imagined, though I don't think the public quite appreciated the irony of it.'

'No,' Rory agreed. 'But Dai did.'

'Still, he rode a winner for us on Pan Piper which took the wind out of Fanshaw's sails. It used to be with him and he'd been telling everyone it wouldn't win from our yard. Did you hear the stewards ordered a pre-race dope test on the favourite?'

'No, I hadn't heard that,' replied Rory, now much more alert.

Patrick shrugged his narrow shoulders. 'Mrs Mundy said he looked fine in the paddock, but later he was running with his tongue hanging out – a bit like Express did at Kempton.'

Rory's head jerked up and he slapped his whip against the side of his boot. 'I wonder if there's a link?'

The head lad looked at him sharply. 'That's what she thought.'

Rory rode up to the gallops on a horse that was new to him. Mrs Mundy, Patrick had said, wanted to hear what he thought of it.

Back at the house later with Patrick, he delivered his views, and hoped to find a few moments with Laura alone. This time the interruption was provided by Henry Straker.

Laura looked up at him with a smile. 'How have you got on?'

Henry sat down wearily and nodded his head. 'She'll be all right.'

'What's this?' Rory asked.

'One of the new fillies arrived from Newmarket with a lump on her ear like a football,' Laura said. 'Wouldn't let anyone near her with a bridle and nothing seemed to reduce it.'

'Well, it will now,' Henry said. 'We had to give her a shot, then I lanced it and drained it. Give her a week and she'll be fine.'

The vet discussed other horses that needed looking at and the blood tests he was to take and analyse that day, anxious, Rory guessed, to avoid any more discussion about the events at Kempton.

Rory, anyway, didn't want to talk about it in front of Laura and he thought that Straker wouldn't have anything new to offer.

Patrick and Henry left together to see the horses out for the next lot, leaving Rory and Laura alone at last.

'How are you feeling?' Rory asked as soon as the door had closed.

Laura pushed Midas's golden head from where it nestled in her lap and stood up. She walked across the room to stare out of the window at the garden where daffodils were beginning to flourish their yellow trumpets. She turned back to look at Rory and her face abruptly crumpled. He felt a guilty tingle of excitement as he watched her struggling to fight back her tears. He knew she wouldn't drop her defences like this for anyone else.

'It's hell. I don't know how much longer I can take the strain of pretending that everything's fine.' Her voice began to tremble. 'But that's the only way I can handle it.'

The moment of weakness passed and Laura took a deep breath. 'How are you getting on?'

'I know more than I did,' Rory said. 'There are a few lines for me to follow.'

'Like what?' Laura didn't sound hopeful.

'I'll tell you if and when I find anything worthwhile. But can you tell me something?'

'What?'

'Has my father-in-law ever expressed any kind of vindictiveness about the horses that you've had from his yard?'

197

Laura thought for a moment. 'Yes, I suppose he has, in the same way that you'd expect anyone to react.'

'With threats of any sort?'

'A bit of loud-mouthed slagging off, but not threats exactly, no. You don't really think he could have had anything to do with it?'

'It's possible. I'm fairly sure that whoever got at the horse only wanted to stop it, not kill it. The fact that some of the stuff was planted in your car would have been for one of two reasons. Either someone was simply laying a red herring to cover their own tracks, or they were deliberately trying to frame you, to get your licence taken away. I've been trying to think who might want that badly enough to go to all that trouble. Can you think of anyone who might?'

Laura gazed bleakly at Rory. 'Right now, I feel the whole world's against me, though I know they're not. Of course there are people who resent the success I've had, especially because I'm a woman. But I really can't think of anyone who'd go to such lengths, not even Mick Fanshaw.'

'Well, think about it, and if you come up with anyone, let me know. I'm going to meet one of Mick's lads at the races today, and I'll see if he can tell me anything. Like I say, it may not be likely, but it is possible.'

Laura nodded half-heartedly. 'Okay. And I'll let you know if I think of anyone.'

Rory wanted to talk to her about the insurance money as well, but he judged she'd had enough for now. He left her to get herself together for visitors – owners, she said – who they heard arriving at the house.

'Keep your chin up,' Rory said, giving her arm an affectionate squeeze. 'We'll get there.'

Olly Mullens had worked for Mick Fanshaw for twenty years. Like a lot of lads, he had started out with dreams of jockey stardom, soon dashed by two fruitless apprentice years. Olly had taken Rory under his wing when he had arrived at Mick's and had hero-worshipped him since he had ridden his first winner for the yard. Since then, Olly had been rewarded for his loyalty to Mick by being made travelling head lad and box driver and he and Rory usually found time for a quick word whenever they met at the races.

That afternoon, Rory found him about to unload a runner in the lorry park at Wincanton racecourse.

'Have you got a minute, Olly?'

'Sure,' the lad answered, dropping the side ramp at his feet.

'This may sound like a crazy question, but it's about Luke Mundy's fall. You know the horse was doped?'

'Of course, it was all over the papers, and Laura Mundy being charged with it and all.'

'Do you think she did it?'

Olly shrugged. 'How would I know? I don't have a clue. But they found the stuff in her car, didn't they?'

'Sure, but someone else could have put it there,' Rory said patiently. 'Look, what I wanted to know was how badly Mick's taken it, losing all those horses to Mrs Mundy, I mean.'

'No worse than anything else. He's sort of resigned now. I'm looking for another job meself.'

'What, you? After all this time?'

'The man's run clean out of money. I don't want to go, but if I'm to have a wage ...'

Rory shook his head. 'I suppose I knew it was as bad as that.'

'That's why you helped him out Tuesday, isn't it?'

Rory had no intention of admitting to anyone what he'd done. 'I was just lucky Bruce forgot to weigh in.'

''Tis only you would do a thing like that for him now.'

Rory abruptly changed the subject. 'Look, can I ask you a straight question about this horse-doping. Do you think Mick had anything to do with framing Laura Mundy?'

The small man spread his hands. 'I don't know. He wouldn't have done, in the old days, but there's no knowing what he'll do now. The man's as down as he's ever been.'

'But fixing Laura wouldn't help him, would it? He wouldn't get the horses back if she lost her licence, would he?'

'I don't know, Rory, and that's the truth.'

Olly Mullens had given him no help, either in confirming or ruling out the possibility of Mick Fanshaw being involved. Rory had been relying more than he realised on some kind of pointer from the lad. He walked back towards the changing room feeling frustrated and ineffectual. He was passing the Clerk of the Course's office as Matt Charters came out.

Matt was sometimes Henry Straker's understudy at the courses where Straker officiated. On an impulse, Rory hailed him.

'Hello, Mr Charters.'

'Oh, hello, Rory. How are you?'

'Fine, thanks. Look, could I have a quick word?'

Charters looked surprised. It was seldom that jockeys needed his services at the races. 'Sure. Now?'

'Yes, if you've got time.'

'Certainly.'

They automatically began to stroll back towards the paddock. None of the people rushing around, getting ready to run their horses or back their selections, took any notice of them.

'What can I do for you?' Charters asked.

'It's just something I'm trying to clear up about Midnight Express.'

'The horse that fell at Kempton?'

'Yes. Weren't you meant to be on duty instead of Straker that day?'

'Yes, I was. I'd mentioned to him the day before that I had a bit of a cold, nothing serious, though, but he insisted that he'd do the duty himself; said I wasn't looking up to it. You know what he's like. He's a very considerate chap, old Henry.'

'Yes, he is. But you'd have been quite happy to go if he hadn't insisted?'

'Certainly. It was only a touch of flu. I don't know why I even mentioned it to him.'

'So you didn't actually ask to be relieved of your duty?'

'No, not at all. As I said, I wasn't that ill, and I enjoy Kempton, but he said we couldn't have the vet going round spreading a cold to all and sundry. Frankly, I had plenty to get on with at my surgery, so I didn't protest too much. Why do you ask?'

Rory looked at him for a moment. 'Oh, no reason

really but thanks all the same. Nice to see you again.'

'And you. Glad to be of assistance!'

Rory left him inspecting the runners parading around the paddock and walked back to get ready for the next race.

He didn't have a ride in the third race that afternoon. He used the time on his mobile phone to catch up on his racing schedule for the rest of the week. Then he phoned Henry Straker's house. Susan answered.

'Hello. It's Rory Gillespie again.'

'Yes?' Susan said flatly.

'I wanted to speak to Henry. Will he be in this evening?'

'No. We're going to Arthur Harris's presentation.'

As Rory had thought, and hoped; knowing that most of the local racing community would be going to see the venerable old trainer honoured.

'Oh. That's a shame. Will you be back late, then?'

'I can't see us getting home much before ten.'

'Oh well, never mind. It wasn't important. I'll try another time.'

'Fine,' Susan said politely.

They said goodbye and hung up.

Rory parked his car in a lane on the other side of the shallow valley where Straker's house stood. Thick, heavy cloud blotted out the moon and deepened the darkness of the night with a relentless drizzle. Rory pulled the green 1:25,000 map of the area from his glove compartment. There were two fields between the lane where he was and the brook – a tributary of the Kennett – which scuttled down the valley floor. The map marked a footbridge into a narrow belt of woodland on the other side, beyond which was a small paddock, and the back of Henry Straker's house, maybe half a mile from where Rory was parked.

He pulled on a pair of waxed leggings and a hooded Barbour, then swapped his shoes for rubber stable boots and slipped out of his car into the damp blackness.

There were no house lights visible anywhere, but he planned to restrict to a minimum the use of the torch he had brought with him.

He found a gate into the field that edged the brook, clambered over, and thanked his luck that it was grass and not corn on the other side.

Without the aid of the light, he headed down the gentle slope to the brook. There wasn't a lot left of the footbridge when he found it, but enough to pick his way across the broken boards with intermittent flashes of his torch.

The woodland on the other side was dense, uncared-for beech and hazel coppice. The map had marked a path which had long since disappeared through lack of use, but he knew that if he headed up the slope away from the brook, he was going more or less the right way.

Five minutes of struggling in the dark through the damp, overgrown woodland brought him to a barbed-wire fence and the small field marked on the map. With his eyes now sensitive to the subtle shades of black that surrounded him, he could just make out the unlighted bulk of the rectory on the far side of the paddock.

He set out across the long wet grass and began to think

about how he was going to get into the empty house.

Halfway across, he heard a muffled bark from inside the house, followed by a clapping noise as a dog came out through a cat-flap to investigate.

He shook his head in admiration at that extra canine sense which could tell a dog of an alien presence without the aid of sight, sound or smell.

The dog – it sounded like a terrier of some sort – barked once or twice. Rory, fifty yards from the house now, stood and waited for it to come to him.

It barked again, more insistently, as it came near.

'Come here,' Rory called in a hushed tone, still not moving. The dog understood that it wasn't being challenged. Its bark became more of a friendly yip as it trotted through the long grass.

Rory offered it the back of his hand. 'Hello, boy,' he muttered.

The dog sniffed the hand, and liked what it smelled.

Rory crouched to stroke the small head, then the damp, wiry body. The dog jumped up and licked his face, as Rory flashed his torch on the name engraved on the metal tag around the dog's neck.

'Okay, Jimmy. Show me the way home.'

Another barbed-wire fence and a small shrubbery separated them from the back of the large house.

Once through, Jimmy trotted ahead to the door by which it had exited and jumped back through the cat-flap.

Rory called softly until Jimmy came back out again. He crouched down and stroked it until he thought it was safe to pick up.

With the friendly terrier nestling against his chest, he turned the handle on the door.

It was locked, as he'd assumed.

He knelt down in front of the cat-flap and inserted an arm through it to see if he could find a key on the inside. He felt around, but couldn't even make contact with the handle.

He put the dog gently on the ground beside him, then lay down so that he could insert his shoulder in through the flap, giving him the use of the full length of his arm. His fingers found first the handle and then, with excitement, a key in the lock. He turned it and felt it click open.

He pulled his arm out, and stood up. If there was no alarm, he was in.

Again, he turned the handle slowly, and this time opened the door. He slipped in with his new canine friend and closed the door behind him before switching on his torch and flashing it around. He was in a room full of dog baskets, boots and washing machines. He shone his light into the upper corners for any signs of an alarm and around the door jamb for wires and connections, but found nothing.

He walked across the room to a door opposite and opened it into a back hall where rows of hooks were cluttered with mackintoshes and all the other wet-weather paraphernalia that outdoor English people keep.

He closed the door, shutting the dog behind him, and went on to make a quick appraisal of the other rooms on the ground floor of the house.

There was a formal dining room, sparkling clean and unused, he judged; next to it was the drawing room where he had sat with Susan and Henry three nights before.

Behind the drawing room was a study with two walls

shelved from top to bottom with rows of veterinary text-books. In front of the window stood a large flat-topped desk and a small chair. To one side of this was a Victorian armchair with a reading lamp beside it.

Henry's surgery was five miles away in the Lambourn valley, but Rory guessed he must bring work home with him. He walked across to the desk and closed the curtains behind it.

On the top, there was a telephone, a small calendar, a leather-edged blotter and a pen stand – nothing else.

Rory pulled open the central drawer between the pedestals. Inside was an A4 diary. He took it out, put it on the desk and began to leaf through it.

In Henry's neat, italic hand were noted various appointments, not, on the whole, professional ones. Rory guessed those were looked after by the surgery staff. There were times and places for dinners, parties, receptions, and fixtures for the Reading boys' football team, sometimes with the results scribbled beside them.

Henry had also entered the names of the racecourses where he officiated on the days when he was, presumably, on duty.

Rory carried on chronologically until he reached the last week of February. On Tuesday, the 27th, was written 'Kempton'.

The word was heavily circled in black, as if someone had been absently using a biro while thinking of something else.

Rory's heart quickened. Fumbling now, he leafed through the next few pages until, on Wednesday 7th March, his eyes picked out the word 'Folkestone', circled again, and beside it, '12.30', the time of the first race that day.

Rory told himself that Straker might have written that to remind himself when he had to be there, but he went right back through the diary. Those were the only two race meetings that were circled.

Convinced that he had a lead now, Rory looked through the whole diary again, then at all the other papers in the top drawer of the desk. But he found nothing that told him any more.

He shut the drawer with frustration, wondering where to look next. His eyes fell on the blotter in front of him. It was liberally covered with doodles – the sort of stylised notes and hieroglyphics that people write when they are talking on the telephone. He held his torch to see what he could decipher.

There were figures, dates, names of drugs – though not xylazine – and, in the top right-hand corner, with the letters heavily traced over several times, the words 'Midnight Express'.

Rory let out an audible grunt of triumph as he stared at it.

He couldn't think how or why Henry Straker – notoriously one of the most honourable men in racing – could be involved in stopping horses, but there had to be more than coincidence in his insistence on giving Charters the day off at Kempton, the two entries in the diary, two pre-race tests – both clean – and the subsequent under-performance of two animals. It had only been Midnight Express's final resting place in the path. lab of the Veterinary College that had revealed the true cause of his demise.

Rory reflected that, without doubt, Henry Straker was the best-placed man in the industry to tamper with a horse. He also realised that he could be leaping to a conclusion very wide of the mark. Two isolated diary entries and a doodle on a jotter – which could have been done after the police had been to see him, or while discussing the test results on the phone – didn't prove anything; nor were they likely to convince the police that they had another potential suspect.

Grimly, he set about searching for more evidence. He didn't know what he was looking for, or where it might be. He glanced at his watch. It was eight thirty. Susan had said they would be back about ten. He'd give them half an hour's grace, which left him only an hour.

During that hour he opened every book, every drawer in the study. He found the Strakers' large, elegant bedroom and searched through every drawer and cupboard.

He found nothing that wasn't entirely explicable by Henry's job as a veterinary surgeon.

Disappointed and frustrated, he went back downstairs and looked for a second time through the drawers of the desk in the study.

It was in a folder of assorted notes and receipts that he found a consignment docket for six fifty-millilitre phials of xylazine, dated 22 February. He picked it up and stared at it by the light of his torch. Then he froze.

The headlights of a car momentarily lit up the bushes outside the study window and he heard the crunch of wheels on gravel.

He held his watch under the light. It was already a quarter to ten. He could hardly believe that he had been in the house so long. The dog barked from the back of the house at the sound of the front door being unlocked. He would have to cross the hall to get back to the scullery by which he'd come in. That wasn't an option now.

Frantically, he looked around the study with a last flash of his torch. The big armchair was angled across the corner of the room. Rory hoped there was enough space behind it to accommodate him in his Barbour and leggings. Footsteps echoed on the flagstones in the hall. In the dark, he clambered silently over the chair. He settled behind it and listened to the vet and his wife making their way through to the back of the house.

'Shut up, Jimmy,' Susan ordered the dog who had started barking again. 'What's the matter with you?'

Rory prayed that neither of them would try the back door, which he hadn't locked behind him. He thought back over the search he had made of the various rooms of the house and tried to remember if there was anything he hadn't replaced as he had found it. With a sudden sagging in his guts, he realised that he hadn't shut the drawer of the desk and that Henry was a tidy, methodical sort of man.

The footsteps came back from the scullery and into the hall.

'I'll be up in a minute, Sue.' Henry's voice was nearer the half-open door of the study.

Rory stopped breathing. He heard the door swing open, and a click as the high, central light came on. With relief, he saw that he was still in shadow.

Henry's footsteps, halfway across the room, faltered.

'What the hell . .?' he gasped loudly.

'What is it, dear?' Susan's voice floated in.

'Er, nothing. Something I'd forgotten about, that's all. I'll be up in a mo,' he said again.

Rory heard him cross over to the desk and rummage through the contents of the top drawer. He recalled that he had replaced the folder where he had found it, under the diary. After a moment, the drawer was pushed back. Henry gave a grunt of self-censure, evidently believing he had left the drawer open himself, and walked out of the room.

The light was switched off and the door closed. Rory breathed more easily and, clutching the incriminating slip of paper in his hand, listened to Henry slowly climbing up the stairs.

He waited where he was for ten minutes. The Strakers' bedroom was on the far side of the house; he could hear no sounds from where he was, but he was confident they had gone to bed.

Cautiously, he raised himself until he could look over the back of the chair. There was no light to be seen under the door. Silently, he climbed out and crept towards where he judged the door to be. Feeling the well-polished panels, he found a large wooden knob and turned it slowly. He swung the door back twelve inches and slipped through.

On the flagstones of the hall, his rubber shoes made a faint squeak. He stopped and listened – no reaction. He reached the door on the far side and managed to open it without a sound, until the dog barked. He slipped in quickly and closed it behind him, muttering to the dog. 'It's okay, boy; it's okay.' He stretched out a hand in the darkness until the animal came to sniff it and recognised it. He crouched down and gathered Jimmy up into his arms, stroking it and tickling it under the chin.

'You can come with me,' he whispered.

In the gloom, his eyes could just make out the glass panels in the back door. Silently, on some kind of coconut matting, he felt his way towards it, still fondling the dog.

He heard Susan's voice from beyond the hall door.

'What *is* it, Jimmy?'

He opened the door, slid through and closed it as light flooded through the glass panes behind him. He reached down, set the cat-flap swinging and tiptoed across the shrubbery towards the paddock fence.

He scrambled over, catching a barb just below his groin, and dropped into the lush, wet grass on the other side. He tucked Jimmy under one arm and sprinted for the woodland on the lower side of the field. More cautiously, he negotiated the next fence, and turned to look back at the house.

Lights still shone from a first-floor window and the glazed back door. But there was no obvious sound of pursuit. A few seconds later, the light downstairs went out, and he guessed that Susan Straker had been ready to believe that the dog had heard a fox or some other four-legged intruder and had slipped out to investigate.

Ten minutes later, the light in the upper room was turned out. Rory gave the dog a last quick stroke and tickle, and dropped him back over the fence into the paddock. With luck, Susan wouldn't check the back door until next morning.

'Home, boy,' he urged. He watched the small dog trot

back towards the house before he turned into the woodland to find his way back to the footbridge across the brook.

Rory's car was undisturbed where he had left it. He pulled off his wet outer garments, got in and rolled a cigarette with shaking hands. He had not really wanted to believe his suspicions that Henry Straker had been responsible for the test on the favourite in yesterday's first race.

Even Matt Charters' information that Henry had insisted on taking his place at Kempton the day Luke Mundy was killed had only made Rory keener to eliminate Henry's name from his list of suspects.

But what he had seen that evening left him convinced that Straker warranted further investigation.

He also knew that that was only part of the answer.

Now he had to find out why. And, possibly, for whom.

Right then, most of all, he wanted to talk to someone about his discovery.

He picked up his phone and dialled Langlands. He hadn't seen Laura since that morning; it felt like a month ago. Her voice, when she answered, sounded unfamiliar.

'Hello?'

'Laura, it's me, Rory.'

'Hi, how's it going?' she asked lightly.

Rory sensed she was doing it deliberately, to stop him from talking openly. He followed her lead.

'Not so bad. I just wanted to confirm the ride on Stargazer tomorrow.'

'He goes, and you're declared.'

'Good. Are you sure he's ready?'

212

'Are you sure you are?' She even managed a laugh.

'Yeah, I'm fine. I've been checking the form of another horse you might like to hear about.'

'Save it till I see you tomorrow,' Laura said quickly.

'Okay.'

He rang off, quickly picked the phone up again and dialled Edward Brickhill's mobile number.

Brickhill answered himself.

'It's Rory Gillespie here.'

'Hello, Rory. Any news on that sick horse?'

'Yes, I think so, though nothing confirmed.'

'Do you want to talk about it?'

'Aye.'

'Can you come here?'

'Where are you, in Sussex?'

'No, London. Do you know where I live?'

'Yes. I'll be there in an hour or so.'

Rory remembered the way and found a parking space in Eaton Place outside the high stucco building whose top two floors comprised the Brickhills' London residence. He hadn't been inside the place for twelve years, but it didn't look as though it had changed at all. The same portraits of great horses and ill-humoured ancestors hung in the same places. The quiet Georgian sideboards and plump sofas looked as though they hadn't been used in the twelve years.

So did the whisky in the decanter from which Edward Brickhill poured him a drink.

Laura's father didn't ask any questions until Rory was settled on one of the sofas in front of an elaborately fake log fire that burned in a classical fireplace.

'So,' he said when he was sure his guest had all he needed, 'what have you found out?'

'I think Midnight Express was got at by the Jockey Club vet,' Rory said hesitantly.

Brickhill's eyes, already sharply focused on Rory, widened very slightly, registering disbelief. 'Henry Straker? I don't believe it. I've known him for years.'

Rory nodded. 'So have I. But I'm sure of it. Have you read yesterday's race report?'

Brickhill shook his head. 'No, why?'

'Laura ran a horse called Pan Piper. He's a good horse and improving, but the form book said that the favourite should have walked all over him. It didn't, though; I watched the race on SIS last night. It started out giving Jimmy McShea a real handful, pinged round the first mile, then started jumping terribly and came home with its tongue hanging out. Pan Piper won easily. But guess what? The stewards had a tip-off that the favourite was got at, and the test was taken by Henry Straker.'

Edward Brickhill looked disappointed but relieved. 'Rory, I don't think that proves anything more than pure coincidence. There's absolutely no reason why that horse shouldn't have been tampered with between Henry taking the test and the start of the race – if indeed he was doped at all.'

'He was; I'm sure of it. Anyway, there's more.'

Rory told him about his visit to the Strakers' house that evening, the entries in the diary, the doodle on the blotter and the delivery slip for the xylazine.

When he had finished, Edward Brickhill didn't say anything. He looked at Rory, then into the fire.

'Look, Mr Brickhill, I know that's not enough to convict him, but it's more than enough to convince me.'

'I don't like coincidences ... But for God's sake ... *Henry? Why?*'

'Whatever the reason, it's got to be something serious.'

'Henry Straker's one of the most honest men I know. He would no more take a bribe than jump over the moon.'

'I heard them talking a bit when they got back this evening.'

'You were still there?'

'Aye, behind an armchair, but that's another story.'

'Do you think Susan knows anything about it.'

'I'm not sure,' Rory sounded doubtful. 'She may do. They're very close, especially since they lost their boys. If I can find out why, I can probably find out who's behind it ... if there is anyone else behind it.'

'Is there anything I can do?'

'I don't think so. I've tried to come up with some connection between the horses that won the races on both occasions, but there's none. In fact, I'm afraid the only common denominator I can find is Laura. Her horse was the first to be doped, and another of her horses won when the second was doped.'

Edward Brickhill looked at him sharply. 'You're not trying to tell me that you think Laura might have had something to do with it after all?'

'Not that she did it; but I think there might be some connection that she doesn't know about. I'm seeing her at the races tomorrow, maybe when I tell her about Straker, she might be able to come up with something. I don't know ...'

Brickhill walked away from the fire and put his glass

on a table behind the sofa. 'Just tread extremely carefully, because you might find you're barking up the wrong tree, and that would be very awkward. Now, I've had some enquiries made among Luke Mundy's staff at Thames Land. His secretary said that the receivers have discovered that he had been gambling on the price of his shares – in a bogus name, of course – and using his inside information, totally illegally. Apparently he had been making substantial profits on it. Just before he died, it looks as though he started on the horses. She didn't know if he'd backed himself on Midnight Express, but she said she wouldn't be at all surprised. He had given her the impression that he was very confident of winning his own race.'

'He had cause to be,' Rory said. 'Even though the horse wouldn't have liked the trip much, he should have walked it in that company.'

'Quite,' Brickhill nodded. 'Anyway, his secretary – Jennifer something – is going to see if she can find out who his bookmaker was. Unfortunately, a lot of the paperwork has already been removed from the office by the receiver, and the Serious Fraud Office have been sniffing around too.' Brickhill picked up his glass and took a long slug of whisky. 'It's typical of Luke. I was always fairly sure there was something wrong with his set-up, but he was an ace juggler, and he had a lot of bottle. It's just his luck that the fraud squad didn't catch up with him until he was well beyond their reach. It seems to me that the vital thing to find out is who he was betting with. I've got someone making enquiries into the firms that make books on share prices to identify any who took significant losses on the Thames Land price. I'll let you know how I get on.' He drained his glass and put it down. 'Now,' he said, making it clear that the interview was over, 'can I offer you a bed for the night?'

Rory declined. In the lift going down he smiled to himself. Until very recently, he had never expected to be asked to stay the night by either of Laura's parents.

Outside, he found his car in the quiet square and with some satisfaction headed back towards the M4.

Chapter Nine

'Where the hell have you been?' Pam asked.

Rory had left the Brickhills' flat after midnight. Pam was waiting for him when he let himself into the house an hour and a half later.

'Do you care?' he asked mildly.

'Of course I bloody care – I am married to you, aren't I?'

'That depends what you mean by "married".'

'You've been with Laura Mundy, haven't you?'

'No. I've been with her father.'

'What the hell are you doing with that pompous fool?'

'Not having sex, which is probably all that worries you.' Rory sighed. He got no pleasure from these confrontations with Pam, but sometimes they were unavoidable. 'Look, if you want to argue all night, I think I'll sleep in the spare room. I've had a long day.'

He walked past her to the stairs and went up to the little room which Pam had overdecorated for visitors who never came.

Despite the schemes and theories filling his head, Rory
slept almost as soon as he had slipped between the sheets
of the guest bed. He was woken by his own internal alarm
clock at six-thirty next morning, and washed and shaved
in Tommy's bathroom. He looked into the boy's room.
'Don't forget, we're going fishing on Saturday,' he said.
''Course I won't forget, Dad. Are you going already?'
'Aye. I've got some horses to work.'
'Okay, 'bye.'
Rory listened for a moment at Pam's door and heard
nothing. Relieved, he went quietly downstairs and out to
his car.

Five minutes later, he was heading down the Lambourn
Valley towards Straker's house.

This time he neither drove up to the house, nor parked
across the valley. He left his car on the grass verge outside
the high stone wall that fronted the old-fashioned garden
and walked through the gate. There were no obvious signs
of life in the house. When he reached the front door, he
pressed the big brass bell for a couple of seconds.

Henry Straker, dressed and shaved, opened the door a
few moments later.

Rory thought he spotted a momentary twitch of appre-
hension in the vet's eyes before he assumed his customary affability.

Rory was suddenly discouraged. He hadn't credited
Straker with any acting ability. He had been relying on
the man's innate honesty to prevent him from disguising
the truth for long.

'Good Lord, Rory, it's rather early for a social call.'
'It's important, Henry. Can I come in?'

A cloud of worry crossed Straker's forehead.

'Well, I am due out now. I'm calling in at Langlands, as a matter of fact.'

'It was partly about Langlands that I wanted to see you. I won't keep you long.'

Straker struggled for a moment, weighing up the position. In the end, he said, 'All right. You'd better come in.'

He opened the door wider and Rory followed him into the hall. Susan's voice came from the back of the house. 'Who is it, dear?'

'It's just Rory Gillespie.' He turned to Rory. 'We'll go into my study. Do you mind if I don't offer you coffee – I don't want to disturb Susan.'

'No, that's fine.' Rory looked around the room where he had hidden the night before. It was far less sinister in the daylight and he was finding it hard to believe what he had found there.

Straker closed the door behind them and waved Rory into the large chair behind which he had crouched less than twelve hours before.

Rory sat. Straker remained standing. 'Well, what can I do for you?'

Rory looked straight into Straker's eyes. 'I want to know why you gave Midnight Express a shot of xylazine before Luke Mundy rode him at Kempton.'

Henry Straker stared back at Rory. He seemed for a moment completely immobile, rigid, unbreathing. The normal healthy glow on his face had turned to a pale grey.

'You want to know *what*?' he asked, his voice conveying indignation and disbelief.

Rory faltered. Suddenly, he wasn't so sure. What, he

thought, if he had made a terrible misjudgement and all the pointers he had found were simply coincidence? It was an appalling thing to charge anyone with, especially someone of Henry's reputation.

Rory cleared his throat. 'I said, why did you inject Midnight Express with xylazine before he ran?'

Straker turned his back on Rory and paced across the room towards the bookshelves on the other side. After a moment, he turned and looked at him with a steady, penetrating eye.

'Rory, we've known each other quite a long time. I considered I knew you well. I've no wish to have a quarrel with you. I think the best thing would be for us to forget that you ever made such an outrageous accusation.'

Rory felt himself quail before Straker's steely directness. Doubts flooded in to wipe out the certainty he had felt about the vet's guilt.

And yet, what about the times in the diary, the delivery note for the xylazine, Midnight Express's name on the blotter, the arrangement to take Charters' place that day at Kempton?

But he couldn't admit that he had broken into the house the evening before and searched the place – not now.

He stood up. 'Okay. I'm sorry. I simply don't see who else it could have been,' he said lamely.

Straker put a hand on Rory's shoulder. 'I understand why you're so keen to find another suspect, but I'm not your man.'

'Who the hell planted that phial in her car, then?' Rory blurted. 'I'm sorry.' He shook his head. 'I just know Laura didn't do it and I don't want to see her go to prison for it.'

'None of us do, Rory. Why do you think I've stuck by her? Like you, I hope very much that she wasn't responsible.'

'I didn't say I hoped she wasn't responsible, I said I know she isn't. I'm sorry to have disturbed you. I'll see myself out.'

Rory climbed back into his car, weary with doubt and remorse. He started the engine and drove back on to the road towards the village to buy some tobacco before going to Laura's. Off the verge, Rory realised that his car was behaving oddly, trying to pull to the left. He turned the radio off to hear the depressing rumble of a flat front tyre.

The lane was too narrow to pull up and let other traffic by, but twenty yards on Rory spotted an opening in the hedge into a small farm track.

He nursed the hobbling vehicle up the road, and turned it a few yards up the muddy track.

Cursing the mud, the car and whoever had left a two-inch tack lying around on the verge, he changed the wheel.

He had the boot open, and was on the point of picking up the punctured wheel to stow it, when he heard a car turn out of Straker's gate.

He stood unnoticed and watched as the vet's Daimler drove past towards the village – the wrong way for Langlands. Maybe he'd had an emergency call?

Rory took a punt. He picked up the damaged wheel, hurled it into the boot without securing it and leapt into the driver's seat. He put the motor into reverse and spun furiously back through the mud and into the lane, just in time to see Straker's Daimler curve out of sight.

He kept his distance until they reached the main road. He let a couple of cars pull in between him and the Daimler and prayed that the vet wouldn't spot him. Unless Straker saw the sign on the side of the vehicle, he probably wouldn't pay much attention to a white Rover, even if he knew what kind of car Rory drove.

Straker carried on, driving quickly down the old Bath Road towards Marlborough. As Rory followed, he tried to sort out what he was doing. Straker's display of indignation in the study had been very convincing. The dignity with which he had dealt with Rory's accusation was exactly what Rory would have expected if he were innocent.

But Rory couldn't ignore what he had seen last night.

A few miles short of Marlborough, Straker turned off the road into the car park of a Little Chef. It seemed an unlikely place for him to have his breakfast. Rory carried on past and pulled into the forecourt of the garage just beyond the eating house.

Parking his car to one side, he got out and walked quickly round the back of the Little Chef. He reached the end of the wall from where he would be able to see Straker's car, and cautiously put his head round the corner.

Straker was still sitting in the Daimler showing no sign of leaving it.

Rory ducked back. Straker hadn't seen him, but sooner or later he would look up. Rory reckoned he would hear if Henry got out of his car. He walked about, out of sight of the car park, as if he were stretching his legs. As he walked, he pulled the last of his tobacco and papers from the pocket of his leather jacket and rolled himself a cigarette.

Several more cars pulled off the main road. Each time, Rory poked his head round the corner to see Straker still sitting in his car, reading a paper.

Impatiently, he wondered what the hell the vet was doing. Of course, it could be something completely innocent – a convenient rendezvous with a client to hand over some prescription or some X-rays – anything.

Rory was beginning to doubt the wisdom of following Straker and considered slipping away and getting to Laura's before the vet when he heard the bubbling rumble of a big bike pull into the car park.

A bike didn't seem a very likely conveyance for anyone meeting Straker, but Rory went back to the corner of the building to sneak a look.

A 1200cc BMW headed straight for the Daimler and pulled up in a space beside it. The rider turned off the engine and propped the bike on its stand. Without removing his full-face helmet, he got off, opened the saddle box behind his seat and pulled out a large brown envelope. He walked round the front of the Daimler and opened the passenger door.

Rory couldn't tell much from the full set of plain black leathers the rider wore. He couldn't even be sure it was a man – slightly built and, without a helmet, maybe five feet eight or nine. Either way, the biker got into Straker's car with confidence and no display of deference to the distinguished vet.

Rory saw them talking, Straker looking straight ahead,

speaking in short bursts, nodding his head, then shaking
it. The conversation lasted little more than three minutes,
after which the biker got out of the Daimler, without the
envelope, walked quickly back to the BMW, swung a leg
over and took off. A few seconds later, Straker went too.
Although he took the same direction – back towards
Hungerford – Rory didn't get the impression that he was
following the bike.

Rory went back to his Rover and drove out on to the
main road. He soon caught up with Straker, though there
was no sign of the bike ahead. The vet was evidently not
in a hurry. Rory followed at the same leisurely rate and
guessed that Henry was now heading for Langlands. He
switched on his phone and prodded Laura's number.

"Morning,' he said when she answered. 'I'm running a
bit late, but I'll be down in time for your second lot. Is
that okay?'

'Sure,' she replied. 'Don't be late.'

Rory knew a back route that cut off the right angle made
by the main roads. Provided there were no tractors on
it, he could get ahead of Straker and arrive at Laura's
before him.

He was lucky. The only farm vehicle he came across
immediately pulled over to let him pass. The tractor driver
looked pleased with himself when he saw, from Rory's
name blazoned on the car, who he'd pulled over for.

At Langlands, Rory was put on a four-year-old gelding
which had shown moderate talent on the flat and which
he was due to ride in its first hurdle race next day at
Uttoxeter. When he could, he liked to sit on a young

horse once or twice before riding it in a race.

He settled the animal on the way up and tried to join in the other lads' gossip. Predictably, this centred on the continuing drama of Laura's arrest and doubts about their own future. The tension in the yard had been heightened, Rory gathered, by a confrontation between Mrs Mundy and the stable jockey. Dai Price had been complaining about the increasing number of rides Rory was being given. The Welshman should have been there that morning, but hadn't turned up. In the circumstances, Rory was grateful for that. Generally, though, the lads seemed reluctant to say too much in front of Rory. His relationship with Laura was apparently common knowledge by now.

Laura was up on the gallops. When Rory pulled up near her after giving the gelding a quick four-furlong gallop, she beckoned him over and he gave up his saddle to a lad who had driven up with her.

'What do you think of him?' Laura asked first.

'He gave me a nice feel. If he stays two miles, he could be useful. How does he jump?'

'He's a natural; sees them and he's off.'

There was a kind of strained normality to their conversation, unnecessary because there was no one else within earshot now that the lad had ridden off, back towards the yard.

'I broke into Henry Straker's place last night,' Rory said with an abrupt change of tone.

Laura, closely watching the next pair of horses drumming up the all-weather gallop towards them, turned to look at him sharply

'You did what?' she asked with disbelief.

'I had a hunch it was Henry, then I was certain, now I'm not sure.'

'But it couldn't possibly be Henry; that's crazy,' she almost shouted.

'Maybe it is; I don't know, but there've been two horses now tested by Henry as a result of tip-offs, and both went on to run bloody oddly. Okay, one we know about because of Professor Douglas's analysis, but the other they assume was clean because Henry had tested it and no one's insisted on a second test.'

'The one at Folkestone, you mean?'

'Yes.'

'No, that favourite ran badly, but not particularly badly. It didn't look much in the paddock. I noticed its tongue was hanging out – like Midnight Express's, but some horses just run like that. I hardly gave it another thought. Anyway, who on earth would Henry be helping?'

'Himself, maybe?'

'Don't be ridiculous. He never has a bet. I'm sorry, Rory, but I think you're barking up completely the wrong tree.'

'Have you got any other trees to suggest then?' Rory asked with a sharpness he immediately regretted. 'And by the way, it would help if you'd told me everything there is to know about the whole business.'

'I have, for God's sake!'

'What about that life insurance, then? Your father mentioned it and Susan Straker told me it was worth two and a half million.'

Laura burst out laughing. 'I don't know who told her that, but she's way out. I can show you the policy – if it ever gets paid – it's worth about four hundred thousand. Quite a lot of money, but peanuts, relatively speaking, if I'm going to lose Langlands and everything else to Luke's creditors – and it looks as though I am. Look, if I'd thought it was relevant I would have told you.'

'Okay,' Rory capitulated. 'But if Henry's got nothing to do with this, I'm getting nowhere fast. I can't tie the thing together at all. I followed him to a meet on the way here this morning. Some guy – at least I presume it was a man – turned up on a big bike, got into Henry's car with an envelope, talked to him for a few minutes, got out and roared off. I thought maybe Henry was just going to hand over some medicine or X-rays or something, but the biker wasn't carrying anything when he got out.'

'That doesn't tell us anything,' Laura said. 'Maybe the biker was delivering X-rays. As you say, he may have been discussing a case or something.'

'Sure, it's possible. Look, after Henry's reaction when I confronted him with it, I felt terrible, but last night I found he'd written the name Midnight Express on his blotter and marked the time of one of the races in his diary. And among a batch of delivery notes, I found he'd had a consignment of xylazine just before the first doping. I thought that was too much of a coincidence.'

'But it could have been just that. I mean, he may have written the horse's name after he'd tested it to remind himself or something.'

Rory sighed. If it was such hard work trying to convince the person he was aiming to help, it would be a lot harder convincing the police – if he ever had enough of a case to put to them. 'I also went to see your father last night. He's looking into Luke's gambling activities. He's discovered that he had been having some very large bets on the share price of Thames Land.'

'How do you mean?'

'Well, some people can't be bothered to go to all the trouble and expense of buying shares to speculate on their movement; they simply gamble on the price changes with a handful of bookies who run that kind of book.'

'My father thinks Luke might have been doing that?'

'He spoke to Luke's secretary; she said the receivers had discovered it. If he was, he was breaking the law, using his inside information. If somebody got to know, they could have used that against him, maybe to blackmail him. And it's possible he had a very large bet on Midnight Express. This secretary seemed to think he had been losing heavily just before he died.'

'I've never seen him so nervous as he was before that race,' Laura said. 'I told you that. I may not have shown it, but I was feeling terrible about the whole thing – having promised the ride to you in the Champion Chase. But I've no idea who he'd have had a bet with.'

'Listen, if we can find that out, we'll know who wanted him stopped. In any normal race, you'd have to look at the horse that eventually won, but in a field like that, there was no certainty that any of them would get round, let alone win. Nobody would bother to nobble the favourite in a hunter chase to make way for another horse.'

'No. You're right. It had to be whoever Luke was betting with.'

'And that could have been anyone. The bet wouldn't have been placed in his own name, I shouldn't think, if it was recorded at all.'

The last lot of horses had galloped past them as they spoke. Laura started to walk back towards the Land Rover.

On the far side of the valley, Rory spotted Henry Straker's Daimler snaking slowly down the lane towards the yard. He glanced at his watch. 'I wonder what he's been doing. He should have been here about half an hour ago.'

'He could have been doing anything,' Laura said. 'He probably made another call on the way. I really think you're wrong about him.'

When they were both in the car, she sat back in the seat and sighed. 'Rory, you've got to find something, somebody. Every day that goes by, more people are thinking it must have been me; I can tell by the way they look away when they see me. I don't know how long I can stand the pressure.'

Rory stretched out a hand and put it on her denim-clad thigh. Gently he squeezed it. 'Don't worry. I've got no intention of letting anyone lock you up. Not after it's taken me twelve years to come to my senses.'

Laura gave him a quick, rueful smile and switched the engine on.

They reached the car park behind the yard at the same time as the vet.

Straker climbed out and nodded at Rory as if it were the first time he'd seen him that morning. Rory saw that he wasn't carrying anything. All the equipment needed to test the horses' blood was kept in Patrick's small office.

Rory waited until the vet had walked round into the yard, talking to Laura, who glanced over her shoulder and made a face of disbelief.

When they were out of sight, he quickly slipped into the Daimler. There was a brown envelope, unmarked, and torn open, on the back seat. He reached back for it and looked inside; it was empty. He searched all the possible places in the car where Straker could have put the contents – in the map and glove compartments, under the seats – but found nothing likely. It was always possible, though unlikely, that Straker had put it in the boot, but Rory felt sure that whatever it was, it was connected with the doping of the horses, and the vet had disposed of it somewhere between the Little Chef and Langlands.

He had been in the car for less than a minute. He got out and walked quickly round into the yard. There was no sign of Laura or Straker. But Declan was just letting himself out of one of the stables.

Rory nodded at him with a smile. 'How's it going then?'

'All right.' The lad strolled across to him and added quietly, 'I got somethin' to tell you.'

Rory, with a look, stopped him from going on. 'Are you bringing a horse up to Uttoxeter this afternoon?'

'Just getting 'im ready now.'

'See me when I get there, before the first.'

The lad nodded co-operatively. 'Okay. See you there.'

The terror of another term at Her Majesty's pleasure gave Arthur Eland the courage to disobey his client once again. He dialled a City number.

His client wasn't pleased.

'I told you I didn't want you to ring me again,' he said. 'Someone's on to us. We're in trouble.'

'Stop worrying. Nothing's going to lead anyone back to you.'

'There's one person who can.'

'Well that won't happen, will it, after your splendid photographic session.'

'I'm not so sure. It's the one link. I think we should get rid of it.'

'Now you're being ridiculous. I have an investment which will yield a few more returns yet. And you'd do yourself more harm than good by doing anything stupid, I can assure you. I'll put you on a bonus when we've made more use of our asset. It's a big week next week and I'm not going to waste it. So, do nothing. I'll ring you with instructions Sunday night.'

The line went dead and Eland stared at the crackling phone for a moment before pressing the plunger to get a fresh line.

With his other hand, he thumbed through a grimy address book.

One of the few benefits of his time in jail was the access it gave him to a national network of practitioners of every conceivable type of illegal service. The serious discouragement of a man's inquisitiveness was easily bought.

A wet westerly swept across the soft green undulations of Uttoxeter racecourse. The sparse Friday crowd – Staffordshire farmers and town people from Derby and the

Potteries – looked dispirited and uninspired as mud-caked jockeys on slithery saddles did their disgruntled best to provide an afternoon's entertainment.

Declan was waiting at the door of the jockeys' changing room when Rory arrived.

'Let's walk down to the stables,' Rory said. 'What have you got?'

'Well, I was thinking of strangers who had been to the yard when the xylazine was found. There were a few, there usually are. But there was this one bloke, looked like he could've been a lad once, come round selling minerals and that. He asked me where Dad was, and I go, "You're out of luck, he's not here," and he goes, "Oh well, I'll call again." I knew I'd seen him before somewhere, but I couldn't think where. I asked Micky Parish, one of the other lads, if he knew him, and he says, "No, but he was at Kempton the day Express got done." And I remembered then, he was poking around the stables that morning. I didn't take no notice then, like I say, he looked like he could've been a lad – you know, not too big, right clothes and everything. But Mick was right, it was definitely the same bloke.'

'What did he look like, then?'

''Ard to say, really. Sort of mousy hair, thinning a bit. Little bum-freezer jacket, brown cords, I think. About forty, maybe. Not the sort of bloke you take much notice of.'

'How did he talk?'

'London, like.'

'I don't suppose he gave you a name?'

'Nah.'

'Can you remember if Mrs Mundy's car was down at the yard then?'

Declan thought for a moment, then nodded. 'Yeh. You was there that morning; Skinny rode your horse back, didn't he, and she came back down with you from the gallops in the Land Rover, dumped you and drove on straight back to the house. She'll often do that, leave her car at the yard if she knows she's coming back down again after.'

Rory nodded. 'Yes, you're right. I was parked next to her car. So when did this bloke turn up?'

'Just after you'd gone.'

'And would he have had time to put something in Laura's car?'

'Easy.'

'Would it have been locked?'

'No, 'course not, not down the yard. I mean, no one would nick it from there, would they?'

Rory nodded, thanked Declan and turned to walk back towards the changing room.

'D'you want me to tell the police about him?'

'Just keep a look out for him, for now. And if you see him again, find out who he is, okay?'

In the absence of most of the southern jockeys, who were at Newton Abbot, Rory had fixed himself a full card for the day. After two unspectacular losing rides, he walked out to the ring to mount up for the third – the novice hurdle – on Stargazer, the young horse Declan had brought up.

He had been through the opposition with Patrick

Hoolihan before setting out from Langlands that morning. If the horse settled, it should provide him with a winner. Viewing the other runners in the flesh now, he didn't change his mind.

The wind had dropped a little, and allowed a steady, misty drizzle to fall and soak into the already spongy turf. But, Rory thought, this ought to suit Stargazer's high action.

And it did.

The horse pulled straight to the front and then relaxed. Rory decided to leave him alone, to see if he would keep going without any opposition in his sights. Stargazer it seemed was perfectly content. He galloped on, seeing the small obstacles and bounding long and low over them.

Passing the stands before the last nine-furlong circuit, Rory turned to find out how far ahead he was. He could barely see the rest of the field through the grey drizzle. He relaxed. He didn't doubt that the rest of them would start to come back to him, but from where he was sitting, there could be only one outcome. Keeping a tight hold, he let Stargazer carry on steadily into the turn. The hurdle on the far side came up to meet them.

The horse saw it but was trying to pull up as it realised it was racing away from the stables. Rory gave it two good cracks down the left shoulder, pulled his whip through and hit it twice more on the other side. He felt that he'd got the horse on an even keel when, without warning, it swerved violently to the left and crashed through the wing of the jump.

The speed with which it changed direction took Rory completely by surprise. He was catapulted sideways out of the saddle and slammed into the wooden stake supporting the white plastic running rail.

Before he had time to feel the pain, he rolled, instinctively, as any experienced, conscious jockey does, and got himself off the track.

As he moved, an excruciating pain pulsed through his left shoulder. With a groan he looked down and recognised the dreaded sight of dislocation.

He saw the bulge of his shoulder bone protruding between his armpit and his chest.

Rory curled his toes tightly, kept his breathing as shallow as possible and tried unsuccessfully to find a position to relieve his agony.

The rest of the field was passing him now, the jockeys showing the businesslike air of people who knew they were now back in with a chance. One of them called, 'You all right?' and sounded as though he meant it.

As Rory was stretchered gently into the ambulance, Terry poked his face through the back door.

'They're going to take you straight to the local knackers,' he said. It was traditional to make light of injuries which were an inescapable part of a jump jockey's life. 'I'll drive your car back and fix a local taxi to take you home. Sorry I won't be able to bring you any flowers.'

Rory met with more sympathy at the hospital. The painkillers given to him by the ambulancemen were beginning to wear off, but he was reluctant to ask for more.

An X-ray confirmed that his shoulder was dislocated. Two white-knuckle minutes with a doctor corrected the problem and the pain disappeared as if by magic. Rory was then given an instruction from the specialist not to ride for at least a fortnight.

Rory nodded even as he told himself there was no way he was going to miss Cheltenham.

Terry had remembered to put Rory's clothes into the ambulance that had brought him from the racecourse. Rory changed back into them, stuffed the muddy breeches and silks into his bag, and told the receptionist on casualty that he was expecting a taxi.

'It's already here, Mr Gillespie,' she told him. 'Came half an hour ago.'

Rory was impressed with Terry's efficiency. He had only been at the hospital for an hour and a half. The last race of the day wouldn't even have started yet. He considered going back to the race-course, but he didn't really feel like driving himself home.

Thanking the smiling nurses, he walked slowly, carrying his bag with his good arm, down to the front lobby of the hospital.

'Mr Gillespie?' A large man was waiting to take his bag. 'How's the arm?' he asked, glancing at the sling.

Rory smiled. 'Better than it looks.'

He followed the man out of the door to a waiting Ford Sierra. The driver opened the back door for him and put his bag on the front passenger seat. Rory climbed in, trying not to shift his shoulder, and settled back into the rear seat. He closed his eyes and hoped he wouldn't be expected to keep up a conversation.

The driver let himself in and they pulled away from the hospital.

Soon they left the small town behind them, heading along the road to Stafford and the M6. To Rory's relief, his driver didn't seem inclined to conversation. Once he was confident they were on the way, he closed his eyes again and tried to sleep.

He had almost succeeded when a change in the car's speed and progress made him jerk his eyelids up to let in the gloom of the late afternoon.

'What's this?' he asked. 'A short cut or what?'

They were travelling along a narrow lane, high-hedged with occasional oaks. Through gaps at gateways, Rory saw small flat fields of empty pasture.

'There's some roadworks ahead on the Stafford road. We'll miss them this way.'

Rory approved and relaxed.

The lane entered a tunnel of mixed woodland. The driver switched on the car's headlights. After a few hundred yards, the lights picked out a Forestry Commission sign announcing a parking area and access to a 'nature trail'.

Abruptly, the car swung off the road on to a patch of muddy gravel. Rory jerked forward and winced at the stab of pain in his shoulder. 'What the hell are we stopping for?' he asked with sudden foreboding. He saw with relief that there was another car in the clearing.

'Thought we'd have a chat,' the driver growled.

Rory froze. A hollow, tingling fear shuddered through his body. There was a fraction of a second when he couldn't move a single muscle as he tried frantically to work out what was happening. Then instinct took over.

He grabbed the handle of the door, yanked it back to

open it. He got his legs out of the car, stood up to look for somewhere to run.

A bulk of human body was blocking his path.

'Oh no, Mr Gillespie. You're not going anywhere yet,' the bulk growled in a flat Black Country voice. 'We need to talk to you . . .'

He provided a full stop to his sentence with a hard fist, deep beneath Rory's rib cage, hitting his sling and sending a wave of nauseating pain through his injured shoulder.

Rory jackknifed and gulped for air. The big fist caught him again on the side of his jaw and sent him sprawling. He lay for a moment, aching, gasping, trying to think.

'You've been poking your nose where it's not wanted. Know what I mean?' The driver's voice this time.

Rory didn't answer the question; he guessed it was rhetorical.

He raised his torso from the ground.

A heavy shoe caught him in the ribs. He collapsed again.

A booted foot exploded into his other side; a kick to his head, to his ribs again, his testicles, his throbbing shoulder.

He stopped thinking. He hadn't even started to fight back, but his job had taught him to deal with pain by blocking out communication from his sensory nerves.

He felt the blows as if detached from his own body. Some instinct, not cowardice, told him that the less he moved, the sooner it would be over.

He lost count of the kicks and any sense of time. When it was over, he couldn't have said if it had taken one minute or ten. But a period of blissful calm followed the final blow. He could hear the wind swishing through the tops of the conifers and budding broadleafs. Even the blood that seeped from his battered gums tasted sweet.

His reverie was broken by the harsh Brummy accent of the man who had been waiting for him.

'D'you understand now? Leave things alone and stop asking questions and we won't need to do this again.'

Rory understood. He didn't think it worth saying.

A boot caught him once more on his bruised ribs.

'Answer me! I want to hear you say you understand.'

Rory groaned. 'I understand.'

'Right, and if you go to the police, next time we won't be so gentle.'

The man underlined his point with a last kick to Rory's torn and bleeding ear.

Through pulsing pain, he heard the feet that had ravaged him crunch across the car park, the slamming of two car doors, motors starting, wheels spinning then finding a grip on the metalled road, engine sounds muffled by the dank woodland and fading to nothing until the only sounds were the wind in the trees and the pattering of raindrops in the puddles.

The drizzle which had been falling most of the day had turned gradually to serious rain. The trees provided some shelter, but Rory became aware that his clothes were sodden through and beginning to chill him.

Throbbing with pain in almost every part of his body, he began to raise himself from the ground, still half expecting to be kicked back down again. On his feet, he staggered to the side of the clearing where there was more shelter. He leaned against a tree and fumbled in his wet leather jacket for tobacco and papers. They were dry enough, but with his damp hands he could only produce a soggy sliver of a cigarette. He sucked at it gratefully, though, gathering the strength and will to walk out of these woods, back to civilisation.

The nurses who had bandaged him up a few hours earlier had been replaced by others, just as gentle and clucking with sympathy.

What terrible bad luck to have a nasty fall, and then be mugged like that – all on the same day!

The nurse at reception said she'd thought there was something funny going on when another taxi had turned up to fetch him. She could certainly give the police a description of the man who had driven him away.

Rory didn't take much persuading that he had to stay in hospital for the night. He phoned Pam and told her he wouldn't be back that night, or riding tomorrow. She sounded indifferent to the news, and said that she was going out and Tommy was staying with a friend in the village.

Laura, when Rory rang her, showed her sympathy by offering to drive up and collect him next morning. She understood what he had meant by 'mugged'. He was grateful, more than he could express over the phone, but told her not to be absurd. She had horses to run, and he could get a taxi.

Laura chose to be absurd.

Rory saw her through a mist of gratitude as she walked

into the small room the hospital had allocated to him for the night.

She watched while he ate some breakfast; left while he dressed, then carried his bag down to her two-door Mercedes.

Rory shivered as they passed the turning up to the woods where he had lain the evening before. He had walked the half-mile down to the turning, and another half-mile along the Stafford–Uttoxeter road before anyone had dared to stop for a battered, wet and bedraggled tramp. A busload of grimy New Age travellers, mistaking him for one of their own, had finally pulled up and driven him back to the hospital.

'That's where it happened,' he said to Laura, nodding towards the turning.

They hadn't spoken about it yet, wanting to get away from it first.

'Do you know who they were?' she asked.

'No. Local contractors, I should think.'

'Are you going to tell the police?'

'I have already, but they'll never find them. They were up from Birmingham and the car was probably stolen.'

'But if they did find them, that would lead straight to whoever's behind Henry.'

'Not a chance. These things are all done at arm's length. Anyway, like I say, they'll never find them.'

'Are you going to go on looking?' Laura asked nervously.

'Of course I am, now I know I'm getting somewhere.'

'I've arranged for Dad to meet us at your house. He phoned last night looking for you. I told him roughly

what had happened. He thinks he's found something.'
    'Good; I need all the help I can get.'

Chapter Ten

They saw the police car outside Camp Farm as soon as Laura turned the Mercedes into the valley.

Rory groaned. 'What the hell do they want? I guess the hospital must have told them you were driving me home.'

'It may not be you they want to see,' Laura said.

She drove on to the forecourt in front of Rory's house. She sprang out; Rory limped. Taffy came bounding out of the house with his tail waving followed by a policeman in uniform and a second in anorak and jeans. They weren't smiling.

The detective spoke first. "Morning, Mr Gillespie. We tried to contact you at the hospital in Uttoxeter but you'd already left.' He turned to Laura. 'And you're Mrs Laura Mundy, I take it.' His manner showed that he was well aware of who she was and her own current relationship with his colleagues in Surrey and Hampshire.

Laura nodded.

'Why did you want me?' Rory asked.

'I'm afraid your house was broken into last night.'

'Good God! But my wife was here.'

'She wasn't, sir,' the policeman stated baldly. 'She returned to the house this morning and found the back door forced and the place turned over.'

'What about the alarm?'

'Apparently it slipped her mind to set it when she went out.'

Rory shook his head. 'Okay. I'd better have a look.'

'If you don't mind my saying so, are you all right, sir?' The policeman looked at the bandages across Rory's ears and the bruises on his face. 'We heard you had a fall yesterday but I didn't know it was so bad.'

'I was mugged after leaving the hospital,' Rory said. 'The local police have got all the details, but there's no real harm done. I didn't have any cash on me.' He walked towards the house disguising his injuries as best he could.

Inside, starting with the kitchen, he found that every drawer in the house had been pulled out and tipped up.

The detective followed him around, making sure he didn't touch anything until the forensic people had been. 'They seem to have left most of the usual things, videos and such like,' he said. 'I'd say they were looking for something particular. Have you any idea what that might have been?'

'Cash, probably,' Rory said quickly. 'I sold a mare for cash the day before yesterday and hadn't had a chance to bank it yet.'

'Was it in a safe, sir?'

'No. I don't have a safe. I don't usually have a lot of cash about the place, not in my business.'

The detective gave a cynical, disbelieving grin. 'Is that so, sir?'

'Yes, it bloody well is so. All my earnings are handled by Weatherby's who pay it straight into my account. But the fellow I sold the horse to was a shady sort of individual.' Rory shrugged. 'Maybe he decided to come and get his money back.'

'We'll check him out if you let us have his name and address.'

'I haven't got a clue. He was a traveller of some sort.'

'Buying horses from you?'

'It wasn't a blood horse – just a nice old coloured pony we had for my son.'

They were in a small room that Rory used as a study. Pam came in as they talked. It was the first Rory had seen of her since he and Laura had arrived at the house. She had evidently been listening outside; she looked as though she was on the point of asking Rory what he was talking about. He managed to stop her with a look which didn't escape the detective. But then, the detective assumed, a jockey would have plenty of dealings in cash; as long as it hadn't been obtained by theft or fraud, it wasn't his affair until the Inland Revenue asked him to bring the jockey in.

'Where was the money, sir?'

'In an envelope. In this drawer.'

Rory pointed at one of the top drawers of the small desk. There was no sign of an envelope among its contents.

'Maybe it's still under the other stuff. We can have a better look after the fellows have dusted it. Now can you tell me if any ornaments or trophies or such like are missing?'

They walked around the house again. All the bronze

statuettes, equine figures and lead crystal bowls that Rory had collected as his share of the big prizes over the years were where they always stood, with their normal coating of dust undisturbed.

When he had assessed as much as he could without touching anything, the policeman took a brief statement from Rory; he had already taken one from Pam. 'That'll do for now. We'll leave you in peace, but don't touch anything until the forensic boys have been.'

'Can't we make a cup of coffee or something?' Pam asked.

'Oh yes. That'll be okay. They should be here soon anyway.'

The police car drove off down the valley, leaving Rory, Pam and Laura standing awkwardly in the kitchen.

'I don't know about you, but I need a bloody drink,' Pam said, reaching a bottle of vodka down from a shelf.

'Me too,' Laura said.

Rory helped himself to a whisky, and the three of them sat down around the table.

'D'you know what the hell's going on?' Pam asked.

Rory nodded. 'I think so.'

'It's to do with her, isn't it?' Pam said, nodding angrily at Laura.

'It's to do with Luke's death,' Rory corrected her.

'Same thing.'

'Pam,' Laura said, and Rory wondered if it was the first time she had spoken to Pam since she had thrown his earrings at her in her father's yard, twelve years before, 'I'm not getting involved in a slanging match with you. Rory's been helping me because he chose to. And it's

248

because he's getting somewhere that he's in trouble.'

'Why? What's he found out?'

'I can't tell you, Pam,' Rory said. 'It wouldn't be fair on you.'

'Don't be so bloody pompous! You can't keep secrets from me. I'm your wife, for God's sake!'

'Talking of secrets,' Rory said, 'are you going to tell me where you were last night?'

Pam made a face and took another swig of vodka. 'I went over to Sheila's when you said you weren't coming home. There wasn't any point hanging around here – Tommy was staying with the Jones's. We had a few drinks, I admit it, and I reckoned I was too pissed to drive home. So I stayed at her house. I wasn't planning to, that's why I never turned on the alarm,' she added as an after-thought. She looked at Rory, then Laura, challenging them to question her version.

Rory didn't believe her, but he let it go.

'It doesn't matter. They didn't find anything to interest them.'

'Why did you give the police all that bullshit about cash from selling a horse, then?'

'I don't know why the hell we were raided last night, but I'm bloody sure it had something to do with whoever doped Midnight Express.'

'And what's all this about you being mugged?'

Before Rory could answer, they were interrupted by the sound of another car pulling into the forecourt.

'This must be the fingerprint blokes,' Pam said. 'They'll find bugger all. People who do this kind of thing don't leave their dabs all over the place.'

'Good morning.' Edward Brickhill walked through the
open back door. 'I see someone didn't wait to be invited
in,' he added, seeing the jemmy marks on the door frame.

''Morning, Dad,' Laura said, rising to greet him. 'Do
you know Rory's wife, Pam?'

'Yes, of course I know Pam. I had horses with her
father for about twenty years. Hello, Pam.'

Rory had also got to his feet. 'Let's go in the other
room, Edward.'

'Don't bother,' Pam said. 'I suppose I'll have to go and
pick up Tommy. You can have your little secret meeting
without me.'

'I don't mind getting him,' Laura said quickly. 'He can
spend the afternoon at the races with me. Perhaps he'd
like to come back in the lorry.'

Rory looked at her gratefully. 'If he's not in the way,
he'd enjoy that; I've got a lot to do before we go to
Wales.' He turned to his wife. 'Pam, if you haven't already
done them, can you deal with the horses. I'm just not
going to have time.'

'And I have, I suppose? I'll go and get Sally to do them.'

She drained her glass, got up and walked sulkily from
the room. No one spoke until they heard her car starting up.

'I take it you haven't told your wife what you've been
doing?' Edward Brickhill said.

'You take it right,' Rory said. 'Laura says you've got
something about Luke's gambling.'

'Yes. I think I have. One of my people made the rounds
yesterday of every bookie who deals in City prices.'

Rory waved him to a chair and they all sat down.
'Drink?' he asked.

'No thanks. Anyway, one of the settling clerks in a firm called Square Mile Sporting said that they'd lost a fairly large amount on the Thames Land price, up till about two months before Luke died. I guess by then he thought things might get less predictable and backed off. Of course, we don't know that it was definitely Luke, but knowing that he was gambling on his price with someone, I think we can assume it was. Then it seems that the same individual, having been paid out somewhere in the region of three hundred thousand, began to back horses, right up until the time Luke was killed, at which point he was about a hundred and fifty thousand down.'

Rory felt himself shiver with excitement. 'What about Midnight Express? Did he have a bet on him?'

Brickhill shook his head. 'There's no record of it, I'm afraid. But he could have had it on with any other book-maker – possibly several; that'll be a lot harder to track down, but I've got someone working on it.'

'But if he was chasing a hundred and fifty grand,' Rory said, 'he'd have had fifty on it. Even if it was spread about, that should show up easily enough. Though I'd have thought he'd have put it on with the firm he owed it to.'

'Not necessarily. After all, he knew they couldn't sue him for the money he already owed them.'

'That's where you're wrong: bets with index makers are fully recoverable, and he'd have hated being warned off.'

'Yes,' Laura agreed. 'He'd have hated that. He would definitely have wanted to settle his account somehow. And now we know what his position was when he died,' she said with a sour grin, 'pulling off a big gamble was the only way. And I've told Rory how desperate he was to win that day.'

'I agree with Laura,' Rory said. 'He'd have had his bet with the same firm, this Square Mile set-up. Maybe he had a private arrangement with the owner of the firm. Do you know who that is?'

'I'd already thought of that, but I'm afraid so far I've drawn a blank. The chief executive of the firm which holds the licence isn't the owner. He's a bright young man who went there from another bookmaking firm about a year ago. But Square Mile Sporting is a private company owned by an investment trust based in Panama. The registered trustees are a pair of Panamanian lawyers.' Brickhill shrugged. 'It's almost impossible to get through that kind of smokescreen, though I wouldn't be surprised if it ultimately belonged to an English operator. It must be set up like that primarily as a cover, because there aren't any real tax advantages.'

'For Christ's sake!' Rory burst out in frustration. 'I'm bloody sure that's all we need to know, and we've found our man.'

Brickhill lifted a shoulder philosophically. 'You may be right, but I'm afraid even if he is we're going to have to find him some other way. And how on earth are we going to prove anything? If it had been an ordinary bookmaker, maybe we'd have had a chance, but this seems just too much of a professional operation.'

Their discussion was interrupted by a series of telephone callers checking on the state of Rory's health, since he had cancelled all his rides that day and the story of his 'mugging' was in some late editions of the papers. He promised all of them that he'd be riding again by the following Tuesday. Laura looked doubtful as she listened, but didn't question it when he finally put the phone down.

Any more discussion was prevented by the arrival of a scene-of-crime officer. Laura went to pick up Tommy on her way back to Langlands. She had left Patrick and her assistant in charge of sending six horses to Sandown that day, but she was anxious to get there to see them run.

The policeman took an hour to find nothing. Rory and Edward Brickhill walked up to the barns, going over and over the possibilities. When they returned to the forecourt in front of the house, Pam had reappeared with Sally, their part-time groom.

'I hope Laura doesn't get back too late with Tommy. He's really excited about your fishing trip and as you're not riding today, I told him you'd be able to set off nice and early.'

Rory groaned to himself, but wouldn't let his wife see his frustration. 'I can't go till this evening anyway. I may not be riding, but I've got a lot of other things to do. We'll leave about seven which means we'll be in Builth by nine thirty, ready to start early on the river tomorrow. Can you pack him a bag for the night?'

'I suppose so. It'll be great for him to have a day out with his dad for a change. A father should spend time with his son, don't you think, Mr Brickhill?'

'Yes, of course. Tommy's a lucky boy.' He opened his car door. 'Rory, we'll talk again later. Try to ring me before you leave for Wales.'

Eland's answer-phone was flashing at him when he arrived back at his house that morning.

He played the tape, not paying much attention to the messages until he heard the deep drawl which he had been waiting for.

'I've got some instructions for you. I'll ring again at twelve. Make sure you're there.'

It was only eleven. Eland didn't even consider ringing back. He'd sweat it out for an hour. When the call came, he would tell him he wasn't doing any more; it was getting too hot.

He sat down and absently picked at the inflamed scab on his hand. It seemed to have got worse in the last few days. His skin was always inclined to erupt when he was under pressure. He mopped his forehead with a grimy handkerchief and, with a shaking hand, poured himself a large tot of rum from a bottle on the coffee table in front of him.

He wished for the hundredth time that he had restricted himself to taking the photographs; that was what he was good at, not all this skulduggery. He could never forget what it was like in prison, and he knew that made him nervous and inept.

He'd had enough. Whatever the man said, he was going to knock this scam on the head; wipe out the elements that could link it all to him.

He'd sent the last batch of pictures yesterday, as he'd been told. They were good shots, as good as he'd ever done, but he was dealing with an unusual sort of victim, and he now had serious doubts that they would be as effective as they should have been.

Besides, he had a horrible suspicion that some of the first ones had gone astray. Even if there was the slightest chance that they had, he had to find them. He'd thought he was going to find them last night; he'd found nothing, but the warning had been delivered. They'd rung him to tell him, and the morning papers had confirmed it.

He let the telephone – two feet in front of him – ring five or six times before he picked it up.

'Hello?' He couldn't disguise the shake in his voice.

'Fancyman. Tuesday.'

'I . . . I don't think he'll do it.'

'Did you send the last photographs?'

'Yes, like you said, yesterday.'

'Then he'll do it. They were brilliant shots.'

'I don't know . . .'

'Listen, just do it. Understand?'

Eland sighed. 'Okay.'

·'There's another thing. Did you have anything to do with that mugging yesterday?'

'What are you talking about?' Eland tried his hardest to feign ignorance.

'You know what I'm talking about.'

'Oh, that. No, 'course not. Why should I have anything to do with that?'

'It doesn't matter. I'll know soon enough. God help you if I get the wrong answer.'

The line was abruptly cut.

Eland held the receiver in his clenched fist and tried to stop himself shaking.

How the hell had he let himself get into this mess?

He hadn't got any choice now. This job was finishing. Too bad about the money.

He prodded the plunger on the phone to get a clear line and jabbed a number.

His call was answered after a few rings.

'I need you tonight,' he said.

He listened for a moment. 'Okay, five hundred, and bring a fresh motor.'

He put the phone down, pleased with himself. At least he'd made a decision. And he'd kept a spare set of contact shots for himself, as insurance.

Rory followed Brickhill down the drive. He told Pam he was going to the physiotherapist, but not where he was going after that.

A good long session with an experienced physio eased the aches and pains from the fall and the beating he'd had. Before he left, he pulled the conspicuous dressings from his head and found that the bleeding had stopped. He still wasn't looking well, but a lot better than he had done earlier that morning.

Once in his car, he applied himself to the one sure lead he had – Henry Straker. Somehow, he had to persuade Straker to tell him what the hell was going on.

He checked round the courses and found that Henry wasn't on duty that day. He rang his house, and was greeted by an answering machine.

He rang the surgery. Mr Straker wasn't in. He had taken his football team to play in Reading. The receptionist didn't know exactly where.

Two o'clock on a Saturday afternoon wasn't a good time to be tracking down a boys' club soccer team. But after half a dozen calls, someone at the library in Reading was able to give Rory the home phone number of the secretary of the club.

The secretary's wife was in. Her husband had gone

with the team to the match on the public playing fields in Reading.

Rory drove to the M4 and pointed his car east.

There were several sets of public playing fields in Reading. By half past three, Rory had found a maroon Daimler in a pitted and puddled parking area off a rough, muddy track lined by overgrown hazel and hawthorn. He had been told that this track led to a dilapidated set of changing rooms which served the playing fields in a public park on the outskirts of the sprawling town.

When he was sure it was Straker's car, Rory backed out and left his car in a side road a hundred yards from the entrance to the track.

He made his way back on foot, down the dripping dark lane – a remnant of the countryside that had been there before the town had swallowed it up. He passed the patch that had been carved out of the hedgerow to accommodate the cars of visitors to the playing fields. Besides Straker's car, there were two minibuses and a couple of cheap old saloons.

A hundred yards further on, he reached the back of the changing rooms. As inconspicuously as he could, he stepped from behind the dilapidated weatherboard building. He found himself looking at a couple of bald soccer pitches. On one of them, two teams of small boys, supported by a dozen or so spectators, were slugging it out in the mud.

Straker was in the middle of the field, looking quite out of character in a navy tracksuit and trainers. Even from a distance, his efforts at refereeing looked half-hearted.

Rory stared at the tall, thin figure and wondered what the hell he was going to do.

He couldn't talk to Straker now – not in the middle of this game, not among the kids he did so much for.

He hadn't come looking for Straker with any firm plan, just the idea that it was only through the vet that he could make any headway. Despite Laura's certainty that Straker wasn't involved, and her father's serious doubts, Rory felt in his guts that what he had found in Straker's house was more than coincidence. But he knew that he couldn't begin to prove it and he had nothing to offer the police.

As he stood there, undecided, the sound of someone coming down the muddy lane impinged on his consciousness. He turned and looked up the track.

Instantly, he sank further back between the changing rooms and the bushes behind them. Picking his way through the puddles and ruts was someone clad entirely in black biking leathers, wearing a full-face helmet, in every respect identical to the person who had met with Straker the previous morning to give him the envelope. This time, though, there was no sign of the big BMW bike. Rory guessed it had been left out on the main road, or more likely, a nearby side road.

Certainly, the biker was moving cautiously, but evidently hadn't spotted Rory. Rory held his breath until the black-clad figure turned into the parking area.

When the biker was out of sight, Rory crossed the track and walked as fast and silently as he could up the same side as the car park.

Fifteen feet from the gap, he stopped and inserted himself into the hedge. Through the budding hawthorn, he could see the black figure crouching beside the Daimler.

Within seconds the biker had picked the lock and opened the door. Still crouching, he pulled something from a pocket and inserted an arm underneath the driver's seat.

The whole operation took no more than twenty seconds before the car door was quietly closed and locked again, and the biker set off quickly down the lane.

Rory had to make a snap decision.

Either he went straight after the biker and followed him, or her, until he found where he came from.

Or he waited to tell Straker that someone had been tampering with his car.

But he knew that by the time he reached his own car, the big bike would be well on its way and uncatchable.

And he didn't want Straker killed.

He waited until the leather-clad figure had turned out of the top of the track before he stepped from his cover in the hedge and ran round to Straker's car. Of course, he couldn't open it – he didn't possess the skill or the tools. He peered into it, at the driver's seat and in front of it, but he couldn't see anything unusual from outside.

He tried wildly to guess what might have been put there – a bomb of some sort, timed, maybe, or triggered by remote control. Whatever it was, he was certain it was intended to do away with the Jockey Club vet.

'Come on, ref,' a boy's voice shrilled hoarsely across the misty pitch. 'How much longer?'

The sound of the young goalie jerked Henry Straker back from the maelstrom of his thoughts. He looked at his watch.

They were a good seven minutes over time. Agitated, he stuck a whistle between his lips and blew it. He tried to remember the score; he'd scarcely noticed the game.

One of his forwards came to the rescue. 'Three-two. Bit close, but at least we won, eh, Mr Straker?'

'Yes, well done. Good game.'

'It's lucky you didn't do anything about Darren's foul.'

'Darren's foul? Oh Lord,' Straker muttered, hoping that the other side's coach hadn't spotted the incident, whatever it was.

Rory ran back down the muddy lane to the football pitch where the game had just come to an end. He carried on towards Henry Straker, who was walking back towards the changing rooms with a group of his boys.

When he saw Rory coming towards him, Straker's step faltered a moment and a look of worried irritation flashed across his face. Rory was close enough by then to see the look, and its quick replacement by a bland, friendly smile.

'Good heavens, Rory, what are you doing here? If you came along to support the team, you'll be glad to hear they managed without your help,' he said, louder than was necessary. 'We won three-two.'

For Straker's sake, Rory went along with the charade.

'A good scoring game, pity I missed it. Took me a while to find the ground. Anyway, now I'm here, I wanted a quick word with you, if that's okay?'

Straker couldn't refuse him without sounding very churlish.

'Well, it'll have to be quick. I've got to get these boys changed and fed. Just let me get my coat from the changing room.'

He disappeared into the old shingle-built pavilion and came out a moment later with a waxed jacket over his tracksuit.

He gave his opposite number an apologetic smile and walked across to Rory, who had moved to a place where they could talk without being overheard.

'For God's sake,' Straker said. 'What do you mean by following me here? I hope it's got nothing to do with your ridiculous allegations yesterday.'

'It might have. I've just been watching someone tampering with your car.' He paused. 'Someone dressed in black bike leathers. They still had their helmet on so I couldn't get a look at their face.'

He saw Straker stiffen. 'What are you saying?'

'You heard. Someone's just planted something in your car – to do you damage. I think you ought to call the police.'

'You must be mistaken. Maybe they were just trying to steal it and couldn't get it started.'

'No, they weren't. Look, are you going to call the police or not?'

'I'm not going to waste their time. Presumably he's gone?'

'Yes, if it was a he. Must have left the bike back on the road. But look, you should have it checked out by a pro. I mean, if it's a bomb or something, you may trigger it.'

'I don't know how you've conceived the idea that anyone should want to kill me. Unless it's the other side's coach.' Straker forced a laugh.

'Look, if you're not going to do anything about it, *I'll* call the police.'

Straker shook his head irritably. 'For God's sake, I'll come and have a look then, but I'm sure you're wrong.'

He called over to one of the men in the party, evidently another supporter of his boys' club. 'Just got to fetch something from my car. I'll be back in a mo.'

He followed Rory silently up the dark track. He pulled out his key to open the door, then hesitated. 'You don't think this device is triggered to the lock?'

'No. He didn't do anything to connect it. He was here barely fifteen seconds. Just put something under your seat.'

Straker unlocked the door and opened it with relief. But he sighed as if it were all a futile waste of time. He leaned down and looked under the seat.

'Can you see anything?' Rory asked. 'If you can, don't touch it.'

Straker straightened his back. 'There's nothing there.'

'Let me have a look.' Rory almost pushed Straker aside and knelt down in the mud next to the car. After a moment of peering into the dark beneath the thick seat, he asked, 'Have you got a torch?'

'Yes, there's one in the glove compartment.'

Taking care not to put any weight on the leather upholstery, Rory leaned across to open the locker in front of the passenger seat. He took out a torch and crouched again to shine it under the driver's seat.

'There is something here,' he announced after a moment. 'It looks like a syringe.'

He lifted his head and placed both hands slightly apart on the soft, well-padded leather of the seat. Gently, he applied some pressure. Between his hands, the almost invisible sharp point of a hypodermic needle protruded up through the leather. He pushed a little harder and liquid spouted from the invisible aperture in the tiny needle's head.

He released the pressure, and the needle retracted from sight. He turned to Straker.

The vet, white-faced, was gaping at the seat. 'Christ! Why the hell should anyone want to do that?'

Rory nodded. 'I'd say that whatever was in that syringe wasn't going to do your health a lot of good. It's the latest joyriders' trick, after they've pinched a car and driven the hell out of it. But I don't think they usually bother to put anything into the syringe.'

He stretched his hand under the seat once more and extracted the weapon. He straightened his back. 'Are you still so sure you don't want to call the police?' he asked.

Straker took the syringe and gazed at it. 'There doesn't seem much point now, really, does there?' he said. 'If a kid's done it for some malicious kind of a lark, how the hell are the police going to find him?'

'But it wasn't a kid; it was an adult, someone who came on a bike, I'd say, not looking for a joy-ride. Come on, Henry, I think it's time you told me what's going on.'

For a moment, Straker looked as though he was going to give in and start talking. Rory held his breath.

But the vet suddenly pulled himself together.

'Listen, Rory, I told you yesterday, I don't know what you're referring to. How do I know you didn't just put the syringe there? I mean, it's very convenient you were just passing when it happened. Why should I believe all this cock-and-bull story about a chap on a motorbike? I don't know what your game is, but kindly stop pestering me.'

The tall man slammed shut the door of his car, stuffed the syringe into a pocket of his Barbour and strode off angrily across the mud and puddles towards the playing fields.

Rory stared after him, shaking his head in frustration. So much for Straker opening up. There was nothing he could do as long as Straker refused to admit what he knew. And he couldn't force him to come clean here. Rory turned and walked back up the track, trying to figure out what to do next. He had to do something.

By the time he'd reached his car, he'd made up his mind to go and see Laura. He didn't ring her. She'd just about be back from Sandown by the time he got to Langlands.

Henry Straker had done his best to oversee the return of his boys to their clubhouse on the other side of town. He tried gracefully to accept their thanks for his indefatigable coaching and support, as well as the tea he'd bought for them all on the way back. It was a fine performance and betrayed nothing of the turmoil in his head.

But when he reached home, the performance had to continue. Susan had just made tea, and produced toast and cake to go with it.

'Come on, Henry, sit down for a minute and relax,' she said considerately.

Disguising his reluctance, he joined her at the kitchen table.

'There are a few letters for you, by the way. The post came after you left this morning,' she went on, to keep the conversation going. She picked up a pile of mail from the dresser behind her and passed it across the table to her husband. He was glad of the excuse not to talk, and began mechanically to open the various envelopes. There were a few bills and confirmations of appointments. On the bottom of the pile was a stiff A4-size envelope. He hesitated a second, then quickly tore open the top. A small piece of paper fell out first. On it were typed the words 'INSTRUCTIONS TO FOLLOW'. He picked it up quickly and glanced across to see if his wife had noticed. But she was busy filling the teapot with more water.

'I'm just going to take this lot into the study,' Straker said with a quaver in his voice.

He stood up and walked across the hall. In his study he sat down at his desk and with trembling fingers began to extract the photograph from the envelope.

Before the black-and-white print was halfway out, a rush of nausea swept through him. Loathing even to touch the repellent photograph, he extracted it, absorbed the full, obscene horror of it and slammed it face down on the desk.

The previous two shots he had received, one through the post, like this, and one delivered by the biker, had been disgustingly graphic – enough to make him turn over every principle he had ever held. But this latest version was much worse.

He didn't know how they had done it, but to prove to anyone else seeing it that he hadn't been a willing partici-pant just didn't seem possible.

With a sob, he buried his face in his hands and let his shoulders heave.

'Are you all right, dear?' Susan's voice was full of concern.

Henry stiffened. Fortunately, he had his back to her. He sniffed loudly. 'Nothing to worry about, just a bit of a cough coming on; running round a wet football pitch all afternoon, I expect.' It took a supreme effort to turn and face her with a rueful smile. 'I'll just put this lot away and come and finish that delicious cake.'

He turned back to the desk, certain that if Susan ever saw the photograph that lay there, she would never be able to spend a minute in the same room with him again, and that the grief it would cause would kill her.

He quickly dropped the envelope and photograph into a drawer of his desk and locked it. He would burn it, like the others, after tea.

Sitting at the kitchen table once more, he said, 'It's going to be a nasty, blustery old sort of night. I think I'll light a fire for you in the drawing room.'

'Oh, yes, Henry. That would be very cosy.'

Laura hadn't arrived back when Rory reached Langlands. But the Filipino cook let him into the small front drawing room and offered to bring him tea.

When she had left the room, he paced around, unable to sit, unable even to think clearly about what he should do next. Someone had tried to kill Henry Straker that day, he was certain of it. Someone who thought that the vet might very soon start talking and provide a link to whoever was pulling the strings.

But Rory couldn't get away from the one major flaw in his supposition – why someone of Henry Straker's unimpeachable good character should be involved in doping horses, especially when that had already led to one man's death and seemed likely to lead to his own. What was he set to gain?

His heart leapt when he heard a car draw up outside. He looked out and saw Laura, on her own, get out of her Mercedes. He walked into the hall to greet her.

She had already seen his car outside. She let herself in through the huge front door, pushed it to with her back and leaned against the ancient oak panels.

'Hi.' She gave him a wan, defeated smile.

'What's happened?' he asked.

'Nothing in particular. I'm just exhausted.'

'And how's Tommy?'

'I think he really enjoyed himself. He's a smashing boy.' Laura smiled. 'I drove him there, and Terry and Declan looked after him. He was adamant about being driven back in the lorry. He shouldn't be too long.'

'But something's bothering you,' he said.

'It's just the strain of it all. What if I go to prison?'

'I'll make sure you don't. You'll get off; I promise you we're going to find who did it.'

She shook her head, not taken in by Rory's false confidence.

'I know you're doing your best; you've been wonderful, but if the police haven't got any further, how the hell are you going to?'

'Come on. Don't be so defeatist,' he rallied. 'I want to tell you where I've got to.'

'I need a drink first,' she said.

'Your maid's gone to get some tea.'

'I'll go and cancel it. Pour me a large vodka and something for yourself.'

Taking her coat off as she went, she disappeared into the maze of corridors that led to the kitchens.

Rory went back into the warm comfort of the small drawing room and poured drinks for them both. Laura came in and closed the door behind her.

'I've told them we're not to be disturbed,' she said. She carried on walking towards Rory. When she reached him, she put her arms around his neck and her lips on his. Their tongues met and hungrily twined around each other, and she hugged him against her warm, tense body.

Rory couldn't remember a kiss so deep or so full of passion. Her flesh became softer as he absorbed her anxiety. When at last their lips reluctantly parted, he still held her in his arms and looked into her chocolate-brown eyes.

'Oh, God!' she whispered. 'I've been wanting to do that for such a long time.'

Rory grinned; he couldn't help himself. Until then, he hadn't been certain.

'Laura,' he breathed, 'you're so wound up.'

'Not now,' she said. 'Not with you. You're strong enough to take it.'

She turned in his arms and he let her go. She picked up her drink and sat on a small sofa. 'Come and sit next to me.'

Rory put himself beside her. For a while they didn't talk as he stroked her long black hair.

'I'm sorry if I seem so ungrateful,' she said after a

while, 'so negative about what you've been doing for me. It's just that I don't want to get my hopes up, and then get nowhere. Anyway, Agnew thinks they might have some trouble proving beyond doubt that I did it.'

'But that's not good enough,' Rory said indignantly. 'You didn't do it and we've got to prove that you didn't. Else the thing'll hang over you for the rest of your life.'

'Well, maybe I deserve it. I mean, I used Luke, didn't I? To get my own back on you, and to satisfy my own ambitions. Do you know, under all that bullying bullshit, I think he was a very insecure man. That's why he was so obsessed with making money and spending it. He used it as a kind of shield from the rest of the world. He would have had absolutely no idea how to cope without money. He'd have hated it, probably rather have died as he did.'

Rory considered this. 'No,' he said after a moment. 'He was a megalomaniac bastard, and don't you forget it. He probably still thought he'd crawl out of the shit and come up smelling of roses.'

'You may be right. I don't know. Anyway, I don't really want to talk about him.' Laura sighed and put an arm up to draw Rory's mouth to hers.

They talked and kissed and caressed, but no more than that. They both knew, without saying it, that that would have to come later. There was no hurry, and when it did come, it would be something much more special than the last time.

They talked a little about what Rory had discovered so far, but Laura was pessimistic. She didn't really believe that he would find out any more than he already had, and she wouldn't be convinced that Henry Straker was involved, or had had an attempt made on his life that afternoon, or that there was any Mr Big lurking behind the whole affair, pulling strings.

Rory didn't press her. He didn't want to spoil the moment. He was enjoying her complete trust and relaxation for once, sure that she wasn't holding anything back from him now.

He had been there with her for an hour when the maid came in to tell them that Tommy was now back at the yard.

Rory got slowly to his feet. 'I'm sorry, I'd better go. I promised we'd set off on our fishing trip tonight.'

'I understand,' Laura said softly. 'I'm just so glad you were able to stay as long as you have. I feel a hell of a lot better than I did.'

Rory knew that she didn't want to let him go, and it took all his paternal instincts to get him out of the house and into his car. Even then, he was reluctant to start the motor. Later, driving home with his son, he felt like a teenage boy who had just discovered love.

They arrived home to a barrage of complaints from Pam, who had been waiting for them.

'What the hell have you been doing?' she asked. 'I was due at Barry Short's drinks party an hour ago.'

'Have you packed all Tommy's stuff?'

'Yes, of course I have. There it is.' She nodded at a pink and yellow nylon bag on the floor.

'Okay,' Rory said, with as much good humour as he could muster. 'Let's go, boy.'

Through the drawing room window, Pam watched the

lights of the Rover bounce down the valley and dialled a number on the mobile phone.

'Hello, they've gone at last. You can come over now,' she giggled, absently pushing up one of her large breasts. There was a brief pause as she listened to a question from the other end. Then, 'No,' she answered, 'not till tomorrow night.'

Tommy, excited to be going at last on the long-promised trip, talked happily for the first half-hour of their journey. Rory let him rattle on, without answering more than he had to.

Gradually, the gaps between Tommy's questions became longer, until, as they crossed the Severn Bridge, they ceased altogether. Rory glanced down at his son, he was fast asleep now. Maybe in the morning, when they got out by the river, he'd be able to push the whole business of Luke Mundy's death and Laura's trouble to the back of his mind and they could concentrate on catching a few salmon.

They carried on quickly up the empty valleys of the Wye and Usk. At Brecon, Rory telephoned the hotel to tell them they would be arriving shortly. Tommy woke from his doze.

'We'll be there soon,' Rory said. 'I bet you'll be glad to get to bed.'

Tommy nodded sleepily.

'Have you had your injection yet?' Rory asked, feeling certain that he must have done.

Struggling to get the words out, Tommy didn't answer for a moment. 'No,' he replied slowly, 'I think Mum forgot to pack it.' Tears began to well in his eyes.

'Oh God!' Rory couldn't hide his exasperation. 'Are you sure?'

'I think so. She asked me to get it out and put it on my chest of drawers, but I don't think she ever went back to get it.'

'The useless . . .' Rory cut himself short. 'Okay let's check before we panic.'

He stopped the car at the side of the quiet road, got out and went round to the boot. He pulled Tommy's bag out and brought it back into the car. There he carefully took everything out, until it was empty. There was no sign of the small bottle of insulin and the syringe with which Tommy fought off the effects of his diabetes.

'We'll have to go back,' he said simply.

'Oh *no*. Dad, do we have to? Can't we get some here?'

'I'm not risking it at this time of night. Look, we'll go back home and get it, then turn right round and drive back, okay? I'm not going to let you miss anything. You'll sleep anyway, won't you?'

'Yeah,' Tommy looked at his father. 'Sorry, Dad.'

Chapter Eleven

A dark red Vauxhall Cavalier, stolen that afternoon from Ealing Broadway Station car park, drove down the valley from Camp Farm. A hundred yards from the main road, the lane became wide enough for two cars to pass.

The driver of the Cavalier saw a pair of headlights turn off the Hungerford road into the lane.

'Who the fuck's this?' Eland said to the man beside him.

'There's another farm up there, ain't there – must be one of them. Relax.' Like Eland, he spoke with the staccato delivery of inner London, which disguised the nervousness they both felt. 'For fuck's sake, this is meant to be your scam! If you don't do nuffin' stupid now, we won't have no trouble. Just take it easy back up to London and we'll dump the motor in Hammersmith. There's no one to tell the filth nothing.'

Eland wasn't so sure, but he hadn't a better plan. The other car was creeping up the lane towards them. He slowed and pulled over until his nearside wheels were on the narrow grass verge. Instinctively, he turned his head away from the oncoming lights until they passed.

'Shit!' his companion hissed. 'Rory Gillespie!'

Eland turned to him, eyes wide, more than nervous now. 'What the fuck are you talking about? How do you know it was him?'

'Didn't you see? His name was plastered all over the side of the car.'

'But was it him driving?'

'Yeah, it was him all right.'

'Then who the fuck was that other geezer?'

'I don't fuckin' know, do I? This is your bloody job, remember? And we never found nuffin'! A right fuckin' bollocks-up!'

'What the hell are we going to do? He'll start yellin' for the filth, and he's seen this car.' Eland's voice had risen in pitch. What had started out as a simple piece of evidence retrieval, well within his scope, had turned into something way out of his depth.

'Stop fuckin' screaming, you berk. We'll have to go back up there and deal with him.'

'No! That's crazy. We'll be walking straight back into it. Let's find a phone, call the nick and tell them we've heard something up there – a few bangs. If they get up there before 'e calls them, they'll think 'e's done it.'

'Are you mad? Do you think we've got time to go driving round looking for a phone box? Come on. Turn this motor round and get back up there. And don't piss about.'

Eland felt his bowels trying to empty themselves.

Everything had gone wrong. Straker had told him Gillespie had some of the photographs, but they'd found nothing, except that the house wasn't empty when it should have been.

Now he'd dug himself into a pit of shit he was never going to get out of. Straker and the jockey were both still alive.

If he went down, he vowed, he wasn't going down alone.

Rory parked beside Pam's Discovery. Leaving Tommy asleep on the passenger seat, he got out quietly and walked towards the back door.

He glanced down the valley. The car he had passed at the bottom had turned round and was coming back up. A flush of fear prickled his skin. It was half past midnight, and he hadn't recognised the car.

He quickened his pace until he reached the door, found it unlocked and let himself in.

'Pam! Pam!' he yelled. There was no answer from Pam, nor any sign of Taffy. He switched on the lights.

The kitchen was a shambles. Every cupboard door had been opened and every jar, tin, packet and bottle swept out on to the floor. He went on through to his study; the mess he had left it in that morning had been added to by every book having been pulled from the shelves, opened and flung in a heap on the floor. His desk had been dismantled, the carpets torn up and pictures taken from their frames.

What the hell were they looking for?

Somebody knew he was on to Straker. He knew that –

it had already earned him the beating in the Staffordshire woods. But they must have thought he knew a lot more than he did – and that somewhere he had the evidence to back it up.

He wished to God he had.

Now they were coming back.

And Tommy was still in the car!

Rory ran out, dimly conscious that Pam should have been around. Her car was here. Maybe someone had picked her up to take her to the party – Dai Price, probably.

The Vauxhall was rattling over the cattle grid across his gateway. He ran to his own car, opened Tommy's door and lifted him out. Tommy groaned and wriggled in his half-sleep. Rory heaved him over his shoulder and began to run towards the house.

But the car had almost reached the forecourt. Changing direction, he headed up towards the barns.

He staggered on under his son's weight. Now the boy was stirring. 'Dad! What are we doing?'

Rory set him down on his feet.

'Sshh!' he hissed. 'Can you run?'

'Why? What's happening?'

'Look, see that car? The men in it want something from me and they're after us. We'll have to go up and hide in the barns until they've gone.'

The idea appealed to Tommy. 'Great! We could hide next to Long Run,' he panted as he trotted along beside Rory.

'That's a bloody good idea.'

They passed the footings of Rory's new barns and carried on to the timber-clad stable yard which they were to replace. Once they'd reached the small three-sided complex they turned to look down the valley. The lights from the house glowed cosily in the black night. There were no sounds of pursuit.

The stallion was housed in a stable which also gave access to a further one beyond, in the corner of the block. More often than not, like now, it was unoccupied.

'Go and get a couple of carrots from the feed shed, and an armful of hay,' Rory told Tommy as he walked quietly to the stallion's stable door.

Long Run stirred and came to put his big handsome head over the door.

'Hello, boy.' Rory put out a hand to stroke the horse's nose. Long Run sniffed and blew in recognition, and expectation. Tommy arrived with the carrots and held one up to the big horse, who sniffed and recognised again and gratefully sucked up the offering.

All the time, Rory kept his eye on the farmhouse below them, where more lights had been turned on as the men searched through the house for him.

He caught a flash of a torch as one of them hunted round the garages and outhouses that clustered at the back.

The wind had dropped to a few occasional gusts, but the quiet up at the yard was shattered by a bang as a squall caught the food-store door which Tommy had left open.

The torch beam swung up the valley, too short to illuminate them, but the faint sound of shouting reached them and the flashlight began to jerk up towards them.

Rory quickly opened the stable door. He and Tommy

slipped in. With a gentle shove from Rory, the stallion obligingly shifted to let them pass. They stuffed the hay into the empty manger and squeezed past the horse to the door of the adjoining stable. Closing the lower door, Rory took the second carrot from Tommy and gave it to Long Run who grasped it between his teeth and stepped back to eat it. Rory closed the upper door and whispered to Tommy, 'Get down and keep quiet.'

From a grille at the back of the box, Rory had a clear view down the valley. The torch was fifty yards from them now, and coming fast.

Tommy was on tiptoes beside him. 'Is that them, Dad?' he asked.

'Yes,' Rory said. 'Now for God's sake, get down and don't say a word, or do anything to upset Long Run.'

He and the boy nestled below the grille, where no torch beam could reach them.

Eventually, on the concrete of the stable yard, they heard steps approach, stop, come on and stop again at each stable.

They heard the mares stirring at the disturbance as the men shone their light into the boxes.

The footsteps stopped outside Long Run. Rory and Tommy could see the flash of the torch above the partition between the two boxes.

A voice reached them clearly. 'Look, there's a door in there, must lead into the corner. Let's take a look.'

'That 'orse looks dangerous.'

'Don't be daft.'

'No, look at him.'

They heard Long Run cross to the stable door, snorting. The men backed off.

'All right,' the first said. 'Let's see if we can get in there round the back.'

A few moments later, the torch beam was shining over Rory and Tommy's heads.

'There's nuffin' in there.'

'I want to make sure.'

The footsteps sounded from the yard again, and stopped at the stable door.

'I'm going in.'

The stable door was unbolted and squeaked as it was opened an inch or two.

There was a shattering, splintering crash as the stallion's hooves lashed out at the inch-thick ply panels that lined his box, and the harsh scuff of his hooves on the ribbed concrete beneath the thick straw bed.

The stable door was slammed shut.

'Christ! It looks bloody wild! I'm not going in there. Gillespie could be anywhere in this fucking valley, for Christ's sake! We'll never find him. Let's get out of here.'

'All right then. We'll do what you said and hope it fuckin' works.'

Rory found he had been holding his breath for the half-minute they had been there. As their footsteps faded, he let it out in a long sigh of relief.

'Okay, Tommy,' he whispered. 'Don't move or make a sound until we've heard their car leaving.'

He felt beside him for the boy and found him trembling. The reality of the danger had evidently got through to him.

When they were certain the car was on its way down the drive, Rory opened the door to Long Run's box and

talked to him as they let themselves out. They could see
the car turning into the main road, and setting off fast
down towards Lambourn. Out of habit, Rory quickly
checked all the horses, closed up the feed store and led
Tommy back down the track to the house.

They had just reached the back door when they saw a
blue flashing light racing along the main road.

Rory waited to see where it was headed. He wasn't
surprised when it turned off and came up towards them.

He and Tommy went into the kitchen. He made Tommy
sit while he went up the back stairs from the kitchen to
the boy's little room and found the insulin and needle
on the chest of drawers.

Two policemen walked in as he came back down.

'Are you Rory Gillespie?' the first asked.

'Sure. How did you know what had happened up here?'

'We don't know what happened up here. We just got a
call that there was some kind of disturbance going on.
Someone reported gunshots.'

'What!' Rory said. 'I didn't hear any gunshots. I got
back and found the place like this, and it was only raided
last night. The two guys came back and chased after us.
We hid in one of the stables until they gave up and
drove off.'

'So there wasn't any shooting?'

'Not that I heard.'

'They've made a right mess of this place. We'd better
have a quick look around.'

'Sure. I haven't had a chance to myself yet.'

He let them go, and organised Tommy's injection. He
was preparing some warm milk for him when the police

appeared. There was a tenseness about them which hadn't been there before.

'Are you telling us you didn't hear any shots?'

'That's what I said.'

The other policeman drew in his breath. 'There are two dead people upstairs – both shot.'

'*What!*' Rory stared at the man who had spoken. 'Who?'

'Don't you know?'

The milk on the hob started to froth noisily over the side of the pan. Rory ignored it. He glanced at Tommy, asleep with his head on the table; at least he wasn't hearing this.

Rory himself was finding it hard to absorb the information. All his instincts were to reject it. He didn't answer the question. In a state of dazed shock, he turned and switched the heat off under the bubbling milk, picked up the pan and poured some into a mug which he placed on the table in front of the sleeping Tommy.

'Are you going to tell us what we're dealing with here or not?'

'I don't know what you're talking about! There's no one else here.'

'Just come and see for yourself.'

'All right,' Rory said, still trying to block the idea from his head. 'I'm coming.'

Leaving Tommy fast asleep at the table, he led the way up the main stairs from the hall. At the top he turned into the corridor towards his bedroom, and stopped, frozen in mid-step.

Halfway along the passage, lying on her back with her

arms flung above her head, was Pam.

Her eyes were open and she was naked.

'Jesus Christ!' he whispered hoarsely. 'Don't let Tommy come upstairs.'

'Can you identify her?'

'Of course I can,' Rory said weakly. 'She's my wife.'

'That's what we thought. Now, can you tell us who the other body is?'

'Where . . . where is it?'

'In the bedroom.'

Rory turned his eyes away from Pam's once soft, warm body and sidled past her to their bedroom.

There was a lump beneath a rumpled top sheet, where a bloodstain, twelve inches across, had spread through the white linen.

The victim's head lay on one side, face towards the door. The familiar sharp features, for once immobile, came as no surprise to Rory.

'Who's that then?' a voice behind him asked.

'He's . . . was Dai Price – a jockey,' he added fatuously.

'Knew him, did you?'

'Oh aye. I knew him. I saved his life on Wednesday.'

The police in Newbury were quite polite when they took him in. They had let him carry Tommy, still sleeping, out to their car and dropped him at his friend's house in the village to spend the rest of the night there.

The two detectives, freshened with cups of strong coffee, questioned Rory rigorously but calmly for two more hours.

He didn't blame them.

They hadn't found him with a smoking gun, but he'd had the opportunity, and a hell of a motive to commit murder, and they had to start somewhere.

But Rory had the advantage that to the experienced eye, the state of the victims and of the house had all the signs of an interrupted burglary, rather than a *crime passionnel*.

In the end, two hours of questioning and the circumstances of Rory's discovery led the detectives to the conclusion that they hadn't sufficient grounds for detaining him.

A police car dropped him at the Joneses' house where Tommy was spending the night, so that he would be there in the morning when his son woke. The forensic investigation would be finished and the bodies removed to the police morgue before he got back home, and they'd need to talk to him again in the morning.

He sensed that he wasn't completely off the hook, though. He sat in a chair in the living room of the small house, with a glass of whisky in front of him, deciding whether to ring Laura or her father.

Though it was half past three in the morning, Edward Brickhill sounded wide awake when Rory got through to him and gave no audible signs of shock when he told him what had happened.

'Don't go into detail now,' he said calmly. 'I'll come down and see you first thing in the morning.'

The numbness he had felt the night before returned to Rory in the morning, followed by physical nausea. Now he was finding it harder to cope with the death of his partner of the last twelve years, despite the almost total erosion of affection between them. Regardless of all her shortcomings in the role, she had still been Tommy's mother. With his thoughts on Tommy, Rory rang his parents in Scotland to tell them what had happened.

The events had taken place too late to make the Sunday papers, and the radio stations were only just beginning to pick up the story. Old Mrs Gillespie had heard nothing about it and seemed to find it almost impossible to believe. Nevertheless, she agreed that her grandson should come and stay with them, as far away as possible from the scene and the local gossip.

Tommy's friend's parents, whom Rory knew only slightly, offered to drive Tommy to Scotland themselves. Rory's gratitude was increased when they also said they would see if they could fix the boy up with some fishing when he got there.

He went up to the small bedroom where Tommy had slept, and sat on his bed.

'Mummy's had a terrible accident,' he started. The boy's top lip began to quiver. Rory took a small hand in his and squeezed it. '. . . and she's died . . . We won't ever see her again.'

He let out a long breath. He had been dreading this job, and had decided the only way to handle it was as honestly as possible.

Tears seeped from the boy's eyes. For a while he looked away and stared at the ceiling, then, calmly, he said, 'I suppose that means we won't be going to Wales now.'

Rory shook his head. 'I'm afraid it does. But we will another time – a real long trip, I promise.'

'Mummy bought me some new Nikes the other day,' Tommy said, finding reasons for missing his mother.

'Did she?' Rory said gently. 'That was nice of her.'

'Will you look after me all the time now?'

'Of course I will.'

It was a damp, cold March morning, but Rory felt insulated from it by the warm, leather-scented interior of Brickhill's Bentley in which he was being driven back to Camp Farm.

'You didn't tell them what you think about Straker, did you?' Edward was asking.

'No, though I would have done if they'd looked like holding me there.'

Brickhill looked relieved. 'Thank God for that. I really want that kept from them until we know for certain that Henry was involved.'

'You still don't believe me, after what I told you.'

'I don't know. But I do know that if Henry *is* involved, it's because somebody's applying some very heavy pressure. We can't risk him being investigated until we really know what's happening.'

Rory shook his head vigorously. 'But, Edward, for God's sake, these people have killed three times now, and your daughter is on the line for one of those deaths.'

'Believe me,' Brickhill said quietly, 'I haven't stopped thinking about that since she was arrested.'

He went on to say that he was making full use of his contacts and his money in looking for connections between Luke's death and his gambling, and he was sure they would soon start to see results.

But Rory wasn't encouraged. 'For Christ's sake, Edward, I think we've got to hand over what we know to the police. If this thing started out as a simple plan to stop Midnight Express from winning, it's got way out of hand now and people are going to be more determined than ever to cover their tracks. I mean, Henry Straker's reputation won't matter much to him if he gets killed, too.'

Rory stood outside his house, thinking that he was getting nowhere fast. He was frustrated and uneasy about Edward Brickhill's anxiety to keep the police away from Straker. For a few minutes, he considered going straight back to the police station, but in the end, something Brickhill had said, 'You could be destroying the man's reputation for ever', echoed in his head.

Still feeling disoriented, he walked round the back of his garage with the vague idea of going to check on the horses before he confronted the police and the mess in his house.

It was then that he discovered the reason for his dog's absence. He found Taffy's wiry black and white body lying stiff and cold behind the garage. From the damage done to the animal's skull, it was impossible to guess what kind of weapon had been used, only that it had been wielded with strength, and unrestrained commitment.

Tears that hadn't come before flowed now from Rory's eyes as he gazed at his lifeless friend.

In a haze of grief, he fetched a spade and buried the guiltless dog.

There were still half a dozen policemen crawling around

the house. They told Rory that Pam and Dai had been removed.

Rory made himself some coffee and sat staring out of the window, up the valley towards his stable block. He ought to have been up there, dealing with his horses, but they seemed completely irrelevant at the moment. He was trying to come to terms with life without Pam; he didn't dare think about Laura.

Exhausted, confused, he sank into a vacuous trance in which all coherent thought was forced from his mind.

He was jerked out of it by the arrival of the two policemen who had interviewed him late into the night.

They wanted to talk to him about the burglary.

Slowly, unwillingly, Rory offered them the same story he had given the previous morning, after the first break-in – someone looking for the cash he had received for the sale of the coloured pony. They were still unconvinced about the source, but seemed prepared to believe in the cash.

'But it won't have been the same people, not after they found nothing the night before.'

Rory shrugged wearily. 'There's nothing else missing.'

'I'm afraid we can't rule out the possibility that the intention was to kill your wife and, er, the jockey. We know you had two visitors last night. Fresh footprints outside confirm that, and that they chased you and the boy up to the barns. And we've had confirmatory sightings of the red Cavalier you described.' The detective paused for a moment, before continuing abruptly, 'Why do you think anyone would want to kill your wife?'

'I don't know,' Rory mumbled.

'I know it's difficult, and I don't like asking this, but did she have other ... boyfriends – someone who might have been jealous of her affair with Dai Price?'

'For Christ's sake,' Rory blurted, finally embarrassed, 'I don't know. Maybe. I didn't even know she was definitely having an affair with Dai.'

'Everyone else did, Mr Gillespie,' the policeman said with unexpected gentleness.

'Well, I suppose I knew there was something going on. To be quite honest, I tried to ignore it. Pam and I hadn't got on well for a long time. I mean, I only stayed with her for the boy's sake; I'm afraid she wasn't much of a mum to him.' Rory was surprised how disloyal to his dead wife he felt, talking to an outsider like this.

'Okay, I'm just asking. Do you think it's possible that happened?'

'I guess it is, but I can't think of anyone in particular.'

'That brings us to the other possible scenario, which is that they didn't realise that the man in the bed wasn't you. In the dark they wouldn't have been able to see and might have made the assumption that it had to be you.'

Rory didn't answer at once, now that the detective had hit the jackpot. He screwed up his face in an effort to look puzzled and startled. 'You mean, do I know of anyone who would want to kill me?'

The policeman nodded.

Rory sighed. 'It's possible. You know I was beaten up after the races at Uttoxeter on Friday; that wasn't a straightforward mugging. I was being warned to leave off asking questions about Luke Mundy's death.'

'What sort of questions had you been asking?'

'Listen, I know damn well Laura didn't dope that horse – it's just not possible – and you guys had stopped looking elsewhere, so I thought I'd bloody well find out what happened.'

'And what have you found out so far?'

'Not a lot.'

'Mr Gillespie, you must have got on to something if these people came to kill you.'

'I haven't. But maybe they think I have,' Rory said, voicing what he'd been thinking for some time.

The detective wasn't convinced. 'Listen, if you know anything and you're holding out on us, you could be charged with obstructing enquiries. My advice is tell us all you know, then leave it to us.'

'I haven't got anything to tell you. All I've done is draw blanks. D'you think I wouldn't tell you if I could give you a name? I mean, if they did want to hit me and didn't get me this time, they'll more than likely try again. Right?'

'Yes, you are right. So it would help us and you if you told us why anyone should want to.'

'I've told you, I don't know.'

The detective shrugged his shoulders. 'If they're after you, it's going to make our job a lot easier when you can tell us why.' He nodded his colleague towards the door. 'We've got to get back. You know where to get in touch with us. In the meantime, you'd better be careful.'

Rory watched them drive back down the lane. All their colleagues had gone now and, knowing that he would never hear Pam's voice about the place again, he found it strangely quiet. He wandered through the house, irresolute and unwilling to start putting right the mayhem caused by the killers.

They'd be back, he was sure of it, and he was crazy not to tell the police about Straker. Luke's death, partly self-inflicted, was one thing, but now double murder. There had to be more of a motive than just a bet. Rory toyed with the idea of letting Straker's reputation take its chance, then thought better of it.

He walked back into the chaos of the kitchen and poured himself a generous slug of Glenmorangie. He sat down at the table and tried to organise his thoughts.

Twice he reached out to pick up the phone and call Laura. Both times he held back. He didn't have anything good to tell her; he didn't want to end up crying on her shoulder, needing her support; it was meant to be the other way round.

The telephone trilled sharply, catching him by surprise. Laura, he thought. She'd have heard by now. He picked it up to talk to her.

'Hello.'

'Rory?' A man's voice; quiet, deep, well bred. He couldn't place it at once.

'Yes. Who's this?'

'It's Henry Straker.' There was an odd timbre to the voice, which somehow disguised it.

'Henry! My God,' Rory blurted.

'I've just heard what happened. I need to speak to you.'

'Okay,' Rory said, quickly recovering himself. 'Where?'

'Do you mind coming here?'

Henry Straker's face seemed to have withered. There was

290

a coating of sweat on the pallid wrinkles of his forehead.

He didn't speak when he opened the door to Rory and beckoned him in with a gloomy smile. He led him into his study and closed the door behind them.

He offered Rory the large chair and sat at his desk.

'I'm desperately sorry this has happened.' It wasn't just sympathy, it was an apology. Rory acknowledged it with a silent nod.

'You see,' Straker went on, 'I'm partly to blame. I'm afraid you've been right all along.' His face seemed to collapse; his large, normally firm grey eyes gave the impression of melting, until he could look at Rory no longer. He turned his bleak gaze to the dripping rhododendrons outside the window. 'I can't tell you what hell it's been. I've handled the whole thing utterly wrong, but . . .' his voice dropped almost to a whisper, 'I had to, for Susan. She just couldn't have . . .' The words faded on his trembling lips.

Rory could feel Straker's pain, but he didn't speak.

'So, I had to do it; nothing could have been further from my instincts.'

Rory held his breath.

'But, those photos!' Straker shook his head hopelessly. 'If she'd seen them, she could never have looked me in the face again.'

He turned his gaze back on Rory.

'Photos?' Rory prompted.

'I don't know how they did it. I remember nothing, nothing about it.'

'About what?'

'The photos they took; they were horrible, despicable;

they made it look as if I were enjoying it.' Straker shook his head in despair. 'The bastards!' he whispered.

'Are you trying to tell me that you've been blackmailed, and you did stop Midnight Express?'

'Yes, yes,' Straker said impatiently. 'Except it wasn't blackmail.'

'How do you mean?'

'I mean, what they had against me was something I didn't do – couldn't possibly have done. I was set up, very cleverly. The bastards had done their homework too; they knew just what would hurt most.'

'What exactly?'

Henry looked at him, pleading for his sympathy. 'I haven't told anyone else about this. In a way it's a hell of a relief, and now I don't think there's any way of avoiding the whole thing coming out. You see, they said if I went to the police and the police believed me and sat on it, they'd send copies of the photos to my wife, the Jockey Club, all the papers and the boys' club. Whatever the truth, my reputation will be shredded; I'll have to resign from every office I hold. I think I could handle that, on my own, but it would destroy Susan. She's had to cope with losing our boys, then bear the fact of her own subsequent barrenness, and she's found that terribly difficult. I'm not even sure that she'd accept my explanation for the photos and what they show.'

'Henry, it may not need to come out. If we can get to whoever's behind it first.'

Henry glanced up at him, surprised by his vehemence.

'But we haven't got a lot of time,' Rory went on, 'and Laura's in trouble.'

'I know,' Straker said guiltily. 'I felt terrible when I heard she'd been charged with Luke's manslaughter. I've tried to show as much loyalty as possible, but . . .'

'But what?'

Straker gave an agonised sigh. 'Oh God! Please don't hold this against me, but it did cross my mind that Laura might have been involved in some way. I mean, you know that she and Luke were at loggerheads most of the time, and Luke was in serious difficulties . . .'

After what he had felt with Laura the day before, Rory didn't want even to consider this again, but he made Straker go on. 'Why do you think she could possibly be involved, though?' he asked.

'It's not fair, really, to mention it – it was almost certainly sheer coincidence – but a couple of weeks before Midnight Express ran, she jokingly asked me what I would give a horse if I wanted to slow it down. It's the sort of question people often ask me, you know, in fun. Well, in the same spirit, I said a ten milligram dose of xylazine would do the trick, and not arouse much suspicion. Then she asked me, seriously, if the same drug would be suitable for tranquillising a tricky horse when it was being clipped – apparently she'd been having trouble with a new mare. I told her it would do, with the right dosage. She asked me to get her a phial of it and I dropped one off the next day.

'The horrible irony is that that's exactly what I was ordered to use by the blackmailer. I'm afraid it occurred to me that she might have tried it out on the horse at home, to see what effect it would have on its performance.

I knew that she wasn't keen on the horse running at Kempton.'

'No,' Rory agreed. 'She wanted to save it for the Champion Chase.'

'But, honestly, Rory, I really don't think she had anything to do with it, and if they got her as far as the dock, I'd have stood up and told them it was me who administered it.'

Rory stared at him, not knowing what to believe. 'Who planted the empty phial in her car, then? That's why the police arrested her.'

Straker sighed. 'It must have been the man on the bike, or someone working for him. He made me give him an empty phial.'

'This guy, this blackmailer, you seem to have seen him a few times. Surely you could have found out something about him?'

Straker shook his head. 'Of course, I tried. But he was always completely covered, with his helmet on and a scarf wrapped across his mouth under the visor. I couldn't even tell you the colour of his eyes. I persuaded a friend of mine in the police to check the number of the bike – I said it had hit my car and driven off, but he came back and told me it was a bogus number – the real vehicle had been written off three months ago. He spoke very little, and of course his voice was muffled by the helmet and the scarf; I certainly wouldn't be able to swear to it if I heard it again. He had a sort of Cockney accent, but that doesn't narrow it down much.'

Rory nodded. It made sense. The blackmailer evidently knew what he was doing, and he'd already shown the lengths to which he would go. If he and Henry were going to stay alive, they were going to have to get to him first, and very soon.

'What I don't really see,' Straker went on, 'is why anyone particularly wanted to stop that horse in that race.'

'That's simple,' Rory said. 'Whoever took the bet Luke had on it.'

'Did he have a bet?'

'We think so. Edward Brickhill's people are pretty sure. The only trouble is, they don't know who with. If we knew that, we'd know everything. There's got to be a bent bookie behind all this somewhere. The problem is, he might be an illegal bookmaker who can't be traced.'

Straker nodded. 'I suppose so.'

But Rory couldn't rid himself of the sickening, disloyal thought that perhaps Laura was still holding back from him, despite the complete trust he had felt yesterday 'If it wasn't done to win a bet, then it was done simply to stop the horse running the race. Anyone other than Luke would have pulled it up after a few furlongs. What would have been the long-term effect on Midnight Express being doped? I mean, how long would it have taken for the horse to recover?' Rory asked.

'It depends entirely on the horse, and how much of the drug was administered,' Straker replied thoughtfully. 'It could take anything from a couple of days to a couple of months. Laura would have been taking one hell of a risk if she'd done the job herself with the Champion Chase in mind.' Straker shook his head. 'I'm sure Laura had nothing to do with it,' he said with conviction now. 'I'm sorry even to have suggested it, when I consider what

I've done myself and everything that's led to.'

'It's okay, I understand. Just tell me what happened, from the beginning.'

The vet looked relieved to confide in someone at last.

'It was about a month ago. I got a call from a man to go and look at a horse in a small livery yard near Sunningdale. Obviously, he gave a false name but he said Mick Fanshaw had recommended me to him. Despite everything, Mick's an old friend of mine, so I agreed; I never thought of checking with Mick. I was due to pick up the Daimler from servicing in Cobham, so it wasn't much out of my way. I found the place – I'd never been there before. I wandered about for a few minutes, called out, but there was no one around, though there were half a dozen horses in the boxes. This chap had told me which stable his horse was in. He'd said he might get there a bit late. Anyway, I thought I'd identified the right box and went in. I was pretty surprised to find that there was just an old cob in there. I'd assumed, as the recommendation had come through Mick, that it would be a blood horse, but I wasn't particularly suspicious or anything – I mean, if the old horse was precious to someone . . . Anyway I thought I might as well get on with examining it and picked up one of his feet. Then suddenly somebody jumped on me and stuffed a rag of chloroform over my face, and that was that – everything went blank.'

'What time of day was it?' Rory asked.

'Just after ten in the morning.'

'What happened after that?'

'They must have given me a jab. I came round about two hours later, feeling like death, being driven along in the back of my own car. I was slumped on the rear seat, so I couldn't see much of where I was going and I didn't want whoever it was to know I'd come round yet – I was still feeling very groggy and not up to any kind of fight. So I kept my eyes shut for most of the journey. The only thing I saw which I could identify was Windsor Castle high on the skyline, so we must have crossed the Thames on the road that links Windsor and Slough. Anyway, ten or fifteen minutes later, the car stopped and the driver got out. I thought he was going to come round to the back, but I heard another car start up and realised he must have gone. I didn't dare look up, in case it wasn't him leaving; it was, though, so I never even saw what kind of car he was in or its number. When I did get up to look around, of course there was no sign of him. I was in one of those parking places in Windsor Great Park. There were a couple of other cars there, but nobody around. I didn't feel up to driving straight away, so I sat there for a bit trying to pull myself together. I couldn't think what had happened, or why I should have been abducted, and apart from being rather dishevelled, I didn't appear to be damaged in any way. My shoes were unlaced and my tie was in my pocket, but nothing had been taken or anything. I was absolutely mystified. I realised I must have been driven somewhere, and I knew we'd come back over the river. As I told you, I'd picked up the car from being serviced that morning, and the garage had marked the mileage on the service sheet which was in the glove compartment. Another thirty-four miles had been added. I reckoned it was about ten miles from Cobham to the yard in Sunningdale, so my round trip must have been twenty-four. I'm afraid that leaves a pretty vast area. I thought about trying to find where I'd been taken, but I didn't know where to begin, and at that stage, I didn't know what the hell was going on. I thought of going back to the yard, but frankly, it occurred to me that whoever it was might have gone back there.'

'Did you go to the police?'

'Yes, of course. But it was all rather embarrassing because I couldn't tell them much. I wasn't injured and nothing had been stolen.'

'Have you been back to the yard since?'

'No, nor to the police, because two days later I got an envelope through the post with the first of the photographs. A few minutes after the post had been, I got a phone call; a man's voice, London accent. He just said that if I contacted the police or tried to do anything to trace where the shots had been taken, they'd be sent to my wife and everyone else.' He placed his hands flat on the desk in front of him, then lifted them in a gesture of helplessness. 'I couldn't take that risk, and when the next call came, telling me to stop Midnight Express, I had to do it.' He shook his head with shame. 'If I'd even thought it could end up with anyone being killed, of course, I'd have taken the risk of them sending the photos. Now two more people are dead. I'll have to give myself up and simply hope for the best.'

Rory ignored this. 'Did they ask you to stop others? That favourite at Folkestone last week?'

Straker nodded. 'But I said I wouldn't do any more. I told the blackmailer I thought you'd guessed what was going on and it wouldn't work again. I'm afraid I told him I thought you'd stolen some of the photos.' Straker turned his eyes from Rory's. 'I'm sorry, I was desperate, and you'd been round asking questions. Yours was the most obvious name and it was plausible to suggest you were doing it for Laura. If I'd dreamt it would lead to all this . . .' He covered his face with his hands once more. 'I realised you suspected I was involved when Charters told me you'd been asking him why he hadn't been on duty at Kempton that day. Then on Friday morning, this man phoned again, just after you'd left, and told me to meet him. That time I was given another photo and instructions in person, by the man on the bike you saw yesterday. From his voice, it was the same person who had phoned me. He wanted me to dope a horse the next day. I said it was impossible because I wasn't on duty and it would look very suspicious if I tried to change that again at short notice.'

'As you did with Charters at Kempton,' Rory added.

Straker nodded. 'I'm afraid so. Anyway, the chap was bloody angry. He said that when I'd seen the photograph, I'd change my mind, and got out of my car. I'd already decided that I wasn't going to dope another horse, whatever happened, but I didn't open the envelope he had given me right away. I was due down at Langlands, but on the way there, I thought I'd better get rid of the photo. I stopped and took it out. It was horrible.' Straker faltered.

'What was it of?' Rory prompted.

'I'm sorry, I just can't tell you. It makes me sick to even think about it. And it was worse than the previous one. I thought about what everyone would say if they saw it – the papers, Susan – it was unthinkable. But I nearly decided there and then to have done with it. I drove to the police station in Newbury and sat outside in my car for about a quarter of an hour. Then I forced myself to get out and walk across to the front entrance. I'm afraid I dithered on the steps for a couple of minutes, and two constables came out and I thought, these people will never believe me, and I went back to the car. I decided I'd have to do this horse after all. But I chucked the photo into a litter bin by the lay-by where I'd stopped and set fire to the whole thing.'

'But you didn't go to the races yesterday?' Rory asked.

'No. I didn't have to. The horse was withdrawn. The man phoned me and told me, but he said there'd be another one, a big one, the following week. I said I wasn't going to do it, and I meant it. I said send the photos to whoever you like. Oddly enough, that seemed to panic him and he started getting very abusive. It occurred to me that maybe the thing was a huge bluff and I put the phone down feeling better, but that didn't last long when I thought how repellent and convincing the photographs had been. I slept terribly and next morning I was at my wits' end again, but I tried to carry on as normal. I'd arranged to go with my soccer team to the game in Reading, which is where you found me. I'm sorry I was so offensive to you again,' the vet said with true contrition, 'particularly as you saved my life . . .'

'What?' Rory asked.

'The syringe under my car seat contained neat strychnine.' The knowledge of how close he'd come to an agonising death showed on the vet's face. 'I analysed it at the surgery. With a small dose straight into the bloodstream, I'd have lasted only a few minutes, no more. I drove back home shaking, and when I got there I found a third photograph that had been posted the day before, I guess before the chap had phoned me. And it was even more horrible than the first two . . .' Straker shook his head. 'They picked the most damaging shot you can imagine. I could hardly cope any more, but I had to. I thought it was better that I should be killed than that Susan should ever see it.'

Rory was beginning to understand the agony that Straker must have been going through. He was suddenly intensely grateful that Edward Brickhill had persuaded him not to tell the police about what he'd found at the vet's house or about the attempt on Straker's life the day before.

Rory gazed at him, relieved but appalled now that Straker had confirmed the extent of his involvement. But he found he didn't want to blame the man, not at all.

'Look, Henry. Try and stall them for the next couple of days. Tell them you'll do another next week. A few more days may get us closer to whoever's doing this.'

Straker nodded bleakly. He didn't believe they could achieve anything.

'They may not phone again and I've got no way of contacting them. When they realise they haven't killed me, which they will have done by now, I imagine they'll try again.'

Rory nodded. 'That makes two of us. The people who came to my place last night must have thought I knew a lot more than I did.'

Straker bowed his head in remorse.

Rory stood up decisively. 'Right, this is what we do. Somehow you're going to have to persuade Susan that both of you have to go and stay somewhere else tonight. If you don't, you could both end up dead. These people aren't just trying to cover their tracks from blackmail and horse-doping, they've got two murder raps chasing them, and they're not going to be worried about a couple more if that'll kill the trail. I'm not going back home; I'm going to stay in a pub tonight. I want you to meet me in Ascot at the racecourse car park, tomorrow morning at eight. We've got to get to where those photos were taken before they get to us. Here's my mobile number if you get held up, but for God's sake, try and be there.'

Straker nodded. 'I'll come,' he said, not disguising the futility he felt.

Chapter Twelve

In the car outside, Rory dialled Laura's number.

After a couple of rings, she answered herself.

'Rory, where are you? I've been trying to get hold of you all afternoon. I've heard the news about Pam and . . . Dai. I can't believe what's happened.'

'I'm coming to see you now. I'll tell you when I get there. And make sure you're on your own.'

Rory drove in through the lodge gates as George Rutherford drove out.

Laura opened the front door of the house to him, greeting him with a warm hug. 'Rory, I'm so sorry.'

'I know. I can't believe what's happened . . . Is there anyone else here?' he asked.

'No. I've just got rid of Rutherford, thank God.' She closed the door behind him and led the way into the small drawing room.

'What did he want?'

'He's been coming on very strong since Luke died. He's

talking about buying the yard for me and getting involved in it himself. He says that now that he's my biggest owner, he feels he has some rights, and, even though Luke tucked him up over a deal, he won't make a claim on the estate if I go into partnership with him.'

'Would he get anywhere claiming?'

'No. The fact of the matter is he could claim on the estate until he's blue in the face but there's not going to be anything left anyway, so I haven't been showing the gratitude that he seems to think I should.' She shrugged. 'Of course, I don't want him taking his horses away but I'm not going to be bullied. Fortunately, the horses are running well so I doubt he'll do anything drastic. But, for God's sake,' she said, abruptly changing her tone, 'what happened last night?'

Rory told her everything that had occurred from the moment he and Tommy had arrived back at the farm. When he began to describe finding Pam's naked body on the landing, she stopped him.

'Rory, for God's sake, I don't think I can take it. How can you be so calm?'

Rory lowered his eyes. 'To be honest, I don't think it's quite hit me. But finding my wife with Dai wasn't too conducive to sympathy.'

'No,' Laura nodded. Then she gave a short cynical laugh. 'George Rutherford asked me if I'd done it.'

'Did you?'

Laura had been looking into the fire. She glanced at him now.

'Of course not. I knew it wasn't necessary.'

'I don't know. I wouldn't have left her, I don't think.

Not while Tommy was still so young.'

'I'm sorry,' Laura said gently. 'That was selfish and insensitive of me.'

'We're both in the same boat. What we are expected to feel and what we actually feel are two different things. Even so, I'll admit, I do feel a sense of emptiness. Numbness, really.'

'What about Tommy?' Laura asked.

'He's bound to miss her, isn't he? But I think he'll get over it in the end. He'll need me a lot more than he already does. But that's okay by me.'

'He's such a good kid. I hope he's okay.'

'Aye,' Rory nodded. 'But if we don't find out what the hell's going on, he's not going to have a dad, either. There's something else I wanted to ask you. Who do you think is Flamenco Dancer's biggest threat in the Champion Chase?'

'I don't think there is a danger, but if I were writing for the *Sporting Life*, I'd say Fancyman, even though he'll be level weights with our horse this time. But what's that got to do with all this?'

'I'm not sure. But let me ask you something else.' He was gazing at her intently now, knowing that he'd have to rely on his judgement of what Laura was thinking over the next few seconds. 'Who told you about the photos of Henry Straker?'

Laura stared back at him blankly.

Desperately, Rory tried to see if there was any discernible subtext to her apparent reaction. He held his breath, and expelled it with a sigh. 'I'm sorry but I needed to know how much you knew.'

'Rory, what the hell are you talking about? What photos of Straker?'

'I thought your father might have told you,' Rory bluffed.

'What photos?'

'I'll tell you another time.' He stood up.

'You still thought I had something to do with it – like the police?'

'I needed to be sure that you didn't. There's so much that points in your direction.' He sighed. 'I'm sorry. It's because I so badly want it not to be you that I have to be really certain. And time's running out.'

'You're not kidding,' Laura said. 'Agnew says the police are no closer to dropping the charges against me. It's not surprising really, is it, when even you don't believe I didn't do it.'

'I do, I promise,' Rory replied in earnest. 'We're doing as much as we can, but we haven't got anything solid to take to the police yet. Tomorrow I may have. I'll let you know.'

Laura stood too and put her arms around Rory's neck. She touched his lips with hers. 'Would you be doing this for me even if you thought I had done it?'

'Probably.'

'That's nice to know. Before you go, I'm sorry to bring things back to the mundanities of life, but without Dai I need a jockey. How long before you're back riding again?'

'I don't know. I haven't used my arm at all; except for doing isometrics.'

Laura looked puzzled.

'You know, exercising the muscles, but not the bones.

I think it should be okay, though.'

'Will you be able to ride Flamenco Dancer or are you going to stick with the Irish horse?'

Rory had a short struggle with his conscience. 'I'll ride yours, if I'm fit. Just this once, I'll let down another trainer. For you.' He grinned. 'Has George backed it?'

'No; he never punts. He says he'd rather rely on prize money – less risky. Actually, it's the glory he's after.'

At eight next morning, Rory waited for Straker in Pam's Discovery. He was outside the empty racecourse car park at Ascot.

When he arrived, the vet looked as though he hadn't slept all night, paler and more haggard than he had been the day before.

He climbed into Rory's car silently, not speaking until they were moving.

'Where are we going?'

'To the yard where you were first picked up.'

The half-dozen horses of various types appeared to be fed, watered and clean bedded, but there was no one around.

Leaving Straker in the car, Rory walked across a small paddock to the nearest house and knocked on the back door.

A young mother in jeans and sweatshirt opened the door with a baby dangling from her hip.

'What is it?'

'I wanted to enquire about the yard.'

'It's my husband you want to see, then. He'll be back

down the yard in about fifteen minutes. You can wait for him there.'

Waiting with Straker made Rory nervous. The strength Straker had shown when issuing his denial to Rory just a few days before had left him. He was a defeated man, ready to give in to forces beyond his control.

Rory knew he would have to get Straker committed to their search if he was going to be any help.

'If you look in front of you on the shelf there, I've got the local Ordnance Survey map. While we're waiting for this guy to turn up, we can narrow the field a bit.'

Straker reached forward for the map and passed it to Rory, who unfolded it and spread it out between them. Rory had already marked the position of the yard where they were.

'Can you show me exactly where you were left in your car?'

The vet looked listlessly at the map and put his finger on a point beside the main road that ran through Windsor Great Park.

'Right,' Rory said, and marked the spot with a pencil. 'I've cut a piece of string twenty-four miles long on this scale.' He produced the string from his pocket and put each end at the two points he'd marked. 'This'll only give us an approximate idea of where you were taken, but it'll narrow down the field a bit. Right, you know from seeing the castle that you were brought back by this road across the river, and presumably along this main road round the south of Windsor. And it looks likely that you were taken from Sunningdale by the same route'.

As accurately as he could, Rory laid the string along the bends and twists of both routes until they converged and ran side by side, under the M4 to a large roundabout on the west side of Slough. A small loop of string was left. Rory measured the loop against the scale chart on the bottom of the map. 'About two miles. Okay, that tells us you were taken no more than a mile by road from that roundabout.'

Straker nodded with a little more enthusiasm. 'But that still leaves a hell of a large populated area.'

'Sure, but it's a start. And the owner of this yard may be able to tell us something about whoever took you. This may be him now.'

An old blue Land Rover was bouncing down the dirt track from the road.

'You stay here. I'll deal with him.'

Rory climbed out of the Discovery and walked towards the approaching vehicle.

The Land Rover pulled up beside him and a heavy-faced man in his late thirties slid the window back.

'Yes, mate?'

'I'm trying to track down a horse. I think it was here for a bit about a month ago.'

The man, alerted by Rory's Scottish accent, looked at him more keenly. 'Aren't you Rory Gillespie?'

Rory nodded. ''Fraid so.'

The man opened his door and jumped down enthusiastically, holding out a hand. 'It's good to meet you, Rory. I'm Roger Williams – always been a fan.'

'Glad to hear it, Roger,' Rory smiled.

'Well, what was it you wanted to know?'

'Did someone take a stable, just for a week or two, about a month ago?'

Roger looked thoughtful for a moment. 'Yeah, there

was a geezer, funny bloke he sounded, never saw him. He paid for two weeks by post and only used the stable for a couple of days, and he certainly didn't have the kind of animal you'd be interested in – some old knackered cob, just come out the field.'

'Still, can you tell me where I can get hold of him?'

'Haven't a clue. He never gave me an address or nothing. He dropped this horse off when I wasn't here and phoned me to ask me to feed and bed it, and picked it up a couple of days later.'

'Well, what was he called?'

Roger laughed. 'Smith, Michael Smith.' He shrugged. 'When people tell you they're called Smith these days, you believe them, don't you?'

Rory grunted. 'So you never saw what kind of a car he came in?'

'Nope. Didn't see him at all.'

'When he talked to you on the phone, could you tell where he came from, by the way he spoke or anything?'

'No, not really. You know, same as me, sort of south-east.'

'Is there anything else you could tell me about him?'

The man shrugged regretfully. 'Sorry, Rory. Anyway what's it all about?'

'Oh, it's nothing. It doesn't sound like the right man, or horse. I think I've been sent on a wild-goose chase. Sorry to have wasted your time.'

'No problem, Rory. 'Ere, you haven't got a good horse you can give me for this week, have you?'

'Sure. Flamenco Dancer in the Champion Chase. He's still good value, and he'll win.'

'Thanks, Rory,' the man burbled enthusiastically as Rory walked back to the Discovery and climbed in.

'That's okay. Thanks for your help.'

'What now?' Straker asked as they drove out of the yard.

'Christ knows.' Rory didn't try to hide his frustration. 'We've got an area to search which may be where the BMW bike comes from. It's not a lot. I was counting on the people at the yard telling us something about the man who rented the stable, but they didn't see him at all. I thought we might have that or his vehicle to go on.'

'I've got an idea,' Straker suddenly blurted with enthusiasm. 'I've just remembered. That old cob I came to see – when I looked at its feet, I noticed they'd been shod with leather.'

Rory turned and looked at the vet, encouraged but not hopeful. 'What was that?'

'His front feet were shod with leather pads between the hoof and the shoe. A blacksmith will sometimes do that if a horse suffers from sore feet.'

'Yeah, sure, but not often.'

'That's what I mean. Hardly ever. So it shouldn't be that difficult to find a dun cob, shod with leather.'

'Great! We need to talk to every blacksmith in the area.' He began turning the Discovery back towards the yard they had just left. 'My new friend Roger will know some and the Yellow Pages will give us a few more.'

Roger Williams seemed pleased to see Rory back again so soon and happily produced his own address book and a recent Yellow Pages. He also offered the use of the phone. Rory set Henry Straker the task of going through the blacksmiths in the directory on Roger's phone, while he went out and tried the other list on his mobile.

There were the names of five farriers in the address book. Three were in, and had no recollection of shoeing a dun cob with leather pads within recent memory, if ever. The other two were out on calls; in both cases, their wives were vague about their exact itinerary. Rory told them both what he wanted and gave them his mobile number, in case their husbands came home sooner than they expected. He put the phone down and cursed. It could be hours before either of them got back.

He went back into Roger Williams' house to hear Straker's voice. 'Well, thanks very much. Sorry to have troubled you.'

'Any luck?' Rory asked.

Straker shook his head. 'No. But I've got a few more to go.'

He dialled another, and drew another blank.

He shrugged and dialled again.

Rory rummaged in his pocket with his good arm, and brought out his tobacco and papers. Roger looked at him nervously. 'Rory, if you don't mind, the wife can't stand smoke in the house.'

Rory nodded. He was used to being treated like a leper for smoking in some households. He let himself out of the front door and lit up. At first, he barely heard the trilling of his car phone, blending as it did with the birdsong from the woodlands all around. But then he became abruptly conscious of its regularity. He turned his ear to listen, and within seconds was pulling open the door of the Discovery and grabbing the handset.

'Hello?'

'Hello. Somebody phoned up wanting to know if I'd put pads on a cob.'

'Yes, yes. That's me. Have you had something in to shoe like that recently?'

'Yeh. That'd be Mrs Morrison-Phillips's. She always wants him padded. Doesn't need it, of course, but she thinks he does.'

'Is he a dun, quite old, about fifteen-two?'

'Yeah. That's him.'

'Great! Can you tell me where his owners live?'

'Morrison-Phillips? Yeah. Silver Birches, Belvedere Lane, round the back of Wentworth Golf Course.'

'That's great. Thanks.'

Rory put the phone down wishing he had been able to show his appreciation more, then ran back to the house to get Straker.

They thanked Roger Williams, who refused anything for the use of his phone, and two minutes later were heading at eighty miles an hour towards the famous golf course.

It didn't take long to find Silver Birches; the trees down the drive told them before they had even seen the sign.

From the road, Rory noticed two well-bred horses grazing in a paddock beside the drive. They drove on past.

'What do you think?' Straker asked. 'If this was our man, surely he'd have used one of those thoroughbreds?'

'Not necessarily.'

'But it's in quite the wrong direction. I'm absolutely certain about seeing the castle.'

'Okay. But if it is where you were taken, they'll know

313

both of us. We can't risk just walking up there.'

'Look,' Straker said, peering back over his shoulder as they passed the property. 'There's some kind of gardener pottering about. I'll go and sound him out.'

Rory stopped and watched Straker, suddenly more buoyant, jump down and walk back to where an old man in dungarees was clearing winter dead wood from a small patch of trees.

Two minutes later, the vet was back.

'No problem,' he said as he climbed back in. 'The dun cob used to live here, but the people, the Morrison-Phillipses, sold it a few weeks ago and it's gone.'

'Did he know who bought it?'

'No. We'll have to go and ask at the house. Apparently the wife's in and she's the one who deals with the horses.'

'You're sure it's not where you were taken?'

'I just don't see how it could be, and the old boy was absolutely genuine.'

'Okay. I hope you're bloody right.'

Mrs Morrison-Phillips looked and sounded like her name. She was well groomed, expensively dressed, about fifty. Rory, on the evidence of the horses in the paddock, wasn't surprised when she recognised him. Fluttering a little at the excitement of having a jockey in her spotless house, she invited them in before they had time to suggest it themselves.

They had told her vaguely that they wanted to talk about one of her horses. She looked very disappointed when she gathered it was the old cob they were interested in.

'I'll be quite honest with you, Mrs Morrison-Phillips . . .'

'Veronica, please,' she interrupted him.

'Veronica. It's the fellow who bought it that we want to talk to.'

'Why, what's happened?'

'Mr Straker here is a top vet – I'm sure you know his name. He and I do a lot of work for the RSPCA, and this animal's turned up in one of their shelters.'

It was an implausible reason for their coming, but Mrs Morrison-Phillips wasn't going to question it. She looked upset. 'Oh no. Is he all right?'

'The horse? Oh yes, he's fine now. Don't worry about that. But we do need to trace the present owner.'

'Well, he was rather an odd little individual. He said he wanted it for his son. He'd brought the boy with him, a very good-looking child, who seemed absolutely smitten by old Samuel. I let them have him for rather less than I'd planned, but I was most concerned about his going to a loving home. I'll certainly have him back straightaway, if he's been abandoned.'

'Oh no, I don't think that's a problem. I think the owner must have been away. Anyway, could you tell me his name?'

'Mr Smith, I think. He paid in cash, you see.'

'You don't have his address, I suppose?' Rory asked, holding out little hope.

'No. I'm afraid not. He simply rang up in answer to my advert and came round. He took the horse away with him there and then.'

'So you don't have a phone number or anything?'

'I'm terribly sorry, no,' Mrs Morrison-Phillips said,

embarrassed at not being able to help the famous jockey.

'Not to worry,' Rory said, controlling his frustration. 'Can you remember what kind of vehicle he came in?'

'Ah, yes, that I can tell you. He had a blue trailer – you know, a Rice or something like that – towed by a dark red Jaguar.'

'Dark red? Metallic or not?'

'Metallic, but quite faded. It was an oldish car; I think one of the old registrations with the letter at the end – a Y.'

'That's a help. He didn't happen to mention how far he had to go, did he?'

'I'm afraid not.'

'Okay, well we think we have an idea of that.' Rory and Straker stood up together.

'Thanks so much for talking to us,' Straker said. 'It's been very helpful indeed. And I'll make sure we let you know what's happened to your old horse, don't worry.'

'You bloody liar,' Rory laughed as they set off back towards Windsor in the Discovery.

'I'm not,' Straker replied with dignity. 'I'll make damn sure I find out what's happened to the animal and write to her.'

'What a gent you are, Henry. Anyway, at least we know our man has an old Jag. That'd need a bit of servicing, and if he lives where we think he does, there's a chance someone round there does it for him.'

'But how do you know he lives there?'

'I don't, but I can't think of any reason why he'd take you there if he didn't. At least it gives us a starting point, that and the BMW bike.'

Twenty minutes later they drove north across the River Thames by the road which bypasses the ancient town of Eton, and under the Slough intersection of the M4.

'If you're right,' Straker said, studying the map, 'this roundabout is within a mile of our target.'

Rory nodded. 'We've got to find a phone book and check the names of the local Jaguar dealers. We may as well start with them.'

Rows of shining cars and a landscaped forecourt suggested unashamedly high rates at the Jaguar and Daimler main dealers.

'I don't think I'd bring a Y-reg Jag here,' Straker observed. 'It wouldn't really be worth it.'

Rory agreed. 'But I'll go in and see the service manager anyway.'

He parked his muddy vehicle in front of the gleaming showroom and jumped out.

A few minutes later, he was back.

'You were right,' he said. 'They very seldom have older models in, but he's given me the names of two other garages who purport to specialise in Jags – both near here.'

Ten minutes later, Rory was talking to the owner of the first of the addresses he'd been given. His well-known face was once again sufficient to persuade the owner to look back through his records to see if he could identify a Y-registered metallic maroon car. No such vehicle had been in over the last year.

The visit to the second garage seemed just as fruitless until the service manager remembered a small one-man-band of a garage, which claimed to specialise in Jaguars, underneath the railway arches of the Windsor–Slough railway viaduct.

Straker was map-reading for Rory. 'That's well within our search area,' he remarked eagerly.

'Sure, but don't get too excited.'

Rory drove gingerly along the rough track beside the viaduct, past a range of various small, scruffy industrial workshops that still flourished beneath the substantial structure of the Victorian engineers of the Great Western Railway.

At the end of the track, announcing itself with several carcasses of deceased Jaguars in the muddy yard outside, were the premises they were looking for.

Rory parked his vehicle among a scattering of scrap iron, got out and picked his way towards the elliptical cavern.

The hiss of a welder from inside the arch encouraged him.

He went in. A pair of legs clad in oil-grimed denim protruded from beneath an old XJS. Blue flashes sprayed from the far side. Rory waited for a pause between bursts before he spoke.

'Hello.'

The legs wriggled away from the car; a torso and a head covered in a welding mask appeared. The oily figure sprang nimbly to its feet, dropped the welder on a work-bench and removed the mask.

'Mornin', mate. What can I do you for?'

He was a youngish man, sharp-eyed and sure of himself.

'I'm looking for someone. I think you might service his car for him.'

'Who's that?'

'I don't know his name. But he lives somewhere round here and drives a maroon XJ6.'

'What's it worth?'

'Not much.'

'A pony?'

Rory nodded and plucked twenty-five pounds from his pocket.

'Bloke's called Eland – Arthur Eland.'

'Have you only got one customer with a car that colour and age?'

'Yeah.'

'What does he look like, then?'

'Average sort of height. Nothing special, about forty-five.'

'What does he do for a living?'

'I don't know. Some sort of photography, I think. There's always loads of empty film boxes and that in the back of the car.' The man gave a conspiratorial snort of laughter. 'And porn. He's into porn. He left some lovely stuff in the boot last time.'

'That sounds like him. Where does he live?'

'I can look up his address, but it'll cost you another pony.'

'No it bloody won't.'

The mechanic made a face and grinned. 'You never get if you don't ask, do you?'

He walked to the back of the arch, to an old desk covered in grimy papers, and found an old-fashioned hard-covered accounts book. He thumbed through it for a moment. 'Here we are. I'll even write it down for you.'

He tore a scrap from the bottom of one of the pages and with a pencil scribbled an address on it. 'There it is.' He passed it to Rory, evidently still pleased with the deal they had done.

Rory glanced at it and felt himself quiver with the excitement of a hound on the scent of a fox. 'Thanks. Here's another twenty,' he offered impulsively.

'Any time.'

'We'll have to get a street plan,' he told Henry Straker as he manoeuvred the Discovery off the muddy forecourt.

'Have you got an address, then?' Straker said, with a tremor in his voice.

'Yes. We've found him.'

They bought a street map of Slough from a corner shop. Straker identified the road they wanted and guided Rory there.

It was a long, quiet cul-de-sac in an uninspired estate of red-brick houses, backing on to open land and, beyond, the motorway.

They drove slowly down the road, past the number Rory had been given. On two strips of concrete in front of a garage stood the Jaguar.

'Bingo!' Rory almost whispered.

They drove on without stopping. The road curved away to the left and ended in a wide, circular turning area. Rory swung the Discovery round and stopped where they could see the Jaguar, but not the house. He turned off the engine and looked across at Straker.

'Okay, Henry. Are you ready for this?'

Straker, pale and nervous, nodded.

'Right. Let's go, then.'

Rory took one of the narrow alleyways that led between the houses to a path that ran all the way along the back of their gardens. He identified the back of Eland's house and waited until he reckoned Straker had reached the front door and rung the bell. Opening the back gate by a simple latch, he walked confidently down an overgrown path to the half-glazed back door of the house. Behind him, the scrubland was empty of humans, and the high hedges of Eland's privacy-conscious neighbours hid him from sight of any of the ground-floor rooms. He'd just have to take a punt that no one was watching from an upper room.

He listened.

He heard a door bell sound at the front of the house.

He waited for three more rings, ten seconds between each ring. Unless Eland was lying low in there, the house was empty. It was as good a chance as they were ever going to get.

Rory looked around for a suitable instrument, picked up a brick which was propping up a sagging water butt and gritted his teeth.

He struck the glass with the end of the brick in a short jab. With a tinkle of broken glass, this produced a small jagged hole above the door handle. He listened for reaction from the neighbours. There was no immediate outcry or sound of new activity. He inserted a hand through the hole, found the key inside the door and let himself in.

He closed the door quickly behind him and walked through a small, smelly kitchen to a narrow front hall.

He could see Straker's silhouette on the reeded glass.

He opened the front door. 'Come in, quick!'

Straker stepped through and closed the door behind him.

'We'd better make sure he's not here first,' Rory whispered.

Henry nodded and they headed up the stairs.

Two minutes later they were back in the hall. 'If he's here, he doesn't want to see anyone,' Straker said.

'He's out. Everything's cold. Right, I'll search. You stand behind the curtain and keep watch. If he comes, we'll scarper.'

Rory, from his preliminary search, had already decided where he was going to look first. He opened the door opposite the living room into what had been built as an integral garage but was now kitted out as a photographic studio.

There was only one piece of furniture – an old metal filing cabinet – suitable for storing prints and negatives.

He walked across to it and tried the top drawer. It was locked. So were the two below it.

He went back to the kitchen and searched around for the largest knife he could find – a heavy, old-fashioned carving knife.

Back in the studio, he inserted the blade between the top of the first drawer and the frame of the cabinet. With a quick surge of strength, he jerked the knife forward. The blade snapped three inches from the handle, creating a much more useful tool.

He jammed it back into the slit, next to the lock, and slowly forced it up again.

With a sharp crack, the blade of the lock slipped free from the frame and Rory pulled the drawer out towards him, right out of its runners so that he could lift it to the ground. The other two came out with even less trouble.

It took him fifteen tense, fumbling minutes to find what he was looking for, a set of monochrome contact sheets at the back of the bottom drawer. He pulled an Anglepoise lamp out from the wall and switched it on. He put the sheet of small prints on a large Perspex light box, and picked up a square magnifying glass lying on it.

A moment later, he saw in clear-cut, well-lit detail just why Henry Straker had been so unwilling to describe the photographs to him.

Eland had shot three rolls of film. Like any experienced photographer, he knew that the more you took, the higher were your chances of the right shot. Shaking his head in disbelief, Rory studied each of the three sheets.

Every single shot was grotesquely compromising, but in the worst of them, the vet was lying naked on a bare mattress; his eyes were closed but there was a sleepy smile on his face, while two equally naked boys, nine or ten years old, manipulated his erect penis.

Rory was more shocked than he would have believed possible. He had heard about paedophilia, read odd pieces in the more sensational Sunday papers, but he had never really believed that this sort of thing actually went on, and he had certainly never seen such graphic illustrations of it.

Even more horrifying was the apparently obvious enjoyment the distinguished veterinary surgeon was deriving from the activity.

It made Henry Straker's otherwise inexplicable behaviour suddenly completely understandable. Even the vet's closest friends would have taken a great deal of convincing that the pictures, or the poses, had been faked.

And outside his job, what Henry Straker was best known for was his charity work with young boys.

Quickly, Rory checked through all the drawers and folders of photographs, containing lurid scenes of every conceivable type of sexual activity, to make certain he had all those which featured Henry Straker. When he was satisfied that there weren't any more there, he scooped up the three sheets and folded them into an inside pocket of his jacket. He also took a photograph of a small, insignificant-looking man being hugged by a tall, naked woman. The picture was inscribed with the words 'To Arthur. Best Wishes, Lucy Leather.'

He checked the rest of the studio and the ground-floor rooms of the house for any clue to who Eland's client might be.

Twenty minutes searching yielded no leads. He suspected that this sort of information, if it existed in any kind of written form, would be on Eland's person, or kept very close to it.

In the living room, on a teak coffee table marked with a circular black burn, he found a small racing diary. He wasn't surprised to see the names of the two horses which Straker had doped written against the dates they had run. On the following day, Tuesday, the name 'Fancyman' had been scrawled.

He slipped the diary into his pocket with the contact

sheets and went to search the upper rooms. He had a foot on the bottom step of the stairs when he heard Henry hiss a warning.

He didn't stop to make sure it was a genuine alarm. In a matter of seconds he was through the kitchen and out of the back door with Henry in time to hear a big-engined bike rev up and cut out on the street at the front of the house. They walked briskly up the path to the back gate and along the rear track to the alley, four houses away, and climbed back inside the Discovery.

'Back it up, quick, so if he comes out he won't see us,' Straker urged.

Rory started the engine and put the car into reverse. He turned and steered back round the curve of the road until the bike and the Jaguar were both out of sight.

Straker lowered his window. 'Turn the engine off so we can hear him if he leaves.'

Rory did as he was asked.

'How do you know he's going anywhere?'

'I don't, but did you make much of a mess in there?'

'Aye, a bit of minor destruction.'

'And did you take anything?'

Rory nodded. He found he didn't want to admit to Straker that he had even seen the photos.

'Then he's going to panic, isn't he? He's not going to ring the police, he's going to go out and look for what's missing. What else would he do?'

'What if he's seen the Discovery?'

'I don't think he registered it; anyway, that's a risk we'll have to take. He won't see it when he comes out, and he won't come this way because it's a dead end. If he did see it just now, he'll assume it was you and probably head off after you.'

Rory nodded. It wasn't a bad bet. 'We'll just have to play it by ear,' he said. 'Anyway, I've got the evidence.'

Straker glanced at him sharply. 'The photos?' he asked with a tremor of shame in his voice.

'Aye. You were right to be worried people would think they were genuine. This bastard Eland certainly knows what he's doing. Judging by what he was keeping in there, this isn't the first time. Trouble is, there's probably another set of prints or negatives somewhere else.'

'At least we've got this far, though,' Straker said. 'I can tell you, I didn't think we had a hope.'

'Sure. We'll just have to see where Eland leads us now. If he goes back to my place, we'll corner him there, then we'll have to let the police take over.'

Straker nodded slowly. 'Yes, you're right.'

As he spoke, they heard the metallic click of a Jaguar starter motor, and the shriek of a loose fan belt.

'He's off,' Straker said. 'Thank God, he hasn't taken the bike.'

Rory started his own engine, and the Discovery inched forward. They caught a glimpse of the Jaguar's tail reversing into the road, then spinning off towards the junction.

Rory waited another thirty seconds before he pulled out. 'Thank God I didn't bring the Rover.'

They pulled away and round the bend in the road just in time to see Eland's car turn left at the junction.

Cautiously, Rory followed, trying to remember everything he'd ever read or seen about tailing cars without being spotted.

He followed the Jaguar up the slip road on to the M4 towards London and let out a sigh of relief as they joined a solid three-lane stream of steadily moving traffic.

Chapter Thirteen

'Hell!' Rory hissed. 'He must have driven like shit off a shovel.'

They were dropping down from the Hammersmith fly-over into west London and they hadn't see a sign of Eland's car in the last ten minutes.

'He couldn't have got off anywhere since we last saw him, could he?' Straker said.

'Yes, he could have turned off at the North Circular.'

The traffic had slowed to three crawling queues. Rory clenched his fists on the steering wheel, trying to contain his frustration at having got so close to his quarry, only to lose the scent.

They had concluded that Eland, panicking, was on his way to see his paymaster.

Now, Rory fought to calm himself, to make a new plan. He picked up his phone and stabbed Edward Brickhill's number.

The financier wasn't answering and Rory was switched through to a secretary at his City office.

'I'm sorry, Mr Brickhill is unavailable at the moment,' a bright, efficient voice fluted back at him. 'If you'd like to leave a message, I'll make sure it reaches him as soon as possible.'

Rory gave her his name, stressed the urgency and gave her the number of his mobile phone. He was putting it angrily back in its cradle when Henry Straker gasped triumphantly, 'Look! That's him, isn't it?'

They were in the left-hand lane, moving faster than the others as cars filtered off. Rory looked where Straker pointed. From the commanding height of the Discovery, he saw the Jaguar. It was in the middle lane, six or seven cars ahead, spewing a faint cloud of black smoke from its exhaust pipes.

'Our mechanic chummy doesn't seem to have made too good a job of servicing it,' Rory laughed with relief. 'I hope the old heap doesn't break down before he gets to his man.'

'How are we going to handle it when we get there?' Straker asked, more positive now.

'We'll just play it by ear, but if we can identify whoever Eland goes to see, Edward Brickhill should be able to help.'

'Edward? What has he got to do with all this?'

'He's not so keen on his daughter being convicted of manslaughter. He's also a big fan of yours; he wouldn't hear of you being remotely involved and he organised a lot of the investigation we've done so far.'

'Thank God for that. I wish I'd known before. Edward's a powerful man to have on our side.'

They were heading down the Earl's Court Road, always

330

keeping in sight of the maroon XJ6, though Rory took no chances by getting too close.

On the Embankment, Eland lost them at two sets of lights. Each time they caught him up, but Straker was getting nervous.

'You'll have to get nearer to him, Rory.'

'But if he susses us, we've blown it.'

'If we lose him we've totally blown it. He's not going to be thinking about being followed now.'

Rory nodded. 'Okay. I'll try to keep one car between us.'

They played Grandmother's Footsteps with the Jaguar the length of the Embankment until they reached the City and turned up by the Mermaid Theatre.

'It looks like we might be getting there,' Rory said, his pulse beginning to race. 'We think our man is connected with a bookie called Square Mile Sporting – runs books on the Footsie index, share prices and that.'

'What's the connection? Do they take bets on horses, too?'

'Oh yes. We think Luke had been having a gamble on the price of his own shares, and taking a lot of money off them. When that all started to fall apart, he carried on with horses and began losing – big money. I mean, like a hundred and fifty grand. What Edward's people haven't found is anyone having a big bet on Midnight Express. But my gut feeling tells me Luke did – a very big one.'

Straker didn't answer.

Rory glanced across at him. The vet had resumed the guilty, haggard look of a few hours before.

'How did I let myself do it?' he said quietly. 'No man's

reputation is worth three lives. And now, the part I played in the interference with two horses will have to come out. I imagine that whatever happens, I'll be struck off.'

'Not necessarily,' Rory said, without believing it. 'Not if the police don't bring charges.' His eyes were fixed on the XJ6, two cars ahead and creeping up Queen Victoria Street.

Abruptly, Eland turned off into a narrow road where there was a small, rare cluster of parking meters, one of which was free. The Jaguar pounced into the space, while Rory cursed and drove on twenty yards. Pulling up, he looked in his mirror.

'He's got out and is heading back up to Queen Victoria Street. You're going to have to follow him – but for God's sake, don't let him see you. Just watch where he goes and follow him as far as you can without letting it show.'

Straker's muscles seemed suddenly to fill out and take on a new alertness. He nodded. 'Right.'

He climbed out of the Discovery and walked slowly up the street behind Eland's disappearing back.

Rory settled down to wait. The misgivings he'd had about sending Straker had dissipated when he saw the man's natural strength and resolve returning.

He tried to stay calm but kept his eyes fixed on his mirror, watching for Straker to come back.

Six minutes later, he was rewarded by the sight of the vet walking briskly and confidently towards him.

Straker opened the door and climbed in.

'Well?' Rory asked.

'I can't tell you his name, but the offices are occupied by the Anglo-Maltese Beef Company. It's on the fifth floor of the block just round the corner. Eland went up to the reception and came out a moment later. He walked across and buzzed the intercom on a private lift to the floor above and was let in. I came back down by the stairs. You're not going to believe what I found.' He looked at Rory jubilantly. 'On the floor below are the offices of Square Mile Sporting. It looks as though you were right.'

Rory grinned.

The phone bleeped.

'Hello,' Rory blurted into it.

'You rang.' Brickhill's voice.

'Thank God. We need some information.'

'What's that?'

'The name of whoever's behind something called the Anglo-Maltese Beef Company. There's a good chance he's connected with Square Mile Sporting – and if he is, that's our man.'

'The Anglo-Maltese Beef Company?'

'Aye. Offices in Queen Victoria Street.'

'Leave it with me.'

Eland fought to control the trembling in his knees as the private lift took him up to the second floor.

The small grey box reached its destination and the door hissed open. Eland stepped out into the soundless, sealed atmosphere. There was no sign of the secretary who had received him before; the place looked deserted.

He faced a large panelled door and felt himself scrutinised by a camera mounted discreetly above the deep architrave. He had been told that he should wait there when he arrived. He tried to stand still and felt a flush of sweat break out across every surface of his body.

The door was opened by the man who had been to visit Eland in Slough a month before. He wasn't wearing a Savile Row suit this time. He was naked from the waist up. Large globules of perspiration glittered through the thick black hair that covered his torso. His bare feet protruded from a soft black towel that was wrapped around his lower half.

His dark eyes burned up and down Eland's slight frame, then beckoned him in. He closed the door. Eland vaguely registered the large room where he had had his last encounter with his client. A slight haze of blue cigar smoke hung like cirrus cloud around the ceiling.

Facing him was a vast window with a southerly view over the tops of the office buildings that dropped away to the river. There was a dead unrealness to the view without its sounds and damp air.

'What do you want?' the large man growled.

There was nothing vulnerable about his semi-nudity.

'We've got to talk,' Eland stuttered.

'Is that so?'

'Yes. Someone raided my place this morning. We're in trouble.'

A rumble of humourless laughter rose from the hairy barrel of the other man's chest.

'We? Oh no.' A large index finger stabbed Eland between his ribs. 'You're in trouble. You fucked it up. Killing those people was very stupid.'

'But it was nothing to do with me,' Eland lied, hoping for inspiration.

'Gillespie's found his way to you. Let me tell you, that's

the end of the trail. If you should think of pointing the finger at me, there is absolutely nothing to implicate me.' He turned and started to walk across the room towards a door on the far side. Eland followed, as if drawn by a magnet. 'And what I can also tell you,' his client continued, 'is that if you try to involve me, you will be killed.' He was through the library and halfway across the bedroom. He turned and looked at Eland with a calm smile. 'You interrupted my sauna. Now leave. I don't want to hear from you again until Fancyman has run tomorrow.'

Eland stood, mid-step, irresolute. Of course, he'd known it would be a waste of time coming here, but he'd had to go to someone.

His client turned and carried on towards a narrow door between two chests of drawers. Before he opened it, he looked back over his shoulder. 'Goodbye. See yourself out.' He watched as Eland turned and walked back into the other room.

Eland padded across the deep carpet and opened the main door to the apartment. He opened it, and closed it.

Silently he turned and gazed, without seeing, through the picture window at the top of Tower Bridge. He waited until he had heard the click of the sauna door closing before he walked back across the footprints he had just left in the pile of the deep velvet Wilton carpet.

He paused at the entrance to the bedroom. He could hear no sounds from beyond the sauna door, sealed and insulated as it was. He saw with satisfaction, from the back of the hinges, that it opened out into the room. And he thanked his luck for the man's penchant for privacy and the lack of a window in the door.

He quickly glanced round to see what tools were at his disposal.

Beside the door to the sauna stood a massive Victorian mahogany chest of eight drawers. He walked across to it quickly and, putting his shoulder to one end, tried to slide it over the deep carpet. Despite the extra strength which the crisis had given him, it wouldn't move.

But he was calm now, and set on his plan. Without any fumbling or clumsiness, he removed the solidly made and heavily loaded drawers one by one and placed them behind him. Although the remaining empty carcass was a substantial piece, he found this time when he put his shoulder to it that after a moment's reluctance it moved slowly over the carpet and across the door of the sauna.

When he was satisfied that it was wedged under the wooden handle as tightly as possible, he efficiently and accurately replaced the eight heavy drawers. The whole operation had taken ninety seconds.

The temperature controls for the sauna were set to the side of the door, just above the top of the chest. He switched the small black dial to its maximum.

To test his barrier, he put his shoulder against the side of the chest and tried to shove it with every ounce of strength he could summon. It didn't budge a centimetre. He stood back, satisfied that even the substantial bulk of the man trapped behind it would not be able to move the door and the chest together.

Finally, he picked up a comb from the top of the chest and wedged the sliding panel of timber over the air slot so that it couldn't be opened from the inside.

He allowed a sulky grin to cross his face. 'Time you

lost some weight, you fat bastard!' he muttered as he padded back through the bedroom, the library and the flashy drawing room to the front door of the apartment.

Out in the lobby, the lift waited with the door open.

A minute later, he stepped out of the warm office building into the soggy, blustering March wind and the noise of the traffic swishing and roaring along Queen Victoria Street.

He turned the corner. The street was empty apart from three cars in the spaces either side of his. He walked quickly down to the Jaguar and got into it. He noticed with automatic relief that he hadn't been awarded a parking ticket, and started the engine.

He was driving west along the Embankment with the Temple on his right when he felt a cold, hard circle press into the thin flesh on the side of his neck.

'You've gone the wrong way, Arthur.'

Eland's hands jerked on the wheel. The courage temporarily granted him in the penthouse had left him. He opened his mouth to speak, but it was too dry for words to come.

'We're going to Bermondsey,' the voice behind went on. 'Cross over Westminster Bridge when you get there.'

It was a man's voice – the voice of a pro.

'Do we wait for Eland to come back out?' Straker asked when Rory had finished talking to Brickhill.

'No. No point. We've done all we can do here for the moment. And while he's in there, he's out of his house. We'll get back there and see what else we can find.'

'Break in again, you mean?' Despite everything he had

done over the last few weeks, Straker's strong regard for the rule of law was still intact.

'Yes. I didn't have time to search upstairs.'

'Okay,' Straker agreed.

They were crawling along the Fulham Road when Rory's phone bleeped.

'Rory?'

'Hello, Edward. What have you got?'

'Nothing yet. This Anglo-Maltese Beef Company, whatever it is, isn't registered at Companies House, or anywhere else, so we're having to go through other channels, using the address – rates, landlords and so on.'

'What will that tell you?'

'It might throw up the name we're looking for. I'll send a snooper round to his office, too, but this character's well skilled in keeping a low profile. What are you doing now?'

'Henry Straker's with me. We're on our way back to the house in Slough where the photos were taken. I've already got one set of prints from there, but we think we could find more leads as to who's employed this guy Eland, the photographer.'

'Well, be careful. The man's already killed twice, so he's got nothing to lose.'

On the way out of London, Rory stopped in the North End Road outside a baker's. Henry went in and bought a bagful of rolls. Neither of them had eaten since the evening before.

Half an hour later, the Discovery nosed into the drab cul-de-sac where Eland's house had stood; where what was left of it now stood.

They couldn't get within fifty yards of it. The road was cordoned off with police tape, and three fire engines revved loudly to pump between them a thousand gallons of water a minute at the blazing, blackened brick box.

Rory gazed at the annihilation of Eland's seedy dwelling and felt his guts quake.

Henry Straker was appalled. 'For God's sake, Rory. This is out of our league. Don't worry about my problems. We're going to have to go to the police now.'

Rory was thinking fast.

'Not yet. If Eland's client is having the place burnt, it's because he doesn't want any trace of the shots or the blackmail to be found – anything that might lead back to him. It's possible the only copies of the shots left are the ones in my pocket. And these people might just come to the conclusion that I've got them.'

'But how are we going to explain what was done to those two horses? How Luke Mundy was killed? Unless we do, Laura's still going to take the rap.'

'As far as the police are concerned there's only Midnight Express to explain. Over to you, Chief Veterinary Officer. Meanwhile,' Rory said, three-point-turning his vehicle, 'I think we'll get out of here.'

Three-quarters of an hour later, a Japanese jeep turned off the road on to a dirt track which marked the course of the ancient Neolithic route along the ridge behind Camp Farm.

The track was hedged with overgrown, straggling hawthorn. It gave little protection from the insistent south-westerly that had been blowing all day, but it was enough to stop the vehicle being seen from the valley to the south, where Rory Gillespie's house and barns nestled.

The two men in the car clad themselves in waxed jackets and rainproof hats and climbed out. Despite the rain, they both wore trainers on their feet. They walked back a hundred yards to a point where a stand of small beeches struggled up to the ridge from a steep, scrub-grown gully. Thirty feet below the ridge, a spring welled from a boggy patch in the thin-soiled sheep pasture. A brook appeared in the gully, where alders and sycamore had been encouraged to grow.

The older of the two men, about forty, with no spare fat and still, grey eyes, consulted the map he held.

'This'll be the best way down,' he said over his shoulder. 'We should be in the trees right down to the yard.'

Ten minutes of slipping down the chalky bed of the busy brook brought them to a point thirty feet from the back of Rory's range of timber-clad stables.

Dennis, the leader of the operation, raised his head over the shallow bank and peered through the spindly tree trunks. He was just able to see the back of the house.

He heard a horse in one of the stables stamp on a bare patch of concrete in his box. Others, wrapped in green canvas rugs, were grazing in the paddock beyond.

There was no sign of any other living being around the yard. Dennis beckoned Mac, his back-up, to follow.

Keeping low, they ran across to the stable block. When they reached it, they worked their way round the back until they could look round the edge with a clear view of the house and the forecourt.

Rory's sign-written Rover and the Discovery stood on the gravel.

Dennis allowed a thin smile to cross his lips. Two targets meant two fees. The contact sheets were worth another grand, and he guessed Gillespie still had them. He'd had the Discovery in sight most of the way from Queen Victoria Street after he'd left Bernie there to deal with Eland. It hadn't stopped anywhere long enough for anyone to dispose of anything and Eland had told Bernie that the photos he'd kept for himself were definitely gone. Dennis wondered what Bernie was doing to the little runt now. He turned to his back-up.

'They're home.'

Mac nodded and felt the adrenaline squirting into his system. He was half his leader's age, and five stone heavier. He'd lost count of how many men he had stalked and, frequently, despatched, but the excitement of it had never diminished. He'd left Glasgow only a month before to work for Dennis. It had been a great move; the quality of the work was so much higher, and much better paid.

He nodded with a smile and felt for the army-issue Browning in his pocket.

Dennis looked at his watch. 'It'll be dark in an hour. We'll wait.'

'What if they go again?'

'We'll have to follow – take whichever car they don't. But there's no way we can get to the house now without showing ourselves. If we're seen, we've got no chance. I'll see what I can do to make sure they stay put.'

He crouched back into the shelter of the stable wall, pulled a small mobile phone from his pocket and dialled a London number.

'Hello. It's Den. How's it goin'?' Dennis laughed at the

reply. 'Good. I'll ring you in about an hour to find out if there's more. Meantime, I want you to do something. Ring our friend down here and tell him you're from Thames Valley CID and you want to see him. Tell him you're coming over and you'll be there in about an hour, and he's not to leave until you get there ... Yes, that'll do fine. Cheers.'

Dennis switched off and put the instrument in his pocket with a satisfied nod. 'That should keep 'em there till it's dark. Christ, I wish that fuckin' horse would give it a break!' he added as Long Run in the box behind them carried on stamping and snorting and whinnying.

'Are you sure you want to stay here?' Rory asked Henry. 'I wouldn't blame you if you didn't.'

'I'm not going to run out now. If they come here, you're going to need help.'

'They'll come,' Rory said with certainty. The grey Toyota had joined the M4 behind them, and left it with them. And Henry had spotted it again, a mile back, as they dropped down into Lambourn.

'But I still think we should call the police,' Henry said.

'We will, once we're sure there aren't any more of those photos anywhere. If you do decide to admit to doping Midnight Express and the other horse, people are bound to think the shots were genuine, aren't they?'

Straker nodded glumly.

Rory went on, 'But if we can get the blame pinned on this Anglo-Maltese Beef bloke, we should be able to get both you and Laura off the hook.'

As he spoke, the telephone rang. He picked it up.

'Yeah, speaking ... Okay, I'll be here.'

He put the phone down and looked at Straker with a shrug. 'That was a man from CID, wants to come and see me here in about an hour. If nothing's happened by then, we'll tell him, okay?'

Straker nodded. 'I haven't much choice, Rory.'

Rory couldn't disguise his relief. 'Right, we'd better get ready.'

Upstairs they switched on a bedroom light and covered the windows of rooms on each side of the house. Rory opened some of them as listening posts, though the wind didn't help. On the ground floor, they turned on the television in the drawing room, lit a fire to give an illusion of normality and drew the curtains.

From a toolshed outside the back door, they selected weapons – an iron wrecking bar and a five-pound club hammer – to supplement Rory's one shotgun.

In the drawing room, the dry chestnut logs were burning well. Rory pulled the sheets of small black-and-white photographs from his pocket and dropped them in the flames.

Both men sensed a symbolic release as they watched the paper curl and disintegrate beneath a violet-blue flame.

Rory turned down the volume on the television and they went back upstairs to survey the landscape on all sides of the house.

The wind had dropped a little as Rory stared up the darkening valley behind the house. Between gusts, he caught the sound of Long Run snorting and whinnying in his stable. After a moment, he went to find Henry on the other side of the house.

'Long Run's making a hell of a fuss about something.

He may just be hungry, but it doesn't sound like it. I think there may be somebody up there.'

Straker came and listened. 'I think you're right, but it could be anything disturbing him. Assuming they don't just drive up, which way will they come?'

'I don't know, it depends what they know about the place, but the best way would be down that gully from the top of the ridge.'

'One of them's come out, look,' Mac hissed with disgust.

They watched a figure in a long coat cross the forecourt and climb into the Discovery.

'Not tall enough for the vet,' Dennis murmured. 'Must be the jockey. We can't do nothing about it. We'll have to deal with him later.'

They saw the car disappear down the lane to the main road and turn towards Hungerford.

Ten minutes later, they came out from behind the stable block.

It was dark now, but the cloud was breaking up and a three-quarter moon shed intermittent pale cream light.

Henry Straker peered out from a black upper room with his eyes tuned to the dark. He had been there twenty minutes, since Rory had left, and he caught the movement clearly.

God, don't let me mess this up, he breathed to himself.

They wouldn't try to come in by the front porch – that would mean opening two doors. This left them a choice of two back doors. Straker had to commit himself to one of them. He reduced the odds in his favour by locking one. The other which he left unlocked gave into a small utility room more suitable for his purposes.

He went through to the drawing room and turned up the volume on the television, which was showing an early-evening game show, with a lot of shrieking laughter and screams of encouragement from the studio audience.

Outside, the two men circled the house like a pair of hunting dogs.

They rejected the front entrance. Close up to the wall, they sidled towards the one lighted, but heavily curtained window on the ground floor.

They listened and caught the sound of laughter and screams of delight, and backed away.

'There's two doors round the back,' Dennis said. 'We'll take one each. If you get to him before me, don't kill him. I need to talk to him first.'

'Right.'

They worked their way round to the back of the house again.

'You take that door,' the Londoner whispered.

Mac slipped across to the small collection of sheds and outhouses that clustered at the back of the house and melted into the dark.

More slowly, his leader circled his way to a door which he guessed from the layout of the windows opened into the kitchen.

Henry Straker stood on a small stool behind the door into the scullery.

He heard the handle turn. His throat dried. With a

shaking arm, he raised the club hammer seven feet from the ground.

When it made contact, it made surprisingly little noise – less than the thud and clatter as the man fell to the quarry-tiled floor.

Surprised and oddly alarmed by his success, Straker stepped off the stool and crouched, shaking, beside his victim. The man seemed to be unconscious but he was still breathing. Straker put down the hammer and felt around the floor until he found the man's gun. He stood up and listened to the sound of the television show, his heart thumping against his chest. Harming anyone, even when they were prepared to do serious damage, was totally alien to Straker.

He waited for a full minute, nervous and unsure.

For God's sake, he told himself, you've got to do something.

The back door was still open, letting in sharp gusts of wind. If anyone was coming that way, they'd have come by now.

Straker walked towards the door that gave into the large central hall of the house. He poked his head through. The light from the drawing room left the corners of the hall in darkness. He took a step forward, holding the Browning in front of him with a shaking hand.

'Drop it or I'll blow your fuckin' head off.'

Straker felt an involuntary wetness dribble between his legs. He dropped the gun and turned his head towards the voice in the kitchen doorway.

'Now kick it across the floor to me.'

Straker kicked it, disgusted at his own cowardice.

The man emerged from the shadows. He had a short-nosed automatic trained on Straker's head and he was smiling.

'Good boy,' he said. 'Now, if you don't want me to hurt you, you can do something else for me. Tell me where the photos are.'

Straker tried to speak. He produced a croaking cough. 'Oh no, you'll have to do better than . . .'

The explosion deafened Straker for a moment.

He watched as the man with the gun dropped it, clutched his stomach and crumpled slowly to the floor. A thin cloud of smoke drifted into the hall, accompanied by the acrid smell of cordite.

Rory, with a finger on the second trigger of his shotgun, stepped over the khaki heap that the man had become.

'Where's the other one?' he asked quickly.

Straker opened his mouth in a startled shout. 'Behind you!'

Rory turned too late. The hammer caught him a hard, glancing blow on the side of the face. His legs sagged and he collapsed to the ground beside his own victim. Through the pain, at a distance from himself somehow, he heard a sharp report, and he was crushed beneath the limp weight of the other man's huge frame.

Unexpectedly, the weight was removed, dragged across him, and Henry was talking to him. 'Rory? Rory? Are you all right?'

Rory's mouth was full of blood and his nose full of mucus. He wanted to tell Henry, but he couldn't.

He felt the vet's arms wriggle beneath him and lift him, carry him, then lower him gently on to a soft surface.

'Okay, don't move,' Straker breathed. 'I'll be back.'

Rory didn't want to move. It hurt too much. He didn't want to open his eyes. He ordered himself to sleep.

Lights from a crystal chandelier which Rory had won in Ireland were shining brightly into his eyes when he flickered them open.

Henry had called the police. The detective inspector who had been at Camp Farm two days before was looking down at him.

'You have been in the wars, haven't you, Mr Gillespie?'

Rory coughed to clear his throat. 'For God's sake, can't you think of anything more original than that?'

The policeman laughed. 'That's good. There's no brain damage then.'

Rory, with his wounds bathed and deftly dressed by the vet, was sore and swollen, but soon able to sit up on his bloodstained sofa.

The man who had hit him was already in hospital, having a bullet from his own gun removed from his left lung.

The second intruder, hit in the back with Eley No. 4 shot from Rory's shotgun at a distance of six feet, was in worse shape, the policeman told Rory. There was a chance he would be paralysed, but he would live.

'Mr Straker's told us what happened, but of course we'll need to hear your version, Mr Gillespie,' the detective said.

Rory glanced at Straker, standing behind the policeman. He shook his head. 'Not yet.'

'That's okay. I've got to get back and talk to your two

visitors. We've done all we need to here. Maybe Mr
Straker would bring you down to the nick in an hour or
so, or I'll come back up. You let me know. But I'll need
to see you this evening.'

'Sure.'

To Rory's relief, they went, leaving the house bright
and silent.

'What did you tell them?' Rory asked as soon as the
police car drove away.

'I told them that someone was trying to blackmail me,'
Straker said simply. 'And that you'd found out who.'

Rory sighed. 'Did you tell them *how* you were being
blackmailed?'

'No. I just said they'd faked some photographs.'

'What about stopping the horses?'

Straker shook his head with shame.

'Thank God for that!' Rory grinned.

'It just means that when they do find out, I'll be in
even more serious trouble.'

'Then we've got to make sure they don't.' Rory smiled.
'Who would they get to run the boys' club football team?
It would be really selfish to admit to the whole thing and
deprive them of a manager.'

'I'd like to believe that, Rory, but the truth's bound to
come out sooner or later. And for God's sake, I did it!'

'You didn't instigate the crime. You did what anyone
else would have done in your position.'

'But, Rory, what about Luke? Your wife, for heaven's
sake?'

'You didn't kill them.'

'Look, I just don't think I can live the lie. And anyway,

when they pick up Eland, he's bound to tell them about me.'

'You told them about Eland?'

'Yes, of course. I had to.'

Rory grunted. 'I suppose you did. Though God knows what they'll deduce from the fact that Eland's house has been burnt to the ground.'

'I said that we guessed he was being paid by someone else.'

'What about Eland's visit to Queen Victoria Street?'

'I thought it might be wiser to wait until we had a name from Edward Brickhill. Of course, when we do, if we pass it on to the police, he's going to tell them about my involvement, if Eland hasn't.'

Rory sank back on to the sofa with a sigh. 'I wish to God you'd left it to me, Henry. We're just going to have to rely on your word against theirs. I thought we'd have heard from Edward by now,' he added. As he spoke, the phone rang. 'That'll be him now.'

Rory stood for the first time since he had been hammered to the ground. He staggered a little, found his balance and limped out to the kitchen to pick up the phone.

'Hello?'

'Hello, it's me.'

'Laura!'

'You sound surprised.'

'I was expecting to hear from your father.'

'What's been going on then?'

'A lot. I can't tell you now. Can you get up here, now?'

'Okay,' she said, picking up the urgency in his voice.

'But just tell me, are you going to be all right to ride Flamenco Dancer tomorrow? I've declared you to ride, but you still haven't passed the doctor.'

With an effort, Rory jerked his mind back to his job. 'I don't know. I've had a bit more damage inflicted.'

'Oh no! Who by?'

'I'll tell you when you come. But look, I'll probably be okay. Will Rutherford mind if I'm not one hundred percent fit?'

Laura gave a hint of a laugh. 'Haven't you heard?'

'Heard what?'

'About George. It's been on all the news on telly. He was found asphyxiated in his own sauna.'

'Bloody hell! When was this?'

'They found him this afternoon in a penthouse in Queen Victoria Street.'

'It wasn't above the Anglo-Maltese Beef Company, was it?' Rory blurted.

'Yes, why?'

'Shit!' Rory hissed breathily.

'Why? What about it?'

'Get yourself round here and I'll tell you.'

'Tell me now.'

'No.'

'I'll be there in twenty minutes.'

'No. Don't kill yourself!'

She laughed and put the phone down.

Straker had followed Rory into the kitchen. He looked at him, eyes wide for information.

'Rutherford!' Rory shouted. 'George Rutherford! He's the man at Anglo-Maltese!'

'Are you sure?'

'Almost positive.'

'I *knew* there was something fishy about him. I never trusted him.' Straker paled. 'He's never going to take the rap for what I did.'

Rory laughed. 'Oh yes he is. He already has. He's dead.' Straker's jaw sagged. 'Dead?'

'Aye. It must have been Eland. Banged him into his sauna and boiled him.' Rory laughed as he opened a bottle of Glenmorangie and poured an inch into two glasses. 'Eland must have been desperate; I guess Rutherford was going to drop him right into the shit on his own without a life belt.'

'My God! Then Eland will really be on the run now. He'll probably try to use those bloody photographs again.'

Rory handed him a glass. 'Just relax. He may not have any and he knows we're on to him. The police are looking for him. He's not going to do anything with those shots now.'

'But he could. He could threaten to send them to the papers; the awful Sunday tabloids would love it!'

Rory understood Straker's panic, but he wasn't going to share it. 'Henry, like I said, if it comes to it, it'll be your word against his as far as the doping goes. What we've got to do now is make sure Rutherford gets the blame.' Rory spoke with a conviction he didn't feel. It would be even harder for the police to extract anything from a dead George Rutherford than a live one. 'And I'm supposed to be riding two horses tomorrow. Where the hell am I going to find a doctor to pass me fit?'

Henry Straker hated lying, and he particularly hated lying to the police.

No, he told them, he had not been asked to pay anything or do anything since the first photos had arrived in the post.

He told them that he'd already reported how he had been drugged and then, with stumbling embarrassment, how the shots had been posed.

The ashes of Eland's house had revealed nothing useful beyond confirming that there had been a photographic studio in the garage. The police accepted Straker's statement that the three photos he had received had been destroyed. They made a note of the descriptions of the boys.

It was Rory who told them about following Eland to Queen Victoria Street, and the offices of the Anglo-Maltese Beef Company.

The Met. were called in. The hunt for Eland was given priority status.

The most senior detective in the Thames Valley police arrived at Newbury police station to talk to Rory.

'We're dealing with three murders here,' he stated baldly. 'To cover up a crime which hadn't been committed.'

'You're wrong there, Chief Superintendent. Luke Mundy's death started all this. I guess he had a lot of money on Midnight Express, and I think you'll find it was with George Rutherford. The horse was doped, lost its footing and killed Mundy, which Mrs Mundy has been charged with. You've got that all wrong. I can tell you Luke was betting heavily, and losing with Square Mile Sporting. If you dig deep enough, you'll find that Square Mile Sporting belonged to Rutherford.'

'And where do you think blackmailing Henry Straker comes into this?'

Rory took a deep breath. 'I think he was set up so that Rutherford could take advantage of his position as Jockey Club Chief Veterinary Officer. Henry Straker has a very high profile both in racing and in his work with children. He's always been outspoken on public and private morals, particularly in racing, which makes his reputation much more vulnerable than most people's. Though the shots were so convincing they could have been very damning, I guess Rutherford didn't bargain for Henry's absolute sense of duty and honour.'

Rory paused, to underline his words, and to see how the detective was taking them. But the policeman's eyes were issuing no messages. Rory shrugged his shoulders.

'Anyway, Henry hadn't done anything, but Luke was dead, and Laura was the main suspect. I began snooping around and I'm afraid that's why my house was raided twice last week when my wife . . . and Dai Price were killed. And again tonight. What started as a simple plan to stop a horse from winning had got totally out of hand. From thinking he'd covered his tracks, Eland suddenly realised he was liable for manslaughter. I guess that when Rutherford knew Eland was on his way up to see him, he ordered all traces of the scam to be destroyed, especially now there were two murders involved. And he thought I had some copies of the photos.'

'Why did you get yourself mixed up in it?'

'Because I knew Laura Mundy wasn't responsible for her husband's death, and she asked me to help her prove it.'

'Don't you think that might have been better left to us?'

Rory grinned. 'No, and apparently I was right. I *knew*

Laura hadn't done it, but as far as your people were concerned, it was bloody obvious she had. As it's turned out, I think I did the right thing.'

'And I'm told it was touch and go for a while that you might have been charged with shooting your wife and Price.'

'Aye, well, I accept it didn't look too good for me when your boys arrived. And I had to lie to them about the reason for the break-in. It's lucky I did, isn't it, because if I'd put you on to Eland, he'd never have led you to Rutherford.'

'And Rutherford would never have been killed,' the detective added drily.

'George Rutherford is no great loss to society.'

'It's not our job to make judgements about victims, merely to prevent and prosecute crime.' The policeman paused. 'But I take your point. Right,' he went on, switching off the tape recorder that had been running, 'I'll have this transcribed, and then you can sign it. Is there anything else you want to add?'

Rory shook his head, and prayed that Henry hadn't had a fit of remorseful honesty in the adjacent room where he was being questioned.

Chapter Fourteen

Rory let himself back into Camp Farm just after ten. He was carrying a bag of hot silver-foil containers from a Chinese takeaway in Newbury. He dumped them on the kitchen table and walked through the hall into the drawing room.

Edward Brickhill stood up. 'As someone's bust your back door again, I let myself in.'

Rory nodded. 'I saw your car. Have you poured yourself a drink?'

'No, but you look as though you need one.'

'You're darn right,' Rory replied and walked across to a drinks cabinet. 'Will you have one now?'

Brickhill nodded. 'I've been trying to get you all evening on the phone. Eventually I tried the police station on the off chance and they told me you were on your way back here. I suppose you've already heard what happened at the Anglo-Maltese Beef Company?'

Rory laughed. 'I heard. Laura told me, but of course she didn't know anything about the connection.'

'Does she now?'

'Sure. I've just seen her. She brought me back from Newbury nick.'

'What the hell were you doing there?'

'It's a long story.'

Rory told him as clearly as he could what had happened that evening. Brickhill didn't interrupt him until he'd described his interrogation by the senior detective.

'Where does this leave Laura?' he asked.

'Still on remand, I'm afraid. They believe that Rutherford was trying to set Straker up, but until they've got something that specifically ties him in with the doping, Laura's their prime target.' Rory shrugged. 'If Henry confesses to it, she'll be off the hook, but Henry would certainly go down. As it stands, they've only really got a circumstantial case against Laura. Unless they can come up with some strong forensic evidence, I don't think they'll stand it up. At the moment, she's prepared to take the risk. Henry says if it looks as though it's going against her, he'll own up.'

Brickhill nodded slowly. 'So we're balanced between a rock and a hard place.'

'Laura's been bloody brave about it, though. She's been under terrible pressure these last few weeks.'

'Is she going to Cheltenham tomorrow?'

Rory grinned. 'Oh aye. She thinks Flamenco Dancer will win. Mind you, it's not certain to run, now its owner is dead.'

'Are you riding it, if it does?' Brickhill looked doubtfully at Rory's bandages.

'Aye, Flamenco Dancer and Shebeen for Laura, and

Dayglow in the Champion Hurdle. I had a good session with the physio on Saturday and she's coming round here tomorrow morning. I think I'll be able to get past the quack.'

'But can you really ride?'

'Sure I can.'

'I hope so, for Laura's sake. Right, I'd better be going. I'll be in touch tomorrow.'

When he could see the Bentley's tail lights travelling down the lane, Rory remembered his Chinese food. He found that it was now only lukewarm. He put it in the oven and while it was heating, picked up the phone to call Tommy in Scotland.

'How's it going, Tommy?' Rory asked gently.

'Oh, okay. But I miss you . . .' There were a few moments of silence before he continued. 'At least I've still got you.'

'Listen, your mum wouldn't have wanted us to be miserable, would she?'

'No.'

'Of course not. So are you all right otherwise?'

'Yeah. I've been fishing and Grandad's been tying more flies with me.' The boy sounded brighter.

'That's great. Make a few for me; we'll use them when we get up to Wales.'

'If we ever get there,' Tommy laughed.

'We'll get there, don't you worry.'

When Rory put the phone down, he couldn't help feeling guilty at the great weight that seemed to have been lifted from him. He looked round at all the things in his house that reminded him of the unhappy life he had been leading and, guilty again, wondered how the hell he had put up with it.

He also tried hard to remember the good things about Pam, in a way he wouldn't have done if she had still been alive.

Whatever her faults, she had always been ready to enjoy life and have a good time. There was absolutely no way she had deserved to be killed.

And he wondered what Tommy would think about a new mum.

After the physiotherapist had been next morning, Laura called for Rory on her way to Cheltenham.

'Hell,' she said as he got into the car, 'you can't go looking like that. Let's go back inside and tidy you up a bit.'

Grumbling, Rory climbed out of the car and let Laura into his house.

'God, what a mess,' she said looking round. 'Where's Taffy?'

Rory gave her a bleak glance. 'They killed him too, the bastards!'

'Oh, no! Oh, Rory, I'm so sorry. I know what it must feel like. I suppose he was trying to guard the house for you.'

Rory nodded. 'Aye.' Then, pulling himself together, 'I'm sorry. I haven't had a chance to clear up after the first break-in, let alone the second and third.'

'And you look a bloody mess yourself. Have you seen the bruises round your eyes?'

Rory laughed. 'I've tried not to look in the mirror.'

'If you go to the races looking like that, someone's going to stop you riding. Are you sure you're up to it anyway?'

'I wouldn't have said I'd do it if I weren't.'

'If you'd got up from a fall looking like that, the quack would have banned you for a few days.'

'Yes, well, I didn't,' Rory said with a grin.

'How's the shoulder?'

For a reply, Rory slowly swung his arm up until it was vertical. He managed it without a wince.

'Very impressive. Are you sure you can do it, though?'

'I'm sure. Stop fussing.'

'Of course I'm fussing. Both the horses you're riding for me today could win.'

The Honorary Medical Officer looked sceptical as Rory stood in front of him in the medical room at Cheltenham racecourse.

'What about those bruises around your eyes?'

'That's nothing, honest, Doc. Just knocked myself on the wing when I came down last week. It's giving me no trouble.'

'All right. Just stand back and lean forward on to the desk with your left arm, and slowly push yourself back up.'

Rory did as he was asked.

'Okay, now raise your arm to the horizontal . . . Okay, now the vertical.'

Rory hoped the doctor couldn't see how tight his jaw was clamped. He managed the manoeuvre without twitching a muscle on his face.

'Okay, let it down slowly,' the doctor ordered.

Rory held his breath and lowered the arm.

'Well,' the doctor said, 'I suppose you're old enough to know better than to go out with a dicky shoulder. Here you are.'

He scribbled a medical certificate and pushed it across the desk to Rory.

'Thanks, Doctor.'

Outside, Rory gave a grunt and circled his shoulder in its socket, thinking that he wasn't quite as old as the doctor supposed.

Declan Hoolihan knew he was going to be on television. He was wearing a new petrol-green fleece jacket he had bought himself for the occasion as he led Flamenco Dancer into the parade ring. He looked after both the horses that Langlands had sent to Cheltenham that day. Over the last six months, he'd done a lot of work on Jimmy – Flamenco Dancer – and even more on Shebeen, who was running in the fourth. As far as he was concerned this was the most important day of the year.

Flamenco Dancer was running in the name of the Executors of the Late Mr George Rutherford. Laura watched with quiet confidence as the gelding walked round the ring with his long, deceptively languid stride.

She just hoped the horse would have the stamina to do most of the work himself; his jockey wasn't going to give him a lot of help. It was the first time in her career she had allowed her emotions to interfere with her choice of jockey. Common sense told her she should have booked someone else.

Laura legged Rory up into the saddle and the tension

rose among the bulging band of spectators round the ring as the race drew nearer.

Rory sensed the atmosphere and wished he could respond to it in the way he usually did, but his adrenal glands had been overworked in the last two weeks. He'd thought several times that morning – at home, in Laura's car on the way – about getting off the ride, but he didn't want to let her down, didn't want her to see him weaken, so to speak, in the final furlong. Rutherford may have been dead, but she still wasn't off the hook.

Flamenco Dancer bounced him down the walkway that led on to the course, aggravating his shoulder as he went. The punters were ten deep on either side, straining for a closer look at their fancies.

Declan unclipped the leading rein from Flamenco Dancer's bit. The gelding gave a couple of steps of showy piaffe before getting back on his quarters and cantering happily away in front of the stands.

Laura and Patrick between them had trained the horse to the peak of its form. It looked in a different league to the other eight runners as they headed back down to the two mile start below the last line of marquees. Apart from standing a couple of inches taller, it had a massive frame that rippled with muscle under its conker-coloured coat. Here was a horse built for jumping at speed and, thankfully for Rory, it was a professional. It didn't pull at all, just took a firm hold of the bit, did what was asked and got on with the job in hand. Now that Rory's body had warmed up, the stiffness began to fade from his muscles. Apart from the worry of his shoulder, he felt fine. The few moments spent circling at the start, waiting for the race to get underway, discussing tactics with the other jockeys, had got the adrenaline flowing quickly around his body. The muscles in his stomach began to contract, his mouth become dry. As the starter called them into line, Rory took several deep breaths, coaxing his body back into working order, letting it take in the oxygen he needed.

Flamenco Dancer had no such problems. As they were coming under orders Rory could sense that the horse was keen to get away. He deliberately let it miss the break, settling it in fifth on the inside.

The going was just on the soft side of good, which Flamenco Dancer liked. As they flew the first three fences, Rory kept glued to the running rail. The horse in front was setting a good, even gallop; all Rory had to do was keep Flamenco Dancer balanced, ensuring that he didn't make any serious mistakes at the fences as the race developed. He didn't mind when he went to the front, as long as he was still there at the winning post.

At the second and final open ditch, the horse in front misjudged his stride and clattered the heavy wooden guard rail. It didn't fall, but for a half-dozen strides it lost its rhythm and Rory eased round, letting Flamenco Dancer move to within six lengths of the leaders.

On the top of the hill on the far side, with three fences still to jump, Rory was breathing right down their necks. He could hardly believe how easily he was travelling. The next couple of tricky downhill fences were always much simpler to negotiate when you weren't under pressure. Rory bided his time, his main concern being that one of the three horses in front might fall and bring him down. With that in mind, he eased Flamenco Dancer to the outside. Four of them in a line flew the third last and raced on towards the next fence. Rory looked across quickly at the trio on his inner; he had each of them cracked. He'd wait until he'd landed safely over the second last and then go for home.

All four horses were travelling at top speed but Rory knew he had won the race; that knowledge made him indecisive and Flamenco Dancer, not getting any particular signals as to where to take off, guessed at the last moment. Only a superb sense of balance kept the horse on its feet as it launched itself much too soon and came down through the stiff birch. The horse's nose almost touched the ground as it struggled to stay upright. Moving its feet quickly it bounced back to catch Rory's body as he came forward. Rory screamed as a vicious stab of pain ripped into his shoulder.

Despite all the massage, the stretched and weakened ligaments hadn't recovered from the damage they'd suffered. The ball had slipped from its socket and every nerve in his shoulder was screaming.

Rory was now nothing more than a passenger. He gripped as tightly as he could with his knees in a desperate attempt to keep the movement of his arm to a minimum. He held both reins in his other hand, crouching over Flamenco Dancer like a drunk as the horse galloped around the long turn towards the last fence. Rory braced himself for the inevitable surge of pain that would come from the jolt of jumping. He tensed his body as Flamenco Dancer ran on gamely. As the horse's feet thudded soundly on to the turf, Rory cried out and fought to stay conscious, but his vision was blurring fast. Winning the race didn't matter any more. His whole body was begging him to stop the pain. Flamenco Dancer stretched his legs to stay with the other horses but carrying a dead weight on his back was too much for him.

Laura knew immediately what had happened and ran down to the course, pushing her way through the crowds.

Now back to the relative comfort of a walk, Rory began to recover. He was being helped by one of the other jockeys when Declan and Laura came running towards him.

'Are you all right?' Laura asked breathlessly, as she reached up to put her hand on Rory's knee, while Declan clipped the lead rein on to the bridle.

'My shoulder,' muttered Rory through his clenched jaw.

'I thought so. You'd better stay on board. It'll be easier than walking back. We'd better get you straight to a doctor.'

'I'm sorry, Laura.' Rory's blue eyes were watering from the pain.

'It doesn't matter. Dad'll be able to buy Flamenco Dancer for twenty grand less than he'd planned!' Laura tried to make light of her disappointment.

Rory forced a laugh through his aching chest. 'What about Shebeen?'

'I'll find someone else to ride him. Don't worry about it.'

'Declan's still got his licence hasn't he, and his allowance?'

'Yes, but he's only had a couple of rides this season.'

'Give him the ride on Shebeen; he'll ride it as well as

anyone else you could get now, and he knows the horse better than anyone.'

Declan held his breath waiting for his boss's reply. Laura looked at him and gave a short laugh. 'Why not?'

From the stands, Rory watched Declan Hoolihan win his first ever race at Cheltenham.

The lad had put his heart and soul into it, and his knowledge of the horse had paid off. The result more than made up for Rory's own failure in the Champion Chase.

A few minutes later in the winner's enclosure, Patrick Hoolihan was red-faced and almost bursting with pride as he led his son in.

When the prize-giving formalities were over Laura and Patrick led the horse back to the stables.

'It was very good of you to give the boy the chance,' Patrick said as he and Laura walked away from the paddock.

'It was Rory's idea, actually. As Declan's done so much work with the horse I thought he'd do as well as anyone else. In fact he did rather better than that.'

'He did, and he's over the moon – all thanks to you.' The little man's blue eyes were shining. 'We've a lot to be grateful to you for, Declan and I, but you can be sure we'll find a way to repay you.'

'He won the race,' Laura said, smiling. 'What more could I ask?'

Patrick looked at her with real admiration. 'Jaysus, you're a strong woman, Mrs M, to be laughing and sad-dling winners with all that's been going on.'

'Not as strong as I seem, Pat,' Laura said soberly. 'If

you really want to know, I've hardly slept a wink in the last fortnight.'

Pat's face clouded. 'I'd not have known, unless you'd told me. Pray God, it'll come to an end soon.'

'I wish I had your faith, Pat.'

Edward Brickhill's green Bentley was parked in front of Langlands when Laura drove in with Rory.

They found him sitting in a large tapestry wing chair in front of a fire of blazing apple logs in the main hall.

'I'm glad you've made yourself at home, Dad.'

'Just getting used to the idea,' Brickhill said.

'What are you talking about?'

'Your late husband's receivers in bankruptcy have accepted my offer for the house and estate. Not a particularly generous offer, but they recognised the dearth of buyers for this type of property in current conditions.'

Laura was astounded. 'But you never said anything about it!'

'Like you, I never see the point of giving away my movements until I have to.'

His daughter leaned down and kissed him. 'You're fantastic. I was dreading having to move out, well, not so much out of here, but out of my yard.'

'You may still have to, if you can't come up with the rent I shall be asking for it,' Brickhill said, deadpan. 'Anyway, we've still got to clear up this other mess. I've been on to Agnew and I'm afraid he says that the police still haven't dropped the charges, though things are looking a bit more promising.'

'How?' Laura asked. 'Unless Henry gives himself up.

And none of us want him to have to do that, do we?'

'No, of course not,' Brickhill agreed. 'Look, it's clear that George Rutherford was behind the doping of Midnight Express. The police took everything away from Rutherford's penthouse in Queen Victoria Street and found an undertaking from Luke to the effect that if Midnight Express didn't win the race, the horse would become the property of George Rutherford. If he did win, all Luke's outstanding debts with Square Mile Sporting would be written off and not pursued.'

'That must have been what I saw them doing here the night George invited himself to dinner!' Laura exclaimed. 'I knew there was something going on. And that's why Luke transferred Midnight Express to my name.'

'But surely,' Rory said, 'if the police know about this bet, it takes the pressure off Laura?'

'Not entirely.' Brickhill shook his head. 'They know that Rutherford was prepared to buy this place and let Laura stay here, and they've been told by the staff here and some of the lads that Luke and Laura weren't getting on at all well. And that still leaves Laura with a motive as strong as Rutherford's. As it happens, it's Agnew's view that the agreement between Luke and Rutherford wouldn't have been a legally binding document. Possibly Rutherford saw it as the only way he was going to get his money. He knew damn well what Luke's position was. I don't know if you know this, but he was able to take back the Chelsea Gaming Club for nothing, though he'd already had seventy percent of the payment for it from Luke.'

'Yes,' Laura said. 'He couldn't help himself gloating

about it to me the other day. Luke must have flipped to
have done a deal like that.'

'They also found details of all Luke's punting on the
share price of Thames Land,' her father said. 'I suspect
Rutherford was holding that over Luke as well. I mean,
Luke could have been seriously run in for insider dealing.
The SFO are desperate to get their teeth into a clear-cut
case like that.' Edward shrugged. 'Poor old Luke. I almost
feel sorry for him now. Transferring the horse to Laura's
name at the last minute wouldn't have worked at all, I'm
afraid. Even if you ever get the insurance money, his
receivers will have a very solid claim to it.'

Rory, with his arm in a sling, listening to the gloomy
tale, tried to guess what Laura was feeling. Despite their
closeness of the last few days, he still couldn't repress a
lingering doubt that he had completely got through to
her. As she and Edward talked, he wandered round the
great oak table that occupied the centre of the hall. At
first unconsciously, his eyes fell on a copy of the *Evening
Standard*, folded with only the front-page headline showing, and beside it, a photograph of Arthur Eland.

Suddenly focusing, he grabbed it, unfolded it and stared
at the story below the picture.

Edward was watching him. 'I thought that might
interest you. That's why I came down.'

'What is it?' Laura asked.

'They've just fished Eland out of the Thames with a
hundredweight of chain wrapped round his legs,' Rory
said as he read the piece. 'They say they'd been searching
for him in connection with Rutherford's murder. They
found him at low tide early this morning. He'd been in

the water between twelve and eighteen hours.' Rory
looked up. 'They're right there. I saw him go into Rutherford's office about three o'clock. Rutherford must have
given the order to kill him before Eland banged him into
the sauna.' Rory gave a grunt of a laugh. 'There's a sort
of nice poetic irony to it, and at least it means that there
aren't any more of those photos of Straker in circulation.'

'Maybe, but that doesn't help Laura much.'

Rory looked at him, then at Laura. 'I think I'll go
down and see if Declan's back from Cheltenham with
the horses.'

He walked across the hall and out of the huge oak
door with Laura and her father staring after him.

'Hello, son. What do you want?' Detective Inspector
Stuart Wood asked as he walked into the room where
the duty sergeant had left Declan Hoolihan. The policeman had taken an hour to drive from his station in Surrey.

They'd been friendly enough to Declan while he waited,
brought him two cups of tea and offered him a few cigarettes. But he'd thought about walking out several times.

Now the detective, the same one who had come with
the Kempton security man to the Axe and Cleaver,
looked quite pleased to see him.

Wood was getting a lot of stick for not holding this
case together. Apart from the empty xylazine phial, the
case against Laura Mundy was looking too circumstantial.
If only, he'd been thinking, they'd found something at
Rutherford's to tie her in.

The lad had come into the local nick, claiming he had
more to say. It had to be worth the trip. And he could

take a drink off his brother in Hartley Wintney on the way home.

'There was something I didn't tell you last time,' the lad mumbled.

'Something you forgot?'

'No.' Declan spoke nervously. 'The man said he'd give me a monkey, cash, and said he'd kill me if I talked.' Declan shrugged.

'What bloke?'

'Eland. The one they pulled out of the river in London.'

The detective perked up. It looked as though it was going to be worth the trip. His chief would owe him a drink if he came back with something hard. He nodded encouragement.

'When did you talk to him, then?'

'At Kempton, that day. After Mrs Mundy had been and looked at the horse. I'd seen him around earlier, but he came up and said he wanted to take a look at the horse. I said, no way; he pulled out one of those long thin knives and prodded me in the gut with it. He said, "You're taking me in there, sunshine." He was only a small bloke, but hard, like.'

'Go on,' the policeman encouraged him. 'Did you let him in?'

Declan nodded, shamefaced. 'When he gave me the money.'

'What did he do?'

'He told me to hold the horse's head while he gave it a jab in the neck. Can't have taken more than ten or fifteen seconds. Then he said, "You tell anyone, and I'll cut your tongue out." That's why I didn't say last time, that and I'd've lost my job at Langlands.'

'Did you actually see Eland inject the horse?'

Declan nodded vigorously.

The detective looked at the lad for a moment, his eyes narrowing. 'Did you ever see him again?'

'Yeh, but he didn't see me, and he never gave me the money. He turned up at the yard, the Friday after. He told Micky he wanted to see Mr Hoolihan, said he was selling minerals. Mr Hoolihan wasn't around, so he went off back to his car.'

The policeman's eyes lit up. 'Where'd he leave his car then?'

'Round the back with the others.'

'Was Mrs Mundy's car there then?'

Declan allowed his brow to pucker as he thought about it. 'Yeh,' he said after a moment, 'yeh, I think it was. Mrs Mundy'd gone back up to the house in the Land Rover.'

The policeman stood up, walked to the door and opened it. 'Sarge,' he shouted, 'I'm going to have to do a formal interview in here. Can you sort me out a couple of tapes?'

Laura watched the first lot pull out of the yard next morning. She felt almost light-hearted. For the first time in weeks, the cloud that had been looming over her life seemed to be breaking up. Agnew had phoned her after her father and Rory had left the night before. He couldn't tell her much, just that the police had confirmed they were pursuing another line of enquiry.

She just hoped it wasn't Henry.

Pat Hoolihan came up quietly behind her in the deserted yard.

'Mrs Mundy, there's something I've been meaning to

give back to you these last couple of weeks.' He felt in the pocket of his tweed jacket and pulled out a small plastic phial, three-quarters full of liquid. He handed it to her.

Laura took it and her heart nearly stopped.

'What . . . what is it?'

'That'd be the stuff you wanted to use to quieten that tricky mare we couldn't clip.'

Laura felt her face redden.

'But where on earth did you find this?' she asked awkwardly.

'That day at Kempton, when I'd to get your keys from your Puffa jacket so's I could drive your car to the hospital, remember?'

Laura didn't need reminding.

'Susan's been staying with her sister in Salcombe since Sunday night,' Henry said when Laura asked after his wife. 'I thought it very likely these people would have another go at me – rightly as it turned out – and didn't want her staying in the house.'

Laura had asked Henry to come to Langlands for dinner with her and Rory that evening, the final day of the Cheltenham Festival. Several things merited celebration.

Langlands had sent out another winner that day. And the police had formally announced that they had dropped their charges against her.

For Rory, the gilt was taken from the first of these events by the fact that he had not been able to play any part in it.

For Henry, the second cause for celebration still left

him with a feeling of dishonour.

On the strength of Declan's new evidence, and the circumstances surrounding the deaths of George Rutherford and Arthur Eland, the police and the Jockey Club were satisfied that they had found the culprits, albeit posthumously. In the circumstances, they weren't charging Declan as an accessory.

Privately, Rory was very glad that there would be no trial where Declan would have to present his evidence in open court. He guessed that was beyond the lad's acting skills.

Rory nodded in reply to Henry. 'There's no question about it, but with Rutherford and Eland dead, there's no danger now.'

'Eland definitely had someone with him when he came to your house – when Pam was killed. The police found two sets of footprints.'

'A contract worker, like the ones Rutherford sent after me on Monday. The police are looking for him. They're doing the two who came after us for attempted murder and they've got a line on whoever put Eland in the Thames. I should think they're quite pleased with themselves.'

The three of them were eating a simple dinner at the round table in Laura's breakfast room. She and Rory wanted to help Henry expunge his crushing sense of guilt. It should have been easier now that Laura was released from suspicion, and Rory had not told him about his conversation with Declan the evening before.

Henry was ready to believe that his life and his reputation were out of danger, but it was clear that no amount of well-reasoned pragmatism would exonerate him in his own eyes. He was more prepared, though, to share the blame.

'I must say,' he conceded, 'now that it's emerged that Eland also doped the horse, I don't feel quite so bad. The dose of xylazine I gave him would never have caused him to come down the way he did. I suppose Eland thought I just wasn't going to do it and was making sure to cover his own back from Rutherford.'

'Exactly,' Rory said. 'We know you'd never have done anything that might possibly have hurt the horse or led to it dumping Luke like that. You must stop blaming yourself, man. I was pretty surprised when Professor Douglas told me the horse had been given too much of the stuff just to slow it down. I was bloody worried when he told me he didn't think it could have been administered by a professional. But now we know what happened.'

'And Eland planted the empty phial in Laura's car. I must admit, Laura, for a while I thought it was the one I'd given you, and I'm afraid it occurred to me . . .' Henry looked at her, embarrassed. 'What *did* you do with the one I gave you?'

Laura stood up and walked out of the room without a word. A few moments later, she reappeared holding a phial, three-quarters full.

'Here it is,' she said. 'As you can see, I only gave the mare a small dose.'

Henry looked puzzled. 'That's funny. You see, the mare's lad told me they'd managed to clip her without it.'

Laura laughed. 'That's what he thinks.'

When Henry left to drive himself home, Laura and Rory went back into her small sitting room. She put her arms around him and gave him a long, tender kiss, careful not to put pressure on his shoulder.

At last she released him and stood back. She put her two hands either side of his sandy, stubbly chin.

'That was delicious,' he said.

She took her hands away and walked towards the drinks table.

She poured a long Glenmorangie for Rory and turned to give it to him. He took it with a wide grin on his battered face.

'That was a brilliant idea,' she went on, 'getting Declan to go to the police with that story. I'd no idea that's what you were doing yesterday evening.'

'It was the only way I could see of getting you off without Henry taking the rap,' Rory said lightly. 'And Declan was very obliging. I told him it was what you wanted and he was so chuffed about winning that race, I think he'd have done anything for you.'

Laura tugged him down on to the sofa beside her and looked into the fire without speaking.

'Rory,' she said after a moment. 'There's something I should tell you.'

'What about?'

'Midnight Express.'

It was Rory's turn to take her chin in his hands. He turned it slowly towards him until they were looking into each others' eyes.

'There's no need,' he whispered. 'I know.'

A selection of compelling thrillers by John Francome

TIP OFF

ROUGH RIDE ✓	£4.99 ☐
STONE COLD	£4.99 ☐
STUD POKER	£4.99 ☐
BLOODSTOCK (with James McGregor)	£4.99 ☐
DECLARED DEAD (with James McGregor)	£4.99 ☐
EAVESDROPPER (with James McGregor)	£4.99 ☐
RIDING HIGH (with James McGregor)	£4.99 ☐

All Headline books are available at your local bookshop or newsagent, or can be ordered direct from the publisher. Just tick the titles you want and fill in the form below. Prices and availability subject to change without notice.

Headline Book Publishing, Cash Sales Department, Bookpoint, 39 Milton Park, Abingdon, OXON, OX14 4TD, UK. If you have a credit card you may order by telephone – 0235 400400.

Please enclose a cheque or postal order made payable to Bookpoint Ltd to the value of the cover price and allow the following for postage and packing:
UK & BFPO: £1.00 for the first book, 50p for the second book and 30p for each additional book ordered up to a maximum charge of £3.00.
OVERSEAS & EIRE: £2.00 for the first book, £1.00 for the second book and 50p for each additional book.

Name ....

Address ....

....

....

If you would prefer to pay by credit card, please complete:
Please debit my Visa/Access/Diner's Card/American Express (delete as applicable) card no:

Signature .... Expiry Date ....